*Gripping Tales of
Intrigue and Suspense:
Signet Double Mysteries*

Murder With a Past
&
Kill As Directed

SIGNET Mysteries You'll Enjoy

- [ ] **SIGNET DOUBLE MYSTERY—TEN DAYS' WONDER by Ellery Queen and THE KING IS DEAD by Ellery Queen.**
(#E9488—$2.25)*

- [ ] **THE DUTCH SHOE MYSTERY by Ellery Queen.**
(#E8578—$1.75)*

- [ ] **THE FRENCH POWDER MYSTERY by Ellery Queen.**
(#E8577—$1.75)*

- [ ] **THE GREEK COFFIN MYSTERY by Ellery Queen.**
(#E8579—$1.75)*

- [ ] **THE ROMAN HAT MYSTERY by Ellery Queen.**
(#E8470—$1.75)*

- [ ] **THE EGYPTIAN CROSS MYSTERY by Ellery Queen.**
(#E8663—$1.75)*

- [ ] **SIGNET DOUBLE MYSTERY—THE DRAGON'S TEETH by Ellery Queen and CALAMITY TOWN by Ellery Queen.**
(#J9208—$1.95)*

- [ ] **SIGNET DOUBLE MYSTERY—THERE WAS AN OLD WOMAN by Ellery Queen and THE ORIGIN OF EVIL by Ellery Queen.**
(#J9306—$1.95)*

- [ ] **SIGNET DOUBLE MYSTERY—THE LOVER by Carter Brown and THE BOMBSHELL by Carter Brown.** (#E9121—$1.75)*

- [ ] **SIGNET DOUBLE MYSTERY—SEX CLINIC by Carter Brown and W.H.O.R.E. by Carter Brown.** (#E8354—$1.75)*

- [ ] **SIGNET DOUBLE MYSTERY—THE BRAZEN by Carter Brown and THE STRIPPER by Carter Brown.** (#J9575—$1.95)

- [ ] **SIGNET DOUBLE MYSTERY—WALK SOFTLY, WITCH by Carter Brown and THE WAYWARD WAHINE by Carter Brown.**
(#E9418—$1.75)

*Price slightly higher in Canada

Buy them at your local bookstore or use this convenient coupon for ordering.

THE NEW AMERICAN LIBRARY, INC.,
P.O. Box 999, Bergenfield, New Jersey 07621

Please send me the SIGNET BOOKS I have checked above. I am enclosing
$_____ (please add $1.00 to this order to cover postage and handling).
Send check or money order—no cash or C.O.D.'s. Prices and numbers are subject to change without notice.

Name _____

Address _____

City _____ State _____ Zip Code _____

Allow 4-6 weeks for delivery.
This offer is subject to withdrawal without notice.

MURDER WITH A PAST

AND

KILL AS DIRECTED

by
Ellery Queen

A SIGNET BOOK
NEW AMERICAN LIBRARY
TIMES MIRROR

NAL BOOKS ARE AVAILABLE AT QUANTITY DISCOUNTS
WHEN USED TO PROMOTE PRODUCTS OR SERVICES. FOR
INFORMATION PLEASE WRITE TO PREMIUM MARKETING DIVISION,
THE NEW AMERICAN LIBRARY, INC., 1633 BROADWAY,
NEW YORK, NEW YORK 10019.

Murder with a Past Copyright, ©, 1963 by Ellery Queen
Kill As Directed Copyright ©, 1963, by Ellery Queen

All rights reserved. For information address
Scott Meredith Literary Agency, Inc.,
845 Third Avenue, New York, New York 10022.

Published by arrangement with Frederic Dannay and the late
Manfred B. Lee. *Murder with a Past* and *Kill As Directed*
also appeared in paperback as separate volumes published by
The New American Library.

SIGNET TRADEMARK REG. U.S. PAT. OFF. AND FOREIGN COUNTRIES
REGISTERED TRADEMARK—MARCA REGISTRADA
HECHO EN CHICAGO, U.S.A.

SIGNET, SIGNET, CLASSICS, MENTOR, PLUME, MERIDIAN AND NAL
BOOKS *are published by The New American Library, Inc.,*
1633 Broadway, New York, New York 10019

FIRST PRINTING (DOUBLE ELLERY QUEEN EDITION), APRIL, 1978

3   4   5   6   7   8   9   10   11

PRINTED IN THE UNITED STATES OF AMERICA

Murder with a Past

Cast of Characters

DAVID TULLY: Rugged architect who tears down the façades of the town's élite and builds a murder case from the rubble. 7

RUTH TULLY: David's missing wife—a slim, dainty, sophisticate wanted for murder. Is she a fugitive from justice, or a victim of injustice? 8

LT. JULIAN SMITH: When murder falls into his carefully manicured hands, his excessive tidiness prompts him to cover it up, rather than dig into it. 8

CRANDALL COX: Gray-faced, slop-bodied caricature of a man with a misplaced third blue-black eye in the flab of his neck. Locus: morgue. 9

NORMA HURST: She hovers delicately between reality and fantasy. 18

SANDRA JEAN AINSWORTH: As tart as her tongue. Her orgies wrapped their tentacles around her sister, Ruth. 19

OLIVER HURST: Norma's long-suffering husband who makes a great show of being normal, but his restless hands are busy: feeling, pulling, scratching, rubbing. 27

MAUDIE BLAKE: A sex pot who boiled too long and then spilled over; she heard too much and talked to the wrong people. 32

ANDREW GORDON: dark, lean, and sullen. "A useless overprotected lunkhead" to his mother, Mercedes, but the object of Sandra Jean's marital machinations. 37

MERCEDES CABBOTT: A much married creature with unpredictable moods and the millions to indulge them. 46

GEORGE CABBOTT: Mercedes' adored third husband. Big, bronzed, and bleached, he wears old jeans, T-shirt, and sneakers as if they were a uniform. 51

JAKE BALLINGER: Crustaceous city editor. A rumpled, baggy-panted newsman of the old school who expects a *quid* for his *quo* and gets it 59

EDDIE HARPER: Prematurely bald TV newscaster who ruthlessly pursues a sensational story. 59

DALRYMPLE: Ingratiating young manager of Wilton Lodge who does not dare evade David's determined investigations. 69

MRS. HOSKINS: A retentive memory and a loose tongue combined to disclose a wicked weekend. 71

1

Dave Tully reached the outskirts of the business district at five o'clock in the afternoon. Trying to make time, he chose River Street and swung into the carstream rushing across the bridge. A cloverleaf intersection a mile beyond split the river of traffic into rivulets. The big beige Imperial took the one going east.

Oleander Drive brought Tully in a gentle climb to the short green hills and, a few minutes later, to the fieldstone pillar whose bronze plaque announced Tully Heights.

The stiffness in his legs—it was a long drive up from the state capital—began to leave him. He felt himself smiling.

Tully Heights never failed to relax him. The Heights had been Dave Tully's baby, from the first inking of the plat to the last brad in the graceful ranchers and splitlevels slipping past the Imperial.

He had done a very good job here, Tully thought. The street layouts held the secret—broad and meandering, following the natural contours of the hills. At the sacrifice of a few lots he had achieved a beautiful individuality. You came upon each house unexpectedly, as if it were alone in the hills—a miniature estate rather than what it was, a unit in a development.

At number 100 Oleander, Tully braked the big car and eagerly turned into the driveway curving to the double garage doors of a redwood and antique brick splitlevel.

The absence of the other car, the general air of emptiness, let him down. Still, she hadn't known he would be getting back at this hour.

Tully got out of the car—a big man, big in the shoulders and small in the waist. His face was square-cut, hearty, with a crinkle-eyed glow under the rather surprising metallic gray of his hair. People invariably glanced at the back of his hand for a tattoo, as in the TV cigarette commercials.

Inside the house he called, "Ruth?"

He expected no answer, and he got none.

As Dave Tully's front door swung closed, a sedate black Plymouth sedan rounded the final bend in Oleander Drive. Behind the wheel sat a rangy, thirtyish man who drove with precision. His features were tidy, almost characterless. The late sun glinted on his dark blond, almost tan, hair, which was smoothly trimmed. He wore a dark suit, a white shirt with a short-tab collar and a conservative necktie. The hands on the steering wheel were squarish, with manicured fingernails.

He stopped the Plymouth behind the beige Imperial and got out—nothing hasty in his manner, but not casually, either.

As he passed the Imperial in the driveway he laid his hand, palm flat, on its hood.

The door chimes halted Tully's progress toward the stainless steel kitchen. He wondered if Ruth had forgotten her key. He hadn't thrown the thumb latch on coming in, and the door was locked.

Passing the front windows, Tully glimpsed the black Plymouth and frowned.

He opened the door and said, "Hello, Julian."

The tidy man stepped inside. "Just getting back, Dave?"

"Five minutes ago."

"How'd you make out in the capital?"

"The bond issue looks good. Let's hope the voters pass it when it comes up. And dredging the river seems feasible. Barge shipping would make a city of us in no time at all. How about a sandwich? I drove straight through, and I'm ready to eat raw dog."

"Thanks, I've got beef waiting at home. But don't mind me."

Tully grinned. "Come on into the kitchen. You can mix me a drink while I roust a Nature Boy Special out of the refrigerator."

Tully let Julian precede him to the kitchen. He clicked coffee on to heat and went about loading two slices of bread with cold cuts and cheese.

Julian Smith's look bothered him. "You want to explain, Julian?"

"Eat your sandwich," the detective said.

"I get the impression it can't wait." Tully stared at him.

Smith watched a sparrow delouse itself on a twig outside the kitchen window. When the bird fluttered and disappeared, blending into the shadows stealing in from the east side of the house, he said, "As a matter of fact, Dave, it can't."

"Business?"

Smith nodded.

Dave Tully set the sandwich down on the work area beside the sink. "Your department is Homicide, Julian. Somebody get himself killed?"

"Yes."

"Well, who?"

"A man named Cranny Cox. The Cranny is short for Crandall."

Tully's broad shoulders loosened, and he laughed. "You had me going there for a second."

"Did I?" the detective said.

"Well, after all. Man hasn't seen his wife in three days and when he gets home there's this character from the mayhem bureau with an official look on his puss." Tully picked up the sandwich and took a man-sized bite.

"The name mean anything to you, Dave?"

"Cranny Cox? Never heard of him. So why the detour on your way home? Of course, we're always glad to have you."

He spoke as if Ruth were standing there in the kitchen with him. Always we, Julian Smith thought. The house had been built for Ruth. Tully was the kind of man who built for the joy of building, and perhaps for that reason he had made a great deal of money out of the Heights. But this house had been a special labor of love.

"Ruth's a little late, isn't she, Dave?"

Tully glanced at the kitchen clock. "She didn't expect me. Probably getting in a positively-the-last rubber of bridge with three other business widows."

"She usually goes on these trips with you, Dave. Why didn't she go this time?"

Dave Tully studied the Homicide man's face with care, and then he set the remains of his sandwich down. "You better stop making like a detective, Julian, and tell me what this is all about. In words of one syllable."

Smith reached into a pocket and brought out something wrapped in white cloth. He unwrapped it cautiously. It was a small revolver.

"This is your gun, Dave."

Tully stared and stared at it. "It is?" he said stupidly.

"You bought and registered it when you moved up here."

"Well, sure. You know perfectly well why. This was the first house I finished in the development, and we were pretty much alone up here for a while. I couldn't have Ruth . . ." He stopped and swallowed. He was angry at the policeman, angry at his own dry mouth and panicky thoughts. "For God's sake, Julian! How'd you get hold of my gun? And what's it got to do with this man Cox, whoever he is? What are you trying to tell me?"

"That it killed him," Smith said. "We fished it out of a sewer near the motel where his body was found."

For some reason Tully found himself groping for the half-eaten sandwich. When he realized what he was doing, he pulled his hand back and gripped the smooth cold edge of the kitchen sink. "What the bloody hell, Julian, are you talking about?"

"I'm sorry, Dave. We've got a pickup on her."

"Pickup on *whom?*"

"Your wife."

"Ruth?" Tully's mouth remained open. "On Ruth?"

"I'm sorry," the detective said again. He pushed away from the window at which he had been standing.

"This is some kind of rib."

"I wish it were, Dave," Smith moved toward the kitchen doorway. "Mind if I look through the house?" He kept moving in the same quiet way without waiting for a reply.

"Look all you want!" Tully shouted after him. "We never even heard of anybody named Crandall Cox! You've just plain flipped, Julian!"

When the detective got to the living room a few minutes later he found Dave Tully standing at the picture window. He had drawn the drapes back as far as they would go, and he was watching the street. His face was a muddier version of his hair.

He turned at Smith's step and asked in a reasonable voice, "Who's this Crandall Cox, Julian?"

"We're not sure yet."

"The gun doesn't mean a damn thing."

"I'm afraid it does, Dave."

"It was just stolen from the house here."

"Did you have a break-in?"

"We must have had."

"'Must have' isn't admissible evidence. Did you?"

"Not that I know of. But—"

"When is the last time you actually saw this gun?"

"How the devil do I know? A long time ago. Look, Julian." Tully was still sounding reasonable. "I don't get this at all. All right, so somehow somebody got hold of my gun and shot this Cox with it. But why Ruth? You ought to know Ruth couldn't kill anybody."

"How would I know that, Dave?" the detective said. "In fact, how would you know it?"

"Damn you, Julian—!" Tully yelled.

"Keep your shirt on. All I meant was that there's a murder potential in everybody."

"Well, even if she could, why *would* she? An absolute stranger!"

"Maybe not so absolute." Julian Smith reached into his inside pocket and his manicured fingers reappeared with a police department envelope. From it he very carefully extracted a sheet of notepaper. He unfolded it and laid it on the coffee table. "I'm breaking all the rules, Dave. Read this. Just don't touch it."

Tully came away from the picture window reluctantly. He bent over the table. It was ordinary white typewriter stationery, its creases slightly worn, its message typed. The date in the upper right hand corner suddenly leaped up at him. If it was to be believed, the letter had been written in the short interval between his meeting with Ruth and their marriage:

Cranny—

You keep away from me, and I mean it. What happened between us is ancient history and you'd better get used to the idea. I've found myself a leading citizen here who's very much interested in me and I think he's going to ask me to marry him. You do anything to spoil my chances and it will be the last thing you *ever* spoil.

I'm serious, Cranny. Just forget I exist and go back to your bedroom-window romances and figuring out ways to dodge an outraged bullet. You stand a better chance of surviving at the hands of some dumb cuckold than you do at mine. *I mean this.*

And five weeks from the date on this thing we were married. . . . The notepaper moved a little under Tully's gust of breath. The detective quickly picked it up by two corners, folded it, and tucked it away.

"Typewritten and unsigned," Tully said unsteadily. "What are you trying to pull, Julian? This can't have anything to do with Ruth."

"Maybe," Smith nodded. "But there are other things, Dave. Cox arrived in town four days ago and registered at the Hobby Motel."

Tully knew the place. The hobby for which it was notorious was as old as Adam. The motel skulked on the edge of town, a combination of tavern, restaurant and hot-pillow joint.

"The day after he checked in, Cox went down to City

Hall and asked to see a marriage license issued to one Ruth Ainsworth and a man whose name he didn't seem to know. When the news of Cox's murder got out, the license clerk called me from City Hall and told me about Cox's marriage-license hunt.

"Then today . . ."

Tully said thickly, "Well, go on, Julian! What about today?"

"Today a woman who had the room next to Cox's came in to tell us that Cox had himself a party last night. She heard a female voice. And at one point, she says, Cox called the woman he had in his room by name. I'm sorry, Dave, but you'll have to know sooner or later. The name Cox was overheard calling his woman-visitor was Ruth."

Tully walked over to a chair. He sat down, his fingertips clawing at the nubby upholstery. His lips were moving, but nothing came out.

"I want you to take a look at this man, Dave. I hate to ask you to do it . . ."

"It's all right," Tully said. He got up and stood there uncertainly.

Julian Smith took the big man's arm gently. "I wish I could spare you this, Dave. But it's possible Cox isn't his real name. You might recognize him."

2

Smith was deft and quick with the whole thing. A local undertaker handled the town's morgue cases. The man known as Crandall Cox lay under a rubber sheet on a table in the workroom of the Henshaw Funeral Home.

Smith's touch on his arm guided Tully through the heavy sweetness of funeral flowers to the room at the rear. The mortician removed the sheet. Before Tully, in all his naked mortality, lay a stranger.

He was a medium-sized man with little fat bloats around the armpits. The flesh sagged all along the line of his jaw. His face was heavy-featured, almost coarse, with a thin, sporty mustache. The hair was black and wavy and came to a widow's peak on the low forehead. There was one blue-black hole in the gray flab of his neck, just below the thyroid cartilage, like a misplaced third eye.

To Tully the late Crandall Cox looked like nothing human.

He tried to visualize Cox with unrelaxed flesh and blood in the tissues of his face, but it was impossible. Even in life he must have looked three-quarters dead—a slug out of some back-alley wall. To think of Ruth—cool, slim, dainty, delectable Ruth—in the arms of this cheap, gray-faced, slop-bodied, slobber-mouthed caricature of a man—made him want to laugh.

Tully looked down at him and thought, You ugly son-of-a-bitch, without any feeling whatever.

"Well?"

Tully turned. "What?" He had forgotten Lieutenant Smith.

"Well, do you recognize him?"

"No."

"You're sure, Dave?"

"Yes."

Somebody opened the door and the flower-smell wriggled in.

"What's the matter?" Julian Smith asked him, eyes on Tully's face.

"It's those damn flowers," he muttered. "Let's get out of here before I throw up."

When they were seated in the unmarked police car, Tully stuck his nose out the window and inhaled.

"Ruth ever mention a man of Cox's description?" the detective asked, starting the car.

"I can answer that one positively absolutely," Tully said without changing expression. "No. How about taking me home, Julian?"

But as they drove off through the gathering darkness, Tully found himself thinking that Ruth had never mentioned much of anything about herself and her life before they had met.

He sat back and shut his eyes. He suddenly felt sleepy.

"Here we are," Smith's voice said.

Tully opened his eyes with a start. They were pulled up behind his Imperial in the driveway of the split-level that had seemed so safe and desirable only an hour ago. The sun had gone down, but the house was dark.

Tully reached for the door-handle.

Smith said, "If you hear from her, Dave, contact me immediately."

Tully looked at him blankly.

"Any other course would be stupid," the Homicide man said. "You realize that, don't you?"

"Yes," Tully said.

"I'll keep Ruth out of the papers as long as possible," the detective said.

"Sure, Julian. Thanks." Tully got out of the car. He was vaguely aware of Smith's hesitation. He shut the door and the detective drove away.

Tully stood still in the middle of the dark yard. He felt very queer—uniquely alone, in a timeless time and a space without margins. Had there ever been a woman named Ruth? Or even a hill, and a house?

Tully shivered and went inside. . . .

He sat in the darkness of his living room going over what Julian Smith had told him on the way to the funeral parlor. The man Cox's body had been found this morning by a Hobby Motel cleaning woman. One of the bathroom towels showed powder burns and multiple bullet holes. The revolver had been wrapped in several folds of the towel to cut down the noise of the shot. He had been shot the night before.

Ruth's face above the towel . . . the tip of her exquisite little nose dead-white, the way it got when she was furious . . .

Tully clutched his temples, but he could not shut out the picture of that imagined motel room, or the voices from his ears.

"Cranny, I told you I never wanted to see you again."

"You won't use that thing, baby. Remember it's li'l ol' Cranny? How's about a drink? Come on, lover, what do you say?"

"You promised me, Cranny. You promised."

"So I promised. So what? Here, have a slug of this . . ."

"Stay back! I warned you, Cranny. You shouldn't have followed me. You shouldn't have called."

"You came running, didn't you? You don't fool me, Ruth. You and me always had a thing going for us . . ."

"I came for only one reason—to make you get out of here and leave me and my husband alone!"

"When you've got it made with this sucker and I can cut myself in?"

"No! I won't let you do it. Not to him, Cranny. I love him . . . Stay back, I tell you!"

"Give me that gun—"

It ended there. It always ended there.

Tully leaned back and sighed, feeling a little better. Ruth indulging in a cheap motel affair for its own sake was simply unthinkable. Especially with a slug like Cox. Yes, even if she had known Cox from somewhere, in the past. Maybe at one time he had been quite different; time and a dissolute life often worked like mold in a damp cellar.

The imaginary dialogue his frantic mind had whipped up could not be too far from the actuality; Tully was sure of it. Cox had been in a position to rake up something about Ruth, something that gave him a hold on her, and she had responded to his motel summons to settle it.

The gun was the giveaway. Ruth would never have taken the gun with her if she had meant to acquiesce in his wishes—obscene, mercenary or otherwise. A woman who intends to climb into bed with an old flame doesn't come to the rendezvous with her husband's loaded revolver.

It was funny how a thing like that—a conclusion so clear—could make a man's spirits perk, even if the corollary was that his wife had committed murder. First things first, Tully thought wryly.

That long-eared bitch of an eavesdropper in the next room hadn't heard a bedroom party going on. She wouldn't have been registered at the Hobby in the first place if she was a decent woman. To Hobby habitués any evidence of a couple alone in one of the rooms would mean only one thing.

And another thing. Why, if the woman's ears were so sharp, hadn't she heard the sound of the shot? The towel could hardly have made an effective silencer; there must have been some report. Yet she had not mentioned the shot to Julian. Or having seen Ruth enter—or, more important, leave—Cox's room next door. There was something off-beat in the apparent fact that Julian's witness, a lone woman of prurient curiosity, would overlook the chance to catch a glimpse of the female of the supposed hot-pillow party as she sneaked out of the next motel room. True, the eavesdropper could have had to leave on a date, although no such thing had been mentioned. Or she could have left her room prematurely to cross the motel courtyard to the tavern for a drink, or a pickup.

But, somehow, none of it added up.

Tully felt a small stir, a faint animal warning. That woman would bear investigation . . .

He got up and put on the lights and went to his den and put on the light there. Then he stood over the telephone table and rapidly dialed a number.

"Yes?" It was Norma Hurst's old-woman voice. Norma was not an old woman; the querulous, almost anile, tone was a recent development.

"Norma? Dave Tully."

"Oh," she said. She sounded disappointed. "How was your trip, Dave?"

"All right. Is Ollie there?"

"He's still at the office, and he knows we have a dinner date, too. . . ." He heard Norma begin to cry.

Through his own preoccupation, Tully felt the old helpless pangs of sympathy. Norma Hurst had been acting oddly for almost a year. The Hursts had had one child, a darling little tow-headed girl with flashing eyes and twinkling legs who was never still. To provide an outlet for her daughter's energies, Norma had bought her a trike. One day the little girl was pedaling wildly down the wrong side of the road when a town garbage truck came around one of Dave Tully's curves and ran over her. The child was killed instantly and horribly. It had taken three men to remove the broken, bloody little body from Norma's arms. Norma could have no other children. She had spent the next five months in a sanitarium.

Tully had never forgotten the day Oliver Hurst had to go to the sanitarium to take his wife home. "Please come with me, Dave," Ollie had begged. "I'm scared to death." "Scared of what, Ollie?" Tully had asked his friend. "They told you Norma's all right now." "The hell they say," Ollie had said bitterly. "I know when Norma's all right and when she isn't. If you ask me, she's never going to be all right—I mean the way she used to be. Dave, I can't get through to her—I don't even know how to talk to her any more. She's always been fond of you. Help me get Norma home." Of course, he had gone. It had been an eerie experience. There had been no outward sign that anything was wrong, but some important ingredient of the old Norma was missing—gone, perhaps forever. Poor Ollie had sat holding her limp hand and chattering away like mad on the trip home. Her only response had been an occasional vague smile.

Tully said into the phone, "Don't upset yourself, Norma. Ollie's undoubtedly on his way home right now, or he'd have called you."

"Why didn't he call me anyway?" Norma wept. "He has no consideration, Dave. I'm so alone all the time—in this awful house—"

"It's one of my best," Tully said fatuously.

"Oh, you know I don't mean that!" To his surprise she stopped crying, sounding angry. "It's just that Ollie keeps avoiding me, and don't tell me he doesn't, Dave Tully!"

"I'll tell you exactly that, Norma. He's the most successful lawyer in town, and he's carrying a tremendous work-load. He spends every minute he possibly can with you."

Norma was silent. For a moment Tully thought she had simply walked away from the phone, as she sometimes did. But then, suddenly, she said, "What did you want Ollie for, Dave?"

It brought Tully back to his own troubles. "Oh, a matter of business, Norma. Would you tell him to give me a ring when he gets home?" He hung up before Norma could ask for Ruth.

Tully sat down at the phone to wait. If ever a man needed legal advice, he thought, it's me right now. Ollie was a damn good lawyer. A little cautious, maybe, but give him time to think a thing through and he was a tough baby to beat.

Tully was still sitting there when he heard somebody moving around in the living room. He jumped up, heart racing. Ruth! Could it possibly be Ruth?

He ran into the living room.

But it was only Sandra Jean.

Sandra Jean was Ruth's sister, and she used her older sister's home as if her name were also Tully, instead of Ainsworth. She was busy at the cowhide-and-bleached mahogany bar when Tully walked in—so absorbed in fixing her Scotch on the rocks that when he said "Hi!" in her ear, she almost dropped the tall glass.

When Sandra Jean saw who it was, she said, "Don't *do* things like that, you creep," giving him one of her characteristic pouty-lipped, moist looks, and turned back to the bar. "You really bugged me, pops. Now I do need one with muscles," and she added a full inch of Scotch to the glass.

"I thought it was Ruth," Tully said. "Do you know where she is?"

"Probably having dinner out," Sandra Jean said, sipping. She gave him a long-lashed, thoughtful look over the rim of her glass. "I guess she didn't expect you home so early. I was kind of working the raised-eyebrow department myself when I saw the car and the lights on—I was just going to look for you when you gave me that verbal goose. But I needed this drink first."

"You're drinking too damned much," Tully said.

"Yes, popsy," Sandra Jean said. "You want to spank the naughty little sister?" She stuck her bottom out at him, laughing.

"Act your age, will you?" Tully sat down wearily.

He wondered only briefly what Sandra Jean was doing there if she had believed he and Ruth weren't home. Ruth's kid sister operated on a sort of emotional radar—"Obey that impulse!" was her motto. She had a key to their house, and if she were in the neighborhood and suddenly felt like a drink, the fact that no one was supposed to be home wouldn't stop her. On the other hand . . .

She was still looking at him over the glass. Tully stirred uncomfortably.

He always had that feeling when he was alone with Sandra Jean. She made him conscious of himself. As if she possessed a secret knowledge, a quivering and unspoken something between them which shamed him, and amused her. The only thing that made it tolerable was his rueful conviction that Sandra Jean affected most men that way.

She turned from the bar and went over to the TV set and clicked it on, sipping all the time. Tully watched her a little warily. She was an attractive kid, all right. "Kid . . ." Some kid! In many ways she was like Ruth—the same clean-line legs, the same nipped-in waist, flow of hips, full shoulders; the same dramatic facial structure, wide-apart eyes, perfect little nose.

Ruth's hair was a sun-drenched auburn and Sandra Jean's was whatever color her frequent whims dictated —right now it was a bangy Cleopatra black—but their real differences were vital, a matter of movement and gesture in carrying out the unconscious commands of their worlds-apart temperaments. If they walked across a room together, observed from either fore or aft Ruth walked like a lady and Sandra Jean like a belly dancer —with the same equipment. There was a smack of sensuality in every move the girl made, almost a naked carnality.

She's going to give some man a hard time, Tully thought dimly. Andy Gordon, if she could wrestle the young nitwit out of mama's clutch. And maybe a procession of others who, like the panting Gordon boy, would mistake Sandra Jean's strip-tease personality for heaven-sent passion. Tully had long suspected that beneath his young sister-in-law's steamy exterior lay a soul of ice.

The blast of the TV jarred him back to the present. He started to get up, but sank back when Sandra Jean turned the sound down low. She dropped into a chair opposite him, sprawling on the end of her spine, her long legs thrust out as far as they would go. She closed one eye and sighted through the amber liquid in her glass.

"Thought I'd wait around for Ruth and muscle in, if you two are going out tonight," she said. "Lover-boy is dancing attendance on mama and left me at loose ends this evening. You don't mind, do you?"

Tully said nothing. Ruth . . . He shut his eyes and

massaged them with the thumb and forefinger of his left hand.

Sandra Jean said suddenly, "Say, what's the matter with you? Trip go sour?"

Tully opened his eyes. "Look, Sandra, don't you have any idea where Ruth is?"

"No. Should I have? You're looking kind of green, Davey. How about a slug of Scotch?"

Tully shook his head and shut his eyes again, wishing she would go away. His temples were pounding. Ruth . . . He tried desperately not to think.

And then a scent insinuated itself into his nostrils, a musky flower-scent that instantly evoked the funeral parlor and the waxworks figure on the mortician's work-table. Tully's eyes flew open. Sandra Jean was stooping over him, careless of the cleft exposed by her low-cut frock, her young breath hot on his face.

"Poor Davey," she moaned, and she stooped lower and put her lips on his surprised mouth, and then she was kissing him hard and thrusting with her tongue.

Something devastating happened to Tully, a reflex of revulsion that made his big hands shoot out and grab the girl's arms and shake her so violently that her head flopped back and forth as if her neck were broken. Sandra Jean yelped softly and dropped her drink; he felt some of the Scotch splash on his trousers. It was the expression on her face, however, that brought Tully to his senses. For a moment she had looked like a terrified child. He shoved her from him and jumped up.

"Don't ever try that on me again, Sandra," he muttered. "Ever, do you understand? Play your erotic games with Andy. I play for keeps." Suddenly he felt ashamed. He turned around and said, "I hope I didn't hurt you."

"But you did." Sandra Jean's moist pout was in evidence again. "You're a brute, do you know that?" She actually wriggled. "Oooh, what a brute. I didn't realize you're so strong, Davey. Shake me again?"

"Oh, shut up," he growled, and walked over to the window. In its reflecting surface he saw the girl staring at his back. Then she shrugged, picked up the remains of the glass, and went off to the kitchen with insolent hips.

The hell with her, Tully thought, staring into the darkness.

Where was Ruth? Why didn't she come home? Or at least call?

Tully set his throbbing forehead against the cool glass. . . .

It was the TV that made him turn around. The early evening newscast had come on, and the newscaster had mentioned the name Crandall Cox.

"Police have made no official statement yet about last night's motel shooting," the man was saying. "But just before air time this reporter learned from an authoritative source that a woman is being sought for questioning, the wife of a prominent local real-estate developer—"

In two strides Tully was at the set, wrenching the dial. The picture and voice faded swiftly.

"So that's it," a voice said behind him.

Tully whirled. It was Sandra Jean with a fresh glass. "What's it?"

"That's why you're acting so funny. It's Ruth they're looking for, isn't it?"

3

The girl sounded perfectly cool. If she was disturbed, it was more a matter of annoyance than worry. Tully gaped at her.

She went over to the bar and proceeded to fix another drink for herself. "It would have to happen now," she complained.

"Now?" Tully repeated blankly.

"I mean, it's darned inconsiderate of Ruth, getting herself involved in a mess just when I was settling my hooks for keeps in lover-boy. It's certainly not going to help me with old lady Cabbott. She'll snatch at this scandal the way a seal goes after a fish."

"I see," Tully said. He felt like grabbing her by the neck and the seat of the panties and heaving her through the picture window. "And that's all you can think about?"

Sandra Jean sat down again in the same sprawled position and sipped her drink. "Oh, come off it, Davey. It's obviously some kind of ridiculous mistake, and anyway Ruth's always been able to take care of herself. Meanwhile, I have to make out with Mercedes Cabbott. She'll look for any excuse to keep Andy and me apart. My sister being hunted by the police is made to order for that old barracuda."

"I guess this just isn't my day," Tully said. He rubbed his forehead with one hand, leaning on the TV set with the other. "What kind of self-centered little slut are you, Sandra?"

Something very hard came into her eyes. But her voice was quite level as she said, "I don't like that, Davey. Don't call me that again."

24

"All right, all right," Tully muttered. "I can't seem to grasp any of this, Sandra. Did Ruth know a Crandall Cox?"

"Ask Ruth that," the girl said.

"Then she did!"

"I didn't say that. Look, Davey." Sandra Jean took a long swallow and then set her glass down. "You think I'm being awfully callous, don't you?"

"I think you're being damned unconcerned about a sister who's knocked herself out for you!"

"I'm not unconcerned," the girl said calmly. "It's just that I'm not worried. I know Ruth a lot better than you do."

"What's that supposed to mean?"

"Nothing. Ruth's always managed just fine. She's done pretty well for herself so far, hasn't she? She's never lost her head in her life. She's far too smart to kill anybody, especially a crumb like this Cranny Cox."

Tully straightened up, staring at her. "Crumb? How do you know he was a crumb?"

"He must have been. Who else but crumbs get themselves shot in cheap motels?"

"You're lying," Tully said. "You do know what this is all about, Sandra. You gave yourself away!"

"I did?" she said. She picked up the glass again.

"Cranny. You called him Cranny."

"So what?"

"How do you know he was called Cranny Cox?"

"The announcer called him that."

"The announcer called him Crandall Cox!"

For the merest instant Sandra Jean seemed perturbed. Then she shrugged and sipped her Scotch. "It's obvious, isn't it? A man named Crandall would be called Cranny, wouldn't he?"

"Who was he, Sandra? What was his connection with Ruth?"

The girl rose. "Really, Davey. Playing detective! You weren't cut out for the role. Good night."

"Not yet!" Tully caught her by the wrist and spun her around. "By God, you know something about this, and you're not leaving here until you tell me!"

25

"Isn't this where I say, 'Please, you're hurting me'?" she said. "For the second time tonight, I might add. Under other circumstances I'd enjoy it. Now I'm bored. Let go of me."

He glared down at her in a dumb rage. She had a special talent for making him feel foolish. He let go and turned abruptly away.

"You're a darling," his wife's sister said sweetly. "Ruth's lucky to have you. About this Cox business, it's Ruth's show. She's innocent, of course, and I'm perfectly sure she'll clear the whole thing up. Try not to worry about it."

"Will you please get out of here!"

"I'm off to the races right *now*," Sandra Jean said. "Where the devil did I throw my purse? Oh, here it is." He heard her going to the door. "You see, Mercedes Cabbott and that stuffed Adonis she picked for a third husband might decide to pack my beloved off on a long trip, and I've got to get in a few licks of my own or lose Andy for good. How mercenary can a girl get! Night, Davey."

He did not reply, and after a moment he heard the door open and close.

Tully went to the bar and poured himself a long jolt of Scotch. He gulped it and poured himself another. Then he sat down and tried to think again.

Sandra Jean had seemed so positive that Ruth would come through this—whatever it was—in one piece. Of course the girl knew all about it. She must have good reasons for respecting Ruth's confidence.

That was the trouble, Tully thought. Those reasons.

He was completely confused. The implications from some of the things Sandra Jean had said . . . If Julian Smith were to phone him this moment to announce that Ruth was in the clear for Cox's murder, could he honestly say that things would be just as they used to be between them?

He swallowed some more of the Scotch.

What had Cox really been to Ruth? He couldn't have been unknown to her—not when his nickname fell so naturally from her younger sister's lips.

Who *was* Cox?

For that matter, *who was Ruth?*

The question invaded and possessed his mind. . . .

Tully was pouring his third Scotch when the phone in the den rang.

It was Oliver Hurst.

"Ollie," Tully said. He felt a deep gratitude.

"What's up, Dave?" the lawyer's rich voice said. "I just got in and Norma says you sounded upset. Anything wrong?"

"Ollie, can you come right over?"

"Now?"

"Now."

"I don't know, Dave. We've got this dinner engagement, and Norma's all over my back as it is for getting home late."

"Ollie, this won't wait. It's a serious personal matter. Believe me, I wouldn't press it or risk upsetting Norma further if it weren't. I've got to talk to you right away."

Hurst was silent. Then Tully heard him say something, and Norma's voice shrilling in the background. "Dave."

"Yes, Ollie."

"I'll be there in a few minutes."

"Thanks!"

Twenty minutes later Tully saw the lights of Hurst's car swing into the driveway. He hurried to the door.

The lawyer's flesh belied the promise of his voice. He was thick-set and moon-faced, and his head was a freckled, almost hairless, egg. But he had fine, light, clear eyes of a deceptive transparency which sometimes made Tully uncomfortable; they were almost the only remains of the lawyer's youth—it was hard to believe, seeing what he had become, that Ollie had been voted the handsomest man in his class in the college yearbook. His hands were never still—pulling an ear, fingering his chin, rubbing his nose, scratching his skull, pinching the skin of his neck.

But if Oliver Hurst had settled into suet and chronic worry, he also—as Tully knew—had guts. He was a fighter. Back when the town had been little more than an overgrown village dependent on the local college of the state university system, Ollie had bulldogged his way through to a first-class education and a law degree. In those years it had been an exceptional achievement for a day-laborer's son. As the town grew, Ollie had had to make his own opportunities; no one made it easy for him. Until David Tully began to throw business his way. That marked Hurst's break-through; now he handled all Tully's legal affairs, and he was the busiest lawyer in town. He owed a great deal to Dave Tully.

Ollie took a quick look around. "Where's the fire, Dave? Everything seems normal."

"Drink?"

"You sound as if I'll need it. What's the trouble?"

Tully splashed some bourbon into a glass. "Ruth."

"Ruth?" Hurst looked puzzled. He merely moistened his lips with the bourbon, as if some sixth sense told him he was going to need his faculties unimpaired. "What d'ye mean Ruth? What kind of trouble could Ruth be in?"

"Have you seen her last night or today? Heard from her?"

"No. You mean you don't know where she is?"

"That's right."

Oliver Hurst sat down, staring at the taller man. "It's more than that, Dave. Come on, let's have it."

"She's apparently mixed up in this motel business."

"What motel business?"

Tully was surprised. He had been so preoccupied with the affair that he had assumed it was universally known. "Haven't you heard the newscast, Ollie?"

"No, I just got home. And you know how Norma feels about the news these days—she'll never let me turn the thing on, can't stand the voices of doom." The lawyer rather deliberately set the glass down. "What is this crud about Ruth and a motel, Dave?" he asked quietly.

Tully said in a bleak voice, "And a dead man."

Hurst stared up at him. "And a *what?*"

"A man named Cox. He was shot to death in the

Hobby Motel last night sometime—body wasn't found till mid-morning."

"So? What's that got to do with Ruth?"

"A gun registered in my name killed him—we kept it in the house here. And a woman in the room next to Cox's says Cox had a gal in his room last night—overheard Cox call her Ruth, she says."

After a moment Ollie Hurst took up the glass of bourbon and drank half its contents. "I see," he said, and he set the glass down again and rose. "How did you learn all this, Dave?"

"Julian Smith told me. He was here looking for Ruth. He has a pickup on her."

"I see," the lawyer said again. He stood frowning, pinching his lips, rubbing his nose, staring at the floor. Finally he looked up. "I don't believe it, Dave. There's something wrong somewhere. It's got to be a mistake."

"That's what I keep telling myself."

"Good God, man, you sound as if you doubt her!"

"Do I?" Tully said.

"Not Ruth, Dave. You ought to know that better than anyone in the world. I can imagine what a shock this is to you, but so-called facts can often be terribly misleading. I'd stake a good deal on Ruth's integrity."

"Then how do you explain those facts?"

"I don't—not yet. But even if Ruth was there last night, there are a dozen possible innocent explanations. Certainly she didn't kill the guy—I can't see Ruth killing a flea, let alone a human being. Who was he, do you know?"

"Who was who?"

"This fellow Cox."

"I haven't any idea," Tully said tiredly. "Julian had me take a look at him over at the funeral parlor. I never saw him before."

Hurst began to walk around the room, deep in thought. "Dave," he said, stopping. "You have no idea where Ruth is? You found no note, no message?"

"No."

"Have you tried calling around?"

"No!" Tully was astounded at the violence of his own

tone. "The last thing I want to do is spread this. Julian promised to keep Ruth's name out of the papers as long as he could. It's true somebody leaked a hint to that damn newscaster, but he's still not naming names. Ollie, I thought I knew her, I thought I knew her!"

"You did. You do."

"Do I? How long did I actually know her before we got married? I don't know a thing about her past. She never talked about it. She could have been a call girl somewhere for all I know."

"That's a fine thing to say about your own wife, Dave! I'm surprised at you—I really am."

"Are you?" Tully heard himself shouting. "What the hell would you know about it? Your wife was never reported in a lousy motel room with a creep—your wife never had a murder charge hanging over her head!"

Ollie Hurst said mildly, "Go ahead, take it out on me if it makes you feel any better."

"I don't know what I called you for! Fat lot of help you are!"

"Here, Dave. Drink this."

It was three fingers of Scotch. Tully started to take it mechanically, but then he shook his head. "I've already tried that. I'm sorry, Ollie, I don't know what's happening to me. A couple of hours ago I was living in a solid world, solid business, solid house, in love with a solid wife. All of a sudden everything's turned to jelly—I can't hold *on* to any of it! I don't know what to think, where to turn, what to do . . ."

"You want me to get a lawyer?"

"A lawyer? What do I need a lawyer for? You're a lawyer, aren't you?"

"This is a criminal case. Actually, I don't think you need a criminal lawyer yet, not till Ruth turns up, anyway. But I'll inquire around and have one on tap. The best way I can help right now is to try to locate Ruth. I could ask around discreetly—"

"No," Tully said in a strained voice. "I'm sorry I even dragged you into this. You'd better get back to Norma and that dinner party of yours. She'll be climbing the walls."

"Wait till I finish my drink before you kick me out, will you?" Ollie Hurst said amiably. He sat down and picked up the glass of bourbon. "Look, Dave, I don't pretend to know much about women. I've got my hands full just keeping poor old Norma going. And I certainly don't know anything about Ruth that you don't know. But maybe I can see her more objectively. That wife of yours is something special—and I don't give a damn if she *was* a call girl, which you and I both know she wasn't! The way she's helped Norma, the way she looks at you when she thinks nobody's watching, her honesty and frankness and kindness to others. . . . Your wife is a lady, Dave, in the only meaningful sense of the word, and if I were to find out different I'd burn my lawbooks and take a job on the county roads. And that's my speech for tonight."

He finished his drink and got to his feet. "Well, I suppose I'll have to tell Norma. Though how I'm going to break the news to her . . ." Hurst sighed and turned to go. "Problems, problems, hey, Dave? But we've got to manage. There's no other choice. Keep in touch, will you? Especially if there's any news about Ruth."

"Good night," Tully muttered.

Was Ollie's judgment right? Except where his own emotions were involved, Ollie knew a lot about women, in spite of his disclaimer. But then why had Sandra Jean insinuated. . . ?

The house, filled with silence, suddenly made itself known to him. Tully found himself looking around, like a child imagining monsters in the next room.

He jumped up. He couldn't stay here doing nothing. There was that woman at the Hobby Motel, his feeling that something was wrong with her story. . . .

4

At one time she must have been pink and firm and cheaply pretty, a sex-pot joyously ready for a tumble. But the years had caught up with her. Her overblown breasts had grown soft and lifeless, her heavy hips supported a thickening middle, and she was getting jowly. She was wearing a flowered wrapper and curlers in her straw-bleached hair, and there was a patina of cold cream on her fat cheeks when she answered Tully's knock on the motel-room door.

She looked at him impudently. "Yes? What is it?"

"Are you Miss Maudie Blake?"

She nodded.

"My name is David Tully. I'd like to talk to you for a few minutes."

"What about?" She was taking automatic inventory, noting the cut of his clothes, the beige Imperial he had parked nearby. If his surname meant anything to her, he could not detect it.

"May I come in?" Tully asked.

"You a cop?"

"No, Miss Blake."

"A girl never knows," she said, poking at her hair. "You don't look like one. What is this, a sales pitch?"

"I'm not selling anything. I'm the husband of the woman named Ruth."

Her eyes closed to slits.

"I know you've made a statement to the police. You don't have to talk to me, Miss Blake. But I'd appreciate it if you would."

He could see her weighing the possibilities, ready for instant retreat or advance. There was an animal cunning about her. He felt his pulse begin to accelerate. His instinct had been right.

"I guess I got a minute, Mr. Tully. Come in."

She stood aside and he entered the motel room. The air was clogged with heavy perfume and powder. The place was close and hot, like an incubator, and it was cluttered with magazines, newspapers and odds and ends of apparel.

The Blake woman shut the door, waddled to the messy dressing table, picked up a pack of cigarettes and lit one. She did not ask him to sit down, or sit down herself. He waited.

"Mr. Tully," she said suddenly. "You ought to know I can't change my story now."

Tully said to himself, Easy, boy, easy. You've got a bite on your line. "You think that's why I came here?"

She made a vague gesture with her dimpled hands. "Why else? I figured this Ruth babe for a chippie. Now that I see the kind of husband she's got, I get a different picture. Class. A bored dame with everything, including round heels." She clucked, shaking her synthetic locks. "It's too bad. How do broads like that hook guys like you?" The fat blonde cocked her head at him. "Just for laughs, how much were you going to offer me?"

"Miss Blake," Tully began, "I don't think you understand—"

"Only thing is, it's too late." She sighed. "You should have beat the cops here. I'm stuck with what I told them."

"And what you told them was the absolute truth?"

"Sure it was." She looked at him steadily. Too steadily?

"Did you actually see the woman?"

"No. I didn't even know he had a woman in there till I heard her say something. These walls are like tissue paper. After that I listened, just for kicks."

"You heard him call her by name, I understand." He had to hold on to himself with all his strength.

"I sure did."

"How many times?"

"Oh, once or twice."

"Then isn't it possible you made a mistake?"

Her wrapper rustled as she undulated toward him. She came close enough for her various odors to sicken him.

"You're really gone on this wife of yours, ain't you, Mr. Tully? I wish I could say I'm not sure, but how could I make a mistake? He said her name loud and clear."

Tully managed to back off without offending her. Why did I have to come here? he thought.

"You want a drink, Mr. Tully?" the woman asked sympathetically. "You look like you could use one."

"No, thanks."

She shook her head. "What a dope, playing around when she has a husband like you. Have they found her yet?"

"No, I mean I don't know. I don't suppose so."

"Maybe she can explain things when they do."

And maybe she can't. "What time did you hear them in there?" Already it was becoming easier to couple them verbally.

Maudie Blake shrugged, everything jiggling. "Earlier part of the evening. I wasn't watching the time."

"Is there anyone else who might have heard them?"

"I guess not. His room's on the end of the row. No room on the other side."

"And you were able to hear him call the woman by name," Tully said. "How is it you didn't hear the shot?"

"I went out before that, I guess—before she let Cranny have it."

He turned to go, his shoulders at a defeated slope. But then he stopped and turned slowly around.

"Cranny," Tully said. *"You just called him Cranny. You knew him!"* He was all over her in an instant, digging his big fingers deep into her floppy arms, glaring down at her. "In fact, you know a hell of a lot more about this than you've let on! Suppose you start telling the truth—"

"Whoa, buster," the woman said. She had gone a little pale around the edges of the cold cream, but her voice was cool and unperturbed. "I could have you up

34

for assault. Calm down, Mr. Tully. You can bruise me any time you want, but not with that look in your eye. Take your hands off me."

"All *right!*" He almost flung her from him in his frustration. "Then you explain why you called him Cranny."

"I must have heard one of the cops call him that." She actually came close to him again and patted his cheek. "I know, she really gave you the knee. You'll get over it. You in the phone book?"

"What?" Tully said, trying to shake his head clear.

"I said you in the phone book."

"Of course. Why?"

"I thought you might have an unlisted number—you look well-heeled enough."

"Why did you ask?"

"Oh, so I could get in touch. In case I thought of something. . . . No, I can't right now," she added hastily, seeing his expression. "But you know how it is. Sometimes a person remembers . . . later."

Tully said tiredly, "Maybe Lieutenant Smith could jog your memory right now, Miss Blake."

"I doubt it," Maudie Blake said, smiling. "I'd just have to tell him the same thing over and over. But I like you, Mr. Tully. And I'm going to set my mind to work real hard to see if I can think of anything else."

Tully stood beside the Imperial immobilized between despair and hope. Some of the Blake woman's statements had had a horribly truthful ring. And yet . . . He kept shaking his head.

After a while he trudged across the parking strip to the office of the motel. Behind the desk was the dried-up old cut-throat who had given him Maudie Blake's room number. The old man was reading the evening *Call.*

"What's it this time?" he grunted, not looking up.

"Sorry to bother you again," Tully said. "But I'd like to know when Miss Blake checked in."

"You would, would you?"

"Yes." Tully began to feel the rumble of anger again. A little more of this and I'll blow like a volcano, he thought.

35

"Can't give out information 'bout our guests."

"A dollar bought me her room number." Tully fished in his wallet and flung two dollar bills on the desk. "When did she check in?"

The old man lowered his newspaper, looked around cautiously, and clawed the two bills out of sight. "Look, mister," he said in a low voice, "this place has been crawlin' with cops. They told me to keep my trap shut. I'll do it this one more time, but that's it." He scuttled over to a card file and went through it fast. "The tenth. That would be four days ago. Now beat it, mister, will you?"

"Thanks," Tully said grimly.

He went out. There was a ferment of exultancy in him now. Maudie Blake had checked in four days ago. The same day as Cox! Surely. . . ? He thought of the Witch in *Macbeth*. "By the pricking of my thumbs . . ." Was it likely that Julian Smith, with all his experience, hadn't seen a possible connection between the Blake woman and the dead man?

The exultancy drained out of him.

Tully plodded over to his car, carefully not looking at the end room of the row. One look on his arrival had been plenty. It was too easy to imagine Ruth stealing up to it, glancing around, knocking surreptitiously. . . .

He drove home in a torment of doubt.

How could a man live in love with a woman and not *know* her? Was Ruth capable of putting on an act that had fooled not only him, but his friends as well? Including a shrewd observer like Ollie Hurst?

It's ridiculous and unreasonable, Tully kept telling himself. The actress didn't live who could carry off such a role for so long.

Ruth had travelled widely. She had finished her education abroad and had a rather cosmopolitan outlook. So she was not particularly interested in the petty social cliques of a small town. She had been quite frank—with him—about her views on living there. But she hadn't minded the smallness so long as she lived there with him, and nobody but him was aware of her attitude. She joined into the life of his set happily, if on her own terms. Practically everyone was crazy about her.

You couldn't paint that sort of honesty into a picture of an adulterous killer.

Or could you?

His doubts were less insistent as he got out of the Imperial in his driveway. The house was still dark. He made a quick, futile search anyway. Then, because he could no longer resist, he began telephoning friends. He explained that he had returned from the capital sooner than he had expected. Was Ruth there?

He received invitations to golf, a dinner, a bridge session, but no clue to his wife's whereabouts. If any of them had heard of the Crandall Cox murder, none had yet connected Ruth with it.

Between calls to others, he kept trying Mercedes Cabbott's number. It continued busy. As he was about to try it for the fourth time, someone rang the doorbell.

Ruth?

But it was only Mercedes Cabbott's son, Andrew Gordon.

Andy wore his usual sulky look. His breath was rich with liquor.

"I was just trying to get your mother, Andy—"

The son of Mercedes Cabbott's second marriage brushed by Tully. He was a dark, lean, sullenly good-looking boy who might have been handsome if his features had had any strength. Tully suddenly realized that Andrew Gordon had a habit of pouting, uncomfortably like Sandra Jean Ainsworth. Too bad his character wasn't as muscular as his body.

"Is Ruth at your place, by any chance?" There was no point in challenging Andy's rudeness. He had been brought up in an atmosphere of special privilege.

"Nah," Andy said. "Where's Sandra Jean?"

"I don't know."

"She said she was stopping by here to kill a loose evening."

"She did. Then she left to look for you."

"Damn," Andy said. "Well, it looks as if neither of us

is having any luck with the Ainsworth sisters tonight. Got a drink handy?"

"You know where it is."

But Tully noticed that Andy went heavy on the water and light on the Scotch. He always acted tighter than he was.

Andy clutched the drink and threw his leg over the arm of a chair.

"I had a real brawl with the old lady," Andy said. "I was supposed to squire her around this evening, but then we got into it. It's that damned George's fault. Can't Mercedes see he married her for the loot?"

Tully knew the petulant statement to be false. George Cabbott, Mercedes's third husband, was a little younger than she, but he had plenty of money of his own. George was a husky, no-nonsense fellow who didn't care a hoot what people thought of him. He wasn't afraid of hard work, public opinion, or anything else. He and Mercedes were genuinely attached to each other, a fact nobody but Tully and a few other perceptive people believed.

"One of these days," Andy promised, "I'm going to push George's nose through the back of his neck."

It might be a pretty good brawl at that, Tully thought. Physically Andrew was gristle, bone and cat-gut. George was a hundred and eighty pounds of rock-crusher.

"I could handle the old lady and marry Sandra Jean," Andy continued to mutter, "if George would keep his nose to himself. He's got my respected mother so worked up against Sandra Jean the old lady'll use any excuse to break us up."

Such as a sister hunted for murder? Tully wondered, and then winced at the absurdity of it.

Andy held his glass up to the light, squinting. To hide the misery? Tully felt sorry for him at that. The boy had had it pretty rough.

In her globe-trotting, gadabout career Mercedes had picked up a string of husbands. By two of these she had borne children. Her daughter Kathleen's father had been a man named Lavery. Andrew was the offspring of Lavery's successor, a mining tycoon named Gordon.

Andy had been a small boy when his half-sister, already a young woman, died in a boating accident. This had been fifteen years ago.

In her daughter's grave Mercedes had buried her maternal common sense. She had never worn an apron in her life, but the strings by which she tied her son to her had been no less hampering. She had protected Andy from everything, including his opportunity to become a man.

"Maybe Sandra Jean ran into Ruth," Andy said. "They'll probably come home together."

"I don't think so," Tully said. "I don't think there's any point in waiting, Andy."

Andy's lip twitched. "Is that a gentle hint to leave?"

"No," Tully said. "Though if you're going to get argumentative, it might be a good idea."

"Everybody, but everybody!" Andy exploded. He looked as if he wanted to throw the glass. "Like a stinking conspiracy. Send Andrew home so mama can tuck him into his itty-bitty bedikins! I'm getting so damned fed up—"

"Look, kid," Tully said, "I've got too much on my own mind tonight to listen to your bellyaching."

"You? What kind of trouble could the noble Dave Tully be in?"

"Skip it."

"First you insult me, then you tell me to skip it! You trying to make me out a nothing?"

"You do a pretty good job of that yourself, Andy."

"You'd better apologize for that," the boy said excitedly. "I'm not going to stand for that—"

"All right, I apologize," Tully said wearily. "Now will you start acting your age?"

"You stop talking to me as if I were still wearing diapers!"

"Well, aren't you? Andy, I've asked you to lay off me tonight. Ruth is in the worst kind of trouble. Some man has been killed in the Hobby Motel and, unbelievable as it is, the police think she killed him. They're looking for her now."

Andrew Gordon's skin underwent a remarkable series

of color changes, from its normal sun-brown through a number of gradations of mud-tan to a final, dirty yellow. There it remained. The boy stared up at Tully as if he had received a fatal wound. Slowly he got to his feet.

"Ruth? Wanted for murder?"

"I told you it was unbelievable."

Mercedes Cabbott's son moistened his lips. "She wouldn't do that to me and Sandra Jean—she couldn't—"

"What?" Tully said, bewildered.

"I always thought that angel-puss of Ruth's was too good to be true," the boy mumbled. "I tagged her for a cheap lay long ago. But to kill the guy and drag Sandra Jean into the papers just when . . . Sure as hell, this is going to blow it with the old lady—"

Andy staggered backward across half the room, landing with a jarring impact against the wall, his hand to the cheek on which Tully's heavy fist had landed.

"Say anything like that about Ruth again and I'll tear that filthy tongue of yours out by the roots."

Tully stood rigid, fighting the steel band tightening about his chest. He kept watching the boy murderously, licking his torn knuckles.

Andy Gordon lurched away from the wall. There was a wild look in his eyes, a sort of crazed happiness.

Tully set himself for a brawl.

It failed to come. Instead, the boy grinned. "So I'm wrong about Ruth, huh? Man, you're as blind as they make 'em."

"I wasn't kidding, Andy. You'd better get out of here now."

"You'd rather not hear it, huh?"

In spite of himself, Tully growled, "Hear what?"

"While you were away upstate, she had a man calling her here. And he wasn't anybody in our crowd, either."

"You're lying," Tully said. "Or making something out of nothing."

"Am I?" Andy Gordon laughed. "Let me ask you one question. I know the answer because I heard the newscast, but I don't know if you did. What was the name of the guy they found shot in the Hobby?"

"Crandall Cox."

40

"So you do know. Good enough! Now you listen to me, big man, because I'm going to give it to you good, where it's going to hurt the most." The young voice crackled with hate. "I was out for a drive with Sandra Jean a couple days ago when she said, 'Let's drop in on my sister and cheer the poor darlin' up.' So we dropped in. Your poor darlin' wasn't home. We helped ourselves to some of your liquor, and just then the phone rang. Sandra Jean told me to answer it, so I did. It was a man with a funny kind of voice—flat and sneery and like he talked out of the side of his mouth. A voice I never heard. He asked for Ruth—he didn't say Mrs. Tully, Dave-boy, he used her first name. I said she wasn't here and asked if he wanted to leave a message. He said, 'I sure do,' and the way he said it—well, 'drooly' would be the only word to describe it. And then he said, 'Tell Ruth that Cranny called,' and he hung up. Crandall Cox —Cranny; get it, Mr. Tully? Do you get it?"

Tully rubbed his eyes. He had an overwhelming wish to lie down and go to sleep and sleep on and on and on.

"Did you tell Sandra about the call?" Tully said.

"Why, sure," Andy Gordon said gayly. "No secrets between *us*. But don't worry, Dave, it's all in the family. *We* won't tell anybody. . . . Say, you throw a pretty good punch, do you know?"

And, still grinning, the boy left.

5

Julian Smith's office at police headquarters was as tidy as Smith himself. He nodded pleasantly to Tully and indicated a chair.

"Don't bother to ask, Dave," the lieutenant said. "The answer is we still haven't found a trace of her."

Tully sank into the chair. "When you phoned me to come right over, Julian, I was hoping—" Tully stopped without hope.

Smith filled two paper cups from a container of coffee and offered one to Tully.

"She hasn't tried to contact you, Dave?"

He shook his head.

The lieutenant regarded him with sympathy. "Not much sleep last night, I take it."

"Not much."

"You look as if you could use some lunch."

"I'm not hungry. Julian, why'd you call me?"

"We have a rundown on Crandall Cox."

Tully set the paper cup down on the Homicide man's desk; it was scalding his hand. He felt as if he weighed a thousand pounds. The headache still drummed between his temples.

"Have you linked Ruth to him?"

The detective said, "Not yet."

"I told you," Tully said. "It's some nightmarish mistake." Where was she? Running? Hiding?

Julian Smith glanced at him again, then picked up some papers from his desk. "You'll be interested to learn that Cox originally came from these parts."

"Really?" It was just something to say.

"As a matter of fact, the name Cox rang a bell the

minute I heard it. This fellow's father, Crandall Cox Senior, owned a big hardware store where the Macklin department store now stands. He—the father, I mean—served a couple of terms on the City Council."

"I don't remember him."

"It was a long time ago. Junior was the apple of his father's eye—a rotten apple, as it turned out. Kicked out of school—he went to college here—wouldn't go into the business, thought the world owed him a living; you know the type. When Cox Senior died and the store was sold, Junior ran through the estate in short order. Spent it mostly on women. Then his mother died. He had no other family here, so Cox liquidated what was left and lit out for bigger fields.

"Through his fingerprints, clothing labels, baggage and a few other leads we got a quick make on him from upstate and a few big cities in neighboring states. He was arrested and tried at least twice for extortion, once on a charge of blackmail, but no convictions." Lieutenant Smith shrugged. "There's probably a big book on him that'll turn up when we've had more time to dig."

"Sounds charming," Tully said dully.

"Until comparatively recently Cox lived pretty well. Off women. Mainly middle-aged widows and well-heeled married women with busy husbands and too much time on their hands."

Tully flushed at that, and Smith went on, looking through his window at the town's main street. "About a year or so ago he began to go to pot physically—kidneys kicked up, an almost fatal pneumonia, a stomach ulcer, heart attack. . . . He wound up in the charity ward of a city hospital, and we're pretty sure he headed for here not long after he was discharged.

"Dave . . . I don't think Cox came back to the old hometown for sentimental reasons. He was sick and broke, and the way I figure it he had a pigeon here ready to pluck—some woman he could blackmail out of a lot of money. And she lost her head and killed him."

"You mean Ruth," Tully said.

"The shoe seems to fit, Dave."

Tully swallowed the dregs of his coffee, crushed the

paper cup and flung it at the window. Smith patiently picked it up, dropped it into his wastebasket and waited.

Tully's skin was gray and his eyes looked as if they had been wiped with sandpaper.

"Thanks for nothing!" he said through his teeth.

"It may not be so bad, Dave. She'd certainly get the sympathy of a jury. Probably could even plead self-defense and get away with it. Why don't you think it over?"

Tully laughed. "You think I'm hiding Ruth?"

"You're head over heels gone on her, pal. It might have warped your better judgment."

"This is one nightmare that seems to have no end." Tully's laugh was more like a bark. "What good would it do me to hide her, Julian?"

"You might be figuring on smuggling her out of the country—Mexico, South America, anywhere. Then turning your assets secretly into cash and slipping away to join her."

"Julian, you can't be serious—"

"Can't I?" the detective said. "Item: We're pretty good at looking for people. Ruth's hiding in no back-street hotel in this town, believe me. Item: You cut short your visit upstate. Why, Dave?"

"I'd finished sooner than I'd expected. I'd only just got back to the house when you drove up and found me!"

"Or you left the capital two hours before you claimed. Figuring normal driving time, there's still about two hours of your return trip we can't account for, Dave. Maybe more, if you really pushed the Imperial."

"You mean," Tully snarled, "I'm a suspect in this case, too?"

"Under the circumstances," Lieutenant Smith said unhappily, "I'm afraid I've got to ask you what you did with those two hours."

Tully drew the back of his hand across his mouth, tasting a clammy slick. It had not occurred to him that he might be under investigation, too.

"For one thing, I got a shave and haircut," he said.

"At the Capitol Hotel barber shop?"

"No, at a place near Monument Square. Not far from the restaurant where I had my breakfast."

Smith reached for a scratch pad and a pencil. "Want to give me the name of the shop?"

"I don't know the name of the shop. I don't remember what the barber looked like, or the shine boy. I didn't realize I'd need them for an alibi or I'd have taken notes, Julian."

"You didn't spend two hours in the shop," the Homicide man said. His face was slightly flushed.

"Of course not! I decided that as long as I was in the capital, I'd take a quick look at the Markham development. The one with the artificial lakes."

"Did you call Mr. Markham?"

"No. He'd have insisted on showing me everything in detail and I'd have lost half a day. I was only interested in his use of the terrain. I drove out there, cruised around, saw what I wanted to see, and then left."

"You drove directly home from there?"

"Yes."

"Okay, Tully, thanks."

Tully drove away from police headquarters depressingly certain that Julian Smith was far from through with him.

It was easy enough to see it from the detective's point of view: Tully returning early from upstate; Ruth, skulking in a darkened house, waiting for her husband, half out of her mind, hysterically confessing in his arms that she had shot a blackmailer; Tully, completely in love with his wife, hiding her without thought of the consequences . . .

Bleakly, he almost wished it were that simple.

6

The mansion—no one ever referred to it as a house—lorded it over the landscape from its eminence above the town. It was a gigantic white-brick edifice with the tall white pillars and sweeping verandas of the Virginia Colonial style, out of place and out of time. But if you could ignore the modern developments clustering about its skirts, and the grimy town far below, it was beautiful.

Tully drove up the winding approach between the immaculate palisades of seventy-foot arborvitae trees, worth a fortune in themselves, catching glimpses of the intricate terracing beyond that kept a crew of landscape gardners busy nine months a year. Then he passed the tennis courts and the Olympic-sized swimming pool. Over the hill behind the house, Tully knew, were stables and riding trails and a ninehole golf course, separated from the rear terrace by an immense acreage as carefully tended as a Londoner's postage-stamp garden.

The English butler—only Mercedes Cabbott would have the nerve to employ an English butler in a community where the acquisition of a cook or even a mere maid was a major triumph—preceded Tully through the gleaming two-story entrance hall and showed him out onto the flagged terrace at the rear of the mansion, overlooking the incredible lawns. Mercedes was seated in flowered grandeur at a white-ribbed glass table, big enough for twelve, before a display of savory-smelling silver-lidded mysteries.

"Good morrow, David," she said.

"Good what?" Tully said, in spite of himself.

"What else can I call it? I don't know whether the hell it's morning or afternoon—whether this is breakfast

Edouarde whipped up for me, or lunch. What is it, Stellers?"

The butler said, dead-pan, "A bit of each, Madam."

"Thank you, Stellers. How about disposing of this grapefruit for me, David? It's laced with sherry. Or would you care for some he-man chow?"

"I only dropped in for a few minutes, Mercedes—" Tully began.

"And a great mercy it is, David—you look half starved. Pull up one of these spidery iron chairs George picked—I can't imagine why! Another place, Stellers, and tell Edouarde to fix Mr. Tully a filet. Medium rare, David, isn't it?"

Tully smiled faintly. "That's right. But really—"

"Shut up, darling. It will make me happy. Don't you want to make me happy?"

Sipping Edouarde's Lucullan coffee, listening to Mercedes Cabbott's brisk small-talk, Tully resigned himself to a long session. She was a tinkling, vivacious little woman, all pinks and whites, with the figure of a young girl and the temperament of a fifteenth century queen. She wore her white hair like a crown and left the dye bottles to commoner females.

No one told Mercedes what to do, not even her husband George Cabbott, whom she adored. She kept whimsical hours, ate when she pleased, abhorred exercise and never gained a pound. She was a many-sided creature with unpredictable moods, and the inherited millions to indulge them. She would suddenly take off for Europe, or India, or some unannounced destination and be gone for months. She would often, without explanation, refuse to support a much-needed community project; yet Tully knew that she just as often made huge anonymous donations to causes or institutions that caught her fancy.

This youthful woman with the imperious blue eyes was old enough to be a grandmother many times over —which she would have been, she had once remarked to him, had her daughter Kathleen Lavery lived. Tully knew how much Mercedes wanted grandchildren— grandchildren of "the right sort." He supposed this had something to do with her ferocious possessiveness toward Andrew Gordon, her only remaining child, and the fierce eye she kept on the girls in whom he showed an interest.

Tully had known Mercedes all his life as most others in town had known her, which was to say not at all. Then his plans to build Tully Heights brought them together. During their negotiations for the purchase of the land he wanted for his development, they had become friends.

It was through Mercedes Cabbott that he had met Ruth Ainsworth. Ruth had exploded into Tully's life when she made a sudden appearance in the storybook mansion as Mercedes's house guest that memorable summer. Mercedes's insistence on making the wedding for them had seemed to touch Ruth deeply; Tully, who had other plans, found himself abandoning them without a struggle.

It was at the wedding that he first met his bride's sister; Sandra Jean had come from somewhere in the East to be Ruth's maid of honor. And in the mansion Sandra Jean had remained, playing a rapidly warming game with Andy Gordon, as a sort of quasi-member of the family. The Ainsworth girls' mother and Mercedes had been intimate friends since their college days, it seemed, and Mercedes had characteristically kept an eye—and often a hand—on her friend's daughters when Mrs. Ainsworth died. Between Mercedes and Ruth there had been an obvious affection; toward Sandra Jean the wealthy woman evinced no such personal involvement. Their relationship was too complex for Tully to grasp.

He had once asked Mercedes, "Sandra Jean seems to bring out the iron in you. Why do you let her stay?"

"Because," Andy's mother had replied sweetly, "here I can keep tabs on what she's up to."

Something Mercedes was saying jolted Tully out of his ruminations.

"Sorry," he said. "I was off on Cloud Nine. What was that again, Mercedes?"

"I said you're not eating your steak. Now let's talk turkey. When are you going to get down to the reason for this visit? I know it's about Ruth."

Tully put down his steak-knife. "How did you know?"

"Darling, two men were here. Policemen. Very discreet and well-mannered. And pathetically anxious to sniff out Ruth's whereabouts."

"Did you tell them?" Tully asked quickly. "Do you know?"

"No, David, to both questions."

"She's in serious trouble," he muttered.

"I gathered as much," she said in a quiet voice. "David, what's it all about? Tell me, please."

"She's suspected of causing a man's death. His name was Crandall Cox."

"That motel shooting?" The little woman had guts of steel. Her eyes turned steely, too. "We shan't let them harm her, shall we, David?"

"Not if I can help it."

"Not if *we* can help it." Mercedes glanced over her shoulders into the house. "I wonder what's keeping George?"

"Mercedes . . . have you heard from Ruth?"

She returned her attention fully to him. "I'm not sure I'd tell you even if I had."

"What do you mean!"

Mercedes Cabbott leaned over and squeezed his big hand with her tiny one; it had surprising strength. "You needn't bark at me, David," she said gently. "You'd have a troubled look of a different sort if your concern were without a doubt. There's a big question in your mind suddenly about Ruth."

"I don't know what you mean," Tully said stiffly.

"You know exactly what I mean. It's Ruth's possible relationship with this worm Cox that's eating away at you, not the absurd allegation that she shot him."

"Well, suppose it is!"

"Then I was right. I don't blame you one little bit, David. It's natural for a man to doubt under such circumstances."

"Is it?" Tully said miserably. "I always thought that if a man loved a woman—"

"Garbage! A man is a man, which means that's a peculiarly vulnerable creature." Mercedes smiled at him. "But I have good news for you, David. Natural as your doubts are, they're unnecessary. I know Ruth through and through. She really loves you. No other man exists for her—"

"Would you make the same statement in the past tense?" he mumbled. "A man, say, named Cox?"

"Do you think you have a right to expect that Ruth was brought up in a bottle?" She squeezed his hand again. "But I'd stake a very great deal on that girl, David. I've never known her to do a vulgar or sordid thing."

Tully sighed. "I'm sorry, Mercedes."

"That's good." The blue steel came back into her eyes. "Because now I can say I'm sorry, too."

He looked up, puzzled. "You? What for?"

"For what I have to do, David. I have to use what weapons fate puts into my hand."

"I don't think I understand."

"In a short time you and Ruth are going to be hip-deep in the worst slops of a sex and murder scandal. I mean publicly. I'm going to have to use it, David."

"That's just what Sandra Jean predicted."

"She did?" Mercedes nodded. "Good for her—she's even shrewder than I gave her credit for. Funny how an angel like Ruth could have such a little bitch of a sister. A bitch, I might add, in continuous heat."

Tully said, without thinking, "It takes two to couple, Mercedes."

For a moment she looked furious. Then she shrugged her pretty shoulders. "Yes, it does, David. I suppose you're justified in taking that tone about Andrew—I haven't always sounded rational about my son. I'm afraid I haven't done a very good job with Andy." Her voice hardened. "But he's all I have left, and he's going to be what I want in spite of himself.

"When I buried Kathleen . . ." Mercedes stopped; for the merest flash of a startling instant, she looked ancient. All Tully could think of was Rider Haggard's Ayesha swiftly crumbling to dust. Then Mercedes was herself again. "I wasn't able to stop mourning Kathleen, David. And when I was left with Andy Junior, the ghost of Kathleen took over. What I mean is . . . I was terrified from that moment on. Terrified that I might lose him, too."

He had never seen Mercedes Cabbott so nakedly distressed.

"I've become increasingly aware of the poor job I've done with Andy. Maybe it was marrying George Cabbott that opened my eyes. Third time the charm, they say. George is the man I should have met and married in the beginning. If he'd been at my side in Andy's formative years, to help me bring Andy up . . ."

"Mercedes."

"No, let me say it, David. I want you to know . . . I honestly don't feel any personal spite toward Sandra Jean. Under other circumstances, in fact, I could like the girl—she's so like me in so many ways. But it's too late all around. Andy is what I've made him, a useless and overprotected lunkhead who doesn't know how to take care of himself. He wouldn't survive six months outside the environment I've created for him. But finally knowing all this doesn't change anything. I love him, and I've got to keep him from coming to serious harm. Sandra Jean would swallow him like a female shark. . . . Have I been awfully selfish, filling your ears with my true confessions when you're in such immediate trouble? Forgive me, David."

"For what?" Tully said. He engulfed her little hand and felt it stiffen in his grasp. She was an island surrounded by an impenetrable reef—a strange and lovely little island full of unexpected hazards. No one, with the possible exception of George Cabbott, had ever really explored her.

At that moment George Cabbott came out on the terrace, and Tully rose, feeling a great relief.

George was a big man, as big as Tully, bronzed and bleached by outdoor living. He wore old jeans, a T-shirt and sneakers as if they were a uniform.

" 'Lo, Dave. Sorry I'm late, sweetheart. I was scrubbing up."

As her husband stooped to kiss her, Mercedes crinkled her little nose.

51

"You've been in the stables again, darling. Sometimes I think I married a horse."

George Cabbott chuckled, and she threw her head back for his kiss. Tully looked away and took the first opportunity to excuse himself.

He had never felt so alone in his life.

Pulling into his driveway, Tully thought he would burst from the pressures building up inside him. He was tired of waiting for Julian Smith to locate Ruth; he had to do something on his own.

And a new fear was gnawing away at him. Was Ruth's continued absence really voluntary? It was possible that she had seen something at the Hobby Motel that had made her a danger to someone. Maybe the police couldn't find her because her body. . . .

Tully ground his teeth and tried to shut out the thought. . . .

Inside the house something was different.

Tully stood holding his breath, trying to sense what it was.

Then he had it. The silence—the silence was gone. With a hoarse cry he made for the master bedroom.

Someone was taking a shower.

He flung himself at the bathroom door.

"Ruth!" he shouted. "Is that you?"

"It's me, Davey—Sandra Jean."

Tully stood there. Finally, he walked out.

He was in the living room when Sandra Jean joined him, her skin warmly moist where it showed beneath the short terrycloth robe. Ruth's robe, damn her! She padded to him, bare legs glistening. Her face was scrubbed shiny, her hair fell in damp ringlets on her forehead. She reminded him so much of Ruth that he had to turn away.

"Mind if I borrow a dress from Ruth, Davey?"

He could have throttled her. He controlled himself. "Help yourself."

"And a cigarette from you?"

He fumbled in his jacket pocket. She stood close to

him, as he lit it for her. Damn her soul, did she have to smell like Ruth, too?

She looked up at him slowly. "Thank you, pops."

She had scarcely bothered to draw the robe together.

"Mmm," she said, inhaling deeply. "This tastes good. Change your brand, Davey?" She laughed, and somehow the robe came apart.

"Sandra Jean," he said softly.

She tilted her head. "Yes?" An amused light danced in her eyes.

"Why the hell," he said in the same soft tone, "don't you go and get dressed?"

The light in her eyes shifted to the other end of the spectrum. She wrapped the robe about her tightly and stamped out of the room.

When she reappeared she was wearing one of Ruth's print dresses and a pair of Ruth's flat-heeled straw shoes. Her glance at Tully was spiteful. She went to the bar and mixed herself a drink.

Tully dropped into a chair. "Waiting for someone?"

"Do you mind, Mr. Tully?"

"I'm not sure I don't. Andy, of course?"

"Of course."

"I should think my house would have lost its charm for him as a trysting place."

"Trysting place!" The girl laughed. "You *are* from Squaresville, aren't you?"

"Strictly," Tully said. "But, Sandra, let's keep our eye on the ball shall we? I don't know what Andy's version was, but last time he was here he made a couple of unpardonable remarks about Ruth. Viciously nasty."

"And you popped him one," Sandra Jean jeered. "But we understand, Davey. You were under a great strain, and all that jazz."

"I still am."

"Andy forgives you. I forgive you. Do you forgive you?"

"I'm sorry I blew my top. But he had it coming."

"Going, as I heard it." Sandra Jean took a thirsty swallow. "You don't care a lot for my fella, do you?"

"I couldn't care less. I wish you'd meet him somewhere else."

"Like in a dirty room in a dirty motel . . . like?"

Mercedes Cabbott is dead right, he thought. This kid is a bitch. "I suppose that's a sisterly reference to Ruth."

"Is *that* what it was?" Sandra Jean asked innocently. "Who's being the nasty little boy now?"

Tully shrugged. He was too exhausted to reply.

Hips on gimbals, Sandra Jean prowled about the room, gesturing with her glass. "You get one thing straight, O Pure in Heart. Nobody wrecks me with Andy, but *nobody*. Mercedes Cabbott can maneuver herself dizzy, you can bar me from this house, but that thar gold strike's mine! Get me?"

"Not that I give a damn," Tully murmured. "But it isn't as if you were penniless."

"Those icky little trust funds Ruth and I interited? They might look like a ten-strike to a girl who had to pull herself up by the runs in her stockings, but it's strictly for the *hoi polloi,* buster. I need as much in a month as that fund brings me in a year."

Something in the way she said it sounded an alert. But he kept his own voice casual.

"You wouldn't be in a financial jam, would you, Sandra?"

"Oh, I owe a few people." She said it indifferently, but he noticed a slight frown.

It came to him in a flash. "Gamblers, maybe?"

"It's none of your business," she said, and he knew he was right. There were several gambling joints just outside the town limits, and Sandra Jean liked to play the wheel. "Anyhow, it hasn't a thing to do with my greedy plans involving Andrew. He's the biggest chance I'll ever get, and I'm not letting him get away from me. You remember that, sweetie."

The door chimed.

Sandra Jean looked at her brother-in-law. "That's my Andy now," she said, "and if you've any idea of telling him what I just said, forget it. In the first place he wouldn't believe it. In the second place, I can get pretty nasty myself, Sir David."

- 54 -

Tully said dryly, "I never had the least doubt of it," and he got up and opened the door.

George Cabbott stood there.

"Oh, George," Tully said.

"Anything new on Ruth?" The big bronzed man had changed from jeans and T-shirt to a conservative suit.

"No."

"If she'd met with any harm, Dave, you'd have heard by this time. By the way, is Sandra Jean here?"

"Here I am," Sandra Jean said. She was standing stock-still in the middle of the living room. "Hi, George. Is something wrong?"

Cabbott said pleasantly, "That would depend on the point of view. I dropped by to tell you you needn't wait for Andy to show up—if, of course, that's what you're doing here."

"I don't think I understand."

"He's having a long, long talk with Mercedes."

"Oh, one of those." Sandra Jean laughed, but Tully noticed that her eyes remained wary.

"I don't think this one is *quite* like the others," Cabbott said. "I'm afraid Mercedes has pretty well made up her mind to cut Junior off without a cent, as the saying goes, in a certain contingency."

"How does that involve me?" the girl said. "Or is that the whole point?"

"Judge for yourself, Sandra," George Cabbott said, and Tully could have sworn there was an undertone of amusement in his voice. "The last thing I heard Mercedes tell Andy as I left was that, in her opinion, if he was old enough to take a wife he was old enough to get a job and support her."

"Now, George," Sandra Jean said, and there was amusement in her voice, too. She can sure put on an act, Tully thought. She's about as amused as a lady spider watching her dinner get away.

George Cabbott merely smiled and left.

55

7

"If that refugee from a TV commercial thinks he can bluff me out of this . . . !" Sandra Jean was raging up and down the room. "I'll show *him*."

"Maybe he's being your very good friend," Tully said.

"And maybe Mercedes Cabbott is a member of the human race! Why, Dave, she put him up to this—isn't it obvious? I'll show her, too!"

There was a bubble of froth at the corner of her mouth. And her sister's predicament, Tully thought bitterly, left her temperature unchanged. That's what she thinks of Ruth.

As if she had picked up the name on her emotional radar, Sandra Jean said suddenly, "I'm not really worried—that woman won't cast her precious sonny-boy adrift—it's the way she treats *me*. You'd think I was Typhoid Mary. The old bitch wouldn't act this way if I were Ruth."

"Well, that's one thing you don't have to worry about," Tully said. "You're not."

His tone seemed to calm her down. "I know I'm not, Davey. It's been thrown up to me all my life. What the hell happened to this drink?" She went over to the bar and got busy again. "It's always been Ruth this and Ruth that, all that's pure and holy. In Mercedes's case it's easy to understand—she latched onto Ruth as a substitute for her daughter Kathleen, who becomes more and more of a saint the longer she's dead—in Mercedes's mind, that is." Sandra Jean took her fresh drink to the sofa and curled up opposite him. "That's all right with me. . . ."

"I don't think it is," Tully said. "I think you hate Ruth. I think you've always hated her."

Sandra Jean looked into her tall glass and considered this. "Maybe I do at that," she said at last. "Maybe I always have, as you say. And that makes me out a stinker for real, doesn't it?"

"Forget it," Tully said, barely waving his hand. "Forget it. I hardly know what I'm saying."

"Look, Davey," the girl said, setting her glass down on the floor. He looked, and he saw a Sandra Jean ten years older, her face drawn down in bitter lines. "Did Ruth ever tell you that our mother died giving birth to me? Till the day he died Daddy never forgave me for it —I was the 'cause,' you see, for Mother's dying. Poor Daddy had a tough time trying not to show it, and it'll give you a short idea of the kind of cookie our father was when I tell you that his solution was to pretend I wasn't there. So I never had a mother, and to my father I was a sort of nothing. Naturally, he gave all his paternal attention—and love—to Ruth, who could do no wrong. That's what I grew up with—a guilt feeling about my mother's death and having my sister thrown in my face. And it's still going on."

"I didn't know that." Tully shaded his burning eyes. He had never more than tolerated Sandra Jean, being polite to her only for his wife's sake; but now he realized that for some time he had even stopped thinking of the girl as a human being. She had become a sort of ambulatory annoyance—a tart-tongued irritant when her sister was around, a menace when she could corner him alone. He could not even flatter himself that she was sexually attracted to him. It was Sandra Jean's way of tearing down everything around her that seemed to have some solidity. Now he understood why. "I'm sorry we haven't got on better, Sandra," Tully said.

"Are you now," the girl said. She had been biting her lips; but now she retracted them in a curl of malice. She stooped and snatched up her glass. "And I love you, too, Davey my lad. *Pros't!*" She tossed down the contents of the glass and deliberately dropped it on the sofa and jumped up. "On that moon-eyed note, dear brother-in-law, you are rid of me for the evening. Any more of it and I'll throw up."

"Where are you going?" It was her way of covering up, he knew, for having momentarily exposed herself.

"Back to the Cabbotts' to play hell with Mercedes's plans. She has no intention of turning Andy loose on an unsuspecting world, but the dumb bunny may not realize it unless there's someone there to tell him. And that's me. Say, call me a cab, will you? I was expecting Andy to drive me back."

Tully silently rose and went into his den and phoned for a taxi. When he returned she was standing at the front door. "You're not such a bad egg, Davey," she said brightly. "Only a little on the raunchy side . . . I had you going with all that autobiographical crud, didn't I, Dave boy?"

"It sounded real to me," Tully smiled faintly.

His smile infuriated her.

"So what!" Sandra Jean snarled. "I don't need you, Ruth or anybody else!"

About ten minutes after Sandra Jean drove away in the cab, the phone rang in the study. Tully raced for it.

"Yes?" he said hoarsely.

"Dave? Julian Smith."

Tully sagged. The detective's tone was good for nothing but more bad news.

"Did Ruth—did you—?"

"No, Dave," Smith said. "No sign of her yet . . . Dave."

"Yes, Julian."

"I'm afraid I've sat on this just as long as it could be sat on. The *Times-Call* and the TV people have it. I simply couldn't keep Ruth's name out of it any longer."

"Thanks anyway, Julian. You've been more than considerate."

"They'll be on your neck any minute. . . . I don't suppose *you've* heard from Ruth?" the Homicide man said suddenly.

"No."

"Dave—"

"I said no!" Tully cried. "God damn it, don't you understand English?"

Smith hung up softly and, after a moment, Tully followed suit. His hands were shaking violently. He was heading for the Scotch when the doorbell chimed.

Tully changed course and sneaked a look out the picture window.

Any minute was right. They were here. The press *and* the TV together. He opened the door.

One of them was the city editor of the *Times-Call*, in person; the other was chief of the news staff of the local television station. David Tully knew them both well. Jake Ballinger was a rumpled, baggy-pantsed old newspaperman from Chicago who had chosen to finish off his illustrious career on a small-town paper; Eddie Harper was a prematurely bald young TV flash who had put the local station on the state map in a big way. If Ballinger and Harper were covering the Cox story in person, Ruth and he were in for it.

They treated Tully very gently, offering sincere-sounding regrets for the occasion of their visit, easing into their questions:

—What do you know about this?

Nothing. I got back from upstate and walked right into the middle of it. I don't know any more about it than you do.

—Where is Mrs. Tully?

I don't know.

—You must have heard from her.

No.

—She didn't leave you a note or anything?

No. But my wife is innocent. That's the only thing I'm sure of.

—What makes you so sure?

Ruth couldn't murder anybody.

—Then you have no proof that Mrs. Tully didn't shoot this man Cox?

I don't need proof. I know her better than anyone in the world. This is all a terrible mixup—mistake of some kind. It will be cleared up when she's found.

—But you have no idea where she is?

No. I told you.

—And you haven't any clue to her present whereabouts?

No, I said!

—How long has Mrs. Tully known Crandall Cox? (this was Jake Ballinger, solicitously.)

I'm not answering any Did-you-stop-beating-your-wife type questions! She didn't know him! At all!

—Do you know that for a fact?

No, I don't know it for a fact—how could I? I know it because she never mentioned a name remotely like that!

—But she must have known him, Mr. Tully (this was the TV news chief, gently). Cox called her by name, according to the witness the police have. By her first name, as I understand it.

—And your gun was used, Dave.

—So Mrs. Tully must have been there, wouldn't you say, Mr. Tully?

I'm saying nothing further—nothing at all!

When the two newsmen were gone, Tully poured himself a stiff shot, and another, and then another. He had handled himself badly, he knew. Done Ruth's cause an actual disservice. Most of all, perhaps, he had resented their pity, as Sandra Jean had resented his.

Standing at the window with the third drink in his hand, Tully felt emotionally naked. Where *was* Ruth? What was she doing? And why? Ruth's cause . . . Did she have a cause?

He tried to keep his thoughts at bay, but they kept hurtling through his mind: Is she only a smoother version of Sandra Jean . . . conning me . . . insinuating herself into Mercedes Cabbott's affections by playing on the old woman's memory of a dead daughter . . . fooling the whole town . . . until an unsavory chapter in her past caught up with her. . .?

The phone rang again. He rushed into the den.

"Hello!"

"The Tully residence?" It was a woman's voice, the wrong woman's. "This is Miss Blake."

"Who? Oh, from the Hobby Motel. Yes?"

60

"I ain't there any more, Mr. Tully. I just moved to Flynn's Inn—too many rubbernecks at the motel. Look, I read the paper. First time I saw you I figured you for class, and now I see by the paper that I was right—you're a real big shot around here."

"What do you want?" Tully asked curtly.

"Well, now, you know I told you I'd think real hard about Cranny Cox. I like to help people if I can."

"Sure you do, Miss Blake." He braced himself; this might be genuine, at that. "And you do remember something now?"

"Why don't you come over to Flynn's Inn and we'll talk about it?"

"Do you know where my wife is?"

"I didn't say *that*."

"Do you!"

She sounded quite unperturbed by his violence. "I like to see who I'm talking to. You better come over here."

"What's your room number?"

She laughed. "Room two two two. Just you come on up . . . alone, Mr. Tully."

"What are you afraid of, Miss Blake?" For a wild instant he suspected some sort of trap.

"Witnesses," she said simply. "You say nothing to nobody and come alone, mister, or don't bother to come at all."

8

She was waiting for him in the doorway of her room. He supposed she had instructed the seedy clerk at the desk in the dusty lobby to warn her of his arrival.

Stretched over her gelatinous figure were skintight slimjims with a pattern of huge pink roses and a knit blouse that sculptured her outsized chest. There was a cigarette in her fat fingers and a tobacco crumb on her lips.

"Anybody with you?" She stepped into the hall and glanced down the dingy stairwell.

"You said to come alone."

She motioned him into her room and followed him in.

She shut and latched the door and leaned back against it, watching him critically—even, Tully thought, anxiously. He glanced around the room; he had never set foot in Flynn's Inn before. Like the hall it was dingy and cramped and dirty, and she had brought with her from the motel room the same odor of stale smoke and cheap perfume. He wondered if he was the intended victim of a badger game—the bed was unmade, the bedclothes tumbled about.

"Have a drink, Mr. Tully?"

"What? Oh—no, thanks. Miss Blake—"

"I never been much on this 'Miss Blake' stuff." The woman went to the dusty bureau and poured herself a shot from a two-thirds empty fifth of rye. "You call me Maudie."

"Look," Tully said. "I don't know what you're up to, but if this is some kind of shakedown racket—"

"Why, Mr. Tully, you got no right to talk to me like

that!" She actually sounded injured. "I just had a story to tell you."

"Then tell it, please, and I'll get out of here."

"A real sad story, I mean." She slung the contents of the shot glass down her throat. "About a girl who needs a loan."

"I'm not a banker or a money-lender," Tully said shortly. "I'm in the market for information and I'll buy it. How much do you want?" He brought out his wallet and waited. Her quick animal eyes pounced on it and sprang away. She went back to the bureau and refilled the glass.

"What's your hurry, Mr. Tully? Why don't you sit down and relax?" Tully looked around, spotted one uncluttered chair, and sat down on it. "That's better," she smiled. "You see, Mr. Tully, I leveled with the cops. My neck ain't stuck out. If I happen to remember an extra detail later, that's natural, ain't it?"

"What detail?"

Her glance was fixed on his right hand, and he looked down. He had forgotten that he was still holding the wallet. "First about that loan I mentioned . . ."

He made an impatient gesture. "How much?"

Maudie Blake said swiftly, "A hundred. Cash. They don't like checks here."

Tully opened his wallet and leafed through its contents. There were three twenties and a few small bills. "All I have on me is seventy-eight dollars."

She walked over to him and deliberately looked into his wallet. "Okay," she said. "Gimme."

He handed her the bills and put his empty wallet away. She made a tight roll of the money and thrust it into the cleft under her blouse.

"Well?" Tully demanded. He felt himself sweating.

She carried her drink to a lumpy chair and sat down, draping her left leg over the arm. She looked at him uneasily and gulped the whisky. She had apparently been drinking for some time; her eyes were beginning to blear and she sounded a little tight.

"You're not going to like this, Mr. Tully," the woman

began slowly. "Remember, I never promised you would. Right?"

"If it's about Crandall Cox," Tully said, "I'm listening."

"And your wife." She blinked and tongued her lips. "She wasn't the only one," she said. "A long time ago . . . well, Cranny used to tell me he didn't give a damn about any of them but me. I didn't believe him even then. But—you know how dames are, Mr. Tully. Or maybe you don't."

Or maybe I don't . . .

Maudie Blake's face drooped all over. "I was the one who was always there—he always had me, and he knew it. Cranny Cox was the kind needed a woman to fall back on when he was scared or broke—something like a dog he could count on no matter what he did. A dog that didn't ask for nothing but a pat on the head once in a while, or even a boot in the rear."

She got up and shuffled back to the bureau and the whisky bottle.

"It must have been rough on you," Tully said. Who cares? he thought. Get on with it!

"Rough? Yes, you could say that, mister . . . yess'r, you could sure say that."

He thought she was going to cry. Instead, her mouth tightened and she seized the bottle and drank directly from it and then took it back to the lumpy chair with her.

"When he got real sick this last time," she said, "I figured I had Cranny for good. Though what I wanted with him I can't tell you. All I knew was . . . I'd sooner have a kick from Cranny Cox than a kiss from any other man I ever knew. And *he* knew it. Goddam that ugly creep, he knew it!"

"Miss Blake," Tully said. "Maudie—"

But she mumbled, "And I was wrong again. I didn't have him, any more than the other times. He still had his great big plans to live it up. He just let me take care of him till he could get back on his feet. Then he robbed me and took off again."

In spite of the sick dread in the pit of his stomach

Tully found himself becoming aware of Maudie Blake as a woman, a hopeless addict of what she herself would hardly dare call love—love for a man who permitted her to shelter and nurse and feed him and give him money, and who then deserted her again.

"Did you know his plans? That he was coming here?"

"He didn't tell me nothing. One day I come home and he was gone, and he didn't come back. No note, no nothing. But I found a bus timetable . . . he'd marked it . . . name of a town, and I remembered he'd once said it was his home town."

"So you followed him?"

"Took the next bus." She hiccupped and giggled, "'Scuse me."

"Why?"

"Huh?" She peered at him owlishly.

"Why did you follow him?"

She seemed surprised. "He needed me."

"If he left you without a word," Tully said, "how did you know he was at the Hobby?" Suddenly he was suspicious.

"I didn't. But I figured him for a cheap motel—I'd only left a few bucks in my flat that he'd lifted. Third motel I tried, there he was, walking across the parking lot."

"I suppose he wasn't very glad to see you?"

"He cussed me out good." She laughed, tilted the bottle again. But it was empty, and she flung it from her. "Later he says okay, you're here you can stay, only keep out of my hair." She laughed again, then scowled and began to struggle out of the chair. "I got to get me another bottle—"

But Tully was towering over her, and she plopped back in alarm. "Cox told you why he'd come here, didn't he?"

"No—"

"You're lying. You've known all along, haven't you?"

Through her fright he saw a glint of cunning. "That ain't what you're buying for seventy-eight bucks, Mr. Tully."

"Would you rather Lieutenant Smith asked you the question?"

"You yell copper and a fat lot of good it'll do you," she muttered. "I'd just have to tell him like I'm telling you: I don't know why Cranny came here, I just followed him, that's all. Is there a law against that?"

Something in Tully's face above her sobered her.

"Now don't you try muscle on me, mister!"

"Cox told you his plan, didn't he?"

"He never—"

"And I was beginning to feel sorry for you! Either you were both in on this from the start, or he cut you in on the action when you showed up at the Hobby!"

She shrank deep into the chair. "No. I swear—"

"Making you share the crime of whatever he was up to would be a kind of insurance for Cox. That's it, isn't it? He didn't trust you, so he assigned part of the job to you. What were you supposed to do, Maudie?" Tully was shaking her now, his fingers deep in her fat shoulders. "What part of the mucky plan did he assign to you? Talk, you bitch!"

It was the sight of her eyes that brought him to his senses. They were bugging out, terrified, from her purpling face; and to Tully's horror he saw that his hands were around her neck. He released her and backed off. She felt her throat unbelievingly.

"You were gonna choke me," she whispered. "I ought to have you arrested for f'lonious assault, that's what I ought to do! . . . But I got a better idea, Mr. Tully."

She was all bitch now, a mountain of triumphant flesh. Tully half turned away, half closed his smarting eyes. The Blake woman got out of the chair and waddled over to him, still feeling her neck.

"I was trying to ease you into it because I thought you were real class and a nice guy and I didn't want to hurt you no more than I had to. But now, Mr. Tully, I'm gonna give it to you good! You know what your seventy-eight bucks bought? You listen!"

He tried to avoid her sour breath, but he could not.

"You drive on up to the Lodge at Wilton Lake—the Lodge, hear? Talk to the people who run it—the maids and the bellhops—take a good long look at the register—"

"What are you talking about?" Tully stammered. "The register for when—what?"

"Two summers ago—first week in June, Mr. Tully," the woman jeered. "Him and her—yeah! Cranny Cox and your wife."

Tully became aware of his surroundings. He was seated behind the wheel of his car in the parking lot of Flynn's Inn. A man came staggering out of the bar and a blare of drunken noise came out with him. Then the door closed and everything was silent again.

He had no recollection of leaving Maudie Blake's room or of getting into the Imperial. He remembered only the ghost of a cackle behind him, as if some witch had laughed in a nightmare . . .

He lit a cigarette mechanically.

The Blake woman was a vicious liar, of course. It couldn't possibly be true. To shack up at a resort hotel with a rotten punk like Crandall Cox. . . . Impossible. Not Ruth. Not a woman as fastidious as Ruth.

Then why had she gone running to the Hobby Motel at Cox's call . . . with a gun . . . two years later?

There's a reason, Tully thought desperately. There's got to be a reason—a reason that takes me off this hook —a reason a man could live with . . .

One thing is sure, he told himself. I know my wife. I'm not going to give that sodden bag of lard the satisfaction of having made me drive up to Wilton Lake on a sneak check. . . .

Two summers ago . . . that was before their marriage, before they had even met. Maybe Ruth *had* been there at the Lodge at the same time as Cox, so what? It could have been the frankest coincidence, something the jealous mind of this Blake virago had seized and built on to house her jealousy. Or else Cox, having met Ruth casually, had done the building to torment Maudie Blake, in the sadistic way of kept men contemptuously sure of their keepers. That was it! Cox had made up the whole story and spilled it to Maudie Blake for laughs, knowing she would fall for it and agonize over it.

So it wouldn't really be doubting Ruth if he did drive up to the Lake and sort of got the feel of the place again. Tully began to think about it even pleasurably. He hadn't been up to the Lake in years . . .

And, of course! He sat up in the car, tingling.

If Ruth *had* spent some time at Wilton Lake two summers ago she could hardly have failed, in her instinctive appreciation of nature, to fall under its spell. It was a beautiful, serene, secluded place, not over-patronized, and at this particular season . . . Why, she might be up there right now! Frightened, maybe, not knowing what to do, not daring to phone, hoping against hope that somehow he would fathom her hide-out and come secretly to her rescue . . .

What am I waiting for? Tully asked himself exultantly.

As he started his car he shut down his mind, refusing to think past the point at which he had stopped.

9

The distance from town to the Lake was a hundred and sixty miles. Tully covered it in under three hours, taking the final twists of the mountain road shortly after nine o'clock.

The Lodge lay at the northern end of the great lake —a rugged, spreading two-story ranch building of ivy-overgrown fieldstone and hand-hewn logs. The west terrace was lighted with copper torches. Cooks in tall chef's hats were serving an outdoor barbecue to the music of a strolling trio of cowboy-clad guitarists. Half the terrace tables were unoccupied.

The beamed lobby with its great fieldstone fireplaces was quiet. An attractive woman of middle age was on duty behind the desk.

"I was to meet my wife here," Tully said. "Do you have a Mrs. Tully registered?"

The woman consulted a register-file. "I'm sorry, sir, she hasn't arrived yet. If you have a reservation, would you like to register for the two of you?"

"No. I want to see the manager."

Tully was hungry-faced and gray. The woman hesitated.

"It's important."

She looked him over carefully. "Just a moment, please." She lifted the wicket, crossed the lobby and disappeared through the tall doors that led to the terrace.

She came back several minutes later with a sunburned young man. He smiled and said, "I'm the manager of the Lodge, Mr. Tully—Dalrymple is the name. Don't worry about your wife's not getting here on schedule. It happens all the time."

"May I speak to you in private, Mr. Dalrymple?"

The young manager's smile became rather fixed.

"Of course. This way, please."

In his office, Dalrymple offered Tully a chair. Tully shook his head, and the manager chose to remain standing, too. He was no longer smiling at all. "I really don't see what the problem is, sir, if it's merely a matter of your wife's being delayed—"

"She may be here already," Tully said.

"I beg your pardon?"

"Registered under another name."

The manager now sat down, slowly. "I see," he said. "I see . . . Of course, Mr. Tully, the management can't accept the least responsibility—"

"I'm not asking you to accept any responsibility. I'm not here to make trouble," Tully said. He pulled his wallet from his pocket and showed Dalrymple a clear snapshot of Ruth. "This is my wife, Mr. Dalrymple. All I want to know: Is she here? Under any name?"

The manager accepted the wallet photo and sat studying it a moment. "No, sir."

"Are you sure?"

"Positive. We're not a large hotel. Vacationers are our stock in trade, and I make it my business to know every guest. I assure you, your wife isn't registered under her own or any other name."

The manager was smiling again. He started to rise. "If that's all, Mr. Tully . . ."

"It's not."

The manager remained in mid-rise.

Tully's pallor had taken on a haggard caste. "Two summers ago . . . the first week of June . . . May I see your register for that period?"

"Certainly not!" The manager completed his rise as if a spring had been released.

"I'll have to insist, Mr. Dalrymple."

"It's absolutely against our rules! I'm sorry, sir—"

"Would you rather I ask the police to take a look for me?"

"Police?" Dalrymple blinked. "Of course, if a crime has been committed—although I assure you, sir, no crime has ever been committed on these premises!—"

"I didn't say it was."

"What kind of crime?" the manager asked abruptly.

Tully hesitated. Then he shrugged. "Murder."

Mr. Dalrymple went oyster-white. "How is the Lodge involved?"

"There's a question as to whether or not a certain man and . . ." Tully licked his lower lip ". . . and the original of this photo visited the Lodge two years ago . . . together . . . or at least at the same time. If I can check it out here and now, Mr. Dalrymple, the police may never come into it at all. Of course, I can't guarantee that. Do you let me see your register or don't you?"

The manager stared at Tully for a long time. Tully withstood his calculating appraisal with indifference. A numbness was setting in, not so much a lack of feeling as a suspension of it.

"Well?"

Dalrymple's glance wavered to Ruth's photo, which was still on the desk between them. He sat down and began to scrutinize it very carefully. "This woman—I mean your wife, Mr. Tully—is she . . . ?"

"Yes." He almost started to add, *But that was before I married her.*

"Two summers ago, eh? I must say the face looks familiar . . . The trouble is, I see so many people come and go—" He rose again, handed the snapshot back to Tully. "What was the man's name?"

Tully found himself able to say, "Cox. Crandall Cox," without choking.

"Wait here, please."

Dalrymple left, shutting the door emphatically behind him. Tully remained where he was. He had not shifted his position six inches since entering the office. He simply stood there, not thinking.

When the manager returned he had with him a dumpy gray-haired woman wearing old-fashioned gold-rimmed eyeglasses.

"Well?" Tully said.

"Well!" Dalrymple inhaled. He said quickly, "We

had a Mr. and Mrs. Crandall Cox registered during the period you mentioned."

"How long did they stay?"

"Three days." The man gestured, and the gray-haired woman stumped forward; she had badly flat feet, Tully noticed, and then he wondered what difference that made, what difference anything made. "This is Mrs. Hoskins, one of our maids, Mr. Tully. Employed here fourteen years. Two years ago she worked the wing where Mr. and Mrs.—where this couple had their suite."

"Suite," Tully said.

"I remember them, all right," the woman said. She had a flat-footed kind of voice, too, as if she had never learned to use it right. "He was the man took an afternoon nap with a cigarette in his hand and burned the new couch in the suite, Mr. Dalrymple, you remember. He'd tied a real good one on—"

"Yes, yes, Mrs. Hoskins, thank you," Dalrymple said.

Tully forced himself to take the photo of Ruth from the desk and across the room to Mrs. Hoskins.

"Is this the woman?"

Mrs. Hoskins adjusted her glasses and peered earnestly. "Looks like her. Yes, sir, I'd say she was the one. It's been a long time, but I always remembered that couple real well even though they was here such a short time. Something about them two—"

"What?" Tully said.

"Well, for one thing, most of the guests the Lodge gets don't drink so much. More refined, like."

Dalrymple coughed nervously. Tully took the photo of Ruth from the woman's worked-out fingers and replaced it in his wallet. He was surprised to find that his own hands were perfectly steady. "Do you remember anything else about them?"

Mrs. Hoskins became quite animated. "Oh, yes, sir! They were real lovey-dovey. Them two are honeymooners, I says to Mrs. Biggle—she was working that wing with me then. Mrs. Biggle says, 'Whoever heard of honeymooners spending all their time getting tanked up?' but I says to her, 'It takes all kinds, and anyway I heard 'em smoothing in there between drinks, like—' not," Mrs. Hoskins added hastily, "that I was listening or anything, but sometimes a maid can't help—"

"All *right,* Mrs. Hoskins," the manager said.

"I don't suppose," Tully said to the gray-haired woman, "you remember hearing the man use the woman's first name?"

"I do indeed," she said, beaming, "Ruth, it sounded like. The gentleman would say it over and over, like he liked it, too."

"That's all, that's all, Mrs. Hoskins," Dalrymple said. "Thank you."

Tully drove away from the hotel sanely enough. But as the lights of the Lodge fell behind, his car seemed to take the bit in its teeth.

He sat like a spectator watching the mountain turns come up and past and away as if on film. Guard railings flashed by, one long blur. The Imperial's engine seemed to gather its powers and streak forward . . .

A stabbing fear jolted Tully's heart.

He jerked his foot from the accelerator in sheer reflex. And went limp and cold.

He drove the rest of the way at a crawl.

The house loomed remote, strange . . . still dark. He got out of the car heavily and let himself in.

As he trudged about turning on lights, the thought came to him that he had forgotten to eat anything. Without hunger he went into the kitchen, put together a sandwich, and sat munching.

The testimony of Maudie Blake might be suspect. But not that of the Lodge manager and the gray-haired maid.

And yet, Tully told himself, it doesn't fit, it simply doesn't fit. Ruth, even a single Ruth, spending three days at a resort hideway with a man like Cox! Unless she was a sort of female Jekyll-Hyde. . . .

The phone rang. Tully put aside the half-eaten sandwich and got up from the kitchen table and went to the wall extension.

"Yes?" He no longer had any real hope that the answering voice might be Ruth's.

"Dave? Norma." Norma Hurst's voice was calmer than usual. Thank you, Lord, thought Tully, for small miracles. "I've been trying to get you."

"I was out, Norma. Anything special?"

"No," Ollie Hurst's wife said, "it's just that I haven't had a chance to talk to you since the news about—since the news. I don't suppose you've heard anything?"

"No."

Norma was silent. Then she said, "Dave, I want you to know we're all with you. I just don't believe Ruth could be involved in a thing like this. Or, if she is, it's entirely different from the way it looks right now."

"Thanks, Norma."

He meant it. Unstable or not, Norma was a good egg. She might keep teetering on the brink of hysteria because of the brutal loss of her only child, but there was solid rock behind the thin edge.

"Norma . . . might I come over?"

"Oh, Dave, would you?"

"I mean now. I know it's late—way past midnight—"

"I insist on it! I know what it means to be alone in the house where . . ." Norma stopped on a barely rising note. "Anyway, Ollie says he wants to talk to you—he didn't get home till an hour ago himself. Have you had anything to eat?"

"Yes, of course—"

"What?"

In spite of himself, Tully grinned. "You've got me, sister. Half a sandwich of I-don't-know-what."

"You come right over, David Tully!"

He found a four-course buffet dinner waiting for him at the Hurst house, in spite of the hour.

Norma was tall and thin and long in the face, and her brown hair was dingy with neglect. Her charm had always lain in eyes of deep beauty and the quick warmth of her smile. The smile had died with the death of her little girl; the beautiful eyes had come more and more to resemble the eyes in photos Tully had seen of Nazi concentration-camp victims—socket-sunken, enormous, haunted and haunting. But tonight she seemed a part of the existing world; Ruth's disappearance and predicament had apparently shocked her back to something like her old plain, friendly self.

Ollie made a great show of being normal, but his always restless hands were busier than ever tonight, feeling, pulling, scratching, rubbing—and the light bounced off his freckled skull like a yellow warning signal.

But there was reassurance in seeing Norma and Ollie together. Angular Norma, plain and warm as homemade bread; stocky Ollie, shrewd, transparent-eyed, in perpetual motion—it had always been hard for Tully to imagine them not married to each other. They were complementary; they had a mutual need, yet an individual stamp. Ollie Hurst had been a hole-in-the-shoe student; Norma had a comfortable income from stocks and real estate she had inherited. Norma herself had once told Tully that Ollie had never touched a penny of her money; it had been a condition of their marriage, at his unarguable insistence.

Ruth and I had some pleasant times in this house, Tully thought. Before little Emmie died. Before Ruth . . .

He shut down tight on that one.

It was impossible to recreate the past, in spite of Norma's surprising recapture of her old self. She fed Tully quietly, while her husband tried to make small talk. But the food stuck in Tully's throat, and Ollie seemed to dry up, and finally an awkward silence fell.

"Suppose we face this instead of pretending it hasn't happened and that Ruth's here," Norma said.

Ollie said, "Nor . . ."

"Oh, shut up, Ollie, this is no time for your office psychology. You do it badly, anyway, when your emotions are involved . . . David." Norma Hurst touched Tully's hand. "Don't lose faith in her."

Tully was grateful. "What do we do about the evidence, Norma? Ignore it?"

"Yes," Norma said, "until Ruth has a chance to explain."

"Cox is no foggy abstract who'll dry up with the sunrise. Cox is real. Or was."

"So is Ruth, Dave. And she still is."

"Norma," Ollie said. "Maybe Dave doesn't want to talk about it."

"I think he does. I think it will do him good. Don't you want to talk, Dave?"

"I need to do more than talk," Tully muttered.

"You need to know you're not alone," Norma said. Her eyes retreated for a moment. "I know."

But now it all came back in a rush, and Tully cried, "She knew Cox. That's a fact. A *fact*."

"How do you know that, Dave?" the lawyer asked quickly.

"Never mind—"

"I don't care what you say," Norma said, and there was a strange tautness in her voice that pulled even Tully around. "Even if she did know him, she's innocent. I won't believe anything else!"

The two men exchanged glances. Then Tully got up and went over to Norma and stooped and kissed her on the forehead. "Of course, Norma, of course. You're a good friend. A great comfort."

But she sat like stone. The old look of panic appeared in her husband's eyes.

"I'm really pooped," Tully said. "I'd better pop back home and hit the sack. Thanks, Norm, for the feed. Ollie—"

"I'll see you out," Ollie said. "Be right back, Nor." At the door he said in a low voice, "Now don't blame yourself, Dave. This has been coming on all day."

"Norma said you wanted to talk to me—"

"I'll drop by in the morning." The lawyer shut the door swiftly. Through the big window as he passed Tully saw Ollie taking his wife's hand with great gentleness. Norma was sitting as they had left her, without expression, except that tears were inching down her face.

10

David Tully had just finished his lonely breakfast when Ollie Hurst drove up. He came in wiping his cranium with a folded handkerchief. His eyes were bloodshot from lack of sleep.

"How's Norma, Ollie?"

"She had a bad night. Apparently this business of Ruth is somehow tied up in her mind with Emmie's death. I finally got her under sedation and asleep, and she seems a lot better this morning."

"I'm sorry as hell, Ollie—"

"Forget it," the lawyer said abruptly. "If it hadn't been that it would have been something else. How about some of that coffee I smell?"

"I've been keeping it hot for you."

They went into the kitchen and Tully poured coffee into two fresh cups.

"No," Ollie said, refusing the cream and sugar, which he usually used in immoderate proportions, "I need it straight this morning," and he gulped a third of it and set his cup down and said, "Anything on Ruth yet?"

"No."

"Dave."

"Yes?"

"Do you know where she is? Are you hiding her?"

Tully glared into the lawyer's crystal eyes. "No. *No.*"

"Okay, okay," Hurst said. "I had to be sure. And you still haven't heard from her?"

"No."

"All right. Then let's talk about the future."

"The future of what?" Tully asked bitterly.

"The future of Ruth."

"What future?"

"Oh, the hell with that defeatist talk," Ollie Hurst snapped. "Look, Dave, I'm a lawyer, and I'm your and Ruth's friend. If you want to wallow in hopelessness that's your funeral—and incidentally it only makes my job tougher. Now what's it going to be? Do I have to do this with you on my back, dead weight, or are we in this together?"

Tully stiffened.

"That's right, hate my guts," Ollie said. "I don't mind. All right. Now I've got us a good criminal lawyer, I mean on tap. I've retained him tentatively, and I've talked the whole thing over with him as it stands. He agrees that there's no point in his coming into this until Ruth turns up or is found. Do you want to know who he is?"

Tully shook his head.

"You mean you actually trust somebody besides yourself? I swan to Marthy! Anyway, his name is Vinzenti and he's top dog upstate in trial work, especially murder cases. I've got to be frank with you, Dave. Vinzenti says that unless Ruth can come up with clear counter-evidence to refute the facts as they now seem to stand, we'll have a real fight on our hands. He also said that the longer she remains in hiding the worse it's going to look for her. That's why I had to ask you again if you know where she is."

"I told you I *don't*."

"I believe you, Dave," the lawyer said soothingly. "I'm just outlining the situation. How about a refill?"

Tully replenished Hurst's cup.

"You haven't touched yours."

Tully drank it.

"The circumstantial case against Ruth is strong," Ollie Hurst went on. "The use of your gun, the testimony of a witness who overheard Cox call his woman-visitor Ruth—and especially Ruth's disappearance after the shooting, add up to a pretty powerful prosecutor's case, according to Vinzenti.

"Against this, he says—barring some unforseeable explanation when Ruth turns up that automatically clears her—the defense will have to try to tear down the evidence. The typewritten unsigned letter, Vinzenti thinks, for instance, is inadmissible, unless the police have turned up an identifiable fingerprint of Ruth's on it. Most of all Vinzenti seems to be counting on the human element. This may well turn out to be, he says, one of those cases in which the law and the evidence prove of less weight than the character of the people involved. The professional leech who preyed on women, the woman of refinement and good reputation who in panic and desperation turned on the beast who was trying to wreck her life—in a setup like that, juries always empathize with the woman, Vinzenti assured me."

Tully laughed. The lawyer looked at him sharply. "What was that for, Dave?"

"Nothing." A woman of refinement and good reputation, Tully thought. Wait till the prosecution gets hold of that Lodge shack-up!

"The hell you say. Dave, if there's something you're holding back . . ."

Tully shook his head. He could not, he could not talk about Ruth and Cox and those three days at the Lodge two years before. Now now. Not yet.

Ollie Hurst continued to study him. Finally, he shrugged. "If you are, Dave, you're being a very foolish guy. Well, we'll have to trust your judgment. Isn't there anything new you can tell me?"

"Yes," Tully said. "We may find help in an unexpected place."

"What do you mean?"

"I've had a session with that witness—the woman, Maudie Blake. She told me something she didn't tell Julian Smith."

"Oh?"

"She and Crandall Cox were old buddy-buddies. He shacked up with her whenever he was on his uppers, or in trouble. The last time he was sick, he let her take care of him till he could get back on his feet, then he lifted some money she'd left around and took off for here. And she followed him. That's how she came to be in the next room at the Hobby."

"She told you all this?"

"That's right."

"Well," the lawyer said softly. "That's interesting. How come she told you, Dave, and not the police?"

"They didn't pay her. I did."

"She asked you for money?"

"Yes."

"How much?"

"A hundred dollars. I only had seventy-eight with me. She took it."

The bald lawyer frowned. He got up and began to walk around the kitchen, pulling his nose, scratching his ear, frowning.

"I don't know, Dave," he said slowly. "That's pretty valuable information to sell for seventy-eight dollars. Unless she's stupid and cheap as hell—"

"She is." Tully wondered what he would say if he knew what else Maudie Blake had sold for the same seventy-eight dollars.

"Did you tell this to Lieutenant Smith?"

"No. Anyway, she said if I told the police she'd simply deny the whole story and stand pat on her original testimony."

Hurst kept shaking his head. "I still don't like it. If she's telling the truth she can deny her head off—the facts can be dug up. She can't be *that* stupid. Dave, you're not telling me the whole story."

"All right, I'm not," Tully burst out. "But don't ask me to talk about the rest—not yet, Ollie. The point is, she can be bought. In fact, I was intending to see her again this morning after you left. I think she knows a hell of a lot more than she told even me."

"You may be getting into something you can't handle, Dave," the lawyer said. "I'd better go with you."

Tully hesitated.

"Maybe I ought to put it this way, Dave," his friend said gently. "If I'm going to help you, I can't do it in the dark, and I'm certainly not going to get a man with Vinzenti's reputation into a case where the defendant's husband is withholding information. Am I in, or out?"

Tully was quiet.

Then his shoulders drooped and he said, "All right, Ollie."

They went in Ollie Hurst's car. Ollie drove, and neither man uttered a sound all the way.

The lawyer parked in the lot beside Flynn's Inn and they got out and went into the dust-dancing lobby.

The same seedy clerk was behind the desk, picking his teeth with a green plastic toothpick while he read a comic book called *She-Cat of Venus*.

"Miss Blake," Tully said. "Maudie Blake?"

"So?" the clerk said.

"She in?"

"Mm-hm," the clerk said, turning a page. "At least I ain't seen her come down. She's one of those afternoon getter-uppers, I guess."

They walked up to the second floor. Tully led the way to the woman's door and rapped. He rapped again.

"She must be sleeping off a drunk," he said to Hurst. "She was tying one on last night when I saw her." He rapped again, shook his head, tried the door. It was locked, and he rattled the knob. "Miss Blake? Maudie?"

"When she ties one on it stays tied, doesn't it?"

"Maybe we'd better come back later, Ollie."

"Let's not and say we did," the lawyer said grimly. He banged on the door with his fist. "Miss Blake!"

There was no response.

"How about asking the desk clerk to ring her room?" Tully suggested.

Ollie Hurst hurried downstairs. A moment later Tully heard the muffled ringing. It kept ringing. Finally it stopped.

Tully began to nurse an uneasy feeling. Ollie was coming back up the stairs with the clerk. They were arguing.

"But I ain't supposed to do that, Mr. Hurst," the clerk was protesting. Apparently Ollie had told the Venusian enthusiast who he was.

"She may be seriously ill," Ollie said. "Suppose she's in a coma or something?"

"Coma my eye," the clerk grumbled; he had a key

with him. "This broad's been lappin' it up like a camel since she got here. If I get into trouble over this, boy—"

"You won't," Tully said. "Open it up."

The clerk unlocked the door, pushed it open a bit, and poked his head into the room.

"Miss Blake—?"

His head retracted like a turtle's. He made a gagging sound and rushed down the stairs.

Tully kicked the door wide.

She was lying in an impossible position on the bed, twisted like a contortionist from the waist down, head hanging far over the side. She was wearing the skintight slimjims with the enormous pink rose design and the knit blouse, just as she had been dressed when he had seen her the day before. The only change was that her feet were bare; one shoe lay near the bed, and the other was half under the radiator near the window. Apparently in an alcoholic collapse she had fallen across the bed, kicking her shoes off as she did so.

A three-quarters-empty bottle of whisky was lying on its side near her right hand. Only a little of it had soaked into the bed.

Neither man made a move to enter the room; they could see only too well from the doorway.

Her synthetic gold hair hung straight down, almost touching the floor; at the roots it was a dirty brown. There was a fish-belly gray-blueness about her stiffened face, a brownish crust at one corner of her open mouth. Her eyes were open, too, staring at infinity.

"That," Tully said with a laugh, "is what you might call dead to the world. How lucky can I get?"

"Dave." Ollie Hurst grasped his arm.

"Don't worry. I have no intention of going in there."

"Dave," the lawyer said again. Tully stepped back and stood slackly in the hall. Hurst reached in, grasped the knob, and pulled the door to. "We'd better notify the police."

11

It was 2:00 P.M. before Julian Smith got back to his office.

Tully was seated near the lieutenant's desk. The tailored Homicide man stopped and looked at him. "Why are you still here, Dave?"

"Where else do I have to go?" Tully was slumped on his tail, his long legs stretched way out, his big hands clenched over his belt.

"How about your office?" Smith went briskly to his desk. "Your business must be going to the dogs."

"Julian, I want to talk to you."

"Sure, Dave," the detective said, glancing through a pile of reports and memoranda. "But right now I'm pretty busy—"

Tully sat up straight. Smith glanced over at him. He immediately pushed the pile of paper aside.

"Okay, Dave."

"Is there an autopsy report yet on the Blake woman?"

"Just a preliminary one."

"What's it look like?"

"The M.E. is pretty sure she died as a result of acute alcoholism. He's making the usual tests for poison, but there are no marks of violence on her, no toxic indications so far except the alcohol."

"So she's going to be written off," Tully said with a peculiar smile, "as an accidental death?"

"In all probability." Smith leaned back in his swivel chair, clasped his manicured hands behind his head. "From the empties in the room and blood analysis, she died when her intake of alcohol passed the critical point. She took one big slug too many—if she had passed out before that, she'd likely have survived. Maudie's tough luck was that she collapsed on the bed before she drank that last one. She landed on her back and she was too near unconsciousness to get up; about all she had the strength to do was lift the bottle to her mouth that last time. Her body tried to heave the stuff but, with her head way back the way it was, only an insignificant amount came up. So . . ." Julian Smith shrugged and sat up. "We get two-three deaths like that a year, Dave, even in a town of this size. Okay?"

"No," David Tully said.

"What d'ye mean no?" the detective demanded.

"I mean no, you've got it all wrong, Julian. Maudie Blake's death was not an accident. It's too damn convenient for somebody."

"Murdered, hm?" Smith seemed unexcited.

"Yes, I think she was murdered."

"And who's the somebody you think murdered her?"

"The same one who murdered Cox."

"You mean," Julian Smith said, "Ruth?"

Tully's face convulsed. He leaped to his feet, upsetting the chair. "Damn you, Julian, I *don't* mean Ruth! Ruth's the pigeon in this thing, don't you see it?"

"Dave," Smith said. "Why don't you drop by your office? Or go home and lie down? You're as wound up as an eight-day clock. What do you say?"

"No!" Tully stood glaring down at him. Suddenly he righted the overturned chair and seated himself in it. "No, Julian, I'm going to sit here till you listen to what I have to say. Or have me thrown out."

Smith hesitated. Then he smiled. "Of course I'll listen, Dave. Shoot."

Tully sat forward immediately. "I've had some time to think since this morning, and I've doped it out. Ruth didn't fire that shot. Someone else did. *Maudie Blake knew that*—knew who really murdered Cox. She implicated Ruth to cover up the killer. And when I came nosing around, Maudie tightened the noose around Ruth's neck to keep me off the right track."

"You mean by sending you up to Wilton Lodge, Dave?"

Tully blinked. "You knew that?"

"I've had one of my men tailing you. We know you went to see Maudie Blake yesterday. We know you then drove up to the Lodge. After you left there, my man tackled the manager. Dalrymple was quite cooperative."

"It's too damn bad," Tully said thickly, "your man didn't stick around Flynn's Inn instead. The Blake woman would still be alive!"

Lieutenant Smith frowned the least bit. "I don't see that that kind of talk is going to get us anywhere, Dave. What's your point?"

"Don't you see it? Why Maudie sent me up to the Lodge? She wasn't interested in the lousy hundred bucks she asked me for, or the seventy-eight I was actually able to cough up. She was after a goldmine! That Wilton Lodge business strengthens the circumstantial case against Ruth. It sends me off in the wrong direction. To that extent it protects the real killer better and so ups the value of what Maudie's selling. Protection, Julian— that's what she had in mind! She was going to hold what she knew over the killer's head and make him pay through the nose for keeping quiet!"

Tully stopped, out of breath, looking at Julian Smith with shining eyes. The shine slowly dulled.

"I'm sorry, Dave," Smith said, shaking his head. "I don't buy it."

"Why not, for God's sake?" Tully cried. "Doesn't it make sense?"

"As a theory, Dave, sure. But it's a theory based on pure assumption, with not a scrap of evidence or a single provable fact to support it—based on two assumptions, actually: that Ruth was not the last one to see Cox, and that Maudie Blake was murdered. There's no evidence that anyone but Ruth visited Cox on the night of his murder, and the medical findings are that the Blake woman died of overdrinking." Smith shrugged. "You know, Dave, unsupported assumptions are tricky things. I could assume something you wouldn't like."

"What's that?" Tully muttered.

"The circumstantial case against your wife rested largely on Maudie Blake's testimony as to what she overheard from her room at the Hobby Motel the night Cox was shot," the detective said. "I could assume that Ruth murdered Maudie—to get rid of a damaging witness. As a matter of fact, Dave, Maudie's death is a bad break for the State . . . and a very good one for Ruth."

Tully sat still. He had not thought of that at all.

"So, you see," Smith said mildly, "as the officer in charge of this case I'd have to welcome evidence that Maudie was murdered, because it would corroborate the assumption that she was murdered by your wife. Fortunately or unfortunately, depending on where you're sitting in this merry-go-round, Maudie was not murdered, so my assumption carries just about as much weight as yours."

Tully was silent.

"Dave, Dave," Lieutenant Smith went on in the same mild tone, "face it—tough as it is, face it. Sick, broke, Cox came back to town to blackmail Ruth. To keep him from wrecking her life, she shot him. Nothing else explains the use of your gun, taken from your house. No other motive has turned up."

Julian Smith rose. "I can't blame you for trying to find an out for Ruth. I'm sure if she were my wife I'd do the same thing—shield or no shield."

He came around the desk.

"I'll tell you what, Dave."

Tully looked up.

"Suppose I take the tail off you. I didn't like having to put you under surveillance in the first place. But in this business you either learn to treat your friends like anybody else or you turn in your shield and take up a milk route. I had to make sure. That Wilton Lodge trip of yours convinces me you really don't know where your wife is."

Tully's lips twisted. "Am I supposed to say thanks, Julian?"

The lieutenant said carefully, "I don't think I get you."

He rose. "You're telling me I'm not going to be tailed any more because you still think I know where Ruth is and may try to contact her—or she me. You're not taking the tail off me, you're doubling it." The detective's barbered cheeks began to show blood. "I don't blame *you,* Julian. You're a good cop. Let me know if you get a lead on my wife."

Julian Smith grinned faintly. "And vice versa?"

"Depends," Tully said. "It all depends."

He picked up his hat and left.

Tully let the automatic part of him take charge of the Imperial's drive home; he had other work for his conscious mind.

He kept trying to visualize the shapeless shadow of the unknown—the stealthy black blob he was now choosing to think of as the real killer of Crandall Cox and Maudie Blake.

If only he could form a picture of him . . . of it. The Blob . . .

After a while Tully gave that up as hopeless. He—it —the Blob might be anyone in the world.

He forced himself to concentrate on the crime.

The Blob had visited Cox that night at the motel after Ruth left. (To go where? But this question Tully killed dead in its tracks.) Maudie Blake overheard, recognized the voice, maybe even saw its owner as he slipped into the room, or out of it afterward. Maudie moved over to Flynn's Inn. She made contact with the killer, told him where she was, demanded a talk . . . It could have taken place either at Flynn's or elsewhere. Wherever it was, Maudie must have laid it on the line: *I know you shot Cranny Cox. I've set up this Ruth with the cops as your pigeon, and I can even make it look worse for her with what I know. But it's gonna cost . . .*

Greedy Maudie Blake. It cost, all right, but not the Blob. It cost Maudie her life. One murder or two—the penalty was the same.

It happened after I left her, Tully thought, after she sent me up to the Lodge. The Blob must have been watching, waiting. I leave, he goes in. Through a side entrance or something, unseen. Then up to her room.

She's pretty loaded by this time. He may have come prepared to strangle her, or to hit her over the head, or smother her with a pillow. But her drunken condition gives him a better idea, a way to kill her that looks like accidental death. . . .

The formless Somebody standing or sitting in Maudie's room. Maybe pretending to drink with her as he discusses her demands. Urging her to drink even more. Until she falls on the bed and passes out.

Then how easy to kill her.

The alcohol-saturated blood already poisoning her liver, kidneys, brain . . . All he has to do is to keep forcing the liquor down her throat as she lies conveniently across the bed with her head over the side and her mouth open. He would have to be careful that she didn't choke to death. A little at a time . . . delicate as an operation, but easy so easy. And finally the alcoholic content of her blood reaches and passes the fatal level.

Dead of an overdose of alcohol. What had Julian Smith said? "We get two-three deaths like that a year."

Obliterate traces of his visit. Trip the tumbler, let the door swing shut, locked.

Easy.

Safe.

(And where was Ruth all this time?)

It gnawed. It gnawed.

Shortly after Tully's return home, a sleek white sports car with the top down dragged to a stop before the house.

The screech of rubber brought him to the front window. Sandra Jean and Andrew Gordon were getting out of the car. They were talking and laughing. Mercedes Cabbott's son made a sweeping gesture: I am master of the world, it said. He stumbled slightly as they started up the walk. Tully wondered how much Andy had had to drink.

Tully opened the front door.

"Hi, pops," Sandra Jean said.

Andy made two fists, did a little shuffle, and threw a one-two at an imaginary opponent. He grinned crookedly at Tully. "Sure it's safe for me to come in, Champ? You pack a mean wallop."

"Andrew, don't be silly." Sandra Jean took him by the arm.

"Come in," Tully said.

They breezed past him into his house, Andy Gordon still shadow-boxing. He's not as drunk as he's acting, Tully thought; he rarely is.

"Oh, Andy, stop that," Sandra Jean said. "We haven't time for games. You can play all you want afterward."

"Afterward?" Tully said. He closed the front door.

"Haven't you heard?" Mercedes's son threw his head back and howled like Tarzan. "The mating call! Mind if I have two or six of your drinks?" He wobbled toward Tully's bar and got busy.

Tully glanced at Ruth's sister.

She nodded. "We're getting married, Davey."

"Oh?"

"Eloping!" the darkly handsome boy chortled. "How's that for an idea, Champ?" He threw himself into an armchair with his drink and stretched his muscular legs, grinning. Tully noticed that he merely sipped from the glass.

"Great," Tully said. "Whose idea was it?"

"Mine, o' course. Got down on my knees to my li'l ol' gal. Didn't I, sugar?" Andy rested his head on the back of the chair and began to sing *O Promise Me*. He broke off to take another sip. Tully glanced contemptuously at Sandra Jean. She laughed in his face and went over to Andy and stooped to rub cheeks with him.

"You certainly did, darling. Nicest proposal I've *ever* had. And so legal, too. Look, I'll be ready in a jiff—"

"Wait a minute," Tully said. "I take it Mercedes knows nothing about this?"

"You take it and you can have it," Andy chuckled. "I s'pose you think I'm afraid of her. No such thing, my friend. Just cutting the old umbilical. I'm old enough to know what I'm doing. Right, my-love-my-dove-my-undefiled?"

"And such muscles, too," Sandra Jean crooned.

"And what's more," the boy said, waving the glass,

"if that louse of a stepfather of mine opens *his* yap—pow! I'll smear him all over the palace floor."

"You'll do no such thing," his bride-to-be smiled, laying her finger over his lips. "This is going to be a civilized elopement. No brawls, no quarrels—just sweetness and light. Mercedes doesn't mean a thing she said. All we have to do is *do* it, Andy. She won't cut you off. She'll come around."

"Not losing a son, but gaining a daughter," Andrew Gordon muttered. "I dunno though, Sandra. The old girl can get awfully tough . . ."

"Everything's going to be just fine, Andy," Sandra Jean murmured, nuzzling his ear. "You just trust Sandra Jean."

"Yeah," the boy said. He pulled her face down and kissed her fiercely.

She struggled, laughing. "Andy! In front of Dave—?"

"Hell with Dave."

"No, now you finish your drink while I get those things together," the girl said firmly. "I'll be right back." She extricated herself, kissed him lightly on the forehead, and hurried out of the living room.

Tully followed her.

She went into his and Ruth's bedroom. Tully went in after her. She wheeled on him.

"Whatever you're intending to say, Dave—I warn you, *don't.*"

"Seeing that this is my bedroom," Tully said, "do you mind if I throw up all over it?"

Her eyes, so beautiful, so like Ruth's, flashed hell's-fire. For a moment he thought she was going to spring at him claws first. But then, with remarkable discipline, she forced herself to smile.

"Davey, I'm sorry. I wouldn't have come except that I have some things of mine here I want to take with me on our honeymoon. I won't be long, and then we'll be out of your hair."

Hair. She had washed a lighter tint into her hair since he had last seen her. He wondered what its original color had been, why she kept changing it.

"Sometimes I think you're not human, Sandra."

"Mercy! And what do we mean by that?" the girl said mockingly. She looked human enough as she turned to walk across the bedroom, her hips rising and falling rhythmically. "Aren't I female-human?"

"On the outside, definitely. But what are you inside?"

"Lover, it goes clear through." She paused at the closet door—Ruth's closet—and turned around. "I know what's bugging you about me, Davey, and it hasn't a bloody thing to do with Andy Gordon or Mercedes Cabbott. You think I'm acting like a bitch because I'm proposing to run off and get married while my sister's in all this trouble. But what do you expect me to do? Sit on Mercedes's terrace and wring my hands? I told you, I can't help Ruth. All I can do is help myself. This is my big chance at sonny-boy. I may never get another."

"You mean it's your big chance at the fortune sonny-boy's slated to come in to."

"Sonny-boy *and* his dough. Look, Dave, I know how you feel about me, but I'm nowhere near as bad as you think I am. Of course Mercedes's money has a lot to do with it. I wouldn't marry Andy if he wasn't coming in to it. But I'm really fond of the kid; I intend to be a good wife; maybe even make a man of him. The big laugh in this thing is that I'll probably turn out the best goddam daughter-in-law Mercedes Cabbott could possibly want for her precious Andrew. End of speech."

She swirled about and yanked the closet door open and walked in and snapped the closet light on. She began to rummage among the garment bags and hangers.

"I know darned well I left my white linen here . . ."

Sandra Jean tilted her head thoughtfully. Tully felt a pang, a stab of recognition. The head-tilt was one of the mannerisms he so loved in Ruth.

He stood there watching the girl. The dim light in the closet played tricks on him. Of course, the hair was different. But if it were darkened to auburn . . . yes, with auburn hair . . .

Something cracked in Tully's head.

Split it wide open.

For an instant he felt dizzy.

He steadied himself in the bedroom doorway.

91

"Sandra." He had trouble with his voice.

"Yes?"

"The natural color of your hair. It's auburn, isn't it?"

Busy going through the garments in the closet, Sandra Jean made a vague affirmative sound.

He began a slow crossing of the room. It was as if he were wading in an undertow. "Two summers ago. In June. Your hair was its natural auburn then, wasn't it?"

"How should I know? Why on earth—?"

She whirled. He was just outside the closet, breathing in heavy gusts, making slow grinding sounds with his teeth. She paled and shrank against Ruth's clothes.

"What's the matter with you?" his wife's sister asked. Her voice was high-pitched suddenly.

Later, Tully was to marvel at his control. All he was conscious of now was the throbbing in his temples and the tickle of sweat as it crept down his nose.

He said thickly, "How long have you known Cranny Cox, Sandra?"

21

Sandra Jean shrank deeper into her sister's clothes closet. "I don't know what you're talking about."

"When did you first meet Cox?"

"I'll let the white dress go for now," she whispered. "I can get it after Andy and I get back."

She made as if to leave the closet. Tully loomed over her. She stopped. Her face was yellow-white now.

"Davey, please. I want to go to Andy."

"Tell me."

"Dave! Let me out of here! Or I'll—"

"What?" David Tully said. "Call Andy? Go ahead. You can tell both of us all about you and Cox. Or yell copper and save me the trouble."

He could see the girl's natural shrewdness take over little by little. She was weighing the probabilities even before the panic was fought down. She smiled up at him.

"I don't know what you're talking about, Dave. You scared me, that's all. You must be out of your mind. Let me pass, will you?"

"Sure," Tully said, stepping aside. She slipped quickly by him. "But I don't think you'll want to go just yet, Sandra. Even if it's only to indulge me a few minutes longer. Don't you want to hear my brain-storm?" She'll have to stay and listen, he thought, if only to find out how much I've guessed.

He was right. Sandra Jean shrugged and said, "Why not?" and sat down at Ruth's vanity, crossing her legs and looking at herself in the mirror. She began to poke at her hair. "But make it snappy, lover, or Andy'll think you've got evil designs on his bride."

"The resemblance," Tully said. "It's been right here

all the time, under my nose, and I didn't see how it answered the question."

"What question?" the girl asked, still plumping up her hair.

"The question of how a woman of Ruth's taste and character could foul herself up with a mucking gigolo like Cox. The answer obviously was that she couldn't. So it had to be you, Sandra. You and Ruth are such look-alikes it hits me every time I see you."

"I suppose there is a resemblance," Sandra Jean said carelessly, "and I can see how you'd figure me for more of a tramp than my beloved sister, but aren't you forgetting something, Davey?" Her eyes in the mirror were watchful.

"No," Tully said, "I'm forgetting nothing, Sandra. You mean the fact that when you were indulging in your nasty little peccadilloes you did it using Ruth's name. I wonder why. To protect yourself? Hiding behind your sister's name would do it, all right. Maybe it had a deeper meaning—"

"Such as, Doctor?" the girl laughed. "As long as we're hallucinating . . ." Her eyes kept giving her away.

"Such as that you've always hated Ruth for being what you couldn't be, and by masquerading under her name in a filthy affair you transferred the filth to her in some perverted kind of way." He shrugged. "The psychiatrists can dig into that. What interests me is that it's the only explanation that makes sense."

Sandra Jean began to search among Ruth's lipsticks for the shade she wanted. "For what?"

"For Wilton Lake, for instance," Tully said. Her hand paused for the slightest instant over a lipstick. Then it resumed its motion and she was applying it to her pouting lips. "That was you up at the Lodge two years ago, Sandra, wasn't it? With Cox? You using Ruth's name and wallowing in a three-day orgy the people up there still remember! That resemblance worked overtime for you, Sandra. I showed one of the maids a photo of Ruth and she said, yes, that was the woman with Cox that summer. It was an honest mistake— seeing a wallet-sized snapshot after the passage of two years, the woman made a logical identification. But I think if we darken your hair and take you up to the Lodge for the old gal to inspect in the flesh . . ."

This time fear flickered in those depths. She set the lipstick down, white-faced again. Tully pressed on remorselessly.

"I don't know why even you took up with a creep like Cox—for the kicks, I guess, rolling around in the gutter to see what it tasted like—but you must have come to your senses, probably gave him some money, and thought you were rid of him. Only it didn't work out that way, Sandra, did it?"

The full lips were drying. Her tongue stole out to wet them.

"Cox wasn't rid of *you*. For some time he let you alone. But then he got sick, and he was broke, and he rummaged around in his dirty little bag of tricks and came up with that weekend. He got in touch with you. And you wrote him a letter—that unsigned typewritten note the police found in his effects: 'Cranny— You keep away from me, and I mean it. What happened between us is ancient history . . . I've found myself a leading citizen here who's very much interested in me and I think he's going to ask me to marry him . . .' That wasn't Ruth referring to me. That was you referring to Andrew Gordon."

He saw her thighs tighten and her rump begin to lift. But then she sank down again.

"You must have scared him off for the time being. Or he was too sick to follow it up. But under Maudie Blake's fat and tender hands he got back on his feet. And he made straight for this town like bad news. And phoned here, asking for Ruth. Andy himself told me that; he took the call when you and he were here and Ruth happened to be out. *Even Cox thought your name was Ruth.*"

Her eyes were darting about now like trapped fish. Tully knew what she was thinking. Not about Ruth. Not about him, or even herself. She was thinking of Mercedes Cabbott's money, and how it was slipping through her fingers.

"That's when you got your big idea, Sandra. You've always had the key to this house. You lifted my gun and went to the Hobby Motel. It was you the Blake woman heard Cox call Ruth. It was you who shot Cox to death."

He could actually see her thoughts snap back to the present. Her head jerked up and she said, "What did you say?"

"I said you murdered Cox."

He thought she was going to faint, and he found himself becoming irritated. Sandra Jean Ainsworth wasn't the fainting type. She was play-acting. Or was she? To hell with her, he thought impatiently.

"Well?"

She shook her head, seemed to be making a great effort. Finally she swallowed, and her lips parted, and her voice cracked as she spoke. "No. No, Davey. It wasn't me."

"You expect me to believe that?" Tully growled. "What do you take me for, a stupid sucker like that oaf in there?"

"Davey, no, no." She got to her feet and went to the bedroom window. She turned to face him, resting her palms on the sill, leaning back so that the curtain framed her head. "This time I'm telling the truth. You've left me no choice."

Tully laughed. "You admit the Wilton Lake shack-up?"

Her head moved ever so slightly.

"You admit typing that note?"

Again.

"You admit stealing my gun? Using Ruth's name? You admit the whole damn thing and expect me to believe you didn't shoot him?"

"I didn't," Sandra Jean said. It sounded real.

Tully was confused again. He sat down on the big bed—*it was king-size, made to order, built especially long, and how tiny Ruth always looked in it and how he used to tease her about it*—just sat there, arms dangling, suddenly without strength or stamina, staring into the past . . . or the future.

"I didn't," a husky voice said in his ear; and he felt the humid tickle of Sandra Jean's breath and the pressure of her body against his back. She had crawled across the bed from the opposite side and seized him softly, like a hostage.

Tully rose violently. The girl fell over backwards with a cry of surprise and pain, exposing her thighs. He reached over and yanked her skirt down so hard the hem ripped.

"Let's keep this clean, you little whore," he said through his teeth. He leaned over the girl, and she scrambled away like a terrified bug, tumbling off the other side of the bed and staring up at him from her knees. "I'm not taking your word for anything, understand me, Sandra? Anything! Not after the vicious deal you've given Ruth."

"Yes, Davey," Sandra Jean whispered.

"You say you didn't shoot Cox—"

"No," she whispered, "no."

"Then who did?"

"I don't know."

"But you admit you were there that night with my gun."

"Yes . . ."

"Why? Why my gun?"

She began to whimper. "I didn't know where else to get one. Davey, I swear that's the only reason—"

"Never mind the swearing bit; it doesn't impress me. If you didn't shoot Cox, why did you take the gun in the first place?" He hardly recognized his own voice now; it was harsh and low, without mercy or humanity. "Answer me!"

She clutched the bed. "To scare him. I wanted to scare him."

"And you say you didn't use the gun?"

"I couldn't, Davey. I was too afraid. He . . . he took the gun away from me. We had a wrestling match over it."

Tully leaned his fists on the bed and glared down at her. "Why did you want to scare him? What was he after?"

"I didn't know when I went there, but I knew Cranny Cox." Sandra Jean's body shook in the slightest shudder. "He was a monster. But a smart monster. I was an idiot to write him about my chance to marry a wealthy man. I might have known he'd try to cash in on it."

"How? By blackmailing you on the strength of those three days at the Lodge? Threatening to tell your husband-to-be about it and so spoil your marriage plans unless you paid up?"

"That's what I thought. But when I accused him of that, he laughed and said he'd hardly break the egg of the golden goose before it hatched. He even offered me a drink and wished me luck with my fiancé."

Tully slowly straightened. It made sense. Why should Cox milk Sandra Jean's modest trust-fund when, by waiting for her to marry a rich man, he would have a fortune to squeeze?

"All right," Tully said.

The girl scrambled to her feet, started to leave.

"All right so far," Tully said, and she stopped in her tracks. "I'm not through with you. So that's all Cox wanted you for, eh? To prepare you for the blackmail to come?"

"Yes, Davey," Sandra Jean breathed. Her eyes were full of fear again.

"And you just walked out of his motel room—leaving my gun behind? Wasn't that a little careless of you, Sandra?"

"You don't understand," she said quickly. "He'd taken it from me and he wouldn't give it back. I wanted it back—I asked him for it. He laughed and said he was keeping it as a memento. I suppose he was afraid I'd change my mind and shoot him after all if he let me get my hands on it again."

Tully brooded.

The girl watched him with anxiety. She took a tentative step toward the bedroom door, stopped as he stirred.

He looked up. "Then what happened to Ruth?"

"I don't know." Her voice rose. "Davey, I don't!"

"Did you see her that night?"

"No—"

"At any time?"

"No, Davey, no."

"You have no explanation for Ruth's disappearance, then? It's simply a great big mystery to you. Right?"

"Yes, Davey. I'm telling you the truth!"

"Sandra." The word had a flat, almost mechanical, timbre. His eyes, sooty with fatigue, stared at her out of a face as rigid as a cheap Hallowe'en mask. "If I find out that you know anything about Ruth's movements that night—where she went—what happened to her—where she is—anything!—I'll kill you. I'll give you one more chance. Where is Ruth?"

She said hoarsely, "I don't know."

For a long time they stood that way.

Then Sandra Jean stirred cautiously.

"Davey. . . ."

"What?"

"May I . . . go now?"

"Go?" Tully looked up. "Go where?"

"To Andy. Remember we had plans to?—"

He stared at her again, shook his head. "You baffle me, Sandra, you really do. There's only one place you're going, and only one man you're going there with—that's to the police, with me."

"I suppose I have to," Sandra Jean said after a while.

"You have to."

"It means postponing our elopement. . ."

Tully said nothing. The girl became reflective. Watching her, Tully marveled at her resiliency. The fear of the immediate past was gone. The trip to the police was an accepted fact. The problem now was apparently how to mend her fences with Andrew Gordon.

She looked up. Problem solved.

"Will you give me a few minutes with Andy?"

He shrugged.

She went to the living room. Tully followed her as far as the hall. He saw her stoop over Mercedes Cabbott's son, who was asleep, kiss him lightly on the forehead, slip into his lap, begin to murmur into his ear.

Sickened, Tully turned away.

A quarter of an hour later he heard Andy Gordon leave. Tully went into the living room.

"Success?"

Sandra Jean was smoking a cigarette in perfect calm. "I think so. He wasn't as miffed as I expected."

"Maybe Andy's not so keen on this connubial connection as he pretends to be."

"Don't be an ass. His tongue is hanging out."

"How much did you tell him?"

"Just enough. I said something'd come up about Ruth's trouble that couldn't wait, and we'd have to elope some other time."

"Just like that. And he fell for it?"

She smiled. "I gave him a Sandra Special before he could think about it. It's a type of kiss I'm thinking of patenting. It produces amnesia."

Tully did not change expression. "Did you tell him you went to see Crandall Cox on the night of the murder?"

"Of course," Sandra Jean said. "I couldn't have him hearing it from another source, could I?"

"What reason did you give Andy for the visit?"

She said hurriedly, "Oh, something or other that wouldn't disturb his dear addled brain too much. Shall we go, Davey?"

He knew then that Sandra Jean had probably ascribed the visit to sisterly duty, something that involved Ruth as the principal—a total and shameless lie. Tully shrugged and went to the door. So long as Sandra set the record on Ruth straight with the police, he didn't care how she bamboozled Andy Gordon and Mercedes Cabbott. They would have to watch out for themselves.

Julian Smith kept them waiting fifteen minutes.

"Sorry," he said, rising from his desk. He offered no explanation for the delay. He looked quickly from Sandra Jean to Tully and back again. "Hello, Miss Ainsworth."

"Hi, Lieutenant." They had a slight acquaintance. "What's up, Dave?" Smith said. "Something on Ruth?"

"In a negative sort of way," Tully said. "May we sit down, Julian?"

"Oh! Please." When they were seated Smith said, "I didn't get that, Dave."

Tully glanced at his sister-in-law. "How do you want it, Sandra? You or me?"

"I'm quite capable of speaking for myself." She seemed so self-possessed Tully's glance sharpened. Julian Smith noted his reaction, slight as it was, and became intent. "I wish to make a statement, Lieutenant. Isn't that the way it's put?"

"Statement about what, Miss Ainsworth?"

Sandra Jean ignored the question. Sitting straight-backed, knees primly together, she took inventory of the Homicide man's office. "Exactly how is it done, Lieutenant Smith? Do you have a stenographer in, or is it taken down on tape?"

Julian Smith said gently, "Don't worry your head about the mechanics of my job, Miss Ainsworth. First tell me what's on your mind. You can always repeat it for the official record."

"Stop stalling, Sandra," Tully said. He knew Smith already had the tape recorder going.

She pouted. But then she folded her hands in her lap and stared down at them. "Ruth wasn't the woman who spent those three days at the Wilton Lake Lodge with Cranny Cox two summers ago. I was the one, using Ruth's name."

Tully was watching the detective's face. It gave no sign of surprise.

"What made you decide to come in with this information, Miss Ainsworth?"

"Well, I've naturally been scared to get involved," Sandra Jean murmured. "But my brother-in-law's convinced me it's the only right and decent thing to do. I mean Ruth's being my sister and all."

Julian Smith swung about. "How did you find out about this, Dave?"

Tully was angry. Great expectations, he thought bitterly. "You don't seem impressed, Julian."

"Would you mind answering my question?"

"I'll answer your damn question," Tully growled. "I found out about it the same way you should have—I figured it out. Ruth and Sandra Jean look a lot alike. It's a couple of years since the people at the Lodge saw the woman with Cox. Ruth isn't capable of a hot-pillow romance with a cheap woman-chasing crook like Cox. So it must have been Sandra Jean. Q.E.D. Simple?"

"Too simple, Dave."

Tully jumped to his feet. "It's the truth!"

"Maybe," Julian Smith said. "And maybe it's a cook-up between you and Miss Ainsworth to cover for your wife and her sister."

13

David Tully cooled off very suddenly—his urge to grab Smith by the neck and shake sense into him died at birth. He had caught a certain look in Sandra Jean's eye, a look of calculation. She was the problem, not Smith. It was dawning on her that the lieutenant's skepticism gave her a possible out even now.

Tully said very quietly to the girl, "If you have any idea of putting on an act for Julian's benefit and finally 'admitting' that you and I hatched up a cock-and-bull story to save Ruth—forget it, Sandra. This is something that can be proved by having Dalrymple and the maid identify you."

"Sit down, Dave," Julian Smith said.

"Sure."

Tully sat down, his stare pinning Sandra Jean to the wall. He could almost see the computer inside her pretty head whirring and clicking to produce the decision.

It was made. Sandra Jean looked bewildered and hurt. "I don't know why you'd say a thing like that, Davey. I'm telling the truth, Lieutenant. I was the one. And, as Dave says, all you have to do to prove it is take me up to the Lodge for a positive identification."

"All right," Smith said. "Let's take it from there. Why did you use your sister's name?"

Sandra Jean said coolly, "Dave has a theory that it's because I've always hated her. It's nothing as Freudian as that. I was eighteen, I thought I was being terribly sophisticated, and since I never expected the story to get out I thought using Ruth's name was a good joke. Now, of course, I see what a bad joke it was."

"So when Cox came to town to blackmail Ruth, it was you he really meant?"

"Obviously. He asked me to come over to his room at the Hobby Motel—"

"The night he was shot?"

"Yes. I went."

"Alone? Or with your sister?"

"As far as I know, Ruth didn't know a thing about it. I went alone, yes."

"With the gun?"

"Yes. I took it from Dave's house. I knew it was there. I've always come and gone in the place as if it were my own home."

"Miss Ainsworth, do you realize the implications of what you're saying?"

"I'm not implying anything," she said. "You're inferring."

He blinked at her, sat forward. "Cox tried to blackmail you, and you used the gun?"

"I did not use the gun. Anyway, he took it from me and wouldn't give it back."

Smith knuckled his jaw. "You did intend to use the gun, however?"

Sandra Jean said calmly, "If I'd intended to shoot Cox, I'd hardly have carried a gun traceable to a member of my family. And I'd certainly have picked a better scene for my crime than a wide-open motel on a busy night. I'd have chosen a safer time, place and weapon, Lieutenant, believe me. I took Dave's gun simply to scare Cox."

The detective's face told nothing. "And did you scare Cox?"

She shrugged. "I guess so. He took a crazy chance and jumped me. He didn't know I couldn't have pulled the trigger even if I'd wanted to. Anyway, he wouldn't give it back to me."

"Then your story is that you didn't shoot Cox."

"It's not a story, Lieutenant. It's a fact."

Smith drummed on his desk. "Tell me, Miss Ainsworth," he said suddenly. "What was Cox asking of you?"

"Nothing."

"Come again?"

"Nothing then." Sandra Jean lowered her head again, modestly. "He knew Andrew Gordon and I were—are . . . well, in love. He was setting me up for a richer haul—after I became Mrs. Gordon." She looked up with a show of anxiety. "I do hope this is all—I mean, confidential, Lieutenant."

"Confidential!" Julian Smith sprang to his feet. "What is this, Dave? Doesn't this girl understand the position she's in? Confidential, she says! Miss Ainsworth, don't you realize that, simply on the strength of what you've already confessed, I have grounds for holding you?"

She smiled.

Smith abruptly sat down again. "There's something crosseyed about this," he complained. Tully had never seen him so upset. He was beginning to feel queasy himself. She had something up her sleeve, but what? I should have known, he thought. She came along too damn meekly!

"You could hold me, perhaps," Sandra Jean said, "but it wouldn't be for long. Cranny Cox was alive when I left him."

"There's only your word for that," Smith snapped.

"Not at all. I can prove it. Or . . . yes, Lieutenant," she said in the sweetest of voices, "I think I'll let you prove it for me."

"Prove that Cox was alive when you left him?"

"Mm-hm." The girl tugged at her skirt. "Oh, dear, I seem to have ripped my hem somewhere . . . You see, Lieutenant, although I went to the Hobby in a cab, I had the man let me out blocks and blocks from the motel and walked the rest of the way. But when I left, I took a taxi right outside the motel. Cranny took me out to the road and actually hailed it for me—handed me into it, in fact, like the gentleman he wasn't. I was all dressed up and I looked like a lady, if I do say so myself. Taxis don't pick up many ladies outside the Hobby, so I'm sure the cabbie will remember me—and Cranny Cox being so gallant and, of course, alive. In fact, I can even give you a description of the taxi man. He was white-haired, about fifty-five years old. . ."

Tully scarcely heard her rattle on, as Julian Smith scribbled furious notes. The cold-blooded little bitch, he thought. She hadn't said a word to him about that!

"Of course," the detective was saying frostily, "even if this checks out, Miss Ainsworth—"

"Oh, it will check out all right, Lieutenant," she smiled.

"—it could mean that you made a deliberate attempt to establish your departure at a time when Cox was seen alive, only to slip back to the motel later and do the shooting. In other words, a phony alibi."

"I suppose it could mean that," Sandra Jean murmured, "only 'could mean' doesn't carry much weight as evidence, Lieutenant, does it? Anyway, my alibi's a lot better than *that*. If you'll find that taxi driver, I'm sure he'll tell you where he took me, and when. He drove me to an all-night party I'd been invited to in the Heights. People named Bangsworth. And there must have been a dozen people there I knew who'll account for every minute of my time. So, you see, Lieutenant, I simply couldn't have shot Cranny Cox."

Tully could only sit there, numb.

Julian Smith sat there, too. He said slowly, "A few minutes ago, Miss Ainsworth, you told me that Cox asked you to visit him at the motel the night he was shot. Just how did he ask you?"

Sandra Jean's brow wrinkled ever so little. "I don't think I understand, Lieutenant."

"I mean, did he write you? Did he phone you?"

"He phoned me."

"Where?"

"At the Cabbotts', where I've been staying."

Smith leaned forward. "But you said he thought your name was Ruth. How could he have looked for Ruth in a place where you're known as Sandra Jean?"

"Oh, that," Sandra Jean said. "Didn't I explain that? Between the time Cranny came to town and the time he phoned me, he did some snooping. That's how he found out my real name and where I was staying, he said."

The unutterable trull. She hadn't told him that, either.

Tully shut his eyes. Andy Gordon had placed Cox's call to the Tully home, when the blackmailer had asked for Ruth, as having come two days before his murder. So at that time Cox must still have been ignorant of Sandra Jean's real name. In those two days, then, Cox had done his homework. But if by the time of his phone call to the Cabbott house he had known that "Ruth" was really Sandra Jean, why had he. . .?

Tully heard scraping chairs. He opened his eyes. Smith and Sandra Jean were on their feet.

"But where are you taking me, Lieutenant?" Sandra Jean was saying, not entirely without alarm.

"On a tour of the cab companies," the detective said, "to make an honest woman of you. Dave, this won't take too long. Though you don't have to wait if you have something else to do."

Tully shook his head. Julian Smith opened his office door and stood aside, and Sandra Jean swept by in rather a hurry, Tully thought, noting that she was careful not to look at him. He could wait. There were only three or four cab companies in town; it wouldn't take long.

It didn't. Barely an hour later Julian Smith marched back into the office. He was alone.

"Where's Sandra Jean?" Tully got to his feet.

Smith homed in on his desk. "She gave me a message for you. 'Tell my darling brother-in-law he needn't wait for me. I'll hop a cab—I have things to do in a rush.' The last I saw, she was streaking for a phone booth. That's quite a sister-in-law you have."

"So her story is true," Tully said slowly.

The detective shrugged and sat down. "The alibi checks. I found the hack the first cab company I hit. He identified her, all right, and corroborated her statement that Cox put her into the cab that night. His trip-sheet in the office checks out for time, too. He described Cox to a *T*. For the record I had him hustled over to the funeral parlor for a look at the body, and I just had a call that he made a positive identification.

"And he did take the girl right from the Hobby to the Bangsworths' at the Heights, as she claims. I phoned

Mrs. Bangsworth and she gives the girl a clean bill. I also phoned three of the people at the party who Sandra Jean said could testify that she hadn't left the house after she got there, and they so testify—the party didn't break up until five a.m., long past the time of the shooting. One of my men is running down the whole list the girl's given me, but that's just going through the motions. There's no question that Cox was alive when she left him at the motel, and she's alibied for every minute after that. She's absolutely in the clear, Dave. Didn't you know that when you brought her in here?"

Tully said, "No," and had to clear his throat. The detective looked at him curiously. "Where does this leave Ruth?"

"You tell me."

"Well, for one thing, Julian, at least now you know it wasn't Ruth who took my gun to the motel."

"There's still that business of the name."

"Name?"

"The name Maudie Blake said she overheard Cox use that night in addressing his visitor—or one of them. According to Sandra Jean, Cox knew well in advance of the visit or visits that her name was really Sandra Jean. So if that night he called some woman Ruth. . ."

Tully bit his lip. He had foolishly hoped that detail would somehow be lost in the shuffle. "That's assuming Sandra told the truth about what went on in the room, Julian."

"Her alibi story checks to the letter. We have to assume the rest of her story is true, too."

"But that means you think my wife came to Cox's room after Sandra left! How do you know she hadn't come and gone—assuming she was there at all!—before Sandra even got there?"

Julian Smith said, "We have the Blake woman's sworn statement as to the time she heard the name Ruth mentioned by Cox in direct address. That time was well past the time we know Miss Ainsworth left. I'm sorry, Dave."

So the Blake woman had lied to him about not remembering the time, too! Tully was striding up and down the office like a prisoner in a cell. "That sworn statement of Maudie Blake's. She's dead, Julian. It seems to me that if it came to a trial—"

"The admissibility of evidence is a matter for the judge and the lawyers, Dave. I can only do my part of the job."

"You've had your case blown right out of your hands!" Tully cried. "Why do you keep persecuting my wife?"

"Because of that name," the lieutenant said doggedly. "Because she's run away. And it's not persecution, Dave; you know better than that. In the light of those two facts I've got to keep after her. You know that, too."

"But you don't even have a motive any more! Not with Sandra's admission that she was the one who spent those three days at the Lodge with Cox."

"I don't have a motive I can prove yet, Dave, that's true." Julian Smith shook his head in distaste. "You make me say it. Ruth did go to Cox's motel. That makes it pretty hard to avoid the conclusion that she knew him. Well, Cox's relationships with women were strictly one thing. So I've got to work on the premise that not only your sister-in-law but your wife, too, was one of his ex-affairs—"

"No!" Tully's face was purple. "No!" His fist came down with a crash on the Homicide man's desk. *"No, no, no!"* His fist kept smashing at the desk impotently.

Smith said nothing more, letting him rage.

After a while, Tully stopped. A choked sound came out of his convulsed throat, and he turned on his heel and strode out of Smith's office.

David Tully paused on the front steps of the municipal building to gulp the fresher air in mouthfuls and work himself back to some semblance of self-control.

He couldn't blame Julian Smith. Julian wasn't emotionally involved with Ruth. He had liked her (although now that he thought of it, Tully recalled that Ruth had always seemed to have reservations about Julian. Was it because she *was* concealing something unsavory about her past, and a policeman made her uncomfortable?). But he had to be a policeman first and a social being second. Julian had no choice.

His rage, Tully knew, had been directed not toward the Homicide man but to himself. He thought he had made peace with his love and faith; now he found himself doubting all over again.

As he stood there inhaling and exhaling, watching and not seeing the traffic go by, he found a thought pushing itself into the forefront of his consciousness. He tried to push it back; it would not stay pushed back.

If . . . *if* Ruth had had an affair with Cox, surely he knew all along that she *was* Ruth and that Sandra Jean *was* Sandra Jean? But the evidence seemed to indicate that Cox didn't become aware of Sandra's masquerade until a day or so before his death. Then the *if* was wrong. Cox didn't know Ruth. He hadn't known Ruth! . . . Unless . . .

Unless he had originally known Ruth under some other name entirely.

It was possible.

If Ruth could be pictured as having somehow got herself to accept Cox's love-making in some remote and hardly imaginable past, she could also be pictured— being Ruth after all—as having done so under a false name. It was more than possible. *If* and *possible* and *false* . . . Tully rested his forehead against the cool stone of the municipal building as his thoughts shattered into pieces that went flying off in all directions.

He started at a touch on his arm.

"Mr. Tully, you feeling all right?" It was a policeman in uniform, without a hat.

"Yes. Sure, Officer. I'm just going." Tully straightened up.

"I came out looking for you. The lieutenant said you'd just left. There's a phone call for you."

"Here?" Who could that be? "Where, Officer?"

"I'll show you."

He followed the policeman back into the building. There was a table behind the desk sergeant's wicket.

"You can take it here, Mr. Tully. I'll switch you in."

The uniformed man sat down at the police switchboard. He said, "Just a minute, ma'am," and plugged in.

Tully thought, Ma'am?

He picked up the phone on the table. "This is David Tully. Who—?"

"Dave! Norma Hurst." It came into his ear all breathy, as if she had been running.

Tully became alert. "Norma? Something wrong?"

"I'm not sure. Mercedes Cabbott called. Ollie was out . . . She wanted Ollie . . . It was really you she wanted. She called trying to locate you." Her sentences tumbled out. Was she having one of her spells again?

"Yes, Norma?" He forced himself to sound untroubled.

"I called all over trying to find you. Then I thought of Police Headquarters. Have they any news of Ruth yet?"

"Not yet, Norma."

"They're listening to us, of course. Aren't they, Dave? I know they are. Can you come over here?"

"Well—"

"Wait, I think I heard Ollie's car. I'll tell him you're coming over."

"Norma. . ."

But she had hung up.

Ollie answered the door. The bald lawyer looked tired and preoccupied.

"Oh, Dave, come in. Norma says she caught you at Police Headquarters."

Tully nodded. He stepped into the Hursts' living room and said, "What's all this about Mercedes trying to locate me? What does she want?"

"She wouldn't say. Just said for me to find you and bring you to her place."

"Ollieeeee?" Norma's thin voice cut through the house. "Is that Dave?"

She burst into the living room with the power of a tornado-driven straw. Tully was shocked by her appearance. She wore a wrinkled dress. Her lank hair was uncombed. Her features seemed to have been honed to cutting edges overnight. Her eyes. . .

111

This was a bad one.

Tully kept himself from staring at her. And at Ollie. At times like this, Ollie went through his own brand of hell.

Norma's nails dug into Tully's hand. "Dave, you must hurry. You must find her quickly."

"Yes, Norma. We'll find her. Now stop worrying."

Ollie slipped his arm about Norma's thin shoulders. "You know we'll do our best, hon. Haven't I told you?"

She collapsed against her husband suddenly. "Mercedes will help you, Dave. She loves Ruth like a daughter. That's why she called. I'm sure that's why."

"Maybe it would be better if Ollie stays here with you."

"No, no, I'm fine. I'll be just fine. That's a promise. Ollie has to go with you, help however he can."

From behind his wife's head Ollie nodded slightly.

"Maybe you're right at that, Norma," Tully said.

Outside, Oliver Hurst mumbled, "It's not good, Dave. I had to humor her. Maybe it'll calm her down. I don't dare cross her when she gets like this. Whose car'll we take?"

"Mine," Tully said. Ollie looked out on his feet.

They got into the Imperial and Tully headed it toward the hills.

"I don't know," Ollie said after a while, shaking his head. "For a while there this hassle about Ruth seemed to shake Norma back to her old self. Now . . . She's worse than she's been in months."

"Why don't you try taking her up to the old place, Ollie? The change may do her good."

The "old place" was a Hurstism for an ancient log house some ten miles from town, deep in the foothills that had come down to Norma from her paternal great-grandfather. He had been an early settler, clearing the land, hewing the logs, digging a root-cellar and building the house with his own hands. It had been kept in a good state of preservation, and the Hursts had used it frequently as a weekend woodland retreat in happier days.

But Ollie Hurst shook his head. "It's the one place

she mustn't go. Isolation is what she wants, a hole to crawl into. The psychiatrists told me to keep her strictly away from there. They want her to be with people."

"That makes sense, I guess."

"She was after me just this morning to take her up there. Reaction from a dream—a nightmare—she had during the night. Must have been a corker; it took me over an hour to quiet her down."

"Nightmare about what, Ollie?"

"It seems she and Ruth were on a roller coaster. The thing kept going faster and faster. Suddenly a little girl —with no face—was in the middle of the track ahead of them on a tricycle. The roller coaster smashed into her, and the little girl wasn't there any more. Then the coaster shot off the end of the track, tumbling through space, which was full of billions of stars. But it was also pitch-dark. Norma was all alone in just black nothing except stars. Ruth had vanished, too."

And that's a fact, David Tully thought.

14

Ollie Hurst trailed Tully and the butler into the foyer of the Colonial mansion. Tully wondered why the lawyer seemed so uncomfortable.

The two men waited in silence.

Mercedes Cabbott appeared, a fresh-scented and girlish vision in skirt and blouse and delicately thonged sandals. Her white hair was exquisitely coifed, as always; her tiny features and lake-blue eyes were set hard.

She looked Oliver Hurst up and down. "How are you, Ollie?" The words sounded as if she had just taken them out of a deep-freeze.

"I'm still here, Mercedes." To Tully's surprise, the lawyer's tone was just as icy.

"And David." She turned, light-footed. "Shall we go out to the terrace?"

They followed her and the butler out. She indicated two of the white iron chairs. "Would you care for a drink?"

Ollie Hurst said, "No, thank you."

Tully said, "I'll pass, too, Mercedes. I'd like to get right to your reason for asking me here. I know it wasn't social."

"That's all, Stellers." Mercedes waited until the butler went back into the house. "Perhaps that's best, David. Actually, George has something to say to you, too— he'll be down as soon as he's through changing." Her lips formed a hard line. "What I wanted to talk to you about concerns Andrew. Do you know where he and Sandra Jean are?"

"No," Tully said. What in hell could George Cabbott

114

want to see him about? "But to the best of my knowledge they're planning to elope."

The only sign Mercedes showed was a slight pallor. "So my bluff didn't work. Well, darling, what am I to do?"

"Do?" Tully said. "I haven't any idea." He did not add what he was thinking: And I couldn't care less.

Very suddenly Andrew Gordon's mother turned to Oliver Hurst. "Ollie? Would you have a suggestion?"

Hurst shifted cautiously in his chair. "Are you asking for my professional opinion, Mercedes?"

"You may bill me for it." There was nothing, utterly nothing, to be learned from her voice.

"All right," said the lawyer. "Are they of legal age?"

"Yes."

"Then I'll be happy to give you my opinion gratis: There isn't anything you can do about it."

Tully had never heard Oliver Hurst speak in quite that tone. It was composed of notes of bitterness, triumph, regret and barely checked temper; they formed a harsh, uncharacteristic chord. And Mercedes Cabbott's blue eyes glittered like lake ice in deep winter at the sound of it. Whatever lay between the two obviously went back a long, long way.

"I might have expected you to say that," Mercedes said.

"You're licked, Mercedes."

"My dear," the young-old woman said softly, "I'm never licked."

The sun bounced off Hurst's bald head as he shifted violently back to his original position. But he did not reply, preferring to examine the hills in the distance.

Mercedes Cabbott rose and drifted to the edge of her terrace. She stood there gripping the iron railing, her back to the two men.

"It's strange how events influence one another," she said. "One brick falls, and a dozen others tumble after it." She turned to face them, and again her voice was as savagely cold as her eyes. "If Ruth hadn't gone away, Sandra Jean wouldn't have become such a problem. But with Ruth gone, the little slut seizes an opportunity she knows may never recur."

There's no point in my putting my two cents in, Tully thought.

They had forgotten he was there. It was strictly a dialogue.

"You asked me for a suggestion, Mercedes," Oliver Hurst said. The savagery in her voice had, oddly enough, purged him. He sounded almost sympathetic. "I'll oblige."

"Well?"

"For once in your life, acknowledge a defeat. Make the best of this, Mercedes. Try to remember that you're not all-wise and all-powerful, after all."

"Have I ever made any such claims?"

Ollie uttered a faint, incredulous laugh. He shook his head. "Don't you know even now what a tyrant you are? And what a helpless parasite you've made out of your son? Sandra Jean isn't the worst fate that could befall Andy. I think it's even possible she might make a man of him out of the little you've left unspoiled."

She had gone white. Her small hands reached backwards and closed around the railing convulsively.

"You have no right to come into my home and say—!"

"I'm here at your invitation, remember? And I didn't speak until I was spoken to." The lawyer crossed his legs easily. His aplomb seemed to increase in direct ratio to her anger. "However, if you want politeness instead of honest talk, I apologize."

Mercedes sniffed with hauteur and came back to her chair. She seemed actually mollified!

Tully was bewildered. What was it between these two? He had never even suspected anything but a most superficial acquaintanceship. But then he thought, What the hell, it has nothing to do with Ruth; and he shrugged.

The rangy shadow of George Cabbott fell across them. His sun-bleached hair curled damply, as if he had just showered. He wore Bermuda shorts and a sports shirt with the tail out.

Cabbott's eyes, which tended to squint from years of

exposure to the sun, widened slightly at the sight of Ollie Hurst. But he merely uttered a pleasant "Hi," stooped over his wife to kiss her—the incongruous thought crossed David Tully's mind of Ferdinand the Bull lowering his massive head to smell a wildflower—and went to the bar-cart near the terrace table. "I take it you gentlemen aren't drinking. Darling?"

"Not just now, George."

"Mind if I have one?"

"What a stupid question for a smart man," Mercedes laughed. The sight of her husband had restored her good humor.

George Cabbott dropped an ice cube into a glass, poured some Scotch in, studying its level critically, then added a few splashes of water from a silver carafe. He joined the group, sitting down and crossing one big blond-felled leg over the other.

"Now, sweetheart, where are we?"

"It's all yours, George." Mercedes gestured helplessly, smiling. "Believe it or not, I haven't the foggiest notion of what George wants to talk to you about, David. When this old bear of mine makes up his mind to do things a certain way, Cleopatra herself couldn't budge him."

"I was told," Cabbott remarked, "to tell you directly, Dave."

"Tell me what?"

Cabbott sipped his Scotch, lowered the glass, agitated it gently. He watched the ice cube slide around. Then he looked up and at Ollie Hurst and said, in a perfectly agreeable voice, "Can you trust this guy, Dave?"

"What?" Tully said, blinking.

"Think nothing of it, Dave," Hurst said. "Nobody trusts a lawyer. Especially on these premises. And especially this lawyer."

"Look, George," Tully said, "I don't know what this is all about, but Ollie Hurst is my friend and my attorney, and anything you may have to say to me you can say in his hearing."

"I don't know," Mercedes's husband said in the same pleasant way. "This might be a special case."

Oliver Hurst gripped the arms of his chair, began to get up. "I think I'd better leave, Dave."

"You sit down," Tully said grimly. "No, Ollie, I mean it! Or I'll leave with you." Hurst sank back. "What's this special-case bit, George? Stop talking like a character in TV."

"If he heard this, Hurst might feel it his professional duty to report it to the police."

"That's a damn nasty thing to say, Cabbott," Ollie Hurst said. He was liver-lipped. "Dave just told you, I'm his attorney. Attorneys don't run to the police to blab about their clients' affairs."

"No offense," Cabbott said with a small smile. "I was given pretty definite instructions."

"Instructions about what, for God's sake?" David Tully cried. "By whom?"

"Ruth."

His head kept swirling like the ice in George Cabbott's glass. The groping thought reached him at last that at some point in recent time he had crossed without noticing it the line between hope and despair. Hope that he might hear from Ruth, that she was even alive.

"Alive," he repeated aloud, turning it over on his tongue as if it were a new taste sensation. His voice rose in a joyous shout. "She's alive!"

"Wait a minute, Dave," Ollie Hurst was saying. He had his remarkable eyes fixed on Cabbott.

"Wait for what? George, where is she?" Tully sprang to his feet. "Come on, George, talk, will you?" He grabbed the big man's shoulders and began to shake him.

Cabbott sat quietly, letting himself be shaken.

"David," Mercedes Cabbott said. *"David."*

"What!"

"You'd better sit down and listen. I have a feeling this isn't good news."

Tully sank back in his chair.

"It happened several hours ago, Dave," George Cabbott said. "I began calling all over town for you, and when Mercedes came back home I got her to do some calling, too."

"And wouldn't say a word about why." She leaned over and squeezed her husband's hand.

"I was at Police Headquarters," Tully said. He wet his lips. "George, for God's sake."

"She telephoned me," Cabbott said. "She wouldn't say from where—"

"Did you ask her?" Ollie Hurst asked curtly.

"Of course. She simply refused to say."

"Are you sure it was Ruth?" the lawyer persisted.

"Her voice." Cabbott shrugged. "Unmistakably."

"Could it have been faked?"

"If it was, it was a perfect imitation."

Tully said hoarsely, "Hold it, Ollie. George, if she wanted to get in touch with me, why didn't she do it directly? Why through you?"

"I asked her the same thing, naturally. She said the police might have your line tapped. Also, she didn't want to chance your talking her out of going away."

"Going . . . away?"

"That's what Ruth said."

"The idiot, the little *idiot*," Mercedes Cabbott said. "Acting noble at a time like this!"

"You mean," David Tully said bleakly, "she's leaving me?"

"I can only tell you what she said, Dave," Cabbott replied in a patient voice. "She said she was sorry for keeping you in the dark so long about her dropping out of sight. She said she was all right physically. She said you wouldn't be hearing from her again until she was safe, perhaps not even then. 'Safe' was her own word, Dave."

"Safe," Tully said. "And she didn't tell you where she was planning to go?"

"No." George Cabbott suddenly drained his glass. "I may as well give you the whole thing, Dave. She said for you to pick up the pieces of your life, and . . . well, she started to cry and said something like, 'Tell Dave he'll always be my sugar-pill,' and then she hung up."

"Her what?"

"Sugar-pill. I take it that's one of her wife-words of endearment? When Mercedes is being especially nice she calls me her hay-bailer."

Ollie Hurst asked, "*Was* that a special word between you and Ruth, Dave?"

"Yes." There was the oddest look on Tully's face. "No imitator would have known about it."

"Then it *was* Ruth." The lawyer abruptly got up. "I think, Cabbott, I'll take one of your drinks after all."

"Help yourself."

"Will you have one, Dave?"

"No. Ollie . . ." Tully got to his feet, too. "I'd like to go now. Make it a quick one, eh?" He crossed the terrace to the doorway, hesitated, turned around. "George."

"Yes, Dave."

"Ruth said nothing at all about Cox? The motel? Anything like that?"

George Cabbott squinted at his empty glass as if it pained him. "That was the last thing I asked her—whether she had shot Cox. That's when she hung up on me. Without answering."

"Thanks, George." Tully walked into the house.

"I'll see you out, David." Mercedes Cabbott rose and hurried after him. Oliver Hurst gulped his drink and followed. Cabbott remained alone on the terrace, staring into his empty glass.

Mercedes and Hurst caught up with Tully on the front steps.

"David, David, I'm sorry."

"I know," Tully said. Her hand in both of his was trembling and cold. He felt very little himself.

"Sorry for a lot of things," Mercedes Cabbott said; and with some surprise Tully noticed that she was glancing Oliver Hurst's way when she said it. But then she said in the old assured way, "I won't keep you. God bless, David," and she went back into her palace.

The two men walked slowly to Tully's car and got in.

"She was talking to you, too, Ollie."

"You noticed that?" And the lawyer was silent. He did not speak again until Tully turned out of the estate into the public road. "I knew her daughter. Kathleen Lavery."

"Oh?"

"Kathleen was a beauty. I was a college kid, and I went head over heels for her. She . . . reciprocated enough to scare Mercedes. I was a nothing, a nobody, without a dime. Mercedes took Kathleen abroad and she was drowned in a boating accident."

"I'm sorry, Ollie."

Hurst shrugged. "It was a long time ago." But Tully noted the gray pallor that had settled over his friend's face.

So now Ollie Hurst had his law practice and his Norma, and Mercedes Cabbott had her Colonial palace to rattle around in and her enigmatic George and her dead —and dying—motherhood.

And I? Tully thought. What do I have?

15

The moment Tully walked into the office Lieutenant Smith said, "There's nothing new." His desk was piled with papers which he rather stealthily covered with a phone book.

"This time you're wrong, Julian." Tully seated himself, uninvited, beside Smith's desk. "You'd better give me a few uninterrupted minutes."

The Homicide man studied him suspiciously. He wore a generally fretful and harassed look today. But then he became relaxed-alert all over; Tully saw it coming over him, like a change of clothing.

The detective picked up his phone and said, "No calls from anybody till I check back," and he hung up and leaned forward on his forearms, clasping his hands. "You've got them, Dave."

"I've heard from Ruth."

Immediately Julian Smith's hands unclasped. He reached for a pencil and pad. "You talked to her yourself?"

"No. It was a message, relayed to me."

"By whom? When?"

"About three-quarters of an hour ago, by George Cabbott. Ollie Hurst was with me. I dropped Ollie off at his home and drove directly here."

"When did Cabbott say he heard from her, and how?"

"Several hours ago. By phone."

"Where was she calling from?"

"She wouldn't say, according to Cabbott."

"Why didn't she get in touch with you in person?"

122

Tully said wearily, "She thought you might have our wire tapped."

"How sure is Cabbott that it was really her voice?"

"He's positive."

Smith grunted. After a moment he looked up from his pad and said, "Well?" with a trace of impatience. "What was her message?"

"The gist of it was that she was physically okay, that she was going away to some place where she'd be safe, and that I should patch up my life and, presumably, forget her."

"In other words, goodbye Charlie." The detective leaned back in his swivel chair, tapping his chin with the pencil. "Well, Dave, in view of that call, was I right about her, or wrong?"

"Wrong," Tully said. "Wrong, Julian."

"You die hard, don't you?" Smith sighed. "All right, I'll play. How does this prove I'm wrong?"

"How did you ever get to be a lieutenant?" Tully said matter-of-factly. "Don't you realize how convenient that message is for the killer of Cox and the Blake woman?"

"Suppose you spell it out for me!" The detective was a bit pink about the ears.

"If Ruth is never found, the goodbye message nails down the lid on her guilt. The all-points goes out like the ripples made by a stone tossed into a lake. The search gets further and further from town here, the ripples gradually weaken and die away. Goodbye Charlie my foot, Julian! Goodbye case—in the unsolved file."

"You still don't make sense, Dave."

"Look!" Tully's eyes were hard. "The whole thing is damn clear to me now—"

"You mean by guess and by God?"

"I mean by logic and proof!"

"Oh?" Julian Smith said.

"Don't bug me, Julian—listen! Either Ruth took off voluntarily, or she was forced into hiding, abducted. Those are the only two choices, aren't they? If she didn't drop out of sight of her own free will, she's being held somewhere under duress!"

"By the real killer of Cox."

"Yes! From which it follows that Ruth is innocent. No, let me keep going. I'll concede the probability that Ruth did go to the Hobby Motel that night. For purposes of my argument, I don't give a damn whether she went there—as you believe—because she was also one of Cox's ex-romances and blackmail victims or—as I believe—because she'd somehow got wind of Sandra Jean's involvement with Cox and followed Sandra to the motel to protect a wild kid sister. Either way, Ruth's *there*, spying. She sees Cox put Sandra into a cab, go back to his room. But before Ruth can leave, she also sees somebody else call on Cox—and it's my guess it's someone she knew or recognized, or she'd never have hung around . . ."

"Pardon," the detective said. "Your version can be improved. Ruth doesn't just hang around outside after her sister leaves; she follows Cranny Cox into his room and talks to him—whether about herself or about Sandra Jean doesn't matter at this point. There's a knock on the door—the somebody else you set up. Ruth is trapped; she can't get out without being spotted by this mysterious new visitor, so Cox lets her hide in the bathroom.

"Cox lets visitor in. Argument. Visitor picks up your gun—lying on the bed, maybe, where Cox tossed it after taking it away from Sandra Jean. Bang! Cox is dead. Ruth cries out or something—anyway, killer finds her hiding there. So he slugs her and spirits her away. Is that it, Dave?"

"Yes, that's it," Tully said eagerly. "And doesn't it make all kinds of sense? For instance: Why doesn't he shoot Ruth, too? Because he sees that she gives him a heaven-sent out. By smuggling her from the motel and keeping her out of circulation, he makes her the logical suspect for the Cox killing. And she takes the heat off him, or any possibility of it."

"And even then he doesn't kill her," Julian Smith said, nodding, "because he's saving her for the psychological moment. Right, Dave?"

"Right! When he figures the time is ripe, he forces her to make contact with me, to tell me she's going to run as fast and as far as she can, and I'm to forget her."

"And how does he force her to do that?"

"Are you kidding, Julian? By threatening to kill her —or, better still, me. Ruth would certainly knuckle under if she thought my life was in danger!"

"And for this killer that's it, isn't it?" Smith murmured.

"Exactly. He's cinched his frame-up and he has no further need of Ruth. But he obviously can't turn her loose, either." Tully said hoarsely, "Don't you see where this leads to, Julian? *He has to kill her, dispose of her so that no trace will ever be found.* Julian, you've got to forget this nonsense about looking for Ruth as a wanted killer. You've got to concentrate every effort on finding her before she becomes another victim! It may be too late already!"

The lieutenant did not stir.

Tully jumped up, yelling. "My God, Julian, are you a complete moron? Isn't it logical? Doesn't it follow?"

"It follows, all right," Smith said. "The trouble is, it follows from a premise you've cut out of the whole cloth. It's built on unsupported assumption."

"What assumption?" Tully cried. "That Ruth is innocent?"

"The assumption basic to that one, that Ruth is being held against her will and was forced to make the call. What's that assumption rest on but plain air?"

Tully leaned over the desk in a bitter sort of triumph. "I wanted you to put it like that, Julian. It rests not on air but on solid fact!"

"Produce it."

"I haven't a sworn affidavit or an inanimate Exhibit A. I have Ruth's own word. She told me."

"She told you?" Julian Smith said sharply. "Told you what?"

"That the message she asked George Cabbott to pass on to me was a fake."

"Interesting if true. How'd she manage to do that?"

"By slipping in a certain word. It sounded like a harmless term of endearment. It was anything but."

The detective frowned. "I don't get you."

"Haven't you and your wife ever used a secret signal, Julian, a word or phrase with a meaning known only to the two of you?"

"Well . . . yes." The lieutenant looked irritated. "If Gert wants to quit a party early because she's bored or something, she'll mention the O'Toole case to me. There never was an O'Toole case. It's our private code for, 'Let's get out of here.'"

Tully nodded. "With Ruth and me it's sugar-pill."

"Sugar-pill?"

"On our honeymoon Ruth told me about some aunt or somebody, a hypochondriac, who was always running to her doctor with imaginary aches and pains. He'd give her pills made out of sugar, and she went away happy. For some reason it tickled me, and I promptly christened sugar-pill our secret word for anything imaginary or untrue. If somebody told a supposedly true story, I'd beam at Ruth and call her my little sugar-pill, and she'd understand from that that I knew or thought the guy was lying his head off. Or if we were introduced to somebody, especially a gal, that Ruth thought I was showing too much of an interest in, she'd say sweetly to me, 'Isn't Miss So-and-So fascinating, sugar-pill?' and I'd get the message: My wife thought the gal was a phony."

"So?"

"The last thing Ruth said to George Cabbott before she hung up was, 'Tell Dave he'll always be my sugar-pill.' That was the tipoff, Julian. Ruth was telling me, 'Don't believe a word of what I've said. This is a phony.' It could only mean she was forced to make the call, told what to say. Does that bear out my theory or doesn't it?"

Smith was silent.

Tully kept looking at him, puzzled.

Finally the lieutenant said, "You wouldn't be making this up, Dave, would you?"

He fought a battle with himself, and won. "No, Julian, I wouldn't and I didn't. But if you doubt me, call Cabbott."

"That wouldn't prove anything. I have only your

word for it that sugar-pill has a secret meaning—the meaning you claim it has—for you and Mrs. Tully."

Tully shook his head and laughed. "The one thing that didn't occur to me was that you'd doubt my word." He shrugged. "Well, that's the only proof I can give you, Julian. I can't see that you and I are going to have much more to say to each other. I've had it."

He made for the office door.

Lieutenant Smith said, "Wait, wait, will you?"

Tully stopped, waited.

"Damn it all, Dave, this puts me in a real spot. It might mean my job . . ." But then the Homicide man got to his feet, and when he spoke again it was with decision. "If your analysis is right, I'll have to reverse my field. And fast, because Ruth is in for it. Go home and stay out of my hair!"

16

Tully went home.

He let himself into the silent house and sank limply into the big chair in the living room. His legs felt like old rubber and a great lassitude had sucked him dry. How long was it since he had come home from the capital—a day, two days, three? He could not remember.

Julian was right. He could do no more. Now it was in the hands of the police . . . now that they were looking for an innocent woman in danger of being murdered instead of for a murderer.

Funny how this thing, Tully thought, has kept testing my faith in Ruth. Down, up, down, up . . . He laid his head far back and stretched his legs gingerly.

Twilight was coming on and the room was sinking into shadow.

First he had destroyed her image. Then he had resurrected its fragments and put them back together. Now she was to be destroyed in the flesh . . . dead . . .

The shadows deepened into near-darkness. The thought of turning on the lights made him wince. Light meant seeing the things they had bought together, lived in, cherished. Light meant Ruth. Better the black gloom and the silence.

The silence.

The silence?

Noiselessly Tully shifted his position in the chair until he was sitting up, ears cocked, straining. There had been something in the silence that made it not quite silence. A sense of presence . . . With one leap he was out of the chair and across the room, his hand shooting out to the light switch.

He whirled.

Norma Hurst stood in the archway that separated the living room from the rear of the house. She must have been standing there, Tully thought, for a long time—perhaps since he had come home.

He felt the flesh of his forearms gather itself into little eruptions of dread.

This was a Norma Hurst he had never seen before. She had combed her drab hair with great care but the result was curiously fumbling. Her long thin face was grotesque with make-up, as if a small child had tried to imitate her mother's toilet. And her eyes . . . her eyes were not Norma's at all. They were overlarge and underbright; they looked blind.

"Norma," Tully said; he tried to make his voice sound natural, but it came out in a croak. "What are you doing here? How did you get in?" She must have climbed through one of the bedroom windows.

Norma put her forefinger to her wildly rouged lips. "Not so loud," she said. "She'll hear me."

Her voice was strange, too. It had a throb in it, a sort of excitement, that gave it an unpleasantly eerie timbre.

"Who'll hear you, Norma?"

"Mother, of course." He saw her shrink a little, as if she were afraid.

It took all his will-power to go to her, smiling, and take her hand. Her flesh was icy. She resisted his pull.

"You're going to take me to her. She's here, I know she's here. I don't want to see her."

"There's no one here but us, Norma."

"You shouldn't call me that."

"What?" Tully said, bewildered. "Call you what?"

"That name. The name of that flat-chested horror."

"You mean . . . Norma?"

"Please," Norma said sharply. "You know perfectly well that my name is Kathleen."

She had plunged over the edge.

Tully knew he must reach the telephone, call for help. Ollie? She must have slipped away from him. Ollie was undoubtedly hunting for her right now. The police? No . . . Dr. Suddreth!

Dr. Suddreth was the nearest thing the Tullys had ever had in the way of a family physician. Suddreth was no psychiatrist, but he would do in an emergency. At least control her, know whom to call . . .

Norma had drifted toward the middle of the living room. Her face was twisted with worry. "I can't seem to remember where Ollie introduced us. Was it at the country club dance last week?"

"Why, yes," Tully said, managing a smile. "Oh! Would you excuse me a moment?"

"For what?" she said with sudden sharpness.

"I forgot. I have a call to make."

"No!" she said. "No—phoning—mother." Her lower lip stuck out resentfully.

"Mother?" he repeated mechanically. How was he to get to the phone?

"As if you don't know! Don't try to fool me. You know very well my mother is Mercedes Lavery." She got into a crouch, looking around, whispering. "She's here, isn't she? You're in this with her! And Ollie calls you his best friend! Where is she hiding? Her glance kept darting about.

"Merce—your mother isn't here," Tully said in a reassuring tone. "And of course I'm Ollie's best friend. Now why don't you sit down and make yourself comfortable while—"

"You are, aren't you?"

"What?"

"Ollie's best friend. Otherwise you wouldn't let us meet here. Mother's made it impossible for us to meet anywhere else."

It was hard to follow the logic of her delusion. The damn phone, so near. But the delusion might be a temporary thing. I can't risk pushing her toward the thin edge of total madness, Tully thought.

She was wandering about the living room now, humming a shapeless little tune. Suddenly she stopped before the bar.

"I want a drink," she said.

"You, Norma—?" He stopped quickly. Surprise had made him forget. Norma didn't drink.

She was looking at him with mean, hopeless resentment. "I ask you once more to stop calling me that *name*. Do you hear me? Do you?"

"Yes. Yes, of course, Kathleen. Sorry."

"Kathleen. That's my name."

"Kathleen."

He wondered if he dared try force. He might be able to wrap her in a blanket or something and tie her up until Dr. Suddreth arrived. No, he thought, she might tumble right over the edge. The safest thing was to humor her as best he could while he figured out a way to make the phone call without upsetting her.

"I want a drink," Norma Hurst said in exactly the same way as before. As if their interchange betweenwhiles had not taken place at all.

"What would you like . . . Kathleen?"

It pleased her. "Now you remember," she said gayly. "Why, Scotch on the rocks. Make it a double."

Norma asking for a double Scotch!

But then a thought struck Tully.

"Sit down, Kathleen. I've got to get some ice from the kitchen for your drink—" He could phone for help from the kitchen extension.

But Norma said, "No ice, thank you."

"You said on the rocks," he said desperately.

"No ice," she repeated.

He poured a huge slug of Scotch into a highball glass and handed it to her, hope returning. Norma didn't drink because she couldn't; hard liquor either made her sick or sleepy. In either event . . .

"Thank you," she said, and held the glass without attempting to drink from it.

"Drink up, Kathleen," Tully said heartily. "You asked for a double."

"Oh, yes," she said in a vague way; and she raised the glass and barely wet her lips. Tully turned and poured himself a drink almost as copious.

"Let's go into my den, Kathleen," he said, forcing another smile. "It's comfier there."

Rather to his surprise, she said, "All right," and ambled along in his wake.

He sat her down in his oversized leather chair and hovered over the telephone without seeming to do so. If only someone would call!

"I suppose you've wondered," Norma said brightly—she was sitting in a stiff position that made him wince—"what I can possibly see in a man like Oliver Hurst."

"Well . . . yes."

"I know everybody does. What people don't realize is that the beautiful Kathleen Lavery—they call me that, don't they?—with all this money and position, is way down deep the unhappiest girl in town. The beautiful Mercedes—they call mother that, too, don't they?—doesn't understand that I need to be needed for myself, for what I am inside, not for what I look like and have. Ollie Hurst needs me as a person—the only man I've ever known who does. What do I care what Ollie looks like? Or that he hasn't a dime? He's mad about *me*. And he always will be."

Under other circumstances Tully would have been fascinated. This is how it must have been, he thought, seen through Norma Hurst's eyes.

"You aren't listening," Norma said. She was still sitting rigid on the edge of the chair, still holding the glassful of untouched Scotch.

"Oh, but I am—Kathleen," he said hastily. "Please go on."

"There! You remembered again." She smiled, a painful surface adjustment of muscle tissue. "Why did you keep calling me that other name? You know, that was cruel of you. Poor Norma can't help being what she is."

"I'm sorry," Tully said. Idly he removed the handset from its cradle. "I mean I'm sorry for—"

"*Will* you stop playing with that phone?" Norma said shrilly. "It makes me nervous." He replaced the handset. "What was I saying? Oh, about Norma. She's so sensitive and high-strung, you know. And *so* unattractive. Of course, she's hopelessly in love with Ollie. The only way she could possibly get him would be to catch him on the rebound while I'm out of the picture. Poor Norma."

So that was it. His skin crawled.

"It may happen, too," Norma said, staring into space over her glass. "That horrible mother of mine! She's offered me a 'compromise.' She's taking me abroad for three months, during which I'm not to see or communicate with Ollie. If I still want him when we get back, mother says, she'll give us our blessing."

"I see," Tully said.

"But I know *her*, the way her mind works. She's figuring on tricking me, the way she always does. Divine Mercedes! If people only *knew* her . . . She'll pretend to be sick, or she'll find some other excuse to keep us in Europe indefinitely. And that will be Norma's chance."

Tully could not help asking, "Then why are you leaving?"

"I have no choice. I'm under age. It's going to be a *battle*. Because I'm going to fight just as hard to talk mother into keeping her word."

"How does Ollie feel about this?"

"Oh, he doesn't know yet. About my going away, I mean. I'll have to tell him soon. The whole story— Where are you going?"

Tully had edged over to the doorway, his mind made up. "To see a man about a dog." It was a phrase, he recalled, popular in Kathleen's day. "Why don't you drink your drink, Kathleen? You've hardly touched it."

She glanced down at the glass with the same vague smile. Tully slipped out of the den. He went quickly into the master bedroom, shut the door without noise, snapped on the light and was over at the night table diving for the telephone book under the bedroom extension in one scrambling leap. Just as he found the *S's* he heard a car turn into his driveway.

By the time Tully managed to leave the bedroom without alarming Norma Hurst and make his way through the rear service door around to the driveway, Ollie Hurst had his ignition and headlights turned off and was coming around the front of his car.

"Ollie."

"Dave, is that you?"

"Yes—"

"Dave, it's happened again—"

"I know."

"She's here?" the lawyer cried.

"Not so loud." He grabbed Ollie's arm. "She's inside. I was just going to call Dr. Suddreth."

"How is she, Dave?"

"Not good."

Oliver Hurst slumped against his car. In the light coming from the bedroom window he looked as if he were going to collapse.

"How far gone is she?"

"She thinks she's Kathleen Lavery."

Ollie was struck dumb. With his head thrust forward and his mouth open and his bald head he looked something like a carp. Then he said, "Kathleen Lavery. Why in God's name . . . ?"

"From what she's been saying, Ollie, I think this goes back a long, long way. Back to her wedding day."

"That was the happiest day of her life!"

"Only on the surface." It was hard for Tully to look at the lawyer. "She's cracked up twice now. Once when little Emmie was killed. Now when Ruth—the best friend Norma ever had—when Ruth's been accused of murder. I'm no expert, Lord knows, but it seems to me this particular gambit began when she married you—when unconsciously she felt that Kathleen's death made her marriage possible. She's carried the load of that guilt around ever since."

"I don't understand," Ollie muttered.

"You'd better start trying," Tully said, more harshly than he intended. "Don't you see how fiercely glad Norma must have felt when Kathleen drowned? But at another level she was shocked at those feelings. I suppose a psychiatrist might say the resulting guilt made it possible for Norma to keep functioning. I don't know—I'm sure it all goes back even further than that. Whatever it is, wherever the hell it stems from, you'd better get her to your psychiatrist fast." Ollie nodded and they hurried toward the service entrance. "Where were you, Ollie?"

"I could see she was working up to something. But I thought she'd be all right if I went for some groceries she mentioned we needed. When I got back from the shopping plaza she was gone. I kept calling around, and hunting for her, till it occurred to me she might have come here. Thinking maybe Ruth was back, or something."

They found Norma in the living room. She was standing at the bar, pouring more Scotch into her glass. It kept slopping over.

She turned and saw her husband and her whole long, taut face screwed up as if she were trying to see through a dense fog.

"Ollie . . . ?"

Hurst's cheeks, gray and slick, twitched as he moved toward her. "Everything's going to be all right," he said nervously. "I'll take you home now, Norma."

She hurled the glass at his head. It sailed past him and smashed against the opposite wall, drenching both men.

"Don't call me that *name!*" Norma screamed. Everything in her face was contorted except her eyes; they remained dull and remote. "It's my mother, isn't it?" she panted. "So she finally got to you, too. She's turned you against me, Ollie. You're all against me!"

"Stop her, Ollie!" Tully shouted.

Hurst was nearer, but her violence had paralyzed him. And Tully was too late. Norma burst through the French doors and disappeared in the darkness of the patio. Tully dashed out after her.

"Ollie, switch on the patio lights!"

The lawyer stumbled to the wall and snapped on the switch. The patio and the grounds beyond lit up like a stage set.

Norma Hurst was crouched under the aluminum awning above the Tullys' fieldstone barbecue pit. The long barbecue knife was in her clutch. Bubbles made a froth at the corner of her mouth.

"My God," Ollie Hurst whispered.

"Save your self-pity for some other time," Tully snapped. "We've got to get that knife away from her. You circle to her right. But *slow.*"

He drifted toward the left. "Kathleen," he said.

"Don't be afraid. No one's going to hurt you. We're here to help you." He kept up the pleasant-toned reassurances, trying to get all her attention. "Why don't you put that thing down? I'd like to talk to you, Kathleen. Kathleen . . . Kathleen . . ."

Ollie Hurst had it almost made. Two steps more . . . He chose that moment to stumble over something in the grass.

As Norma began to whirl, Tully rushed her, grabbed the knife close to the handle, and twisted. To his amazement, the knife refused to come away. Then he felt her other hand clawing at his face and he was fighting for his life.

"Ollie—!" he choked. "Pin her arms!"

Her husband got behind her mechanically, threw his arms about her. She was making blubbering sounds now, like an animal, her teeth glittering in the strong lights. Tully got both hands on the half of the knife and wrenched. He staggered back as she suddenly released it, lost his balance and fell heavily to the grass. Instead of struggling aimlessly she doubled over and brought her right heel up in a vicious backward kick. Ollie Hurst let out a whooshing *oomph!* and then a yelp and sat down.

She was free.

Gasping, she began to scramble up the slope of hillside beyond the perimeter of the lights. Tully flung the knife as far as he could in the opposite direction and dashed after her, launching himself in a flying tackle. They both fell, face down.

"I'll kill you. I'll kill you," Norma Hurst shrieked. She slithered about in his clutch like a fish, everything going at once, arms, hands, fingernails, legs, feet, teeth.

There was only one thing to do, and Tully did it. He got his right hand free and punched her in the jaw.

17

When the private ambulance drove away Ollie Hurst, looking eighty years old, got into his car and began to back out of the driveway. Tully walked along, one hand on the driver's door.

"Let me know what the psychiatrist says, Ollie."

The lawyer swallowed. "Dave . . ."

"Forget it. If you need me, call."

Tully waited at the edge of the road until Oliver Hurst's car disappeared around the curve. Then he went into the house and made for the phone in the den.

"Julian? Dave Tully. I've got to see you."

"What about?" The Homicide man sounded tired and peevish. "I was just getting set at the TV."

"It's important, Julian. May I come right over?"

"To my house? My wife's walking around half-naked. Where you calling from?"

"Home."

"I'll come over there."

Tully hung up and went into the kitchen and dug around in the refrigerator. Nothing but cold cuts. He made a face and set the kettle on to boil. He was just pouring hot water into the big mug with the word PAPA on it when he heard Julian Smith's car pull into the driveway.

He let the detective in and said, "How about a cup of coffee? I know you don't drink."

"Instant?" The detective was in rumpled slacks. He needed a shave.

"That's all there is in the house."

"The hell with it," Smith said.

He followed Tully into the kitchen and sat down wearily. "How'd you get those scratches on your cheek?"

Tully set the kettle back on the electric range and sat down to his coffee. "That's the reason I want to talk to you, Julian. Norma Hurst did that."

"Norma Hurst?" The lieutenant stared at him.

"I found her here when I got home. She's gone off the deep end again, Julian. She thinks she's Kathleen Lavery."

Julian Smith slowly took out a crumpled pack of cigarettes. "Kathleen Lavery . . . She was Mercedes Cabbott's daughter, wasn't she? Died in a boating accident in Europe somewhere?"

"That's right."

Smith looked puzzled. He lit his last cigarette, made a ball of the empty package, glanced around, then stuck the paper ball in his pocket. "What happened, Dave?"

"Ollie went out food-shopping and she took off. I had to handle her with kid gloves, and she did quite a bit of talking—as Kathleen. Finally Ollie got around to looking for her here. She went completely off her rocker and into a violent phase—got hold of my barbecue knife, and I had to knock her out. Delusions of persecution."

"Where is she now?"

"At Pittman, the private sanitarium. Ollie called for an ambulance. That's the place she was in after their child died."

The detective looked around for an ashtray, saw none, and tipped the ash into his cupped hand. "I don't get it, Dave. I'm sorry, of course, for both of them, but why did you have to get me out at this hour of the night to tell me about it?"

"Because I think what happened tonight is tied into the Cox case."

Smith looked around again for an ashtray. "Don't you have an ashtray?" he asked irritably. Tully got up and went into the den and brought back an ashtray. It seemed to make the Homicide man feel better. He emptied his hand of ashes and tapped some more from his cigarette into the tray and said in a good-humored tone,

138

"You sure you aren't the one who's gone off his rocker, Dave?"

"I'm saner than you are, with your damn compulsive neatness," Tully snapped. "Here's what I learned via Norma's delusion tonight: Kathleen Lavery and Ollie Hurst were in love with each other. In fact, they planned to get married. Mercedes characteristically interfered—talked Kathleen into a three-month separation from Ollie in Europe. The whole thing became academic when the girl was drowned in Switzerland."

"So?" the lieutenant asked, unimpressed. "What's that ancient history got to do with this Cox crumb's murder at the Hobby Motel a few nights ago?"

Tully said slowly, "I think Crandall Cox's killing had its origins in that ancient history. He may have come back here to shake down Sandra Jean—"

"And Ruth?"

"Okay, and Ruth!—but his killing had nothing to do with either one of them. *I think Cox was murdered by Kathleen Lavery.*"

Julian Smith blinked. "Are you nuts, Dave, or am I?"

"Listen to me, will you?" Tully said tensely. "Norma's lived all her married life with the guilty knowledge that she got Ollie Hurst only because Kathleen Lavery died. The guilt has built up to the point where apparently Norma feels the compulsion to deny that the girl died at all. But in the real world the girl *is* dead. The only way Norma can resurrect her is to slip into a deluded state and become Kathleen herself.

"Now look!" Tully leaned over the table toward the silent Homicide man. "Cranny Cox was born and brought up in this town. He was a no-good and a girl-chaser from his teens. If you dig deeply enough, Julian, I'm betting you'll find that in those days Cox chased Kathleen Lavery and, what's more, caught her and made time with her.

"Norma knows this—"

"How?"

"How the hell do I know how?" Tully cried. "Maybe Kathleen told Ollie after they fell for each other, and

Ollie told Norma when they got married. Anyway, the other day Cox comes back here. Somehow Norma finds out, probably through Ruth. But Norma's already nursing the delusion that she's Kathleen. She goes to see Cox that night—*as Kathleen*. Cox doesn't realize he's dealing with a mental case, tells her to get lost or something—almost certainly, being Cox, laughs in her face when she calls herself Kathleen. It triggers Norma's violence—I saw it happen tonight. And there's the gun, my gun, within reach. Julian, I tell you the answer to this puzzle is that Norma Hurst shot Cox while she thought she was a girl dead God knows how many years!"

"And your wife?" Julian Smith asked.

"You mean what's happened to her?"

"That's exactly what I mean."

"But don't you see?" Tully cried. "In the grip of that delusion Norma's as strong as a man—and a damn strong man at that! I had to clip her on the chin because I couldn't subdue her any other way, and you know I'm no weakling, Julian. I tell you Norma took Ruth forcibly to some hiding place, maybe tied her up and gagged her. Maybe the doctors can give Norma one of those new drugs they're using on mental patients, find out where Ruth is before she starves to death! I know, Julian, it sounds pretty wild—"

Smith leaned over and touched Tully's hand. "Relax, Dave, or you'll be needing a paddy wagon yourself. I've got a fullscale search going for Ruth on a round-the-clock basis. She'll be found."

"Then you don't buy this Norma-Kathleen theory," Tully said bitterly.

"No, Dave," the lieutenant said.

"Why the hell not!"

"Well, for one thing, that telephone call from Ruth. If she's innocent, the killer forced her to make that call. It's not the kind of behavior a mental case like Norma would evince, from what I know about such cases. It isn't the type of aberration that sets up a pigeon to cover up a killing. If Norma's type of psychopath had done it, she'd probably have shot Ruth on the spot and gone on a rampage and shot at every living thing in sight. I'm sorry, Dave."

Tully sagged in his chair. "So I'm back where I started," he muttered. "There's an out for everybody in this thing but Ruth."

He got up heavily and went to the kitchen window. The house suddenly felt like a prison.

"By the way," Julian Smith's voice said from behind him, "Ruth's picture is being telecast over every TV station in the state tonight. It may help."

"May. Will it?"

"I've seen it happen, Dave. A gas station attendant, a waitress in a diner, a pedestrian on a street corner—we'll get plenty of calls, and we won't ignore one of them." Tully felt the detective's hand on his shoulder. "Why don't you take a pill and hit the sack? I promise to wake you up personally if there's any news at all."

"Go to hell," Tully said.

18

After Smith's departure Tully prowled about the house. A new thought had come to plague him, of having recently seen or heard something meaningful. A word, a key, a clue—an open-sesame that with one push would reveal the truth.

But what was it?

He holed up in the den, trying desperately to raise from the dead whatever-it-was. He sat stiff and strained until sweat slicked his forehead. Finally he muttered a curse on all darkness.

Tully heaved himself out of the chair and went to the phone. He dialed Information for the home telephone number of the city editor of the *Times-Call*, Jake Ballinger.

"Dave Tully?" Ballinger was yawning. "Something?"

"Well, for one thing I want to thank you for the way you've handled the Cox story, Jake," Tully said. "I mean as regards my wife."

"We've printed the facts. I left my tabloid techniques back in Chicago." The rumble sounded interested. "What's up, Dave?"

"I need a favor. Will you let me go through your files?"

Ballinger said immediately, "Meet me outside the shop."

A jalopy was parked before the newspaper building when Tully drove up. The bulky newspaperman promptly hopped out. He looked as expectant as an old birddog.

"What's the yarn, Dave? I expect quid for my quo."

"I haven't one—yet."

Ballinger gave Tully a sharp look and led the way into the partly darkened building. The rumble of press machinery was giving the old floors the shakes. Upstairs, a crew of three was still on watch in the newsroom. Locally, the paper was published as the morning *Times* and the afternoon *Call,* with a *Times-Call* appearing on Sundays.

The old man plodded past the newsroom on his flat feet to a glass-partitioned office. He opened the door and snapped on a light. Tiers of laden shelves reached to the ceiling.

"We're running cuts of your wife in the morning edition," Ballinger said. "Headquarters request. I gather the gendarmes of our unfair city don't think Mrs. T.'s so guilty any more. Why, Lieutenant Smith sayeth not. Any news?"

"She's not guilty at all, Jake."

Ballinger kept eyeing him. "This is our morgue. What are you after, Dave?"

"Kathleen Lavery."

"Lavery . . ." Ballinger's hard blue eyes turned inward. "Oh, yes. Why?"

"I'm not sure," Tully said. "I think Cox had other reasons for returning."

"Such as?"

Tully shrugged. "He staked his life on coming back here. He must have had a pretty solid expectation of loot—real loot—to take such a risk."

"And you think it goes back to Kathleen Lavery?"

"I don't know what to think, Jake. This is from desperation. Maybe your files have the answer."

Ballinger rummaged through a card-index file, drew a card out, moved to the shelves. Consulting the card, he fished nearly a dozen small, flat cardboard boxes from the shelves. He opened them one by one and from each took out a round flat tin.

"Let's take these over to the viewer, Dave."

"Microfilm?"

The old newspaperman chuckled. "Unto even a one-horse town cometh technology."

Tully trailed Ballinger to the microfilm viewer. Ballinger turned the projector on and slipped the top film into place. A front page of the *Times* sprang into being on the viewer's frosted plate.

"Watch the heads, Dave. We click from page to page till we hit the story relating to our subject."

For forty-five minutes David Tully watched a beautiful young girl grow up. The Laverys leaving for Europe. The Laverys returning from Europe. Young Miss Kathleen Lavery entertaining with a Christmas party at the country club, under the chaperonage of Mrs. Mercedes Lavery. At fourteen—taking a blue ribbon at the horse show—the budding teenager pictured sitting her sleek mount seemed to Tully a lonely little figure. Swimming on her school team in an intra-state competition. Entering a Junior tennis tournament in England. Story after story...

And then her death.

"Hold that, Jake."

Ballinger held it, looking curious. Tully skimmed through the story. "... vacationing in Switzerland with her mother. Miss Lavery was pronounced dead from accidental drowning after her boat capsized on Lake St. Cyr. Her body was washed up on the lake shore shortly after dawn yesterday morning, Swiss time. It was found by a group of early morning swimmers..."

Tully scanned the rest of the file. It concerned the girl's funeral, and a final obit recounting her short history and family connections.

"That's it. Ballinger clicked off the viewer.

Tully mumbled: "No mention of Crandall Cox."

"Why should there be?"

"He preyed on women most of his life, specializing in the upper crust. I thought he might have done a job on the Lavery girl. She was certainly the richest and most vulnerable target in this town."

"He'd have had a pretty tough time," the old newspaperman said dryly, "worming his way into her set, from what it used to be like in those days."

Tully scowled, watching Ballinger stow away the films. "By the way," he said suddenly. "How did Kathleen happen to drown? She was an expert swimmer, according to one of these stories. Or were you still in Chicago at that time, Jake?"

"No, I'd been here about six months when it happened. It was a big story. Anyone or anything connected with Mercedes has always been a big story here." The old man shrugged. "There was a lot of back-of-the-hand talk, because the Swiss authorities didn't come up with any clearcut explanation for the accident. There'd been a squall of sorts, and the girl had taken the boat out alone, presumably—they finally decided that when the boat upset she got a crack on the head, or a cramp. Or swam around in circles in the dark till she was exhausted."

"It doesn't sell me," Tully said.

Jake Ballinger looked at him. "Are you suggesting that the bonnie Kathleen was murdered?"

"How the devil do I know what I'm suggesting?" Tully exploded.

He and Ballinger went down into the street.

"Thanks, Jake."

"For what?" the old editor rumbled.

In spite of himself, David Tully grinned. "For nothing, I guess."

Back at home Tully thought and thought, and finally he resorted to the telephone again. He hesitated only a moment. Had Sandra Jean already taken Andrew Gordon across a state line to get married? Although that would be pretty fast work even for Sandra Jean . . . He dialed the Cabbott number.

The butler answered.

Tully asked for Mr. Gordon.

Andy came on. "What do *you* want?" His voice was guarded.

"I'm relaying a message from Sandra Jean."

"Not so loud!"

"She wants to meet you here—in my house—right away." He used the most conspiratorial tone he could contrive.

"But I was supposed to meet her at the Blue Iris in a half hour!" The boy sounded in an agony of indecision.

"Look, Junior, I'm simply telling you what Sandra said. I don't give a damn whether you meet her or not."

Tully ended the conversation with a slam. He ran to the picture window and waited.

Twelve minutes later headlights swung into his driveway. Tully had the front door open before Andy could ring.

"Come in, fly," Tully said.

"What?" the boy said blankly.

"I said come in."

Andy Gordon came in. His eyes were bloodshot and his dark young face looked puffy and hung over.

"Where's Sandra Jean?" He looked around suspiciously.

"She isn't here," Tully said.

"What d'ye mean she isn't here?" Andy cried. "You said—"

"I wanted to talk to somebody about Kathleen Lavery," Tully said.

The boy blinked and blinked. "What the hell is this?"

"I decided your stepfather George probably doesn't know, and your mother would be too tough. That leaves you, Andy."

The big muscular young body seemed to swell. "I'm not so tough, is that what you mean?"

"You're not tough at all, Andy."

The boy came at him like a blind bull. Tully sidestepped and hooked hard. Blood spurted from Andy's nose. He hit the floor hard. He grabbed at his nose, looked at his blood-smeared hand with terror, and began to cry.

"That's more like it, kid," Tully said. "Because the next time you swing on me it'll cost you a mouthful of teeth."

"Damn you!" Andy Gordon wept. "I'll kill you . . ."

"I haven't got the time to let you. I want answers, Andy, and I want them straight and now."

"Answers to *what?*" the boy said viciously.

"It's about Kathleen."

19

"Crandall Cox and Kathleen," Tully said. "Did they know each other?"

"How would I know?"

"She knew Ollie Hurst, even thought of marrying him. She knew Cox too, didn't she?"

"I tell you I don't know! Man oh man, I'll fix you for this, Dave—"

"Stick to the subject at hand. Mercedes took Kathleen abroad to keep her from marrying Ollie. Did Cox figure any way in that?"

"I don't know!"

"You do know," Tully said. "Mercedes runs a pretty taut ship. She's held Kathleen's fate up to you since you were in diapers—I mean, as a horrible example of what comes from crossing mama. Right, Andy?"

Andy was pressing a handkerchief to his nose. "Wait till she hears about *this*."

"I'm not impressed any more," Tully said. "I have a wife to get back. Are you going to talk?"

"The papers—" Andy shrank back.

"I read the papers, Andy. They printed the official handouts. Your half-sister was a good enough swimmer to be on her school swimming team. She didn't drown accidentally, now, did she?"

Andy glared up at him. Whatever it was that he saw in Tully's eyes, it made his own eyes shift.

"No. She didn't."

"Well," said Tully. Then he said, "And she wasn't murdered, either. The Swiss police are among the best in the world. They wouldn't have missed that."

"I don't follow you," the boy said sullenly.

"Kathleen was the daughter of a millionaire American. And there was no proof her death wasn't an accident. Under the circumstances, didn't the Swiss authorities decide to let it go at that?"

"I don't know what you're talking about."

Tully stooped over him and said softly, "Kathleen killed herself, Andy, didn't she? Took that boat out in a squall and deliberately upset it and let herself go under? Probably leaving a suicide note that Mercedes destroyed. Isn't that the truth about Kathleen?"

The boy's voice was little more than a whisper. "Yes."

"Why, Andy? Why did Kathleen kill herself?"

"She'd found out she was pregnant."

"Thank you very much, Mr. Gordon."

Mercedes Cabbott's son shot to his feet and darted toward the door. Before Tully could move Andy was out of the house.

A moment later his car roared its belated defiance as it escaped.

Tully went into the utility washroom off the kitchen and plunged his face into a basinful of cold water. Then he went into the kitchen and looked up the number of the Pittman sanitarium and dialed it and asked if Mr. Oliver Hurst was still there, and how was Mrs. Hurst? He was told that Mr. Hurst had left not long before and sorry, we can give out no information about our patients.

Tully broke the connection, began to dial Ollie Hurst's home number, thought better of it, and hung up.

He got into the Imperial and drove over to the Hurst house.

Ollie answered the door. He looked like hell.

"Dave. I was just going to call you."

"How is Norma?"

"Quiet under sedation. The doctor kicked me out. Come on in. Something up?"

"Yes. I hate to ask this of you, Ollie—you look about as beat as I feel!—but would you do me a favor?"

"Don't be an idiot," Ollie Hurst said crossly. "What?"

"I'm going up to the Cabbott ménage to see

Mercedes. I'd like you to be present when I tackle her."

"About what?"

"I'll explain later. Will you come?"

Ollie stood there. "You put me on a spot, Dave. I'm not comfortable in that house."

"I wish I could spare you," Tully said. "But Ollie, I've got to have you there."

"All right."

Ollie went for his jacket and tie. Tully got into his car and waited. Finally the lights went off and the lawyer came out and climbed in beside Tully. Tully turned the car around and headed for the hills.

As the Imperial turned into the Cabbott grounds Ollie Hurst said suddenly, "This isn't about Ruth, is it, Dave?"

"No."

"Then I don't see—"

"That is, not directly." Tully's mouth set in a grim line. "Everything I've been doing in the past few days has been about Ruth one way or the other, Ollie."

Hurst nodded and settled back. He appeared shrunken, half the size he had been.

It was George Cabbott who opened the door. The blond giant looked angry and formidable.

"We've been expecting you," Cabbott said. "Come in."

"Then you do know the story," Tully said.

"I do now!"

Mercedes's husband did not even glance at Oliver Hurst. He led them through the house to the terrace. Mercedes was waiting for them at the king-size terrace table. She looked odd in the weird lighting of the insect-repellent bulbs.

"It was quite horrid of you, David," Mercedes said in a high, tight voice.

"Yes," George Cabbott growled, "you sure had one hell of a nerve. Why don't you take me on for a change?"

"You didn't try to clobber me, George," Tully said. He looked around. A cigarette was smoldering in an ash tray on the table; neither Mercedes nor George Cabbott smoked. "I take it Andy's declared himself on the side of discretion. He's updated you, Mercedes?"

"My son felt he should tell me that you'd forced certain information from him," she said frigidly. "Did you have to trick him into coming to your house?"

"And why Andy?" George Cabbott demanded. "If you wanted information, why didn't you ask Mercedes, like a man?"

"Do you think she'd have told me?"

"Of course I wouldn't have," Mercedes said. She had not once glanced Ollie Hurst's way. He stood just outside the circle of grisly light, a forlorn shadow.

"If you want to break a chain," Tully said sententiously, "choose the weakest link. Confucious or Sherlock Holmes or somebody, wasn't it?"

Mercedes poured herself a drink from the heavy silver cocktail shaker. Tully noted that her hands were trembling. She did not offer any to him or Hurst, or even ask them to sit down. She drank in hard gulps. Her husband stood by, watchful as a paid guard.

"All right, David. Now that you've broken the chain, what do you intend to do?"

"Get the rest of the story straight."

"Then the police?"

"I'm afraid so."

She poured another drink. George Cabbott took the glass from her hand and flung its contents out into the black lawn. She glanced at him, and he shook his head very slightly.

"How much will be made public, David?"

Tully shrugged. "The irreducible minimum, as far as I'm concerned."

"After all these years you'd destroy her image . . . blacken her name?"

"I can't destroy or blacken, Mercedes," Tully said. "That was done long ago, by others."

The beautiful young-old woman sank into a chair, her back growing a queer hump. Her husband leaned over and took her impeccable little hand. It lay there lifelessly.

"Why?" George Cabbott asked. "That's what I don't

understand, Dave. What purpose does this serve?" He asked it in a determinedly reasonable tone, like a representative of management in a labor dispute.

"The cause of life, liberty and the pursuit of happiness," Tully replied. "My wife's."

Ollie Hurst stirred, stepped forward. In the light he looked like a ghost. "Dave. What did Andrew tell you?"

"The truth about Kathleen's death. When Mercedes strong-armed her into going abroad, Kathleen discovered that she was pregnant. She killed herself."

The lawyer stared at him. Then he shuffled over to the table and took the shaker and Mercedes's glass and poured. He set the shaker down carefully and drank slowly and thirstily. The tiniest frown appeared between Mercedes's graceful brows. "What else do you know, Dave?"

"You tell me, Ollie. Was Kathleen's child yours?"

"Yes."

"Did she know she was pregnant when her mother took her to Europe?"

"No. Kathleen wrote me from Switzerland. Her letter reached me after the news that she'd drowned. I knew she had committed suicide." Ollie Hurst stared out into the darkness.

"I suspected the baby was yours," Tully said thoughtfully. "If it had been Crandall Cox's—"

"You—shut—up," Mercedes Cabbott whispered. "You shut your filthy mouth!"

"If it had been Cox's," Tully said, "he'd have tried to cash in on it right away. Of course, he must have found out. How did he find out, do you suppose, Ollie?"

He saw the fine sweat appear on Hurst's bald head.

"The letter," Tully said softly. "Of course! The letter you just said Kathleen wrote you. Didn't you and Cox both go to college here? It must have been around the same time—"

"It was," Mercedes Cabbott said. "Oh, it was! And now I remember, Oliver. You and Crandall Cox roomed together during one semester."

"I'm going great guns, Ollie," Tully said. "I'm really hitting it now. That's it, sure. Cox swiped that letter

151

from you, and he kept it like an insurance policy all these years. You probably thought you'd lost it. Isn't that it, Ollie?"

The lawyer said hoarsely, "Dave." He licked his lips and said again, "Dave."

But Tully said, "It was Kathleen's secret that brought Cranny Cox back here after fifteen years. He didn't come back to put the bite on you, Mercedes—he was desperate, and he'd saved that letter for a desperate day, but he knew how tough you could be, and he'd look for a softer touch.

"You, Ollie. You've done well for yourself—he'd have investigated *that* for sure. You're a respected member of the community. Your legal practice lies here. You have a vulnerable wife. He'd have played on all that, Ollie—counted on its making you pay through the nose to keep that letter from being published, ruining you socially, destroying your livelihood, maybe turning your wife into a hopeless lunatic.

"The one thing he didn't count on," Tully went on, and he had to steel himself with all his strength to keep from betraying the pity and sorrow and disgust he felt, "the one thing Cox didn't count on was the lengths to which you'd go to hold on to what he was threatening. And the fact that you're a lawyer and know that a blackmailer never stops.

"It was you who killed Cox, wasn't it, Ollie?"

20

The man with the shining bald head was silent. Suddenly he looked strange—older, thinner, less substantial. Mercedes Cabbott and her husband were regarding him as if they had never seen him before.

As perhaps they haven't, Tully thought.

"It would have been a pretty simple case if Cox hadn't been so greedy," Tully said into the silence, and then he shrugged. "But then he wouldn't have been Cox, would he? He came to town to blackmail you, Ollie, but while he was here he thought he'd do a little business with Sandra Jean, too . . . whom he knew as Ruth. He must have set up the appointment with Sandra Jean first —a little incidental he thought he'd get out of the way. I wondered why he didn't try to get some money out of Sandra on the spot—why he was willing to let her off the hook until she married Andy and he'd have something worth his while to go after. Now it's obvious. He didn't need Sandra's immediate pittance; he had a much bigger fish tugging on his line. So Sandra came and went, and then you came at *your* appointed time, Ollie."

He saw Ollie Hurst swallow, as if to gather sufficient moisture in his mouth to lubricate his voice. Before the lawyer could speak, Tully went on.

"You came, Ollie, and the gun Cox had taken away from Sandra was right there, and whether you came prepared to kill Cox or the sight of the gun set you off, you managed to grab it and cover him and wrap a towel around it and shoot him dead."

"And Ruth walked in on *that?*" Mercedes said in soft horror.

"She did, didn't she, Ollie?" Tully said. "She'd followed Sandra to the motel, seen her leave, saw you go into Cox's room, and she must have sensed that Cox had some hold on you, too. And with some quixotic idea of helping you—she's always liked and looked up to you, Ollie; you remember that, don't you?—Ruth barged into that room after you. And found you standing over Cox's dead body with the gun in your hand. It must have been your voice Maudie Blake heard calling Ruth by name, not Cox's—listening through that thin wall to the whole thing, Maudie must have made a lightning decision to lie for you and cover for you, Ollie, so that you'd have to pay *her* off. As you did, when you slipped into her room at Flynn's Inn subsequently and forced a lethal dose of booze down her drunken throat."

He was no longer Ollie Hurst at all, but a standing corpse, a breathing dead man, so still and stiff he might have been a corpse in fact. I wonder, Tully thought, if he even hears me now.

George Cabbott drew a quavery sort of breath and exhaled it noisily. "How do you know all this, Dave?"

"It follows from one simple thing, so simple I hardly noticed it at the time." Tully's breath came out under tension, too. "Ollie made a tremendous mistake. The night I went to Flynn's Inn at Maudie Blake's request, she told me she'd 'just' moved over there from the Hobby Motel. The next morning—the morning Ollie and I found her dead—we went in Ollie's car, Ollie driving. Never once the night before in Ollie's house, never once that morning in my house, did I mention the fact that Maudie Blake was no longer at the Hobby Motel, but had moved. And on the drive to Flynn's neither of us said a single word. *Yet Ollie drove directly to Flynn's Inn.*

"I didn't realize until much later how significant that was," Tully ground on. "In fact, I didn't remember it at all. Until, that is, I began to put the pieces together about Ollie's relationship fifteen years ago with Kathleen. Then it popped out, and it hit me between the eyes. That business with Kathleen concealed a possible motive for Ollie to have killed Cox. The knowledge he shouldn't have had—of where Maudie Blake had holed in—put him right smack in that room at Flynn's Inn—pouring a lethal dose of liquor down Maudie's gullet. It's not evidence, but I'm not after evidence—let Julian Smith and the prosecutor's office worry about that. In fact, what I'm after—"

"Dave," the corpse said. "Dave, you've got to understand I didn't know that gun belonged to you. All I saw was a gun—and that damn leering face . . . It was over—I was committed—before I really had time to think. And there he was, dead, and afterward that Blake horror—trying to squeeze me, too. . . ." Ollie Hurst said dully, "Didn't she realize that a man who's killed once finds it easy to kill a second time? I had to kill her. She knew. She knew everything."

"And Ruth?" Tully said. "And Ruth, Ollie?"

"Ruth . . . She walked in . . . I couldn't kill Ruth. Not Ruth. My friend. Norma's friend. Your wife. . . ."

Tully crouched slightly. He heard his breath whistling up from his lungs, tasted the foul taste of undiluted hatred in his mouth. "You couldn't kill Ruth, Ollie? Do you think you can still pull the old-pal act with me?" He dimly heard his own voice shouting. "You didn't kill Ruth then for one reason only: You needed her as your fall guy! And when you thought you were in the clear and you had Ruth all set up to take the rap for you—did you kill Ruth, too? *Did you, Ollie? Where did you put her? Where have you got her hidden? Alive or dead?*"

"Dave, no! I'll take him!"

It was George Cabbott who sprang between them, reaching for the lawyer with his bronze arms.

It was impossible, but Ollie Hurst moved faster. Tully saw the blur of his hand snatching the cocktail shaker from the table, the weirdly colored line of light it made as the shaker struck Cabbott squarely in the face. The big man went down with an expression of great surprise. Blood began to pump from his mouth.

And Ollie Hurst—portly, bald Ollie Hurst—twisted his clumsy body and grabbed the terrace railing and vaulted over it like a gazelle and disappeared in the darkness.

Mercedes Cabbott dropped to her knees beside her husband with a faint cry.

Then Tully found himself on the black lawn, running.

He could not see Ollie, and he had to stop and listen for the thud of Ollie's feet on the turf. He ran, and stopped, and listened, and ran again. When the thudding sounds turned into snapping dry-stick sounds, Tully knew that the lawyer had reached the gravel driveway before the house and was sprinting across it.

How long he chased his quarry Tully had no notion. It seemed endless, and it seemed no time at all. He ran and stopped and ran like a man in a dream, where time did not exist.

At one point he made contact. He remembered seeing the flying figure suddenly, hearing the horrid labor of his lungs, launching himself into space from behind like a swimmer at the start of a race, watching Ollie beyond all reason twisting his chubby body sidewise in a slow-motion film, feeling his shoulder slam glancingly against Ollie's rib cage, pitching forward on his face with his hands extended to break his fall, feeling the jarring impact of his shoulder on the lawn, feeling himself tumbling over and coming to rest on his back, one vast windless pain.

The next thing David Tully became conscious of was running down a long slope after the fleeing lawyer. At the bottom of the slope stretched the Cabbott stables. His first reasoned thought came to him: Ollie Hurst had no plan, no destination. He was simply running, running in a blind instinct to prolong the sweet oblivion between crime and punishment. And he was dangerous. Now he was really dangerous.

Tully took longer strides. He was running easily now. It was no effort at all. He was only a few yards behind Ollie Hurst when the lawyer ducked into the hay-barn.

Tully plowed to a dead stop just outside the barn door. He listened, trying to hear over his own breathing. And he heard. He heard the huge and heaving gasps of an animal run to earth, incapable of further flight, cornered.

"Ollie," David Tully said. "Ollie, I'm coming in."
Nothing but the gasps.

"Don't try anything, Ollie. I'm not going to hurt you. But you're going to tell me what I have to know."

There was a slobbering break in the gasps, and then they resumed.

Tully stood still.

Suddenly there was moonlight. It shone through the open door into the barn. He could not see Ollie from where he was standing.

"Ollie, I'm coming in."

Most of the barn was dark.

"Ollie?" Tully said. "Don't try to hide from me. I see you."

"No . . . you . . . don't."

Tully whirled. The gasping voice had come from behind him.

Ollie Hurst was crouched in the doorway. His torso was still heaving for oxygen, his mouth wide open, the moonlight bouncing off his teeth and wet skull and streaming cheeks. There was a pitchfork in his hands and its tines were a foot from Tully's throat.

"I don't want this, Dave," Ollie gasped. "I didn't ask for this. I've got to keep running as long as I can. The keys, Dave. Give me the keys to your car."

The shining needles of steel moved back and forth slightly, came closer.

Tully did not move. "Is Ruth alive?"

"Of course she's alive—"

"Where is she, Ollie? Where are you hiding her?" He wanted to believe. He so desperately wanted to believe.

"The keys," Ollie Hurst said again. "I'll get them one way or another, Dave. I'll get them if I have to kill you. Toss me those keys."

"Sure, Ollie. If you'll tell me where Ruth is."

"First the keys."

"No deal," Tully said. Was he lying? If Ruth were dead, wouldn't Ollie tell the hiding place in return for the keys without bargaining? He must be telling the truth. . .

And suddenly it came to him, as the other revelations

had come to him, in a flash, whole and perfect. The tines were very close to his throat now, and he had to fight to ignore them.

"Or would this be it, Ollie? Where would an amateur like you find a hideout for your kidnap victim on the spur of the moment? You couldn't have made any preparations. It would have to exist—safe, isolated, ready for use.

"There's a place like that available to you, Ollie," Tully said, "the only place you could take her that fits the specifications. The place you and Norma call the old place, that Norma's great-grandfather built up in the hills. That's why you talked Norma out of going up there . . . The root-cellar would be a good spot. Ruth's in the root-cellar of the old place, isn't she, Ollie?"

The tines wavered. "Dave," Ollie Hurst said faintly. "Please—"

"George has phoned the police by this time, Ollie," Tully said. He felt as big and sure as a mountain. "Julian Smith . . . Ollie, listen! Hear it?"

It was the creeping hysteria of a police siren from far away.

"What's the use?" Tully asked the rigid man softly. "You'll only get yourself killed if you run. It isn't over by a damn sight, Ollie. Not while you've still got friends. Like me. And even Ruth. Give it to me?"

He carefully extended his hand.

Oliver Hurst collapsed. Everything gave way at once, head, arms, legs.

Tully took the pitchfork away from him.

"Ruth?"
He heard a gagged, frantic moan.
Tully smashed in the root-cellar door.

Kill As Directed

Cast of Characters

HARRISON BROWN, M.D.—His passion for money taught him that the right office in the right neighborhood makes for meeting the "right" people............ 7

TONY MITCHELL, LL.B.—Kurt Gresham's dapper attorney, a criminal lawyer who was especially "civil" to a client 9

KURT GRESHAM—Cherubic looking multimillionaire, who was as harmless as a big fat round H-Bomb....... 14

KAREN GRESHAM—Kurt's copper-haired, green-eyed wife, who wouldn't deal unless she had the whole deck... 15

DETECTIVE LIEUTENANT GALIVAN—The pipe-smoking "fatherly" type, who upsets routines with routine investigations 19

DR. ALFRED MCGEE STONE—Tall, thin director of the Taugus Institute, he "had no fat"................ 39

Dr. Peter Gross—Respected pedagogue, he was one of Harrison Brown's biggest boosters.................. 49

Mrs. Bernice Stone—Wife of Dr. Stone, a quick-eyed, plump little hen, who "had no lean".............. 88

Uncle Joe—Always ready to do a favor for a friend—for a price................................... 96

Franklin Gregory Archibald Smith—The mortician who arranged for the disposal of "Uncle Joe's brother's ashes"; he knew how to urn a fast buck........ 102

Mr. O'Brien—A giant of a house detective with a broken nose, who found a crowd in a suite for one........ 122

One

Shoulders, back, chest and thighs, arms and hands and feet—Dr. Brown was big in all departments. Even his nose was big. Once it had been big and straight. Now it was big and crooked, his football trophy.

Dr. Brown had dark eyes and dark hair. His look was dark, too, a chronic darkness; sullen, quite boyishly sullen. It went with his hair, darkly rumpled from running his big fingers through it in chronic desperation.

Dr. Brown's friends called him Harry. Dr. Harry (for Harrison) Brown was thirty years old, and he considered himself a failure. Had he been able, like many fellow healers of his acquaintance, to sock it away in a safe-deposit box, he would have considered himself a success. Yet Dr. Harry (for Harrison) Brown was not a shallow man. He was simply in the grip of a disease that strikes men, shallow or deep, impartially.

Dr. Harry Brown's passion for money came from a lifetime of not having enough of it. "Not enough" is a relative term; Harry Brown's not-enough had been relative to a background of exposure to too many too-much people. The friends of his father had been rich, and Harry's friends had been their sons. Harry had gone to a rich man's prep school on a scholarship; scholarships did not provide convertibles, charge accounts and fat allowances. At his Ivy League college he had roomed with the sons of the rich and dated the daughters of the rich; on holidays he had been seduced into their homes. He had been fed by their French chefs and served by their English butlers. He had slept on their silk sheets, and under them. He had sat on their antiques, buried his shoes in their rugs, gaped at their art investments, driven their foreign cars, ridden their thoroughbreds, taken the helm of their yachts. He had grown up swallowing daily doses of envy as others swallowed vitamin pills. Envy had sustained him and given him the strength to envy more. Envy had sent him through medical school. Envy had chosen and furnished his office.

But there its efficacy had stopped. Envy seemed powerless to provide him with a practice.

Dr. Harry Brown was intelligent. He knew that a practice, a lucrative New York practice, was merely a matter of time. He was only two years out of his residency. But time meant patience, and patience could not be cultivated in the acid soil of envy. Intelligence did not help; it was an empty watering can.

Dr. Harry Brown sat alone in his office, his spacious office with the private street entrance, in the impressive apartment building on Central Park West; sat alone in the office gleaming with the latest and most expensive medical equipment; sat alone waiting for the telephone call.

It was seven o'clock of a pleasant evening in May. Outside, the city was beginning to wrap itself in the warm dusk. He sat in a dusk of his own; only his desk lamp was on, and he had swiveled its business end toward the wall. He was slumped in his genuine leather swivel chair, long legs sprawled under the desk, morose, glowering, in a tension sweat.

Who would have believed it? Two years of getting nowhere.

Patients today: two. A kid from the next apartment house with an infected finger; a pregnant teenager who wanted an abortion—this one he had sent packing without even charging a fee. One patient yesterday, a passer-by off the street with something in his eye. None at all the day before. And the day before that, the repeater. Hallelujah. The guy hadn't yet paid for his first visit two months ago. The deadbeats smelled out the new doctors. Even assuming that this character paid, that made the grand total of $30 gross for four days. $7.50 a day. Big deal. The rawest office boy these days would turn that down with a sneer.

Who would have believed it? Two years not merely of getting nowhere, but of sliding downhill. Two years of watching the thirty thousand dollars from his father's life insurance shrink like ice on a hot tin roof. It was all gone, and a lot besides. He was over his head in debt.

Who would have believed it? Unmarried. No family hanging around his neck. No one to look out for but himself. And he couldn't do even that.

It wasn't as if he were an incompetent. He was a good

doctor. He had proved that in his residency. But how did you spread the gospel? Maybe I should have set up in Los Angeles, he thought wryly, where some doctors use neon signs and advertise in the newspapers.

It was evident now that he had made a bad mistake in opening an office in New York. The yawpers about the "shortage of doctors" had never tried to make a go of it in Manhattan. Why, there were two other doctors in this very building, established men. Seven, excluding himself, in two short blocks. And this kind of office, in this kind of neighborhood, produced a chain reaction. The address dictated expensive clothes, perfect grooming. The clothes *and* the address made a glittering new car mandatory. And all for what? To impress whom? The kid with the finger? The transient with the eye? The terrified girl with the illegal belly? The dead beat? And to maintain this empty show he had to live in a hole in Greenwich Village, with hardly enough furnishings for a monk's cell. . . .

The phone rang.

"Harry?" It was Tony Mitchell, all right.

"Yes," Dr. Brown said.

"Oh, in one of *those* moods."

"What's the score, Tony?" he asked abruptly.

"Dinner at eight. At the Big Dipper. Reservation in the name of Gresham—they lay out the purple carpet instead of the red when you mention it, and purple's my favorite color. So put on your best bib and tucker, Harry."

"How many of us?"

"Three. You, me, delicious Mrs. Gresham."

"What about Gresham?"

"Did I leave the old boy out? Maybe he'll come, maybe he won't. You know Kurt—business before pleasure. Pleased?"

"I don't know what you mean," Dr. Harry Brown said.

"Sure you don't," Tony Mitchell chuckled. "Look, son, don't horse around with little ol' me. I'm chaperoning tonight, and I know it, and I know you know I know it."

"Stop it, Tony."

"Shall I prescribe, Doctor? Four or five vodka martinis and our radiant Karen of Gresh as a chaser. Whoops! That slipped out. Who is the hunter, O Physician, and who the hunted?"

In spite of himself, Harry Brown felt better. "Sounds to me as if you've had your four or five already."

"And so I have, and so I have. Listen, pal, I've got to go get pretty. See you at eight."

The Big Dipper, he thought as he hung up. No less! Leave it to Tony Mitchell. Nothing but the best. Well, Tony could certainly afford it. Many a lawyer in town would have exchanged his entire clientele for Mr. and Mrs. Kurt Gresham.

The Big Dipper . . . Harry Brown rose. For the past month he had been his own chef, opening cans at home in the Village and heating their contents. It was the only way he could take Karen Gresham out; Karen was used to the best—well, to the most expensive, anyway. Tonight Tony Mitchell would pay, or Kurt Gresham if he showed up. Not that they'd let him, but he couldn't even go through the motions of reaching for the check. A dinner for four at the Big Dipper, with cocktails and wine and adequate tips to the *maître d'* and waiters, would come to almost a hundred and fifty dollars—two weeks' salary for Dr. Harrison Brown's yawning day-shift receptionist.

Dr. Harrison Brown shuffled about, flicking on lights. In his gleaming examining room he opened a cabinet drawer, took out a fifth of whisky, poured himself a shot, gulped it down and, replacing bottle and glass, went into one of the two dressing rooms, the one with the full bathroom. As he stripped, as he stepped under the shower and soaped himself and turned on the needle spray and felt his body come alive, Dr. Harrison Brown thought about Anthony Mitchell, Esquire, Attorney-at-Law . . . thought about luck, and its quirks. For it had been chance, pure and complex, that had thrown him back into the orbit of that incandescent, hurtling personality.

Law had been Harry Brown's father's profession, too—slow, meticulous, painfully honest Simon Brown; old Sime Brown, never in court, a law-book man, a brilliant brief man, everybody's counsel on appeal; student, scholar, sickly, toward the last doddering; a man of great learning and greater wisdom and greatest principle. Attorney Simon Brown, widower, without personal ambition, deeply devoted to his only child, his son, deeply committed to encouraging that son to study medicine, to become a successful physician and so to be able to enjoy those things in life which meant so little to him. Or perhaps, as Harry Brown suspected, his father had cultivated a personal indifference toward material satisfactions because he had long ago recognized his incapability of achieving them. But for his son. . . . It explained why he had kept himself impoverished in order to expose his son to the environment of wealth.

Daddy-o, Harry Brown thought bitterly, you played me a dirty trick. Who had said, "Wisdom is folly"? It was the stupidest thing the wise man had ever done.

It was in his father's office—during a short vacation, while he was still in medical school—that Harry Brown had first met Tony Mitchell. Tony, seven years Harry's senior, was already a criminal lawyer with a future; he brought his brief work to Simon Brown. He was handsome, zestful, sophisticated, quick-witted, sardonic, gay, an electric personality—all the things that Harry was not.

"Your old man's a genius, did you know that?" Tony Mitchell had said to Harry Brown in his baritone chuckle. He was reputed to have an extraordinary courtroom voice. "And I take advantage of him, pick his brains." For one moment young Mitchell had turned serious. "It's unfair as hell. But . . . You know what's wrong with your father, Harry? He's too damned *shy*."

It was an indictment, Simon Brown had remarked dryly later, that would never be drawn against Anthony Mitchell, Esquire.

But Harry had liked him. And, of course, envied him.

They had become friends quickly, gone out together. They made an interesting pair. Where Harry was serious, Tony was ebullient. Where Harry was awkward with women, Tony collected them like moths. They complemented each other, even physically. Harry's big, bulky, rugged body was the perfect foil for Tony Mitchell's quicksilver slenderness.

But then Harry had had to go back to school, and Simon Brown died, and the friendship died, too, as quickly as it had been born. They drifted apart and soon lost track of each other.

Harry Brown stepped out of the shower and toweled himself viciously. Then he shaved and got into the change of clothing he kept in the bathroom closet. Against tonight's eventuality he had stored fresh linen, black shoes and socks, a custom-tailored midnight blue suit and a solidly dark blue French silk tie. Knotting the tie before the mirror, he asked himself, How do I stand? And how much longer can I keep up the front?

Not long, he knew. He was over his head in the two classic troubles: money trouble and woman trouble.

He had planned everything so conscientiously. The thirty thousand dollars had looked as impregnable a reserve as the gold in Fort Knox. He was interested in two fields, internal medicine and surgery; he had figured that two years of private practice would determine which way he would go. And choosing the "right" neighborhood for his office the most modern equipment, the slick car, the posh clothes —these had seemed the logical means to his goal, and the devil take the cost.

The devil had taken the cost without providing the anticipated *quid pro quo*. After two years, nothing had come to a head. The surplus of patients implicit in a shortage of doctors had shunned Dr. Harrison Brown in droves. Patients had materialized, but in insufficient numbers. This week was not typical; he had had far better ones; but, on the average, income and outgo were ludicrously out of balance. He saw, too late, that establishing a lucrative practice was going to take far longer than he had calculated. Time meant money. And his money was running out.

And then, four months ago, a chance encounter in a bar with Anthony Mitchell had breathed life back into his hopes just as they were heaving their last gasp.

One stare, and Tony Mitchell was all over him like Old Grad at the class reunion. "Harry boy! My God, it's Harry! How are you? Where've you been hiding out?"

They had double-dated for weeks, got high together, done the town—having more fun than Harry Brown could remember. Then one night, alone in Mitchell's apartment, the lawyer had said suddenly, "All right, Harry, it's time you took your hair down. What gives? Where's it pressing? You put on a pretty good act, but seeing through acts is standard procedure in the courtroom, and I can spot one a mile away. You in trouble? Do something foolish? Let's have it."

So Harrison Brown, M.D., had told Anthony Mitchell, LL.B., all about it. From the beginning to date. His ambitions, his plans, his training, his decisions, his frustrations, his grim prospects. And he told of terror by night and by day; of the first doubts, then the growing fear, then the panic . . .

"Okay, enough," Tony Mitchell said crisply. "I want to sleep on this, Harry."

"You?" Harry had exclaimed. "What can you do?"

"Plenty. Just give me—oh, a couple of days. Can you be at my office Thursday at noon?"

"Yes—"

"Here's my card."

"But, Tony—"

"Look, let me do the worrying. It's my business to worry about peoples' troubles. That's what I get paid for. Only for you it's on the house. See you Thursday."

At noon on Thursday, Dr. Brown had presented himself at Anthony Mitchell's surprisingly businesslike office on Fifth Avenue. No playboy here. The office girls had clearly been picked for efficiency, not looks; the law clerks were intent on their work. "Sit down, Harry," Tony Mitchell said in a tone Harry Brown had never heard from him before.

Harry sat down and fumbled for a cigaret, wondering what was coming.

"I've considered your problem," the lawyer said, leaning back in his chair, "and I approve your plan. It's perfectly sound for its long-range objective. It wouldn't be for a cluck, but you're no cluck."

"How would you know that?" Dr. Harry Brown said. "For all you know, I might be a medical misfit."

"I've looked you up," said Mitchell quietly, "and you're not. I'm satisfied that, professionally, you can make it big. The one weakness of your plan was insufficient capitalization. You didn't realize how long a pull it was going to be."

"I sure as hell didn't."

"The problem gets down to this: To get where you're going, you need more fuel than you figured. Once you build up enough speed, the fuel question drops out as a factor. Harry, you're going to have to go to the bank."

"For what?"

"For a big fat loan."

Harry Brown laughed. "And what'll they give it to me on, Tony, my good looks?"

Tony Mitchell grinned back. "If that was your collateral, you couldn't borrow the down payment on Jack Benny's Maxwell." But then he became all business again. "I think another thirty thousand would do it, Harry. If you were careful, it ought to get you over the hump."

Dr. Harrison Brown suddenly realized that he was trying to light the cigaret. He lit it, looking at his friend through the smoke. "You know a bank that will lend me thirty thousand dollars without collateral?"

"Sure. Mine."

"Don't tell me you own a bank!"

"Not quite," said Tony, smiling. "What I have in mind is to sign as co-maker. You'll get it."

"Now wait a minute, Tony," Harry protested. "I couldn't let you do that."

"Why not?"

"If I fell flat on my face—"

"You're not going to fall flat on your face. I consider you a lead-pipe cinch, given enough time. Thirty G's should do it. Also, I'm going to protect my investment by seeing what I can do to throw some well-heeled patients your way."

"Let me think about it, Tony." He tried to control his voice.

"There's nothing to think about." Tony Mitchell jumped out of his chair. "Let's go, Harry."

"Go? Where?"

"To my bank. They're waiting for us."

"Tony—"

"Oh, shut up. What are friends for? On your feet, kid."

So he had let himself be rushed into it, confused with reborn hope and unutterable gratitude. There had been no trouble about the loan; four months had gone by and nothing had changed, really, except that the condemned man had been granted a reprieve. Oh, there had been some changes, but they had scarcely improved his position. In fact, Harry Brown mused, they had worsened it.

Tony Mitchell had been as good as his word about the "well-heeled" patients. Dr. Brown, on Mitchell's generous recommendation, found himself the personal physician of the first rich patients of his career, Mr. and Mrs. Kurt Gresham.

Kurt Gresham was a multimillionaire. He owned an import-export company with world-wide outlets and a huge annual income. Gresham's offices were in the Empire State Building.

The millionaire was a cardiac, chronically overweight from compulsive eating; his medical needs called for frequent examination and adjustment of medication. His doctor was an old man on the verge of retirement; he was transferring his patients gradually to other physicians, and Kurt Gresahm's time had come.

"Tony Mitchell's told me a lot about you, Dr. Brown," Gresham had said during their first interview. "And I've done some poking around of my own. After all, it's my heart that's involved; I don't want to make a mistake."

"Why don't you transfer to a heart specialist?" Harry Brown had asked him abruptly.

The stout millionaire had smiled. "I like that, Doctor. But old Doc Welliver has always said it wasn't necessary. Now maybe he told me that to hang on to a good thing, but I don't think so. Anyway, what I've learned about you I'm satisfied with. Do you take me on?"

"I'll answer that question, Mr. Gresham, after I've learned about your heart. I'll want to see Dr. Welliver's records on you, and I'll want a day of your time."

"You name it." The millionaire had seemed pleased.

He had gone into Gresham's case with great care. In the end he had decided that there was nothing involved which he could not handle. And, again, the millionaire had seemed pleased.

So their professional relationship had begun well. If only, Harry Brown thought glumly, it had stayed that way!

For there was Mrs. Gresham—the fourth Mrs. Gresham, according to Tony Mitchell. Karen of Gresh, as Tony called her. Delicious Karen . . .

Delicious Karen was the woman trouble.

Dr. Harrison Brown got to the Big Dipper at ten minutes past eight. Tony and Karen were already there, lapping up martinis, at a table against the banquette. Karen was seated on the banquette, with Tony opposite her.

"Notice that I've reserved the place of honor for you," Tony said, his beautiful teeth laughing-white against his sunlamp-burned skin. "With Cupid sitting across the table beaming." To the waiter who had moved the table aside to allow Harry to slip in beside Karen, Tony said, "Two vodka martinis for the doctor here, and another round for Mrs. Gresham and me."

"Where's Kurt?" Harry said. On the banquette seat, protected by the cloth, Karen's hand was searching for his.

"Oh, these beetle-brows," Tony said softly. "You always make the lovelies. Why wasn't I born with the gene of beetle-brows?"

"Oh, shut up, Tony," Karen Gresham said. "Kurt's not coming, Harry. He just called. Tied up at home working on whatever he works on. Disappointed?" She turned her enormous green eyes his way. Below the cloth her hand was brushing his lightly, hungrily.

"Not disappointed, and not not," Harry said. There it

15

was again, the havoc to his nervous system. On the excuse of reaching for his cigarets, he withdrew his hand.

"Forgive him the syntax, honey," Tony Mitchell said. "Doctors get that way from writing prescriptions."

"I think Harry's disappointed," said Karen, smiling. There was the slightest pucker between her brows. "Kurt fascinates him. Doesn't he, Harry?"

Harry said nothing except, "Your health." He picked up one of the two cocktail glasses the waiter was setting before him and gulped down half of it.

"That's a hell of a toast for a would-be successful doctor," Tony said. "And say what you want about that husband of yours, Karen, he's a fascinating monster. The most fascinating in my experience, which has dealt with monsters almost exclusively."

"To Kurt Gresham, Monster De Luxe," murmured Karen, and she sipped her fresh martini.

"Might's well order," said the lawyer; the waiter had his pencil patiently poised. "Duck, that's it. Duck Aldebaranis—truly out of this world. How about you two?"

"I don't care," Karen said.

Harry shrugged.

"Shrimp first? With that crazy sauce? Lovers? I'm speaking!"

"Oh, you order, Tony," Karen said.

"Yes." Harry observed her over the rim of his glass. That fascinating old monster certainly had an eye for women. She was exquisite, and when she sat beside her husband he became grotesque; Karen was almost half Kurt Gresham's age. What hath God bought, he thought bitterly.

Yes, exquisite. The facial bones so delicate, with the fragility of fine china, and something of its translucence. The thoroughbred way in which she held her head, with its swirl of incredible copper hair. The great green wide-apart, innocent, worldly, inscrutable, enchanting eyes. The flesh under that tight green gown with its daring décolleté cut. . . . The gown must have cost his income for months. The emerald necklace making love to her throat was probably worth more than his father's insurance policy had brought. Yes, old Gresham knew how to pick his women—and how to keep them . . . For one lightning moment Dr. Harrison Brown thought: Was *she* what had got into his blood? Or was it what she represented—the symbol of everything he had fiercely yearned for all his life?

16

They were well served and they ate while Tony Mitchell joked and ragged them. Through it all Harry was conscious only of the heat of her pressing thigh, the caresses of her secretive fingers. They lingered over dessert and coffee and Drambuie, and then, after the table was cleared, they drank more coffee and more Drambuie; and he got a little drunk, and his tongue loosened, and he even laughed several times. And then, at about eleven o'clock, Tony said, "Did you come in your car, Harry?"

"Yes."

"Then suppose you take the lady home. I've got to get a good night's sleep tonight—I'm due in court in the morning on a tricky case. You don't mind, do you, Karen? And don't bother to lie. Waiter?"

They left Tony Mitchell paying the check.

He drove her home and double-parked in the gloom of Park Avenue near the Gresham's duplex. She threw herself into his arms, kissing, straining, clinging. "I love you, I love you, I love you..."

Harry Brown said nothing. He clutched her and said nothing. What was there to say?

"What are we going to do, darling? What are we going to do?"

He made no answer. He had no answer.

Then she said, "He's going out of town for the weekend. I'll see you Friday night and Saturday night and Sunday night. Alone. No one else. Yes? Yes, Harry?"

"Yes."

"Good night."

"I'll take you in."

"Not tonight, darling. See you Friday. I'll call you the moment he's gone."

He drove downtown, guilt rumbling within him. Was he in love? Was he? He was certainly infatuated. But love... marriage...? She had been honest with him: She had married a rich old man quite simply for his riches—God knew he could understand that!—and she could not face the thought of losing it. Gresham would give her no grounds for divorce; he was mad about her. And if she should provide the grounds, she would get nothing. And yet... *I love you, Harry. What are we going to do?*

He slid into the parking space before his house on Barrow Street and locked the car.

The dingy lobby was empty. He rode the creaky self-service elevator to the third floor, unlocked his apartment door, locked it behind him, snapped the light switch in the vestibule, threw his hat into the hall closet and went into the living room, fumbling for the switch. He found it and flicked it on and saw the girl.

She was slight and blonde, staring up at him with wide-open eyes from the armchair. She wore a plain black suit, a white blouse, and black patent-leather shoes that glittered in the light. He had never seen her before.

"Hello?" Dr. Harry Brown said with a frown. "Who are you? How did you get into my apartment?"

She did not answer. Just stared up at him.

Then he knew.

He went to her swiftly.

She was dead.

Two

The man in charge reminded him comfortably of his father—an elderly, very tall, grizzled and slightly stooped man, in clothes that hung as though they were a size too large for him. His gray eyes were clear, compassionate and weary, his voice slow, deep-toned, without urgency. He had introduced himself as Detective Lieutenant Galivan. While the technicians were busy with their apparatus, Galivan talked quietly with him.

"You're sure you've never seen her before, Doctor?"

"Never in my life."

"Do you have any idea who she might be?"

"Not the slightest."

"A patient, maybe?"

"Absolutely not."

"Someone who might have come to your office *with* a patient?"

"It's possible, I suppose. All I can tell you is that, to the best of my recollection, I've never laid eyes on her before."

"And you have no idea—no idea at all—what she's doing in your apartment?"

"It ought to be obvious," Harry Brown said angrily. "Even to a cop. She's dead in my apartment."

"Whoa, Doctor. Take it easy. If you're telling the truth—"

"Are you doubting me, for God's sake?"

"— then I can understand your state of mind." The detective showed his small tobacco-yellowed teeth in a smile. "But please try to understand mine. If you're telling the truth, as I started to say, this doesn't make much sense, does it? A woman you never laid eyes on turning up dead in your apartment?"

"No, it doesn't. But here she is."

Galivan looked at him. Harry Brown felt as if he were

19

being gone over by a vacuum cleaner. "Your door was locked?"

"Yes! Locked when I left this morning, locked when I got back tonight."

"And you've never given anyone a duplicate key to the lock?"

"I've already answered that! Not even the janitor has a key. I installed that lock myself when I took the apartment."

"Sure is a funny one," the detective murmured. He took out a pipe and a tobacco pouch and deliberately filled the pipe. Harry Brown waited, seething. Only when he had his pipe going smoothly did Galivan go on. "By the way, the Assistant Medical Examiner says she's been dead for a number of hours."

"I know that," said Harry sarcastically. "I'm a physician, remember?"

"And you say you haven't been back here all day?"

"That's right. I left at eleven this morning."

"She hasn't been dead nearly that long, so that's one in your favor, Doc. If you're telling the truth, that is. You sure you didn't come back here during the day?"

He fought for control. "I'm sure, yes."

"How about this evening?"

"I had dinner out with friends."

"Well, wouldn't you have had to come back to change your clothes?"

"I did that at my office. Showered, shaved, got into fresh clothing at about seven o'clock."

"We can check that, Dr. Brown."

"You do that!"

Galivan smiled again. "Murphy?" A bulky crewcut young plainclothesman strolled over. "Dr. Brown says he showered, shaved and changed his clothes in his office at seven o'clock this evening. He's going to give you the key to his office—right, Doctor?"

In silence Harry unhooked the key from his key ring and handed it to Murphy.

"What's the address?" the plainclothesman asked mildly.

Harry told him.

Murphy nodded and strolled out.

"Young Murphy's pretty good at that sort of thing, Doc," Galivan murmured. "I hope you're telling the truth." Harry compressed his lips. He was suddenly very tired.

"And then," the detective continued, "you went out to dinner. Where?"

"The Big Dipper. Met my friends there at a little after eight—Anthony Mitchell, he's a lawyer, and a Mrs. Gresham, a patient of mine whom I know socially through Mr. Mitchell." He tried to keep his voice at the same level of mere annoyance. They mustn't suspect about Karen and him; they mustn't find out. "I dropped Mrs. Gresham off at her apartment house on Park Avenue around eleven P.M., then drove on home to find this."

"You put in the call to us, Doc, how long after you found her?"

"Seconds, my friend, seconds."

"I see. This Mr. Mitchell and Mrs. Gresham—can I have their addresses?"

"I don't see why you have to drag my friends into this!"

"Nobody's dragging anybody into anything, Dr. Brown. It's just a routine checkout of your story. Their addresses?"

Harry gave him Tony's address and Karen's address.

The detective jotted them down, puffing on his pipe. "Oh, by the way, Doctor," he mumbled as he wrote. "Do much of a business in abortions?"

Harry looked at the man, speechless. Then he burst into laughter.

"There's something funny in what I said?" Lieutenant Galivan asked slowly, taking the pipe out of his mouth.

"Hilarious! You don't know how hilarious, Lieutenant. The answer is no. I don't handle abortions, and I don't recommend pregnant girls or women to any doctor who does. In fact, I wouldn't know where to send such a patient if I wanted to."

Galivan continued to look at him. "Do you know a doctor who would send such a patient to *you* if *he* wanted to?"

"Oh, I see what you're driving at. You think the dead girl. . ." Harry shrugged. "No, I don't."

One of the technicians came up to them and said, "We're through here, Lieutenant."

"Any luck, Closkey?"

The man glanced at Harry. "No," he said, and went away.

"There are no signs of violence on the body, incidentally," Lieutenant Galivan said to Harry. "Have you any idea, as a doctor, what she died of?"

"I'm going to leave the medical opinions to your Medical Examiner's office, Lieutenant."

"Oh, they'll do an autopsy. I just wondered if you knew. Willing to come downtown with us, by the way?"

"Do I have a choice?"

"Sure," said Galivan, puffing hard. "You can come voluntarily, or I can get legal about it."

Harry Brown looked at him in absolute incredulity. "Do I understand that you're detaining me? As a suspect?"

"Suspect? Suspect for what, Doc?"

"How should I know? For murder, I suppose!"

"Oh, you think she was murdered?" Galivan asked.

"Well, wasn't she?"

"Was she?"

"Oh, hell," said Harry.

"Look, Dr. Brown," the detective said. "This could be a rough deal for you all around. Whether you're telling the truth or lying." He actually sounded sympathetic. "I'm not going to bull you. I know a doctor can't afford to get personally mixed up in a police investigation. But I can't help myself any more than you can. As bad as it might be for you professionally, it'll be a whole lot worse if you're withholding information."

"I'm *not* withholding information!" exploded Dr. Harrison Brown. "How many times do I have to repeat that? What do you want me to do, tell you I know the girl when I don't? This is as much a mystery to me as it is to you!"

Surprisingly, Lieutenant Galivan said, "I'm inclined to believe you. Only a nut would dream up a story like this under these circumstances. Of course, it may be that's what you are, Doc—a nut. We'll check that out, too. In fact, you're going to have to be checked from every angle we can think up. Nothing personal, you understand. Let's go."

At the precinct station Galivan took him upstairs to a square, bare, shabby room. "Before we go through the formalities, I'm going to leave you alone here to think."

"Think?" cried Harry. "About what, for heaven's sake?"

The lieutenant looked thoughtful. "Well, if you're telling the truth, Doc, some son of a bitch played a real socker of a joke on you. For your own good you'd better start rummaging through your head for some patient, or so-called friend, or anyone else you may know who'd be cockeyed enough, or mean enough, to put you in the middle of a mess like this."

Galivan went out and closed the door. Dr. Harrison Brown sat down on a hard chair scarred with cigaret burns and scratchwork art.

And he began to think.

He had not thought sixty seconds when he knew it must have been the work of Kurt Gresham.

Two weeks ago his phone had rung at midnight. He had sat up in bed and fumbled for the receiver and Kurt Gresham's voice had come through, contained, precise, almost prissy: "Harry? Harry, can you get up to your office right away?"

"What is it? What's wrong?"

"An emergency. How soon, Harry?"

"Give me thirty minutes."

Twenty-four minutes later he was in his office and five minutes after that the bell rang and Dr. Brown opened the street door to admit Kurt Gresham and a steel-faced man supporting a woman with a face the color of well-aged cheese.

The woman was fat and tight-lipped; she wore an expensive evening gown, and in her naked shoulder, just under the skin, there was a bullet. It had required hardly more than first aid: a simple probe to extricate the bullet, a clamp, a shot to prevent infection. The steel-faced man had taken the woman away, neither of them having uttered a sound; and then Kurt Gresham had said, "Neat and quick, Harry. I like the way you work."

"Mr. Gresham—"

"Kurt, Harry," Gresham had said gently. "We're friends, aren't we?"

"All right—Kurt." He had the most curious feeling of entrapment. "You're going to have to tell me what this is all about."

"I am?" Gresham had said, just as gently.

"Of course! The woman suffered a gunshot wound. The law says all such wounds have to be reported to the police department by the attending physician."

"I know what the law says, Harry. You'll do me a great personal favor if you don't report it."

Harry Brown had stared at him. "You can't be serious. I could have my license revoked."

"Yes," the millionaire had smiled, "but that won't happen. I absolutely guarantee the discretion of everyone involved. Naturally, I don't expect you to run even the slightest risk without adequate compensation. Will this be of help?"

He laid a check down on Harry's desk. It was for five hundred dollars.

"No," Dr. Harry Brown said.

"The woman is not implicated in anything criminal, Harry. She was an innocent bystander—"

"Then she has nothing to worry about," Harry said abruptly, "and neither have you."

"Harry, listen, will you? Will you please listen? Let me have my say."

"Go ahead and have it. But I'm not going to jeopardize my medical license—"

"For a measley five hundred dollars?" The fat man looked hurt. "Harry, have you misjudged me to that extent? This is just a token fee. Listen, I own a large number of night clubs. Does that surprise you? Here in New York. A couple in Washington. Several in Philadelphia, Chicago, Miami. Nobody knows I own these clubs; my ownership is hidden behind a complicated corporate setup. I want it that way, I need it that way. See, I'm not holding anything back."

Listening to the smooth, precise voice, watching the bland and fleshy face, Harry felt a knotty hardness form in the pit of his stomach. "I don't like it, Mr. Gresham—"

"Kurt."

"Kurt. The answer is still no."

"But why, Harry? Lots of businessmen put surplus funds to work in other enterprises—"

"And hide them?"

"Why not? Why should I complicate my business life by letting it be known that I also own a string of night clubs? Anyway, that's the way I prefer it."

"You mean," said Harry tightly, "because your anonymous sideline produces an occasional gunshot wound?"

"That's part of it," Gresham said without hesitation. "Every once in a while somebody gets out of line in a club, in spite of my people's precautions, has too much to drink, starts a brawl. Not often, Harry. And sometimes that somebody turns out to be packing a gun. So, occasionally, somebody gets hurt and needs medical attention. Night clubs operate under license, the way doctors do; and a shooting or other violence jeopardizes the license. At the least, it makes us subject to investigation. I don't want my clubs investigated—it might reveal my ownership. And that's something, as I said, that I want to remain under cover. I've gone to a lot of trouble to keep it that way. One of my precautions has been to retain a physician to take care of just such incidents on a strictly confidential basis. Dr. Welliver did it for me for years. Now that he's retired, I'd like you—"

"No."

"Dr. Welliver never got into trouble. I can protect you—"

"No."

Gresham did not seem offended. "Well, let's drop it for the time being. Of course, it's been something of a shock to you. It's my fault, Harry; I should have prepared you. But please remember I'm not asking you to commit any crimes, just to give me your confidential help on the rare occasions—"

"No."

"I won't accept that till you've had time to think it over, Harry. Let me repeat: You'll be very well paid—"

"No!"

But he had let Kurt Gresham walk out of his office in the small hours that night, leaving the check for five hundred dollars on the desk. And he had slipped the check into his drawer after Gresham's departure, not destroying it. And he had not reported the wounded woman, or her two subsequent visits for routine treatment—both late at night, long after hours. And the following week he had unlocked the desk drawer, slipped the check into his pocket and had gone over to his bank and cashed it. . . .

Yes, the mysterious dead girl was connected with Kurt Gresham in some way, with one of his night clubs. It had to be; there was simply no other explanation. But how she had got into his apartment, and for what purpose; and why had Gresham said nothing to him about it in advance —to these questions Dr. Harry Brown had no answer.

He was sure of only one thing: he was in something way over his head—in something deep, dark and dirty.

The door of the bare precinct room opened and Detective Lieutenant Galivan came in. "Well, Doctor? Remember anything?"

"Nothing," Dr. Brown said.

"Your office checked out, by the way. You showered,

shaved and changed all right. Here's your key." Harry took it. "Oh. What are your office hours?"

"Twelve to two, four to seven. Otherwise, by appointment."

"Now about the lady," Galivan said. "We have some interesting facts."

"Yes, Lieutenant?"

"Unfortunately, we found no purse, so we don't know her name or where she lives. But the clothes are expensive and her body looks like a beautician's ad. Recall a woman whose initials are L. M.?"

Harry thought, "One or two patients, maybe. Why, Lieutenant?"

"L. M. was embroidered on her panties. You've prescribed narcotics in your practice, haven't you, Doctor?"

"Naturally." The sudden question jerked his head up.

"A lot?"

"No more than normal."

"Kept records?"

"Of course."

"We're going to have to check them tonight. We're also going to go through them for female patients with the initials L. M. Sorry to give you such a rough night, Doc."

"What's all this about narcotics?" Harry asked casually. At least he hoped he sounded casual.

"The girl died of an overdose of heroin. She was an addict, a mainliner. Whenever you're ready, Doc. First we'll take your formal statement."

A police stenographer took his statement in the squad room, and then Galivan, young Murphy and two other policemen took him uptown to his office, where his records were closely examined.

"Clean on the narcotics, from the looks of it," Galivan said.

"Thank you," Harry said without enthusiasm.

There were three female patients with the initials L. M., all from the previous year. Despite the hour, Galivan telephoned them.

They all answered their phones, very much alive.

"That's it, Doc," Galivan said. "It's out of your hands now and in mine. I'll keep in touch. Give you a lift home?"

Six days later, exactly at noon, Detective Lieutenant Galivan strolled into Dr. Harrison Brown's office.

"You've identified her," Harry said.

"Finally," Galivan answered, sitting down with a slight groan. "Routine turned the trick. Her suit, which looked pretty new, had a Lord & Taylor label. We checked all their charge accounts back two years of women-customers with the initials L. M. No dice, alive or dead and buried. So we had to wade through cash sales slips by the thousands. Police work is so glamourous. And then we made her—Lynne Maxwell, Lynne with an *e*. Ring a bell, Dr. Brown?"

"Lynne Maxwell." Harry shook his head. "Not even a tinkle."

"What a town this is," said the detective sadly. "Live and die practically next door, and you might just as well have been on the moon."

"What do you mean, Lieutenant?" Harry asked sharply.

"She was a neighbor of yours. I mean, practically. Lived on Bank Street. Artist. Studio like a movie set."

"Artist," frowned Harry. "How come nobody missed her?"

"Well, first, she lived alone. Second, she was very rich, inherited dough. Came from Denver, Colorado. Third, she was unmarried. Fourth, she had no steady guy, kept to herself. One like that can disappear for a long time without raising questions. Twenty-nine years old. Shame, huh?"

"Rotten shame."

"The few people she knew say she spent money like water, mostly on herself; had a lover once in a while, nothing serious—bascially a loner, no real attachments. By the way, not one of her acquaintances could link her to Dr. Harrison Brown. They never heard of Dr. Harrison Brown. That ought to please you, Doc."

"It doesn't please me or displease me. I've told you the truth about the girl from the start."

"Don't get hot, Doc. That's why I came all the way up here to fill you in."

"Thanks, Lieutenant," Harry said mechanically, "but this thing has been bothering the hell out of me. How would you like to come home and find a dead girl you never saw or heard of before in your living room?"

"I wouldn't like it."

"I don't like it, either. I've had my lock changed, but if someone was able to get past one lock, a second one won't protect me. I don't sleep well."

"I don't blame you." The detective sounded genuinely

sorry for him. "So I guess you'll be glad to hear that we're keeping this case open."

Harry stared. "Why, Lieutenant?"

"You."

"Me?"

Galivan rubbed a knuckle on his chin. "Doctor, I'm Homicide. Now it's true that this case doesn't look like a homicide. This Lynne Maxwell killed herself, intentionally or accidentally, by injecting more junk into her body than it could tolerate. She died in her studio, or she died in the street, or maybe she even died in your apartment. If it was her studio or the street, somebody would have to deposit her in your place. Why? Or if she died in your apartment, what was she doing there? How did she get in? And why did she come? See what I mean, Doc?"

"Yes," Harry said gloomily.

"So—case open instead of closed. Accidental death or suicide, the fact remains that you found her in your apartment, and it's an unexplained fact. When it's unexplained, whatever it is, you can't close the book on it. And brother, it sure is bugging me."

"You and me both, Lieutenant."

"Well, that's about it, Doc." Galivan rose. "If anything further pops on this, no matter what or when, please let me know right away."

"Of course, Lieutenant."

He was in the midst of examining a patient, at one o'clock, when his office girl buzzed him.

"Mr. Gresham is on the line, Doctor. Can you speak to him?"

"Not now," Harry said. "Tell him I'll call back."

"He says it's important—"

"I'm examining a patient," he snapped. "I'll call back."

Gresham sounded displeased when Harry finally called. "I said it was important, Harry."

"I don't take calls in the middle of an examination, Kurt," said Harry. "What do you want?"

"I want to see you."

"You do?" said Harry. "That's a coincidence. I want to see you, too."

There was a silence. Then he heard Gresham chuckle. "Well. That makes it cozy. So you figured it out, Harry?"

"Figured what out?"

"About Lynne Maxwell?"

It was Harry's turn to be silent. He felt confused and angry and helpless all at the same time.

Finally he said curtly, "When and where?"

"Three o'clock? My office?" asked the prissy voice.

"I'll be there."

Three

Dr. Harry Brown looked him over. Really for the first time.

He was a big man, globular. He had a round ruddy face, soft, white, womanish hair and eyes clear and colorless as sun on ice. The tip of his big nose was round and the little red-lipped mouth was round. He looked guileless, good-natured, almost cherubic. He was about as harmless as a big fat round H-bomb, Dr. Harry Brown thought.

"Harry," Kurt Gresham began, "I'm going to make a confession to you. Try to win you over. If I fail, no hard feelings. But I warn you now. If you breach my confidence by so much as a word. . . ." The millionaire shook his head; everything shook with it. "I wouldn't like that at all. Harry, I'm not a man of violence. Quite the contrary. I consider violence the first resort of the stupid. The only times I have indulged in violence were those times when nothing less would serve—the last resort. Do I make myself clear, Harry?"

"Perfectly. You're threatening to have me murdered if I don't keep my mouth shut."

The girlish lips opened out into a little round smile. "Crude, Harry. But I see we understand each other."

"The hell we do, Gresham. I don't give a damn about your 'confession,' as you put it. I want to know just one thing: why did you have the dead body of that Maxwell girl planted in my apartment?"

Gresham blinked. "You're really a very clever young man, Harry. However, I'd like, if I may, to develop this in my own time and way—"

"The hell with your time and way! Answer my question!"

The silky white brows drew together sulkily, the colorless round eyes flattened and slitted. For an absurd mo-

30

ment Harry Brown thought of pediatrics and the baskets of fat little baby faces just before feedings, preparing to cry. But there was nothing infantile in Gresham's tone; it was hard, greedy, paranoiac. "You have the gall to talk to me that way? Nobody talks to me that way, Doctor. *Nobody. Nobody!*" The last word was almost a shout. And then the brows drew apart and the eyes and face became round again. "I'm sorry, Harry. You mustn't make me angry. A bad heart and a bad temper don't mix, do they?"

"I'm not here as your doctor. What about Lynne Maxwell?"

"Harry, I admire you. You're rough and tough. I want you on my side."

"What about Lynne Maxwell?"

"I'll come to that, Harry. But first I want to talk to you about myself. About you. About our future together."

"We have no future together, Gresham."

"How do you know, my boy?"

"What about Lynne Maxwell?"

"Please, Harry. I beg your attention."

Dr. Harrison Brown sat back in the enveloping armchair and looked past Gresham's globular head and out through the wide windows at the blank blue sky. They were high up, on the fifty-fifth floor. He wondered dully what was coming.

"Do you know what business I'm in, Harry?"

"Import-export." He shook a cigaret from a package, dug in a pocket for matches.

"Do you know the chief product I import?"

"Now how would I know that?" He found the matches, tore one from the packet and struck it.

"Heroin."

Harry's hand remained in air, the match flickering.

"Light your cigaret, Harry," said Kurt Gresham, smiling. "You'll burn your fingers."

He lit the cigaret, carefully deposited the charred match in a shiny jade ash tray. "Heroin?" he said. My God, he thought, my God.

"You sound shocked," said the fat man, still smiling.

"How should I sound, Gresham? Amused?" He jumped up.

The millionaire folded his hands comfortably. "You're so young, Harry. You have so much to learn. No, sit down, please. I want you to hear me out."

"I've heard all I want to hear!"

"Will it hurt you to listen for a few minutes? Please. Sit down."

"All right." Harry flung himself down. "But if you think I'm going to tie myself up to a dope racketeer—! I know what narcotics addiction does to the human body. And I have some idea of how you slugs work. Giving out free samples to high school kids through your pushers, getting them hooked, then pushing them into a life of crime to get the money for their daily fixes—"

"Oh, my, Dr. Brown, you do know a lot, don't you?" said Kurt Gresham, the whole globe shaking silently. "You know it all. Shall I tell you something, Dr. Brown? You don't know *anything*. Not about me, anyway. Not about my kind of narcotics operation."

"And what kind would that be?" Harry sneered. "Philanthropic?"

"No," said the millionaire, "but I perform a social service just the same."

"Social service!" Harry choked.

"Social service," said Gresham, nodding. "Have you any idea how many hundreds of thousands of habitual users of narcotics in this country are *not* high school children who were hooked by unscrupulous pushers and dealers? are *not* degenerates? are *not* beatniks out for kicks? are *not* the dirt of society? My clients are all upright, respectable, useful and, in many cases, distinguished people who, in one way or another—a lot of them through illness—became addicted to drugs, just as you're addicted to that nicotine you're inhaling right now. I don't sell to criminals, Harry. I have no connection with the dope rackets or racketeers. I'm a maverick operation. A specialist, you might say, with a specialized trade."

"Of all the rationalizations—!"

"Realism, Harry. I'm preventing the proliferation of criminals."

"By engaging in the criminal dope traffic!"

"No; by providing narcotics rations to those respectable people who need them in order to continue to lead useful, respectable lives. If not for me, they'd have to traffic with the criminal element—buy inferior drugs, drastically cut to produce a bigger volume and profit—become prey to underworld blackmail. If not for me, Harry."

"Oh, so now the supplying of junk is to be considered

an act of benevolence? Is that how you'd like me to think of you? As a humanitarian?"

"In a way. Basically, I am a businessman in a large and profitable business. But I'm no less a humanitarian than the successful publisher who makes a profit selling Bibles."

"That's one hell of a comparison!"

"As good as any. Psychiatrists think so, the higher echelon of welfare workers think so, the government of England thinks so."

"Nothing you can say—"

"In Britain an addict is treated not as a criminal, but as a sick man, which is what he is. He needn't deal with criminals there, or become a criminal himself in order to satisfy the craving induced by the habit. In Britain the addict may go to a doctor and receive his ration of the drug by prescription, all quite legally. Once our federal authorities and Congress realize that that's the only way to cope with the problem, my services won't be needed and the underworld will lose a major source of its income."

"There are moral kudos even in the peddling of junk. That's what you'd like me to believe?"

"I insist you believe it, my boy. You're intelligent enough to understand, if you'll open your mind."

"I'm listening, Gresham, but I'm afraid my mind is closed. Junk peddling is junk peddling."

"Of course your mind is closed. You've been raised in an atmosphere of legalistic bias. During Prohibition, for example, you were told that the manufacture, transportation and sale of liquor was a horrid crime. Then the Eighteenth Amendment was repealed, and suddenly liquor became respectable again. I'll bet you still can't take a drink without having guilt feelings about it."

"Liquor and narcotics are hardly the same thing," Harry snorted. "There's no danger of alcoholism unless there are underlying psychological causes. But anyone can become a narcotics addict simply through excessive dosage."

"All the more reason for recognizing that it's a medical, not a criminal, problem. And it's bound to be recognized, Harry. Sooner or later we'll have the British system here and I'll be out of business. Meanwhile I'm serving a socially desirable purpose that ought to be served by the government."

"Man, if ever I heard sophistry . . . !"

"Not true. There is nothing unsound in my argument; it's not a rationalization. Admittedly, I've made a great deal of money in the commission of acts now considered unlawful, but they're not unethical acts. It's our antiquated laws that are wrong, not I."

Harry Brown looked at his watch. "Would you kindly come to the point, Gresham? I have to get back to my office."

Kurt Gresham pinched at the pink jowls beneath his small round chin. "Harry, I want you to stop thinking of me in terms of gangsters, pushers, despoilers of teenagers and all that. I'm not a conscienceless corrupter of human beings, believe me. For thirty-five years I've been serving the needs of statesmen, writers, artists, actors, architects, judges, businessmen, financiers, society people—"

"God Almighty."

"I supply only the best, the worthiest; my potential clients are screened by experts; I accept only people of means and discretion; and there are so many, so many..."

Dr. Harrison Brown sat silent.

In the silence, Kurt Gresham selected a long thin cigar from a humidor, lit it carefully, blew aromatic smoke.

In spite of himself, Harry said curiously, "You say you've been in this racket—pardon me, humanitarian service—for thirty-five years. How did you get started? What gave you the idea? Mind telling me?"

"Not at all. My father was in the import-export business in a modest way—getting along, not rich, not poor. He died at the age of seventy-nine, and all his adult life he was a heroin addict. Through his international contacts he was able to buy supplies of the drug for his private use: they were brought in for him by a trusted European representative during legitimate business trips. It was because of my father that the idea struck me—what an ideal solution this method would be to the problem of supplying respectable addicts with their necessary drugs—and, of course, how profitable. When my father died and I took over the business, I began to work on my idea—very slowly and carefully. Today I have a small but airtight organization of hand-picked people."

"Hand-picked, am I?"

"Over a period of thirty-five years I have had to make replacements, of course: employees had died, grown old, retired. You're old Dr. Welliver's replacement, I hope—I sincerely hope, Harry. For both our sakes."

Something in the fat man's tone made Harry's scalp prickle. "Does Mrs. Gresham know about all of this?"

"Of course not. Karen is my wife, not a business associate. But to get back to you, Harry. I've studied you; I've had you most carefully investigated. I know all about you: about your father's struggle to make you what he couldn't be; about your compulsive drive for success and wealth—all about you, Harry."

"My God, how . . . ?"

"My staff is made up of experts—each of whom knows only an essential few of his colleagues, by the way, as you will be my expert in your field, knowing virtually none of the others. I even know of your recent loan. . . ." The fat man opened a drawer of his desk, extracted a rectangle of blue paper and tossed it across to Harry. "Your loan has been paid. That's the cancelled note. I cannot afford to have any member of my little official family in debt. You see, Harry, just by agreeing to this little conference, you're ahead thirty thousand dollars."

Harry stared at the blue rectangle.

"Put it away, Harry," Gresham said. "Or tear it up."

Dr. Harrison Brown looked up from the blue paper so tightly held in his hand. "What do you want of me?" he croaked.

"Don't look at me that way, Harry. I'm not the Devil, and I'm not asking you to sell your soul."

"What do you want of me?"

"Put that note away, will you?"

Harry stuffed it into a pocket. "What do you want of me, Gresham?"

"Absurdly little, in fact. You'll continue to build up your practice independently, but to give you freedom from financial worries I'm going to put you on an annual retainer—ostensibly for being my family physician. You'll be called on no more than five or six times a year for the confidential jobs—they don't happen often; sometimes a full year's gone by without the need for a job like the one you did on that woman."

"So much for so little? That can't be the whole thing, Gresham—"

"But it is. I'm willing to pay handsomely just to know that I have a doctor I can depend on in an emergency."

"I've got to get to my office," Harry said, rising. "I have office hours—"

"I've already had your office girl called, Harry. You're delayed, important case. And it is, isn't it?"

35

Harry sank back, staring at him. Gresham puffed on his cigar.

"Now, Harry," he said briskly, "I want you to understand how this thing works because, even though you're a minor cog in the machine, even the minor cogs are important to keep the machine running smoothly.

"Gresham and Company, Import and Export, has been in business for seventy years. We're a firm of excellent reputation, doing a good business in a lawful manner. However, certain key people secretly pick up the narcotics I need in Europe and the Orient; and the other key people deliver it to me together with the legitimate goods we import. We never take chances. We never smuggle in big shipments, for instance, because we don't have to. We're in business day in and day out, and so small quantities can be brought in day in and day out; no splurges, no large purchases, nothing that attracts attention; never any trouble in thirty-five years. Is that much clear?"

"Yes."

Gresham deposited a long ash delicately in a tray. "Distribution and sales naturally pose more dangerous problems. I've already indicated that the selection of the client is done by experts. The client must be of the highest moral character and of sound financial background—people who are willing to pay as much for our discretion as for the drugs. As for the actual transactions—"

"Your night-club chain," Harry exclaimed.

"Exactly." The millionaire crushed out his cigar and leaned back in his huge baronial chair. "I don't go west of the Mississippi. My distribution points—drops, if you will—are here in New York, in Philadelphia, in Washington, Miami and in Chicago. In each of these cities, under dummy ownership, I own several small, exclusive clubs. In each club the manager is one of my key people, and it's the manager who makes the delivery and accepts payment—in cash, naturally. And there you have it, my boy. Oh, I should add what must be obvious—I have a doctor on my payroll in each of the five cities. Is there anything else you would like to know, Harry?"

Harry Brown was silent again. Then he mumbled, "That woman with the bullet wound I treated. Who was she, a client?"

"Good heavens, no!" Gresham said; he actually sounded shocked. "We don't have that kind of client, Harry. She's an employee. Sometimes there's violence in our ranks, no matter how careful we are. As I said, it doesn't happen often. When it does, we take extraordinary measures to keep it within the family, so to speak."

"And," asked Harry dryly, "if the little family misunderstanding happens to wind up in a murder, Gresham? What's your family doctor expected to do with the corpse —grind it up for hamburger?"

"Harry," said the millionaire in a pained voice. "In the unfortunate event that an individual dies in one of these episodes, we take him off your hands. You have nothing to do with—ah—disposal. Actually, it's happened only half a dozen times in the last twenty, twenty-five years— and in three different cities, at that. Don't worry about things of that sort. We have resources and connections that would astonish you. Anything else?"

"Yes." Harry Brown said grimly. "The matter of—"

"Oh, excuse me," Gresham said. "I almost forgot your retainer." He took a check from his desk drawer and reached over to lay it softly before Harry. "For a year in advance, Harry. Twenty-five thousand dollars."

Dr. Harrison Brown stared down at it. He grew very pale. He did not touch the check.

"And you'll earn more, Doctor. I paid you five hundred dollars when you treated the lady with the bullet nick. That was chicken feed—I didn't want to startle you. Hereafter, on the rare occasion when you'll have to treat one of our special patients, you'll receive a fee of five thousand dollars per patient. Such fees will be in addition to your yearly retainer. And now, what were you going to ask me?"

Harry thought bitterly, You clever bastard. He looked up from the check and said, "Lynne Maxwell. I want an explanation."

"Oh! Yes, of course, Harry," said Kurt Gresham, and his round mouth flattened sadly. "Most, most unfortunate thing. I won't conceal it from you. She was a client. The first case of its kind we've ever had. She tried to commit suicide by taking a deliberate overdose. And then, as often happens, regretted it. She phoned the manager of the club where she always made the pickup—and, of course, under the unusual circumstances, he quickly got word to me. I got a couple of my security people to drive over to her apartment. They found her dead."

"So you had them plant her body in my place, Gresham," Harry said wearily.

"I'm so sorry, Harry." The colorless eyes remained round and without guile. "But I did feel I had to impress you with our—ah—resources. I wanted you to realize that we can go through locked doors and perform miracles with dead bodies—depositing them, for example, where they don't belong."

"In other words, I'd better accept your proposal, or you'll frame me for something nice and ripe."

"Harry, did I say anything like that? Or imply it? It was simply a demonstration, preliminary to this talk."

Dr. Harrison Brown rose, picked up the check for twenty-five thousand dollars, stored it in his wallet and put his wallet away. He left Gresham smiling.

Outside, in the warm Fifth Avenue sunshine, Dr. Brown shivered. It was not from fear. It was from self-disgust. He had simply been unable to resist the money.

Four

In time, Dr. Harrison Brown became aware of the compassion of Lieutenant Galivan, or of what he believed to be his compassion. This belief in Galivan's compassion did not spring from any overt act on the lieutenant's part; to the contrary. For four weeks and a fraction thereof, nothing appeared in the newspapers about Lynne Maxwell.

To this absence of news about the dead girl Dr. Brown gave much thought. The corpse of a Greenwich Village artist found in an apartment where she did not belong would be sensational news anywhere. Then why wasn't there one word about it in the papers? Obviously because Galivan had sat on the story. The lieutenant was wise and experienced; the lieutenant was compassionate. God bless the lieutenant, said the doctor silently. He would never again have to hear the name Lynne Maxwell.

But he did hear it again, four weeks and a fraction after the event, on a Sunday night following an afternoon of golf at Taugus in Connecticut.

The Greshams, members of the Taugus Company Club, had put him up for membership and he had been accepted: he could now afford it. He played golf on most Sunday afternoons, and this Sunday afternoon the fourth player was to be Dr. Alfred McGee Stone, another member of the club.

"Stone? I don't know him," Harry said.

"He's dying to meet you," Kurt Gresham said.

"Why?"

Tony Mitchell said, "Maybe he thinks you're grist for his mill."

"What's his mill?"

"He's director of the Taugus Institute."

"What's that?"

"It's charity," Karen Gresham said.

Tony Mitchell said, "Maybe he's heard of *you*, Harry. Wants to pluck you from the ranks and institutionalize you."

"Nonsense," Karen Gresham said. "These jokers are giving you the business, Harry."

"No, really," Kurt Gresham said. "Dr. Stone's been asking about Harry ever since I mentioned his name."

Dr. Alfred McGee Stone was tall, wire-thin and bald, with a good sunburn, wolfish teeth, an Arab's nose and rimless glasses which kept slipping down his beak. He acknowledged his introduction to Harry heartily: his clasp was powerful and a little impatient. The rest had been golf. Dr. Stone played a whale of a game, all in silence.

But at the bar in the clubhouse afterward, they had been alone for a while and Stone said, "Harrison Brown. I've heard about you."

Harry squinted. "From whom?"

"Dr. Peter Alexander Gross. The astonishing Pete Gross. I understand you were one of his wonder kids."

"Dr. Peter Gross! How is he?"

"As always. Indestructible."

Dr. Peter Alexander Gross had been his professor of surgery, one of those legendary teachers who inspire worship. Harry had not forgotten their many wonderful nights of talk.

"I love that man," Harry said simply.

"He thinks a lot of you, Brown."

"That's very kind of him." I wonder, he thought, what Dr. Peter Alexander Gross would think of his *wünderkind* now. . . . Harry said abruptly, "What's this all about, Dr. Stone?"

Stone used a bony middle finger to push his glasses up on his bridgeless nose. "Dr. Gross and I have been discussing you . . ." But just then Kurt Gresham, showered, shaved and pinkly cherubic, came ambling toward them. "Look," the physician said. "We need a talk, a long talk, and this is neither the time nor the place. I come into New York every Tuesday. May I drop in on you?"

"Of course, Doctor."

"This Tuesday?"

"Certainly."

"One o'clock all right? At your office?"

"One o'clock will be fine."

Then Kurt Gresham was upon them. "Tony and Karen are outside on the patio. Let's join them, gentlemen."

"Why wasn't Mr. Mitchell your fourth, Kurt?" Dr. Stone asked.

"Tony doesn't play golf, Doctor."

"Then why is he here?" Dr. Stone seemed puzzled.

"He likes my wife," chuckled the millionaire, "among other females. And he likes my money, and he and Harry are old friends. Those are three pretty good reasons on a beautiful day, even if he doesn't like golf. Oh, there they are . . ."

In the warm yellow sunshine, over a glass-topped table, the four men and Karen Gresham had cocktails.

"See here," said Dr. Stone suddenly. "Why don't you all stay up here and make an evening of it as my guests? We'll have dinner . . ."

"How sad," said Gresham. "I can't, Doctor, I have a business appointment in the city at seven."

"On a Sunday?" exclaimed Stone.

Karen said, "Always on a Sunday."

"Well, at least let's have luncheon," said Dr. Stone. "The chef extends himself for me. He needs a gallstone operation . . ."

They were back in the city, at the Gresham apartment, by six o'clock. Kurt Gresham went immediately to change, the others to freshen. They met again in the drawing room at six-thirty, Gresham in business suit and carying a brief case. "I should be back by nine or ten." He kissed his wife's cheek. "Have fun."

When he was gone, Karen Gresham said, "Now we'll narrow it down further. You two have fun. I'll attend to the servants." She smiled without prejudice, a sweet smile for the doctor, a sweet smile for the lawyer, and left the room.

"Attend to the servants?" said Dr. Harry Brown. "I don't get it, Tony."

"Do you have servants, Doctor?" asked Tony Mitchell solemnly.

"No servants, Counselor."

"So you don't get it. Servants need attending to."

"Like how?"

"Like do you know how many servants there are in this palatial dump?"

"I know there's a cook. And there's the Filipino houseman."

"Also m'lady's personal maid. Also a chambermaid."

"What attending do they need?"

"Quitting time is seven o'clock."

"You mean they don't live in?"

"They don't live in."

"But I know some of them have quarters here—"

"They stay over only when there's a formal dinner or a late party."

"That's an odd arrangement."

"Karen prefers it that way. They make her feel uncomfortable, especially when she's left alone here with them, as she so often is. You've got to remember that Karen wasn't to the manor born. She's only been Karen of Gresh for a couple of years. She's still not used to being married to a fat cat."

She came back in skin-tight green slacks and a low-cut green blouse.

She did a pirouette. "Like?" she said.

"Wow," said Tony Mitchell.

"Thank you, kind sir." She turned her smile on Harry. "No comment, Doctor?"

"I don't have Tony's line."

"Wouldn't fit you, kid," the lawyer grinned. "You're the deep-think, stern-type character the women go overboard for. They just ride along with me."

"Oh, I don't know," Karen teased. "There's *something* underneath that glossy veneer. What do you think, Harry?"

"I've never been able to dig deep enough to find out."

"Lay off the scalpel," said Tony.

"But I *am* inclined to think all that lightness is surface stuff. Underneath—" Harry smiled, "who knows? Whatever it is, our friend the counselor is mighty careful not to let it show."

"Will you kindly let me off the operating table?" Tony said. "Karen, I'm hungry."

She kissed each of them lightly on the lips. "Coming up. And while mamma whips up some Canadian bacon and scrambled eggs and gobs of toast, and daddy's off somewhere making another million, my two beaux can go into the dining room and set the table."

Later, they had Irish coffee in the drawing room, an inspiration of Tony Mitchell's.

"Delicious," said Karen Gresham. "What's the recipe, Counselor?"

"You start, not surprisingly, with good hot black coffee. Got that?"

42

"Yes, sir."

"Pour the steaming brew into the mug. Sugar to taste, stir well. Add a jigger of Irish whisky, stir likewise. Plop a voluptuous blob of thick whipped cream on top and do not stir at all. Lick and love. So how come you haven't mentioned Lynne Maxwell to us, Harry?"

Dr. Harrison Brown, sipping through the cool whipped cream, suddenly scalded his throat. He choked and set his cup down and fumbled for his cigarets.

"How come—*what?*"

"Baby, I've had experts trying to stall me. Hell, it's more than a month now and we haven't said a word, waiting for you to open up. There's a time limit on everything, pal. We're dying of curiosity."

"Lynne Maxwell," said Dr. Harrison Brown, smoking rapidly.

"It's at least four weeks since that cop came to us. Galivan. Good cop, Galivan. One of the best."

"Oh, you know him?" Harry said fatuously. Of course they must have been wondering. He had forgotten that Galivan had checked his alibi.

"Sure I know him. We work the same beat, except that we're on opposite sides of the street." Mitchell looked at his watch. "It's ten minutes to nine, buddy. I'm going to keep chattering for another five minutes to ease you up, then, wham! Cross-examination—" The lawyer was scrutinizing Harry with an anxiety that belied his tone. He said quietly, "Of course, Harry, you don't have to say a damned thing about it if you don't want to."

Karen had her knees crossed high, and her huge green eyes were intent over the coffee cup.

"Why haven't you told us, Harry?" Karen asked.

"Because I didn't think it was anyone's business but mine."

"Surly beggar, isn't he?" murmured Tony.

"Tony, I didn't want to drag you and Karen—"

"But you did, Harry, when you told Lieutenant Galivan about being with me and Karen that night. Didn't you think he was going to check your story out?"

"I know," said Harry ruefully. "I guess I just wanted to put the whole thing out of my mind. But how did you find out the girl's name? Did Galivan tell you?"

"Sure he did," said Tony Mitchell. "Remember, this is my kind of racket. When he asked for a written statement from this lady, this lady was smart enough to insist on consulting her lawyer. Imagine Galivan's surprise when her lawyer turned out to be the very gent he wanted to question along with her. Said lawyer wouldn't give his own statement, or authorize a statement from his client, the lady, unless he was informed what it was all about. So the lieutenant, for whom I've done a favor or two in my time, told me the story in confidence. Incidentally, Harry, if you're still worried, you don't have to be. You cleared al the way—except with us."

Harry Brown looked from Tony Mitchell to Karen Gresham and back again. Neither was smiling. "What's that supposed to mean?"

"Well, you were in trouble, weren't you?"

"Yes."

"And we're supposed to be your friends."

"Yes."

"And we were involved as your witness."

"Well—"

"Well, what, Harry? I'd have spoken to you immediately, but Karen didn't think we should pry. She felt you were disturbed about it, that in time you'd come around to talking to us."

Karen said, "I don't think, Tony, you should have brought it up."

"The hell with that," Mitchell said. "I'm his friend. And a lawyer. Harry, what's this all about?"

What could he say? What could he tell them but lies?

He felt trapped in his chair, and he stood up awkwardly and began to walk around on stiff legs.

"There's very little I can add to what Lieutenant Galivan told you, Tony—"

"Did he tell you the cause of death?"

"Overdose of heroin."

"That's right. Did you have anything to do with that, Harry?"

"Nothing."

"Well, was she a patient of yours, or what?"

"Not a patient."

"Then what?"

Harry did not look at Karen. "A . . . friend."

"She must have been a pretty good friend."

Karen said, "Don't, Tony."

"Yes," said Harry Brown. "She was. Once."

"All right. How'd she wind up in your apartment?"

Harry Brown filled his lungs and suddenly sat down

44

again. "Once she had a key to my place. It was a long time ago, it was over, I'd forgotten all about it. Then, that night, with an overdose in her, she came to my flat. Who knows why a drug addict does anything? Anyway she must have let herself in, and when I came home I found her there. Dead."

"What about the key?" the lawyer asked.

"It was in her hand. I took it."

"Why did you do a damned fool thing like that?"

"Actually I don't know. I remember feeling sort of numb. We can't predict, can we, how any of us will react to a totally unfamiliar crisis? I suppose I didn't want to be involved . . . intimately involved."

"But man, her body was there, right there in your apartment! How intimately involved can you get?"

"I did it, it was done."

"And the police?"

"I simply told them I didn't know who she was or how she'd got into the apartment. I knew I had nothing to do with it and I knew I could prove that I hadn't been home . . ."

The doorbell rang.

Harry sprang to his feet as though released and went to the door with Karen following him, and in the little entrance-foyer she threw her arms around him and clung.

"You're a liar," she whispered.

"Karen . . ." He could feel her body vibrating with passion and anxiety.

"You were lying about Lynne Maxwell. I know."

"Karen . . .'

"You're in terrible trouble, Harry. I know that, too. I love you."

And then she opened the door for her husband.

Five

Dr. Harrison Brown woke from a nightmare and could not sleep again. He touched the button of the night lamp and saw that it was three o'clock. He snapped off the light, got out of bed, pushed a window up another inch and stood in the darkness looking out. But then he became aware of the sweat-soaked pajamas. He lowered the Venetian blind, tilted it for privacy, put on the light again and went to the bathroom and took a shower.

Ever since that day he had talked with Kurt Gresham in Gresham's office, he had been clogged with fright—oppressive, a weight interior. But now it was out. It had been a fright of circumstance, of self and conscience, a fright of future, all internal: but now it was even worse, because it had to be examined for cause.

And Karen . . . she had known he was lying about Lynne Maxwell last night. How could she possibly have known? And what had she meant?—"You're in terrible trouble, Harry. I know that, too."

With Gresham home, the evening had turned gay. Friends had been telephoned and invited; there had been music and drinks, dancing and games—flirtations; and, of course, no further talk about Lynne Maxwell.

Harry Brown put on fresh pajamas and made coffee and drank it in the living room, chain-smoking all the while.

He had to admire them. They could turn it off and on at will; he could not. They laughed and joked, and played and danced, and flirted and told outrageous stories; but he knew that Tony Mitchell had concealed offense, and perhaps Karen also.

He had simply not been able to take them into his confidence. What could he have said to Karen—his mistress—about Lynne Maxwell? How could he have explained her presence in his apartment? A jealous woman would instantly jump to the false conclusion that Lynne Maxwell had a key to his apartment. At the worst, she would accuse him of a concurrent affair; at best, an old affair coming back to life. So he had hoped against hope that Galivan, in checking his alibi, would not reveal the cause of his inquiry. He had not confided in Tony because Tony was so close to Karen. And after his conversation with Gresham, he could not speak at all, for any reason. From now on, Dr. Harrison Brown saw with bitter clarity, dissembling and dishonesty would be the guidelines of his existence.

Unless he could get out of what he had got himself into.

The thirty thousand dollar note Kurt Gresham had paid off he could—perhaps again with Tony Mitchell's co-signature—reinstate at the bank, returning the money to Gresham. The twenty-five thousand dollar check he had accepted from the millionaire . . . there was nothing really wrong with that, Dr. Harry Brown told himself; many wealthy men with chronic illnesses paid their doctors fat annual retainers. . . .

But then he shook his head. It was no good. He wasn't getting the twenty-five G's for checking Gresham over regularly and taking prothrombins and fiddling with Dicumerol dosages and quinidine; he was getting it for being a monkey on a string. No, he'd have to give that back, too. Cut loose entirely.

But would Gresham let him go?

At this point Dr. Harry Brown stopped fantasizing. That old, ill, eccentric, highly intelligent purveyor of narcotics to rich and famous addicts could be expected to show the sympathy of a shark. He had let his latest medical puppet in on the secrets of his organization; he would hardly allow the puppet to jerk free. The incident of the dead girl was proof enough of that.

He's got me hooked, Dr. Harry Brown brooded. As hooked as any of his clients. And if I try to unhook myself, the best I can hope for is a little visit from Mr. Kurt Gresham's "security people," the worst, a one-way ticket to the bottom of the East River. Harry Brown had no answers.

Did Tony Mitchell have answers?

Tony Mitchell. Kurt Gresham's lawyer. Did Tony Mitchell have any idea of the real business of Gresham and

Company, Import and Export? Harry Brown doubted that, on the ground that Tony Mitchell was too smart to involve himself in criminal activities. But . . . was he? Bright, glib, surface-scintillating—how smart *was* Tony? True, he was a highly successful criminal lawyer with a good reputation; he had a large income, he lived high. But suppose it had been Gresham and Company that put Tony in orbit? Suppose Kurt Gresham had picked up his New York attorney as he had just picked up his New York doctor? It was possible, possible. After all, Tony was a criminal lawyer; wasn't that significant? The ordinary legal matters of a legitimate business surely called for an ordinary attorney. But the illegitimate matters . . .

Dr. Harry Brown slumped wretchedly.

Yes, it had developed into a gay party: Gresham, cordial; Tony, jaunty; Karen, charming. They could turn it off and on: only Dr. Harrison Brown had been the morose outsider. And there had been something else—Tony flirting openly with Karen under the round and colorless eyes of the permissive old husband. Harry Brown had felt the prick of jealousy. Was there something between Karen and Tony? Had there ever been? Certainly they made a plausible pair—handsome Tony, beautiful Karen, both clever, sophisticated, debonair, enchanting. Where in hell did Dr. Harry Brown fit in?—Dr. Brown the plodder, the close-mouthed, the deep-think character . . . the ambitious stooge?

Dr. Brown got up and went to his medicine cabinet. He swallowed a sleeping pill and crawled into bed.

He slept fitfully, with more nightmares.

In a nightmare, he heard her.

"You're in terrible trouble, Harry. I know that, too. I love you."

Six

He called her from his apartment at eleven o'clock; from his office at twelve o'clock; and at two; and at four. Each time he was told that she was not at home, and each time he left a message for her to call back.

It had been, for him, a busy day. Six patients, all routine office calls, no house calls. He had not left his office; he had even sent out for his lunch.

Now at a quarter past four the phone shrilled and he seized it. But it was not Karen Gresham. It was, incredibly, a familiar booming baritone.

"Harry? Peter Gross."

"Dr. Gross!"

"How are you, Harry?"

"Never mind how I am." Suddenly he felt ashamed. "How are *you*?"

"Busy, busy. Working hard?"

"Not too."

"Doing what?"

"Practicing medicine."

"G.P.?"

"G.P."

"That's a goddam shame. I've got nothing against the G.P., only you fiddling around with general practice is like Isaac Stern getting a job playing in a Hungarian cabaret. Are you getting rich, Harry?"

"No, Doctor."

"So you don't even have that excuse. Has Alf Stone talked with you yet?"

"He's dropping in tomorrow."

"Well, you listen to him, Harry. I believe it's important for you. Do you hear me?"

"Yes, sir."

"Do you remember Lewis Blanchette?"

49

"Of course." Dr. Lewis Blanchette, before his retirement, had been one of the most famous surgeons in the United States, a giant of surgical techniques.

"Do you know what's happened to Lewis?"

"Last I heard, he'd retired."

"From private practice only. He's a mere sixty. In his prime. You know what he's doing now, Harry?"

"No, sir."

"He's chief of surgery at Taugus Institute." There was a pause and then Dr. Peter Gross said, "I want you to listen carefully to Alfred Stone, Harry. As a favor to yourself." Dr. Gross characteristically hung up without a goodbye.

Dr. Harrison Brown leaned back in his new-smelling leather swivel chair. The office was dim and cool with shadows, the sunlight diffused and diminished against the drawn blinds. Dr. Peter Gross knew him well and fondly. He remembered their long evenings at Gross's home on campus, talking about his ambitions, his needs. Gross had urged upon him a career in surgery. "You have the nerves, Harry, the hands . . ." But to become a surgeon took long years of apprenticeship. He did not have the time; he wanted to get rich quick; it was a need, a sickness. Harry had been honest with the old man and Gross had been wrathfully patient and understanding; they had parted with affection.

The phone rang again.

"Harry?" Karen. At last.

"I've been calling you—"

"I know. But I've been with Kurt all day. I'm with him now. Sneaked off to call."

"I want to see you."

"And I want to see you."

"Tonight?"

"Impossible."

"Then when?"

"Tomorrow. Tomorrow he's going to Philadelphia for a couple of days. I'll be free to spend as much time with you as you like."

"How about as much time as *you* like?"

"Harry, what's the matter?"

"I'm in trouble. Don't you remember telling me?"

"Oh." Quietly she said, "I didn't realize you were referring to that. We'll talk about it tomorrow."

"What time? Where?"

"Pick me up at home at eight o'clock. Bring the car."

"All right."

"I can't talk any more now, darling."

"Okay."

"Love you."

"Okay."

She hung up.

He heard the outside buzzer. His receptionist announced a patient through the intercom. It was a woman, a repeater, a hypochondriac who was developing a dependence on him. He took a long time with her, soothing, reassuring, prescribing a placebo. After that, there were no patients, no calls, no anything. His receptionist went off and his part-time evening girl came on, and she did her nails while he read medical journals until seven. At seven-ten, while he was washing up—the girl was already gone—he heard the buzzer. Wiping his hands on the way, he opened the door to Tony Mitchell.

"Hi, buddy-boy," said Tony. "Figured you'd still be around. Had to see a client up in this neighborhood. Hungry?"

"I could do with a bite."

"Always the enthusiast. My God, Harry, don't you ever smile?"

"When there's something to smile about."

"Finish your ablutions." He strolled after Harry, tall and elegant in slim-trousered, thin-striped brown tropical worsted and a brown leghorn with a rakish ribbon. Tanned, smooth-shaven, clean-jawed, clear-eyed, he looked like a model for *Esquire*.

Dr. Harrison Brown looked his friend over as he got into his jacket. "You're pretty well satisfied with life, aren't you, Tony?"

"Why shouldn't I be? I've got everything I want—"

Dr. Brown said sharply, "Let's start with some cocktails."

Over martinis at a jammed bar in a posh little bistro off Fifth Avenue, Tony Mitchell said, "How about eating Italian?"

"I don't care."

"I know a little place—"

"You know all the little places."

"Picking on me today, baby? Getting even for yesterday?"

Harry frowned. "Yesterday?"

"Last night. Lynne Maxwell."

"Cut," Harry said.

"For the time being. We'll pick it up later."

"Where's your little place?"

"Down your neck of the woods. A jewel of a joint."

The place was in an old Village brownstone. They walked down four steps and through a long corridor, and into a big quiet room. It was plain, well-lighted, uncrowded, uncluttered, with large tables and booths, and plenty of leg-room. The food was North Italian, not too hot, delicious.

"This *is* good," Harry said.

"Praise from Harry Brown! Now *that's* something."

"What's it called?"

"I never saw a name, but we call it Giobbe's, because Giobbe—Job—owns it. Giobbe's the little guy with the bushy blond hair who seated us. It's a family operation. His mother and father and mother-in-law and father-in-law are all in the kitchen. The waiters are either brothers or cousins or uncles. So you want to talk about Lynne Maxwell?"

"No."

The waiter brought espresso coffee still brewing in the pot. "Let him drip a little bit yet," he said and went away. Tony said, "Would you rather talk about a thirty-thousand dollar loan that's been paid in full?"

Another waiter came over and removed the plates and brushed the crumbs from the table. There was still wine in the Chianti bottle, and he left the bottle and wine glasses. Harry poured himself some more wine.

Tony said, with no trace of banter, "What in hell's wrong with you lately?"

"What symptoms have I displayed, Doctor Mitchell?" Harry polished off the contents of his glass and reached for the bottle again.

"You've been living in a world of your own. You think a Lynne Maxwell thing disappears into thin air just because you don't talk about it? A big loan gets itself paid off and you don't say one damned word. I was co-maker on that loan, baby, remember? The bank notifies me that it's suddenly all paid up. I'm curious, so I go over for a little chit-chat. Seems it was paid in cash, interest and all, and the note picked up. Didn't you think I'd learn about it?"

"Well . . ." Harry drank all the wine in the glass. "There

52

was a man, see, who once owed my father a lot of money and never paid up. This man had been in to see me a few times and, well, I told him about the loan and something of my problems. Seems he'd made a pile—anyway, conscience or something made him pay off the note. I should have explained, Tony, but—hell, I've been in turmoil . . ."

Tony Mitchell's eyes were long and oval-shaped, so black that the pupils merged with the irises. They were opaque and gave off a sheen that told nothing. "What man, Harry?" he asked softly.

"I'd rather not say."

Tony tapped the top of the espresso pot. The sound of the dripping had stopped. "Check," he said, and smiled; and then he said, "And the turmoil? Karen?"

Harry did not reply.

Tony poured the steaming brew into their cups. "Okay. With a guy like you especially, I dig that. The guilt, the whole bit. Interrogation closed. You're a close-mouthed bastard, but just remember I'm a friend. For in case."

"Pot calling the kettle black."

"Come again?" Tony's chin tilted up.

"I'm closed-mouthed and you're loquacious, a real garrulous guy. But what comes out? Nothing."

"You're losing me, baby."

"There's Karen."

"So?"

"And there's Karen's husband."

"So?"

"You know them a lot longer than I do."

"So? So?"

"You know what you've told me about them?"

"What?"

"Nothing, that's what. A lot of nothing, Tony."

Tony sipped his espresso, frowning. "You worried about the old man?"

"Should I be?" Harry looked straight at him.

"No." Tony Mitchell returned the look steadily.

"Why not?"

"Because he's a smart old man. Because he's a smart old man married to a young wife. So he's permissive. He lets her run. He lets her enjoy. He'll never interfere unless it gets wide open, a scandal."

"How do you know?"

"I know the guy."

"How well?"

"Well."

"How long, Tony?"

"Ten years."

"How long do you know *her*?"

"About three. I met her when she was managing a night club in Philly."

"Managing a night club?" Harry gripped the cup.

"She never told you?"

"I never asked."

"Well, then ask. You don't have to pump me about her. But if you're worried about the old man, don't."

Harry lit a cigaret, carefully. "Tony. Would you say Kurt could be . . . dangerous?"

The black eyes looked curious. "Dangerous?"

"Well, I'm . . . going with Karen." What a stupid, callow way to say it. Especially since he had not meant that at all.

"I told you, Harry, he's permissive. Yes, if you crossed him I think he'd be dangerous. But a little adultery . . . I think he thinks she's entitled. Wide open, no. Discreet, yes. He knows she'll always come home to Big Daddy."

Harry inhaled cigaret smoke. "Where does he go?"

"What?"

"Every Monday, Wednesday, Friday and Sunday evening. For a couple of hours. Without fail."

"With fail. If he's out of town, he doesn't go."

"But where?"

"Business."

"Every Monday, Wednesday, Friday—even Sunday?"

"*His* business."

"But you're his lawyer—"

"That's right. Not his partner."

"You never asked?"

"Why should I ask?"

"How'd you meet him originally, Tony?"

"As a client."

"Ten years ago?"

"Ten years ago, as a client."

Harry drank coffee. He rubbed out his cigaret. "You're a criminal lawyer."

"That I am."

"Is Gresham a criminal?"

Tony's white teeth flashed in a smile. "That's a phony syllogism, pal. I'm a criminal lawyer. I have clients. Therefore, all my clients are criminals. Nonsense." Now Tony lit a cigaret. "As a matter of fact, I did meet him through one of my criminal-type clients. They guy was a broker who'd got into trouble with SEC. They prosecuted, and I got him off. Gresham had done business with this guy, and he admired the job I did. So he retained me on certain civil matters, and that's how I became his lawyer—on civil matters, pal, not criminal. It's a pleasure to hear you talk, even if all you're doing is asking questions. Anything else, Mr. District Attorney?"

"I am sorry," said Harry.

"Sorry? For what?"

"For pushing."

"Push any time, bud. It's good finding out you're alive."

"You wish something?" said the waiter.

"Plenty," said Dr. Harrison Brown. "But I don't think I can get it here."

"We'll settle," smiled Tony Mitchell, "for another pot of espresso."

Seven

On Tuesday there were five patients. It was a hot day; summer had come early to New York, and he was thankful for the quiet, expensive air conditioning of his office. Between patients he sat with his ankles crossed and wondered what his receptionist thought about her employer's "practice." At twelve-thirty, Dr. Stone telephoned to apologize and request postponement of their meeting to seven P.M. Harry readily agreed; only when he had hung up did he remember his appointment with Karen for eight o'clock. He decided that he would tell the good doctor he had to make a house call at eight. He remembered, guiltily, Peter Gross's admonition to "listen" to Dr. Stone. Hell, he thought, I can listen fast. He wondered what Dr. Stone could possibly want to talk to him about, and shrugged.

Promptly at two o'clock he left his office, telling his receptionist that he could not possibly be back before four-thirty. "If anybody calls," he said, "don't make any appointment before half-past four."

"Yes, Doctor," she said.

What a farce, he thought.

He went out, to nowhere.

He had lunch of roast beef, spinach and potatoes at the Automat. Tony Mitchell wouldn't be caught dead in the Automat. The hell with Tony Mitchell.

Afterward, he walked over to his bank and cashed a check for two hundred dollars. He could never predict how much an evening with Karen would cost him; she was an expensive date. Then he strolled to Central Park and sat on a bench in the sun and thought about Kurt Gresham and Karen and Tony Mitchell. And himself.

What had he learned last night about his pal Tony? What actually had he hoped to learn? Two things: whether

Mitchell knew of Gresham's narcotics business; and, if so, was he party to any of it? Dr. Brown laughed, in the sun, on the bench. Lies beget lies: he was now even lying to himself. There had been a much more important question in his mind last night: was there, or had there ever been, anything between Tony and Karen?

And what had he learned? Nothing.

Perhaps because there was nothing to learn.

It was quite possible that in ten years Tony had learned nothing of Gresham's real business, if, as he claimed, he had been handling ordinary civil matters arising out of Gresham's legitimate import-export business. On the other hand, Gresham's narcotics organization, with its complex of trusted key people, would certainly have to include lawyers. Was Tony one of them? If so, his coming to the rescue—introducing his old friend Dr. Brown to the Greshams, and everything that followed—made Mitchell Gresham's recruiter. That meant that Tony knew the whole story of his involvement with Gresham and was deliberately playing dumb.

So Mitchell wasn't involved, or he was involved. There was no way of telling.

Harry Brown sighed.

Tony and Karen?

Tony said he had known her for three years, which meant since before her marriage to Gresham . . . had met her *while she was managing a night club in Philadelphia.*

Karen had never mentioned that. Now that Dr. Harrison Brown came to think of it, his ladylove had never mentioned a word about her background.

A night club in Philadelphia! Where Kurt Gresham owned several clubs! And then, not long afterward, Gresham married her.

Coincidence? Dr. Brown squirmed and perspired on his bench in Central Park.

It was possible. It was even likely, unless a man were a fool. It was likely, considering subsequent events, that the Philadelphia night club Karen had been managing was a night club owned by Kurt Gresham. And if that were so . . .

Dr. Brown got up from the bench and began to walk fast in the hot sunshine. It was as if he were trying to escape from the logic of his own thoughts. But there was no escape. Gresham had told him that the managers of his night clubs were key pieces in the machinery of his narcotics trade. So Karen must have been one of them. First as an employee, then as Gresham's wife—why, she must know as much about Gresham's dope operation as the old man did! Was that why she had said to him on Sunday night, "You're in terrible trouble, Harry. I know that, too. I love you"?

He could feel the sweat coursing down his legs. Tonight. Tonight he would . . .

Dr. Alfred McGee Stone came promptly at seven. "I want to apologize again . . ." Dr. Stone began.

"Please, Doctor, it's all right," Harry said as he led the way to his consultation room. "If anyone should apologize, it's I. I find I have an important consultation at a patient's home at eight o'clock; I'll have to leave at seven-thirty. It's only just come up, or I'd have called you."

"Then I'll be brief," Dr. Stone said. "This is only an exploratory talk, anyway." He patted his sunburned bald head with a handkerchief, settled his rimless glasses high on the bridge of his nose and smiled. "I believe you know of my connection with Taugus Institute?"

"Of course, Doctor. You're the director."

"Do you know anything about the Institute?"

"Not much."

"It's a private charitable institution, well endowed. The original grant of land, buildings and equipment came as a bequest from Anders Johnson when he died; Anders Johnson, Senior, the multimillionaire. We receive periodic grants from others, private individuals as well as foundations. We have the most advanced equipment and our staff is superlative. We have a large staff in permanent residence—physicians, surgeons and nurses besides the usual institutional help—and then there are those who contribute their services part time. The grounds are beautiful, the food is excellent, and there's a special residential area of lovely cottages for the permanent staff. So much for the over-all layout, Dr. Brown."

Dr. Brown glanced furtively at the clock on the wall.

"Our charities are for the middle-income groups exclusively."

"Beg pardon?" Harry said.

"Not for the poor, not for the rich."

"For the middle income? *Charities?*"

Dr. Stone smiled. "A poor word. Our services, then. You, as a doctor, know very well that those who suffer most financially in the event of serious illness are people of middle income. The indigent can get the best treatment from the most skilled physicians without charge at the public hospitals. The rich, of course, can afford to pay for the most protracted illness. But for the middle-income group serious illness is usually a disaster. That's what the Taugus Institute is geared to prevent. It's the first institution of its kind, the first to provide unlimited services without charge beyond a reasonable—I might say nominal —fee, paid by the patient on acceptance."

"But," Harry said, " 'middle income' is a pretty elastic term. What criteria do you use in your selections, Dr. Stone?"

"The family physician makes an application to Institute for the patient, and our investigators go to work. The type and degree of illness are balanced against the savings and income of the family; and upon the report of our investigators, we accept or reject. And now, if you please, Dr. Brown, *my* first question. Are you in sympathy with the project? I may as well warn you that we have been called everything from proponents of socialized medicine to outright Communists—which, by the way, old Anders Johnson foresaw, to his considerable amusement. He was one of the world's most rugged individualists. How do you feel about it?"

Harry said slowly, "Suppose I were to say I'm sympathetic to the idea. Let me be blunt, Doctor. What's the point?"

Dr. Stone looked at him keenly. "Do you know who our chief of surgery is?"

"Dr. Lewis Blanchette. Dr. Gross told me."

"Gross has talked to you?" exclaimed Dr. Stone.

"He called me to say I was to listen to you."

"The old devil." Stone laughed. "Born manipulator. Well, Lewis Blanchette wants a permanent assistant-in-residence, to work directly under him. A young man. I don't have to tell you what that would mean professionally."

"Yes?" Harry Brown said.

"Blanchette and Gross have been lifelong friends. It seems that Peter Gross has recommended you to Blanchette for the post. How does it strike you? By the way, you'd have till the first of the year to get your affairs in order. Well, Doctor?"

"I'll think about it." Harry said.

Dr. Stone's lips tightened. He pushed his glasses excitedly up on his nose. "Are you rejecting the offer just like that? Out of hand?"

"I said I'd think about it, Dr. Stone. I didn't say I'm turning it down."

"Doctor, I've been an administrator for a long time now. I can recognize a turndown when I hear it. I think, in all justice to yourself, you ought to listen to the terms, the conditions, a quick rundown of the pros and cons."

"Of course, Doctor." Harry glanced at the clock again. Dr. Stone noticed, and his tone took on an edge.

"First, pro. A young surgeon, working in close daily contact with Dr. Lewis Blanchette, would receive the finest training in the world. Agreed?"

"Yes."

"Not only training, but reputation. Agreed?"

"Yes."

"Now the cons. First, if you're acceptable to Dr. Blanchette, you'll be bound by contract."

"For how long?"

"Seven years. At the end of seven years you may leave. We would hope you would not, that you'd stay on. However, the choice would be yours, Dr. Brown."

'After seven years," said Dr. Brown. "And at what salary, Dr. Stone?"

"Well, you must remember we're financed very largely by endowments," the bald doctor said rather quickly. "Ten thousand a year."

Harry suppressed a wry smile. A fine way to get rich.

"That is, to start," Dr. Stone went on. "There'd be annual increases—you'd be making fifteen thousand at the end of the seven years. But it wouldn't cost you anything for rent or food—you'd have one of the cottages, and if you married you'd be given larger quarters. And, of course, fringe benefits—six weeks' vacation, pension plan, sick leave and all the rest of it. Oh, and I'd like to add one thing more, Dr. Brown."

Smooth operator, Harry thought. "Yes, Doctor?" he asked politely.

"We would hope, as I said, that you'd remain with us. But if you didn't, let me point out that seven years at the Institute, working with Lewis Blanchette, would make you,

If it's money you're interested in—" smooth and perceptive, Harry thought; or else old Gross has armed him, "you'd be a rich man in short order. Blanchette's associate for seven years would have the most widely known and respected reputation, and I don't have to tell you what a lucrative field surgery is for a top man. Sorry if I sound crass, but as long as I am giving you the picture ... No offense, Dr. Brown?"

"No offense," said Dr. Brown with a straight face.

Seven years ... By that time, he thought, he would be close to forty.

Who in hell needs it when you're old? I want it *now*. Seven years tied down by contract. For ten thousand a year to a maximum of fifteen. With "benefits." He felt like saying, Dr. Stone, right now I have from one patient— *one* patient—a retainer of twenty-five thousand dollars a year. I'm launched, I'm on my way. By the time I'm forty I'll have it all, all!

Or will I? thought Dr. Harrison Brown. Maybe I'll be in jail. Or dead ...

He passed a hand over his forehead.

"Something?" said Dr. Stone.

"Headache," said Dr. Brown.

"I haven't let up on you, have I?" Dr. Stone rose, and Dr. Brown rose with him. "May I come again? Some Tuesday when I'm in town?"

"Please do, Doctor."

"And you'll give some thought to this?"

"Naturally."

"I know I threw in a great deal all at once. Talk to Gross. If you wish, I'll arrange an appointment for you with Blanchette."

"I'll think about it, Dr. Stone. And thank you."

They shook hands, and Harry let him out and locked the door behind him.

He undressed, showered, shaved, put on fresh clothes, locked the office, jumped into his car and drove blindly through the humid streets to Park Avenue. At five minutes after eight he pulled into the curb near the canopy of the Greshams' apartment building. He was about to turn his keys over to the doorman when he saw her in the lobby. Waiting.

She waved.

He waved.

She came out to him.

Eight

She wore a white linen dress: short sleeveless; white needle-heeled pumps; no stockings; she carried a white linen jacket and a small white purse.

Her long legs and bare arms were the color of warm fresh toast. With her copper hair pulled back in a ponytail, with just a touch of pink on her lips and no other make-up, she looked very young.

The dress was tight, and she tugged at the skirt in getting into his car. He caught a flash of brown thigh and felt his throat thicken and his heart pound and a stirring in his groin. Then she was sitting beside him, close, pulling at the skirt, lips parted.

"Hi." She had a deep voice, intimate, hardly more than a whisper.

"Hi," he said. "Hungry?"

"Starved."

"Me, too. Where would you like to eat?"

"Not Giobbe's," she said.

He looked at her, startled.

She laughed. "Tony phoned me today," she said.

"Then you know the place."

"Of course. You know Tony. Always discovering places, and what Tony discovers Tony gives a real workout. Yes, darling, I've been to Giobbe's. I've been, and been, and been."

The car was cruising up Park Avenue. "Where, then?"

"Up and out," she said. "Up and out and far away, where it's cool. In the country. I want to eat with you, drink with you, dance with you *and* sleep with you. I want all night with you tonight. I'm not going back home."

"Westchester?" he said. "Connecticut?"

"I know what. Jersey. There's a place—Heavenly Grotto. Hellish name, but a heavenly place. Good music, good décor, good food, good candlelight. Kurt took me there once before we were married. There's a heavenly motel nearby, too. Kurt and I stayed there in separate cabins. Tonight, one cabin."

Did she expect him to believe that? "Do you know how to go?" he asked.

"Cross the George Washington Bridge. I'll direct you from there. God, I've been longing for this. It's so damned hot. The weather's been beastly."

"Yes."

"Cool, where we're going. Cool and delicious."

He made a left turn and drove across the park and over to the West Side Highway. Already it was cooler in the breeze coming from the Hudson. They could see the bridge in the distance, thin as a lavaliere displayed in space.

"Miss me?" she said. "Since Sunday?"

"Yes."

"And before Sunday? Miss being alone with me?"

"Yes."

"Like my idea?"

"What idea?"

"Heavenly Grotto, and the Golden Cave."

"Golden Cave?"

"That's the name of the motel." She giggled. "Isn't that the craziest name for a motel?"

"I wish I'd known," he said.

"Known what?"

"Motel."

"Look, my laconic lover, you'll have to stop being cryptic. You wish you'd known *what* about the motel?"

"That we were going to stay overnight."

"Why?"

"I'd have brought a change of clothing, a bag, something."

"Oh, now please, Doctor, you're not preparing for surgery. This is off the cuff, an impulse, fun! How come you're so romantic in bed, but with your feet on the ground you're nowhere? How come?"

"Cut," he said.

"You won't be wearing your clothes much, anyway, sweetheart. Mostly they'll be hanging. We'll check in first at the Golden Cave, mister and missus, and freshen up; then we'll go eat and dance and drink and talk; then we'll go back to the cavelet and hang up our clothes and let 'em hang. Love me, lover?"

"Yes."

"That's why my servants don't sleep in."

"What?" he said. "What?"

"Servants who sleep in know when the lady of the house sleeps out."

"Yes," he said, and he thought: You've been married for two years, and you know me for four or five months; with whom were you sleeping out before me, my love? "We've got a lot to talk about tonight," he said.

"You bet," Karen said cheerfully. She opened her purse and took two cigarets from a pack and lit both, putting one between his lips.

She moved away from him, snuggled down, stretched her legs, laid her head on the back rest and half-closed her eyes.

They smoked in silence until they crossed the bridge.

The Golden Cave was gold; all the cabins were gold with white roofs. Harry parked in front of the office and went in and signed the register: Mr. and Mrs. Harrison Brown.

"How long you staying?" asked the clerk. He was a small, neat, sunburned man.

"Overnight."

"That'll be thirteen dollars."

Harry paid.

"Cabin 4, this way, please," said the man. Outside he said, "Park in front of the cabin. I'll walk."

He walked. Harry drove. Karen sat lazily.

In Cabin 4 the sunburned man said, "Anything you want—soft drink, cigarets, telephone—just ask at the office. Somebody's there all night. Check-out time is tomorrow morning, eleven o'clock. Here's your key. Thank you very much. Come again."

Alone, they freshened up. They did not touch each other. They talked about the beautiful night, the comforts of the spic-and-span cabin.

They drove over to the Heavenly Grotto, which was not a grotto but a two-story stone building with a purple neon sign outside. The candlelit restaurant was a maze of small rooms. The tables were covered with lavender tablecloths; there was a dance floor and a string orchestra and, rimming the room, a balcony with a wrought-iron grille. The place was crowded with well-dressed diners.

The white-jacketed *maître d'* immediately said, "There's more privacy in the booths on the balcony, sir."

"Balcony," Harry said. Were they that obvious?

He led them toward the steep wrought-iron stairway. "The captain will take over. His name is Danny."

"Thank you," Harry said.

The stairway was narrow, and Karen preceded him. The *maître d'* remained at the foot of the stairs; Harry knew without glancing back that the man was admiring Karen's legs. And why not? he thought. She has beautiful legs. She's a beautiful woman. Let him enjoy himself. For him it's free.

The upstairs captain led them to a booth, lit new candles and left them in the lavender glow. A waiter came with lavender menus. "Drinks first?"

"Gimlet," Karen said. "Double."

"Two doubles," Harry said.

The waiter went away. The music was soft and professional. The place was clean, airy, not noisy. Even before the drink came, Harry felt himself starting to relax. After the drink, he was in complete command.

The waiter came again. "Do you wish to order now?"

"No," Karen said. She pushed aside the menus. "I'll have another gimlet."

"Double again?" said the waiter.

"Double," Karen said.

Harry nodded.

They drank more slowly this time. Their knees were touching. "All right, Karen, let's have it," Harry said.

"What?" Karen said.

" 'You're in terrible trouble, Harry.' " He mimicked her voice and intonation.

"Oh, that," she said.

"That," he said.

"I'll have to start from way back."

"Go ahead."

"Would you rather eat first?"

"There's plenty of time."

"Funny. A drink is supposed to stimulate the appetite."

"Maybe two drinks kills it."

"How about four?"

"Four?"

"Actually, darling, we're on our fourth. Doubles."

65

"Karen, you're stalling."

"You bet I am."

"Why?"

"Trouble isn't pleasant. You're in a lot of it. I'm in trouble, too, but not so much, and anyway, I'm used to it." She smiled crookedly. "I've been stalling for weeks now."

"Well, you can stop right now. What did you mean, Karen?"

She put down the gimlet and reached for a cigaret. He held a match to it.

"Thanks, darling. Well, it starts with a kid going to college in Los Angeles. Me. Father dead, mother working as a waitress. She was an old woman; it had been a late marriage, I was an only child. Well, I was graduated with a B.A. from U.C.L.A. Now what in hell does a girl do with a Bachelor of Arts degree?"

"Any number of things."

"All of them piddling."

"What did you want?"

"Money. Real money, and the sooner the better."

It was Dr. Harry Brown's turn to smile crookedly.

"We were always just scraping along. Even as a kid I dreamed of living easy and rich, à la Hollywood pipe dreams. How does a girl with a Bachelor of Arts degree make a pipe dream come true? Get right up there in the big money?"

"She marries it, if she's pretty enough."

"Do you think I'm pretty enough?"

"You're beautiful," he said bitterly.

"I went where the money was. I'd taken stenography and typing, and I got good secretarial jobs in big outfits, with big people. I kept looking for a rich husband, and I struck out. The loaded ones were either already married or gunshy; they all wanted to sleep with me, but without benefit of clergy. Then my mother died. I chucked the whole secretarial bit and became a dancer."

"Dancer?"

"A stripper."

"You?" Harry stared at her. "Wasn't that a waste?"

"Look, Junior. My high I.Q. and my B.A. degree found no customers. I took inventory and decided I had more negotiable assets—what you lechers call a luscious hunk of stuff. And I was twenty-five by then, and time was awastin'."

"No love?"

"Pardon?"

"Twenty-five, and you hadn't fallen in love?"

"I thought so, two or three times. They turned out to be jerks. I can't stand a jerk. I've never been in love."

"Never?"

"Until you, of course, darling." She leaned over and smiled and squeezed his hand.

After a moment Harry withdrew his hand to light a cigaret. "So you were twenty-five and you became a stripper."

"With my equipment it was the easiest way in. There's a lot of money in knowing how to take your clothes off. It's an art. In fact, there are schools that teach it."

"I didn't know that," said Dr. Brown. "There's a lot I don't know."

"Well, there are. I had some money saved, and I went to the best school I could find."

"And you learned how to take your clothes off."

She laughed. "There's more to it than *that*. And if you're any good, they place you after graduation. I was good and they placed me. I did the whole wheel."

"Wheel?"

"Los Angeles, San Francisco, Reno, Vegas, New Orleans, Detroit, Chicago, Dallas, Houston, Miami, New York, Philly. The strip circuit. I earned three, four hundred a week, which gave me the kind of clothes I wanted. And I met well-heeled Johns and hooked them for cars, apartments, furs, jewels, bank accounts—while all the time I kept my line out for the one big fish with the ring in his nose. Pardon me if I brag a little, darling. There were few strippers around with my equipment. I'm not talking about merely body—I'm talking about the I.Q. and the degree, too. I was really a rarity in the profession. A gal who could discuss Renaisance painting and the Angry Young Men as well as bump and grind. Oh, I knocked around, and got knocked around—an educated bum, you might say. But I was a lady, and they all knew it."

She was silent for a while, and Harry beckoned the waiter. "Another round," he said. "Make these singles. Go on," he said to Karen.

"I found myself working in a Philadelphia club. A man named Kurt Gresham showed a great interest in me—he was there very often. I didn't find out he owned the joint till a long time later." She laughed again. "He was big,

67

the kind of fish I'd dreamed about, a millionaire. He'd obviously gone overboard for the whole woman—the body, the face, the youth; later I found out that he checked out my background, U.C.L.A. the B.A., everything. I played him very cool, darling; he got the stiff arm all the way. And he flipped. Grabbed hook, line and sinker."

She picked up the fresh gimlet. "My luck had finally turned. But I knew I had to play Kurt carefully, or he'd get away. He got nowhere with me sexually. I hooked him in the head, where he lived."

Harry sipped his drink very slowly. He did not want to get drunk. Not yet, anyway.

"He was more than twice my age," Karen murmured, "and three times married—divorced from his first wife; the other two had died. The more he pitched, the more reserved I got. When he was hot, I was cool. The more physical he got, the more intellectual I got. I think it was the brains that finally landed him. He pulled me off the floor and made me assistant manager of the club. I played along; the salary was good; I knew my fish was hooked and having his run. And then he propositioned me."

"With what?"

She looked at him coolly. "You know damned well with what."

"I do?"

"Coyness doesn't become you, you hairy ape. We're letting our hair down now, my love."

"We are?"

"Yes," she snapped. "For our mutual protection."

Harry finished his drink. He was fighting the happy feeling. "So?" he said.

"Bit by bit, he sounded me out. Oh, I know him now. He'd done all the checking; he knew money was my weakness. I was his pigeon—just as *you* are, Harry. Of course, I had one advantage you and the other pigeons don't have. He wanted to use me, as he's now using you, but he was also in love with me. Finally, he let me in on the whole story, and I was either in or out. Do you know what out means with Kurt, Harry?"

"What?"

"It means you're dead." When he did not reply, Karen said, "Where was I?"

"You had the whole story. You were propositioned."

"He knew—don't ever underestimate him, Kurt is a

genius—he knew with me, just as he knew with you, that I wouldn't refuse him. I didn't."

"You became manager of the club." He was tearing a cigaret butt to shreds.

"With all the duties appertaining thereto. I state here and now that in the entire illustrious career of Kurt Gresham, I have the unique distinction of having been the only lady-manager of any of his night clubs. My salary was a thousand bucks a week *cum* bonus. I hadn't yet gaffed my fish, but I had him banging his snout against the boat. When I got him, it was on my terms."

"What terms?"

"I'm hungry now, Harry."

"Oh. A cliff hanger."

"The next episode will concern you. But you'd better eat first, my love."

He shrugged and tried to catch the waiter's eye.

"I want us to eat, and I want us to dance, and I want us to get just a little bit drunk. We've got all night."

Nine

Karen Gresham, back in Cabin 4 at the Golden Cave, said to Dr. Harry Brown, "You go ask, my love. I'm parched."

"Me, I'm also parched, my love."

"So go ask."

"Sure," said Dr. Harry Brown. "What've I got to lose?" He was having a little trouble with his final consonants.

He went out of the cabin and weaved to OFFICE. The sunburned man was sitting soberly in an easy chair, reading a newspaper.

"Hi," said Harry.

"Hi," said the man.

"Can I buy some booze?" said Harry.

"Booze, Doctor?" He folded the paper and laid it on the arm of the chair, showing yellow dentures.

"Doctor?" said Harry Brown.

"MD plates on the car," explained the clerk. "You said booze, Doctor?"

"That's what I said," said the doctor.

"Booze," said the clerk, rising, "is located eight miles due north, which is where you'll find the nearest package store. Which figures to be closed by now."

"Which is why I'm asking you."

"Well, I like a snort once in a while, Doctor, so I guess you'd have to figure I have booze, yes."

"Vodka, maybe?"

"So happens I do have vodka, Doctor."

"Sell me a bottle."

"Now you know better'n that, Doctor. That's illegal."

"I'll tell you what," said the doctor. "As you observed, I am a doctor. Doctor, medicine. I prescribed vodka. For myself. What do you say, friend? How much for a bottle of vodka medicine?"

"Can't sell without a license, Doctor," said the clerk, showing pulpy gums. "But I could give you some."

"Ah."

"If you buy what goes along with it."

"Limes?"

"I have better than limes, Doctor. Bottle of Rose's Lime Juice. Imported from England. I also have ice cubes."

"Could I buy the bottle of Rose's Lime Juice and the ice cubes?"

"Sure. That's legal. But, this time of night, expensive."

"And would you then donate the bottle of vodka?"

"I have nothing but respect for doctors, Doctor. I'd like you to accept it as a token of my respect."

"For how much?"

"For thirty bucks."

"Thirty bucks!"

"They're top-quality ice cubes, Doctor."

"Better be," said the doctor. He produced his wallet, and the sunburned man produced his token of respect.

Her dress was hung away. She was wearing bra and briefs and shoes, and the catch was off the ponytail; her massed hair surrounded her face like a sunset. She took the tray from Harry and said, "You have persuasive ways, don't you?"

"Thirty bucks," Harry said. He took off his jacket.

"Even so, he doesn't know you from Adam. You could be an inspector or something."

"He saw the New York MD plates." He ripped off his tie and his shirt. "Do you have a comb?"

She gave him a comb from her handbag. He went to the lavatory and washed with cold water and combed his hair. When he came back, the gimlets were ready. They clinked glasses.

"To us," Karen smiled. There was excitement in her eyes.

"Us," he said.

The room was warm. He opened the windows and tilted the blinds, transferred his cigarets and matches from his jacket to his trousers. Then he sat down with his drink on the shiny plastic-covered armchair. She stretched out on the bed. The squeak made her laugh.

"A squeaky bed in a motel. Am I a pervert, darling? The idea tickles me." She laughed again, drank thirstily, and then there was no more laughter. "You parked there for the night, O hairy one?"

"I'm waiting for the next episode," Harry said.

"Where was I?" She made a face.

"You were managing a night club in Philadelphia at a thousand dollars a week, and the big boss was in love with you."

"Yes, all the way. He wanted to get married."

"And so you married him and lived happily ever after."

"Not that fast. We ran into a technical difficulty."

"What held it up?"

"Money."

"The root of all evil."

"Not money *per se*. Everybody misquotes that proverb. *The love of money is the root of all evil.* I Timothy-something."

"So?"

"So Kurt wanted to get married, and I held out. I think at first he was surprised—he thought I'd jump into his arms at the smell of a ring. When he saw I was serious—he's a really smart old man—he said, 'All right, let's talk about a deal.'"

"And you held him up for a bundle."

"No. I told him the truth. I told him what I wanted out of life—money, ease, status. I told him I didn't love him, that if I married him it would be because, as his wife, I could have all three. I told him I'd try to be a good wife, but I warned him I liked men. I told him he was old. I told him I'd probably cheat on him. If he'd marry me on those terms, I'd accept."

"Pardon me," said Harry, "if I reach for the salt."

"He lapped it up, darling. You don't know Kurt. He's a man who hates to be fooled. He appreciates straight talk. He thought it over, and then he said he understood. He said he wasn't a jealous man. He said he was old and used-up and had a bum heart; he didn't expect me to love him. He said he wanted to own me; and in order to own, you have to buy."

Thinly Harry said, "Was he to get a bill of sale?"

"The marriage certificate."

"And what were you to get?"

"A hundred thousand dollars in cash."

"Cheap. Dirt cheap."

"Don't get bitchy, lover, you're not the type. How about stirring up some more sauce?" Karen held out her empty glass. He got up and in silence made new drinks, lit a cigaret for her, put an ash tray beside her on the bed. He lit a cigaret for himself, and went back to his chair. "That was only to be the down payment," Karen said comfortably. "Petty cash for emergencies. There was more, much more, in the offing. Like millions."

"Millions?" Harry said, staring at her body.

"Millions."

"He agreed to turn over millions?"

"I didn't say that."

"But didn't you just say . . . ?"

For some reason his tone inflamed her. Her eyes flashed and she cried, "Listen, damn you! Listen, won't you?"

"Sorry." Harry smoked his cigaret.

"We continued our business conference. He wanted to buy me, so the terms became the issue. I went back to his being an old man. He could die suddenly and I'd be left with the short end of the stick. He said his will would take care of me. I said a will could be changed. He talked about a widow's dower right. I said, 'And suppose you died broke?' The more I dickered, the more respect he showed for me. I won't bore you with all the details. We had a number of talks."

"And the final deal?"

"Three million dollars in cash was deposited in a bank in escrow. On Kurt's death the three million becomes mine. The trust is irrevocable except for one condition—if I divorce him. Otherwise, he can't touch it."

"Suppose he divorces you?"

"The trust stands. I insisted on that, and he agreed. He wanted to own me in the worst way."

"He got his wish, didn't he?" said Harry. "Maybe he's not as smart as he has everybody thinking. Was Tony Mitchell your lawyer?" he asked suddenly.

Karen stretched in a lazy-cat way, and laughed. "Now don't be a complete dope, Doctor. Tony Mitchell was *his* lawyer."

"And yours?"

"No one remotely connected with Kurt Gresham, I assure you. I was very careful about that. I retained a top attorney and, after the agreement was all drawn up, I secretly double-checked with another top man."

Harry shook his head. "You're quite a woman, Karen. So when Kurt dies, you come into three million dollars, do you?"

"Oh, more than that, lover. I'd get the widow's mighty mite by law, and then, of course, there'd be his will. I don't know what's in it, but I could conceivably come into everything."

"And how much would that be?"

"Oh, fabulous scads," she said dreamily. "Who knows?" She raised her glass and sipped, and over its brim her green eyes flicked at him like a whip. "But I'd settle for the three million, the way I feel right now."

A queer little chill ran down Dr. Harrison Brown's back. "I thought you said you couldn't get the three million unless he died."

"That's right," said Karen. Then she said softly, "Lover."

It seemed to Dr. Harrison Brown that the room was baking over an invisible fire.

"What do you mean?" he asked in a croak.

She murmured, "What you're thinking I mean."

"You mean . . . you wish he were dead?"

"I wish he were dead. Yes, Harry. How's his heart?"

"Pumping," he said. "Karen."

"Yes, darling?"

"If you were free . . . would you marry me?"

"Yes. Yes."

He was silent. She was silent. They drank. They smoked.

Karen got off the bed and went into the bathroom and he heard her washing. She came back with a wet towel and, wiping his face tenderly, kissed his damp forehead. Then she took his glass and freshened their drinks and went back to the bed. It squeaked. "Now we come to you," she said.

"Me," he said. "Yes. What about me?"

"You're in," she said. "And you don't belong. I feel sorry for you."

"In what?" he said.

"Already you're afraid to talk, even to me."

"In what?" he said.

"One word will do the job."

"Say the word."

"Heroin."

"I'm in," he said. "Is Tony?"

"I don't know."

He grinned. "Oh, come on."

"I tell you I don't. If Kurt propositioned him, Tony's in. Otherwise, he's only Kurt's lawyer on legitimate stuff."

"What does that mean?"

"It means that once Kurt makes up his mind to proposition you, you're either in, or you're dead." She drank and wiped her face with the towel and hung it around her neck.

"How did you know about me?" Harry grunted.

"I asked Kurt."

"How come?"

"Lynne Maxwell."

The name was like a cold shower. But on a cold day. "Yes?" Harry said. His skin was actually pimpling.

"When Tony got Lieutenant Galivan to spill the story, I mean when Galivan was checking your alibi, I immediately recognized the fine Italian-or-whatever-the-hell-it-is hand of my dear husband. You see, I knew Lynne Maxwell."

"*You* knew her?" he cried.

"I'm still part of the screening apparatus, darling," Karen smiled. "Especially valuable now that I move in exalted circles as Mrs. Kurt Gresham of Park Avenue. I did the prospective-client screening on Lynne Maxwell. Undercover Gal, that's me. When Lynne was found dead in your apartment, I knew Kurt had selected his New York medical replacement for old Doc Welliver. That's the way my husband works. I asked him, and he told me."

"And you mean to say that if I'd turned him down—"

"Harry dear, you *are* sweet. He'd opened up to you, hadn't he? Could he afford to let you say no and walk out on him? How do you think Kurt's been able to keep his operation secret for so many years? But I gather that in your case he wasn't taking much of a chance."

"I still find it hard to believe," Harry said. "So damned melodramatic. Or are you pulling my leg?"

"I wish I were." She sat up on the bed and unhooked her brassiere and flung it away. She walked over to him and stooped over his chair and kissed him. His lips were cold and she slipped onto his lap and drew his head down to her.

"He didn't tell you about his liquidation department, did he? Or maybe he did and you didn't believe him. It's permanently staffed with experts, and I mean experts. If Kurt decides you're dangerous, you have the damnedest accident. You slip in the tub and break your neck, or you get a dizzy spell and fall off a subway platform just as the express is coming in, or you're found in Central Park dead from a mugging, with your cash missing, or you step in front of a truck, or you take an overdose of sleeping pills with the clear evidence that you're deeply in debt, or . . . oh, I can't think of all the ways you can die without the nasty word 'murder' coming into it. I can't, but Kurt's liquidation department can." She put her palms on his face and pulled it back from her moist, fragrant body and said, "Now I want you to kiss me."

"I want to talk."

"We've got all night to talk," she murmured. "We're finally touching, Harry, finally making contact. It's . . . exciting. It's so exciting. Harry, kiss me. Take me."

He kissed her. He took her.

Ten

Later, side by side in the darkness, they talked.

"He'd have killed me, would he?" Harry muttered.

"You're sweet. Violent yourself, capable of violence, but sweet, darling. Harry, get this through your head. Move wrong, talk wrong, smell wrong, and Kurt's specialists dispose of you. What's more, you can't get out. You're in for the rest of your life."

"What about Dr. Welliver? He's getting out, isn't he?"

"No. He just thinks he is. He's still under all the old restraints. If he doesn't know that, he won't live long enough to realize it. Incidentally, I don't think he's half as feeble as he makes out. I think old Doc Welliver has put on an act for some time, maneuvering for retirement."

"Sick of the whole thing after all these years?"

"You are an innocent, aren't you? No, because I think he thinks a crack has developed in the operation and he wants to get out from under before the whole thing comes crashing down. And you know what, Harry dearest? I think doc's got something. And you know another thing, my hairy baby? I think so does Kurt."

"What do you mean?"

Karen was silent. Then he felt her shoulder, snugged against his, twitch in a shrug. "I've gone this far, I may as well go the whole route. Harry, do you have any idea where Kurt goes every Monday, Wednesday, Friday and Sunday evening?"

"How the hell should I know? He hasn't told me much inside stuff. I don't even know how much of it is true. I've caught him in one lie already."

"What's that?"

"He told me you're his wife, period. That you know nothing about the dope operation."

She laughed. "Four nights a week he goes to the Starhurst."

"Starhurst? What's that?"

"A rundown but respectable old hotel at 83rd Street and Columbus. Kurt's maintained a suite there for many years. On the first floor—he walks up—Suite 101."

"Suite for what?"

"Business. He never spends more time there than is absolutely necessary. Kurt's one of those on-the-minute men. He demands absolute punctuality from his visitors."

"What visitors?"

"Don't get ahead of me. He gets to his suite at the Starhurst precisely at five minutes to seven, and precisely at seven his visitor arrives."

"What visitor?"

"The manager of one of Kurt's clubs—from New York, or Chicago, or Philly, or Washington or Miami. They rotate, never more than one manager an evening. Kurt comes with a brief case, the manager comes with a brief case. Kurt walks up, the manager walks up five minutes later. The stairway is to the right of the hotel entrance, through a short corridor. The desk and elevators are at the rear of the lobby, so the chances are nobody sees either of them go in and up. But even if somebody did—two well-dressed men, carrying respectable brief cases, five minutes apart—"

"What's the point, Karen?"

She twisted in the dark; she was perspiring again, and her naked shoulder slid against his as if it were greased. "Give me a cigaret, please, darling."

Harry groped on the night table. He gave her a cigaret, lit a match. She was frowning. She took only a few puffs and handed the cigaret back to him. He extinguished it in the ash tray on the table.

"In Kurt's brief case is a fresh supply of junk for the manager, put up in retail packets," Karen said in a mechanical undertone. "In the manager's brief case is the dope take from his club since his last visit, all cash. The contents of the brief cases are exchanged, facts and figures are gone over, and the manager leaves. Five minutes later Kurt locks up and leaves, too. And that's it."

Harry stirred restlessly in the humid darkness. She laid a gentle hand on him, as if to soothe and reassure him.

"Six months ago, for the first time in the history of the operation, one of the Washington managers—a quiet middle-aged little man named Carona, who looks like a filing clerk—failed to show up at the Starhurst for his appointment."

"Skipped with the take?"

"Nobody Kurt clears for a managerial job ever skips, Harry. No, Carona failed to show because, when his plane touched down in New York, he was arrested by two city detectives."

"With a brief case full of money?"

"No. The manager never carries the money on him. I don't know just what the system is—I think it comes on ahead some way and the manager picks it up after he gets off the plane. It wasn't the money. What bothered Kurt was the fact that Carona was picked up on a twenty-year-old charge."

"What kind of charge?"

"Felony murder. A policeman was killed during a liquor-store heist twenty years ago. Two men were in the holdup. The cop killed one of them; the other killed the cop and got away. The one who got away was Carona."

"And Kurt took him into the organization with *that* hanging over his head?" Harry asked incredulously.

"Carona was never linked to the killing—or the heist, for that matter. He was never identified—wasn't even hauled in for questioning. They simply didn't know who the killer was. There were no witnesses; the cop and the confederate died instantly. He made a clean getaway."

"Then how come the New York police pick him up for the crime twenty years later?"

"That's the bugging question. Carona claims he's never told anyone about it except Kurt. He told that to his lawyer. All the lawyer's been able to find out is that the police were suddenly tipped. The only theory that makes sense is that Carona's wife tipped them. He says he never told her, but he could be lying. Carona's been playing around with a blonde recently and his wife found out. Anyway, what's been sticking in Kurt's craw is that the district attorney was able to ram an indictment through the grand jury. And Carona's been refused bail. It doesn't wash. There's something behind this—and it could create the crack I mentioned."

"Who's Carona's lawyer?" asked Harry. "Tony?"

"My God, no. One of Kurt's undercover puppets. A real talent. Bobby Trenton."

He stiffened. "You don't mean Robert Cope Trenton, the ex-judge?"

"That's the baby, baby."

"I don't believe it," Harry exclaimed. "Why, Judge Trenton writes books on constitutional law. He has an international reputation."

"I told you Kurt picks only the best. Don't ask me how he got Trenton on his payroll—probably framed him for something. Anyway, Bobby says there's no real case against Carona; he guarantees an acquittal. So—why did they pick Carona up? Why did they phony through an indictment?"

"The crack in the monolith, eh?"

"That's what Kurt thinks. Somewhere something leaked —maybe in Europe, maybe in the Middle East or in Asia —and Carona's picked up. Bobby Trenton's told him it's a phony, that he has nothing to worry about, that the only reason for the whole thing is to squeeze some information out of him about the operation. It's been made clear to him that all he has to do is keep his mouth shut, that he'll be cleared, and there will be a hefty bonus for him when he is. But he's a dead man. And that's what Doc Welliver was really worried about—that Carona knows he's a dead man and *might* talk."

"I don't understand."

"Kurt's had his best men out in the field, inspecting, feeling for the crack. He's going abroad himself in September to mend whatever needs mending. But it's obvious that Carona is now a real liability. While Judge Trenton holds his hand, Kurt's arranging for his liquidation. A jail killing takes time—I mean, a killing that looks like an accident, that can't be traced back to the organization. It's being arranged, but it takes time."

"Christ," said Harry without impiety, sweating in the darkness.

"That's why I'm telling you, darling. You got in at just the wrong time. If trouble came, I doubt if you could statnd up to it. I know you, Harry. You aren't geared for this kind of thing. If Carona talks before he can be eliminated, the whole operation goes sky-high and they'd have you singing like a canary in no time. Kurt made a bad mistake in picking you. He doesn't know it yet. We've got to pray he never does."

"Maybe I'm not as weak a sister as you seem to think—"

"Darling," she said softly, "don't be angry. You've got

all the strength a woman could ask for. But not the kind an involvement in a racket calls for. You're too basically decent and honest. Darling, tell me. How come you allowed yourself to get sucked in?"

"I suffer from the same disease you do," said Harry in a dull bitterness.

"Money?"

"I'm sick with it."

She flung her arms around him. "Why the hell did I have to meet you? I was going great. All I could think of was the money—the money I've got, the money I'm going to get. Now all I can think of is you, damn you. I love you. I met you too late—"

"Let's not kid ourselves, Karen. You wouldn't have let me get to first base as a penniless doctor over his head in debt. And if you were a stripper living on her paychecks, I'd have passed you over. And both of us for the same reason. We're sick. We're infected."

"Let's not talk any more," Karen whispered.

They clung in the darkness. It was hot. But not that hot. This was tension sweat. The sweat of fear.

He said savagely, "What happens when he's dead?"

"Carona? The crack is found and mended, and business goes on as usual."

"I'm not talking about Carona."

She pressed against him, hands slipping on the wetness of his body, fingernails biting into his skin. "I wish he were. Dead. Dead. For your release as well as for mine. I'd marry you in a minute. We could be money-sick together, and we'd have three million dollars to cure us. Maybe a whole lot more. Harry, we'd be free, quit and clear and and cured . . . He's old, used-up, nearing the end, and we're young and at the beginning. Harry," she whispered. Her hands slid fiercely along his body. "Harry, we'd have it all—and each other—and no more hiding in lousy motels . . ."

But then she took her hands away and sighed and turned from him.

She turned from him and he turned from her and they lay on their sides, backs damply touching; they did not talk again until morning, when the motel room was bright with sun. But in the night before sleep—hot, wet, touching, mouth dry, blood thumping—Harry Brown became committed.

Eleven

For days he fought the thought back. As he pushed it down in one area of his brain, it rose in another. It invaded and occupied his work, such as it was. It intruded on his sleep, interfered with his meals, his drinking, even his sex life; he was now frequently impotent when he was with her, and irritable, and the fact that she soothed him, and understood, only seemed to make it worse. He lost weight, there was a tightness about his mouth, his eyes acquired a glitter that appalled him. I'm beginning to look like a psychotic, he told himself. And it *is* psychotic. Who thinks of murder but a lunatic? How in God's name did I get into this mess? Caught, lashed, hog-tied in a criminal conspiracy. He, Harry Brown. Harrison Brown, M.D. And thinking thoughts of murder to get out of it!

It's ridiculous, he thought. It isn't happening. I've got to shake this off. Get out from under. Somehow.

The phone call settled it.

It came on a broiling Monday at one o'clock in the afternoon. Kurt Gresham's voice curtseyed over the wire: "Harry? How are you, boy?"

"All right," Harry said.

"Harry, can you come over to the office today?"

"What time, Kurt?" That voice made him sick.

"Two-thirty fit into your schedule?"

"Yes."

"Thank you so much, Harry." The snick of Gresham's connection being broken sounded like something out of an execution.

At two-thirty Dr. Brown was ushered into the presence. The presence was garbed in cool blue, with a startling white tie. The pink globular face was crinkled with pleasure.

"Ah, Harry, right on the dot. That's good. How are you, boy?"

"All right. What's more to the point, how are *you*?"

"I know, you're going to scold me for not keeping my last two appointments."

"That's not very smart, Kurt."

"I know, I know," Gresham sighed. "Press of business. Small emergencies. But they add up, Harry. I can't even plan on leaving the city this summer except for weekends. But in September"—he smiled cheerily—"we'll be going off on a nice long vacation."

"Oh?" said Harry. Karen hadn't said anything about going with him. He settled back in his chair. The office was deliciously cool. The view from the fifty-fifth floor was entrancing.

"Harry."

"Yes? Oh, I beg your pardon."

"You like beautiful things, don't you?"

"Yes."

"There's so much beauty in the world. Unfortunately, a great deal of it is so expensive, eh, my boy?"

"Yes." What was Gresham driving at?

The millionaire raised the lid of the humidor on his desk.

"Cigar?"

"No, thanks."

The little round, red-lipped mouth thrust the cigar straight out as the little pudgy pink hand held a lighter to it. Gresham puffed slowly, smiling. Then he took the cigar out between thumb and forefinger.

"Do you have a passport, Harry?"

"No."

"We'll arrange that for you."

Harry blinked. "A passport? What for?"

Holding the cigar between thumb and forefinger, palm exposed, fingers curled daintily, Gresham puffed again. Then he said, "For our vacation, of course."

Harry almost laughed. "You mean it's me you're expecting to go with you?"

The pinkish globe crinkled benignly. "On September first I'm leaving on a trip to Europe and the Far East. I'll be gone six weeks, possibly two months. With a bad heart, I naturally want my doctor to accompany me. As my doctor you'll be paid a generous fee; as my guest, all expenses paid. Sound attractive, Harry?"

"And all I have to do is take care of you?"

Gresham chuckled. "There may be another chore or two. We'll cross that bridge when we build it."

What now? Harry thought. Am I promoted to be one of his executioners? He's been working me in slowly from the very first meeting, spinning the web, tightening, closing it. He's sure of me now; I'm one of his boys.

A perverse impulse made Harry say, "I'm afraid it's not possible, Kurt."

"Let's not play games, Harry." The pink deepened, the tone soured.

"I'm a doctor, Kurt. I can't walk out on my patients."

The cigar was dropped into an ash tray. "You're a difficult young man, aren't you?"

"I don't think so," Harry said innocently, wondering as he said it what he thought he was doing. Why was he baiting Gresham? He knew he could not win. I'm like a kid playing with matches, he thought—I know it's dangerous, but it excites me.

"Harry, you can be very valuable to me, and I to you. I have big plans for you." So Big Man was still giving it the soft sell. "So let's not waste time fencing. Think of me as a father . . ."

Who, Harry thought, is kidding whom? "What about my patients, Dad?"

That did it. He saw Gresham's ears take fire while the rest of the fat face became the color of ash and the unpigmented eyes hardened into slag. "I'm giving you plenty of notice, Harry. Doctors can always turn over their patients to other doctors. Make your arrangements."

"And if I don't?" I'm trying to commit suicide, Harry thought, that's it. He had an almost overwhelming desire to get up and go around Gresham's desk and tip the big chair over and put his foot on the big round face, and grind.

"Harry." The prissy voice was now guttural, the grayed jowls shaking, the little womanly red mouth puckering. "You cut out this kid stuff, understand? You'd better take the blinders off. You listen to me."

So Karen was right. "You talk as if I have no choice."

"You don't!"

Harry took time out to locate his cigarets and make a ritual out of lighting one. Then he said quietly, "All right, Kurt, spell it out for me."

"I'll do just that, Harry. You've been drafted, and your

hitch is for life. *My* life, Harry. No, you have no choice. Go AWOL and you're a sudden casualty of the war. Indulge in loose talk, and you'll find yourself up against the wall smoking your last cigaret. But be a good little soldier and do what you're told, and you'll get all sorts of citations."

"Can you translate that from poetry into prose?"

"All right. I want you, I've got you, I'll pay for you. But all the time you're getting rich you'd better remember one thing: You can't get out. How is my spelling, Harry?"

Harry was silent. Then he said, "I suppose there's nothing left for me to do but ask: How rich?"

The ears faded to their normal shell pink, the ashes took on a glow, the slag melted and became Gresham's eyes again. "Now that's what I've been waiting to hear, Harry! You had me worried for a while. I find myself liking you more and more, I suppose because you stand up on your hind legs and talk back to the old boy. . . . Why, I should think this first year should gross you more than fifty thousand." He lit another cigar.

"How do you figure that?"

"Oh, I didn't tell you. Just for going abroad with me, Harry, you're going to earn an extra fee of twenty-five thousand dollars. And that's only the start. Next year you should make at least a hundred thousand. Your take will keep rising, unless I'm all wrong about you, and I don't think I am. I have a feeling you've got the makings of one of my little upstairs group—my board of directors. In fact, it wouldn't surprise me if you became a director in record-quick time. Sound good to you, boy?"

"Very good indeed, Pappy."

"Then I have another goodie for you to think about," Kurt Gresham beamed. "The moment you're voted onto my board of directors, you're included in my will."

"Your will?" exclaimed Harry. The surprise in his voice was genuine.

"Ah, that throws you, does it? In our kind of operation I can't work out a pension plan—" out of the fresh cigar smoke came a fat chuckle—"so I provide a form of social security for my faithful inner circle. My nine board members—you'd make the tenth—are down for half a million dollars apiece when I die. Do you know how much I'm worth, Harry?"

"I have no idea."

"To tell you the truth, neither do I. Probably a hundred

million. A lot depends on the state of the market. Most of it is in blue-chip investments. So it means very little to me to leave my best people half a million apiece. Actually, they're all better off having me alive—salaries and bonuses are high, Harry, high. It will pay you to make every effort to keep this pumper of mine operating—your earnings over my lifetime will far exceed the half million you could expect on my death. However, it's comforting to know it will be there when the fountain goes dry—eh, Harry?"

"I . . . Kurt, I don't know what to say."

Gresham kept beaming at him.

You liar. Harry thought. You conscienceless, megalomaniacal liar! You're building me up to a dirty job, probably murder—dangling carrots in front of my nose while you lead me to the slaughterhouse.

"Then we understand each other, Harry?" Gresham simpered.

"Yes, Kurt."

"And you're my doctor?"

"I'm your doctor."

"All the way?"

"All the way."

"You're going on a vacation with me?"

"I am."

"You'll be paid in full before we go. Need any money now?"

"No."

"That's it, then, boy. I have certain problems, but we'll discuss those during our trip. Today I enjoyed. You're a rough one, kid, you forced my hand. You'll be an asset to Gresham and Company." The fat man heaved himself out of his chair and came around the desk. Harry rose. "Thank you so much for coming," Gresham said.

He put an arm around Harry's shoulder and walked him toward the door.

"Love from Karen," he said in the same warm affectionate tone.

"Oh?" Harry could not suppress a start. If Kurt Gresham felt it, he gave no sign.

"You've been seeing a lot of Karen lately."

"She's a charming woman," Harry said stupidly.

"Look out for Tony."

Harry stammered, "I . . . beg pardon?"

"Tony Mitchell."

"Oh," said Harry.

"Jealousy is an indecent emotion, Harry. It has no respect for the proprieties. Discretion, my boy, discretion and a decent respect for the opinions of mankind. Especially husbands. Eh?"

Gresham laughed.

Harry laughed.

The short fat arm around him tightened in a hug that for an instant alarmed Harry.

But then Kurt Gresham let him go.

Twelve

One Tuesday afternoon, at five o'clock, Dr. Alfred McGee Stone dropped into the office of Dr. Harrison Brown.

"My wife's in town, shopping," said Dr. Stone. "I was wondering if you could join us for dinner."

"Sure thing, Doctor," said Dr. Brown.

"Eight o'clock all right?"

"Fine."

"By the way, if you have any suggestions . . . My wife is always looking for new places to eat. If there's some special restaurant you know—"

"How about Giobbe's? It's a wonderful Italian place in Greenwich Village . . ."

Mrs. Stone turned out to be a plump little hen of a woman with bright, quick eyes. She clucked over every dish at Giobbe's.

"You know, Doctor," she said to Harry, "I'm here only as Alfred's excuse. Ordinarily a woman would resent being used that way, but this food is so divine—"

"Bernice." Dr. Stone tapped his lips with his napkin, rather embarrassed. Then he laughed. "well, it's true, Doctor. Have you been giving any thought to my proposal?"

"Yes," Harry said politely.

"No decision yet, I take it."

"No."

"Well, there's plenty of time. When you do come to a decision, though, I hope you'll call me at once."

"Naturally, Doctor."

Dr. Stone began talking about the Taugus Institute. "I will admit," he said after a while, "that the one possible drawback from your standpoint is the matter of income. I take it you're an ambitious young fellow. I don't mean to sound like somebody out of a soap opera, Doctor, but a lot of money and happiness don't necessarily go together."

"Happiness?" Harry said, holding on to his glass of Chianti. "Do you know a happy man, Dr. Stone?"

"A great many of them. Don't you?"

"He's too young to be happy," said Bernice Stone.

"Peter Gross is happy," said Dr. Alfred Stone. "Lewis Blanchette is happy. I'm happy. I love my wife and children and grandchildren. I like my work. I'm not rich, but I have enough to give my family a decent life, with some left over for books and recordings and golf and taking my wife out to overeat occasionally. What more could a man want?"

Harry was silent.

"Aren't you happy, Dr. Brown?" asked the plump little woman.

"I suppose not, Mrs. Stone."

"You join us at the Institute," Dr. Stone said. "You're not happy because you're not satisfying your innermost needs. Are you?"

"I suppose not, Dr. Stone." He felt like a fool.

"May I call you Harry?" the director of the Taugus Institute asked with a smile.

"Of course," said Harry.

He was committed. He no longer fought it; it was no longer unreal. He was committed to pit himself against a wily old adversary who had all the weapons on his side.

I have only one advantage, Dr. Harrison Brown thought: the adversary doesn't know he's in a fight. To the death. I have no choice—he told me that himself. So I'm locked in the arena, and I've got to kill or be killed—be killed slowly. At least he'll die all at once . . . The concept of himself in the role of murderer no longer struck him as psychotic. He could look at himself in the mirror again. He could think his plans out without squirming . . . well, much.

He was sleeping better, working better, loving better.

He did not talk of his plans to Karen. She knew. She had told him about the Starhurst routine in detail. If she did not realize consciously why she had done that, she knew all the same.

He was committed to murdering Kurt Gresham. As the man's doctor it could be a simple matter. But as the man's doctor it could also be a dangerous matter. And as the man's wife's lover . . . He stood to gain the widow, the millions, the dream he had dreamed all his life. Gresham's death must not lead, even in theory, to Dr. Harrison Brown's door.

So it had to be murder—crass, vulgar, apparently without finesse. Murder as far removed from Dr. Brown as a Chicago alley mugging. Murder not as a crime of passion by an amateur, but as a deliberate underworld assassination. A doctor would obviously use a doctor's weapon—poison, or an injection, or some pharmacological means deriving from the victim's coronary. Therefore—sudden death by a gangster's weapon.

This, then, was the first problem.

The weapon called for was clearly a gun. But he had no gun. To procure one legally was to invite investigation. The question was therefore how to procure one illegally, without a license. It should be an untraceable gun, if possible, its serial number destroyed beyond resurrection—a professional killer's weapon. Because, clearly, it had to be found near the body to establish the professional nature of the killer.

Where did a physician practicing medicine out of a Central Park West office get hold of such a gun?

Thirteen

On a sticky Friday evening, Tony Mitchell phoned. "How about the weekend, Harry, just you and me? I'll take the boat and we'll sail up to Montauk. The Greshams are away for the weekend."

"I know," said Harry Brown. "They flew up to some hundred-dollar-a-day joint in Maine."

"You know everything, don't you, Doctor?"

"You bet," said Dr. Brown.

"Pick you up early tomorrow?"

"How early?"

"Six o'clock."

"Brother, that's early. Okay, Tony, I'll be ready."

Tony Mitchell's boat was a cabin cruiser, deepsea, roomy, racy. They fished and swam off Montauk and ate and drank on board, and then in the evening they moored at the hotel pier and checked in to a two-room suite. They showered and napped and changed into dinner clothes and had dinner in the outdoor restaurant and flirted with two tanned girls in billowing dresses. In a night club afterward, they danced and tippled and Tony told jokes and the tanned girls laughed, and they danced and tippled some more, and then Tony and his girl disappeared, and Harry went back to the hotel with his girl, kissed her good night and went up to the suite and undressed and showered again and went to sleep. In the morning he awoke once and peered in to Tony's room. When he saw that Tony's bed was undisturbed, Harry went to the bathroom and rinsed his mouth and then got back into bed.

In the afternoon Tony said, "The hell with the boat. Let's live it up here at the hotel. Swim in the pool, leer at the girls in the bikinis. In July it's just too damned hot for fishing. Agreed?"

"Agreed."

"You know, I miss the Greshams. That old bastard fascinates me. And Karen *is* lovely."

"Yes."

"Oh, we're back on the one-syllable kick. Hangover?"

"Yes."

"Let's eat by the pool."

By the pool Tony said, "How come you get nut-brown right away? Me, first I get red."

"I'm swarthy. Say, Tony, how do people kill people?"

"What?"

"How do people kill people?"

"You're not hung over, Harry, you're still drunk. Whittle those vittles. You'll feel better."

Tony took inventory while they ate at the umbrella table. "Now that's more like it! Look at that over there— the tall one in the white bathing suit, near the diving board. I think I'll make it."

"How do people kill people?" Harry said.

Tony stared at him. "Say, what's with you today?"

"I was thinking about it last night," Harry said, smiling. "In the restaurant, in the night club. Looking around at all those people. Wondering how many of them wanted to kill somebody—a wife, a husband, anybody. Did you ever feel like killing somebody, Tony?"

"Sure. You. Right now!"

"No, I mean suppose you did."

"Did *what*?"

"Want to kill me. How would you go about it?"

"These are the thoughts you were thinking last night, Dr. Brown?"

"Well, I was a little loaded by the time I got back to the room," Harry laughed.

"Brother, you must have been! What time did you get back?"

"Early."

"Aha," said Tony Mitchell. "Whose room, ours or the little blonde's?"

"Ours."

"How was she?"

"I don't know. I dumped her and hit the hay. Now, come on, Tony, satisfy my curiosity. How would you do it?"

"How would I do *what*?"

"Kill me. Would you use a gun?"

"Oh, cut it out," he lawyer groaned. "You're still carrying a load—up to the gunwales. Better take something for it. My God, that little blonde chick was yours for the asking. Are you sick or something, Harry?"

"Now you sit here like a nice little doctor and wait for your medicine, while I ankle on over to the diving board." Tony rose and winked. "I shall return with the girl in white. Watch how it's done, old boy."

"Where would you get the gun?"

"What gun?"

"The gun to shoot me. I suppose you'd want one that couldn't be traced. Where would a respectable lawyer get hold of an untraceable gun?"

"Why would I want to shoot you?"

"Any reason. You hate me."

"Not me, baby. I wouldn't kill you."

"Under any circumstances?"

Tony's dark eyes turned cold. "Under any circumstances, baby. Nothing is worth the risk. Not if you're sane. Look, Harry, take your alcoholic speculations somewhere else. Maybe this amuses you. It doesn't me."

Harry laughed. "The great criminal lawyer refuses to give away a trade secret."

"What trade secret?"

"Where you'd get a gun."

"I wouldn't," Tony said shortly. Then he laughed, too. "Son, I'm getting you back in shape right now. Waiter?"

A waiter came up. "Yes, sir?"

"Bring my friend here a Bloody Mary. A double. He's in a bad way."

"Yes, sir," said the waiter, and he went away grinning.

Fourteen

He missed Karen. When he phoned on Monday he was told the Greshams were not due back in the city until Wednesday. When he phoned on Wednesday she talked to him almost curtly: she would not be able to see him until Saturday.

On Saturday she called him; and in the hot and dripping evening she came to him at his apartment. She was pale in spite of her long weekend; she was dressed in unrelieved black. She did not kiss him when he opened the door for her.

"Have fun in Maine?" Harry asked.

"We just lounged around and rested. How are *you*?"

"All right."

Her great green eyes were in shadow, puckered with tension. "I want a drink, darling."

"Vodka?"

"Gin and tonic. Lots of gin."

He went to the kitchen and came back with the drinks in two tall glasses. She was smoking. She rose instantly and came over and took one glass from him. She turned as though to go back to her chair. Then she turned back and said, very quietly, "I'm glad you made up your mind."

"About what?"

"I saw Tony. He told me about your weekend at Montauk."

"What about it?"

She licked at the glass, set it down, squeezed her cigaret out in an ash tray.

"You know how Tony runs on. He was telling me about the crazy things people say when they're drunk. Harry Brown gets stoned and right away starts trying to pump his pal the criminal lawyer about how people kill people —where somebody who wanted to commit a murder would get hold of a gun that couldn't be traced. Tony said he was glad he was the one you asked—anybody else, he said, might have taken you seriously. Wasn't that sort of a stupid thing to do, darling—asking so transparently?"

"I don't know what you're talking about," Harry said. "It was just babbling."

She picked up her glass and drank and looked at him over the rim. "Yes, darling," she murmured.

He drank, too. "Incidentally," he said, "how come you found the time to see Tony but not me?"

"Because I love you, and Tony is—well, Tony."

"I don't follow."

"Kurt's been in and out, office and home, unpredictably. I've had to keep available. That Carona mess is an emergency, and Kurt is spending most of his time on it. The trip to Maine wasn't to relax. It was so he could see some people, ostensibly vacationers, about the Carona matter, about a possible inside investigation of Gresham and Company, and about Kurt's trip to Europe in September. You know you're going with him?"

"I know," Harry said. "But you had time to see Tony."

"Jealous?" she smiled.

"I've been aching, Karen. In all the right places." Harry came to her, leaned over.

"Please, darling, not now." She lit another cigaret, inhaled deeply, let the smoke out in a gush. From behind the smoke she said, "Tony is one of Kurt's lawyers. He comes with Kurt to the apartment. Kurt gets called away. So Tony and I have a chance to talk for a few minutes. Don't be silly . . . You know, Harry, I'm glad. And yet I feel ashamed."

"What?" Harry said.

"It shouldn't be you. I'm the one who ought to do it. But I just don't have that kind of courage."

He said shortly, "Let's not talk about it."

"We've got to. If I weren't such a damn coward . . ." She finished the gin and tonic. "It isn't as if I couldn't arrange to have it done. I've met all kinds in my dainty career. But when you buy a thing like that you're wide open to blackmail. From the frying pan to the fire. Who needs it? Harry . . ."

"What?"

"You're his doctor . . ."

"No," Harry said. Then he began to walk around the room, silent. Her eyes followed him anxiously. He stopped and turned to face her. "All right, if you insist on discussing it. There must be no possible connection with me. Not a medical method at all. It's got to look like the exact opposite. A gangland job—what do they call it?—a hit."

She said in a low voice, "Yes. I hadn't thought . . . But I wish—"

"Look, Karen. I believe I'd have to do this even if you weren't involved: either do it or be a monkey on a string for the rest of my life. I never had a choice. I was pulled in, not knowing what I was getting into, and then it was too late. Stay in or go out feet first. Kurt made that quite clear. The way I figure it, it's either committing one big crime now and being free, or an indefinite series of little ones working for Kurt, with the threat of death hanging over my head night and day. Stop castigating yourself. I'm fighting for my life—for our lives."

She reached rather blindly for the glass before she realized that it was empty. She sat there looking into it. "Harry . . . what do you need?"

"A gun equipped with a silencer. And, of course, cartridges. The gun and silencer with all traceable markings removed beyond even chemical detection. Professional stuff. I want that gun to be found."

"You shouldn't have said anything to Tony. You should have come to me in the first place. I can get them for you, Harry."

"Your connections . . . I never thought of that." He saw her turning the empty glass over and over in her hands. He said, "Another drink?"

"Please."

He kissed her hands and took the glass into the kitchen and came back with a bubbling refill. She drank thirstily as he stood over her. She took the glass from her lips and looked up at him and said, "Go away, darling—over there, where you were . . . There'll be no connection with me, either. A long time ago I was the love apple of the eye of a certain big shot in Frisco. In my strip days. He was crazy for me. Want to know what my professional name was then?"

"What?"

"Jackie Jill. Cute? All strippers have cute—or nutty—names. He knew me as Jackie Jill and I knew him as Uncle Joe, period. He couldn't possibly associate me with Mrs. Kurt Gresham of New York. Don't laugh, but he's basically a sentimentalist. He stopped carrying the torch for me ages ago, but he'll remember Jackie Jill."

"I don't like it," muttered Harry.

She laughed. "If you're worried about the flame reviving, don't be. I can reach Uncle Joe, and I'm positive I can arrange to get you what you need. Without danger to either of us. He'd do it as a favor for Jackie Jill, and no questions asked. It's his way of doing business; he has no interest in what use the material is put to. It's a matter of demand and supply; as far as Uncle Joe is concerned, the matter ends there. To use your word, Harry—professional."

"How would you work it?"

"I'll call him long-distance from a pay phone, as Jackie Jill. I still have his unlisted phone number. Uncle Joe owes me a few favors from way back, and he knows he can depend on my discretion. His interest will end there. Shoud I do this, Harry?"

"Do it, but be careful."

"And then?"

"I don't know yet. I think the Starhurst. That time schedule you told me about—he sticks to it?"

"Meticulously."

"He comes at five minutes to seven?"

"On the dot."

"And the visitor at seven?"

"Promptly. Not a minute before or after. He's drilled that into them so that now it's second nature."

"That gives him five minutes alone," Harry said. "It ought to be enough—it has to be . . . I think—yes, we'll work out an alibi for me, just in case I'm questioned or investigated. . . ."

"Harry."

"Yes?"

"There's something I've got to tell you."

The mixture of distress, defiance and shame in her voice made his head come up sharply. "What's that?"

"I've got to tell you now . . ."

"What?"

"If anything should go wrong—"

"Yes?"

"I'll lie. I'll ditch you. I know me. I'll leave you high and dry. Holding the bag. I'll say it was all your idea—that you forced me into it. . . . I told you, darling, I love you, and I do. But I know me, and I'll look to save my own skin, love or no love. I want you to understand that now, before this goes any further..."

He looked at her across half the room. "You're a remarkable woman, Karen."

"I'm a dirty coward."

"Thank you."

"For what?"

"For being honest with me. But don't worry. Nothing will go wrong."

"But the police—they'll press, they'll squeeze. They have ways..."

"They won't get the chance."

"But Harry, think. Now. Before..."

"I've thought, Karen," Dr. Harrison Brown said. "I'm going to kill him because I have to. If it goes wrong, I'll kill myself."

On Sunday night the Kurt Greshams threw a party at their Park Avenue apartment. It was a gay party, in formal dress; Mrs. Kurt Gresham was radiant in a stunning Cassini original. The affable host announced to his guests that on September first he was going off to Europe for a couple of months in the company of his new personal physician. "If I were young I'd take my wife, or a sweetheart, or perhaps my wife *and* a sweetheart. But I'm old, so I have to take my doctor instead. So it goes."

There was laughter, and applause, and the hostess invited her guests into the glittering dining room for supper and champagne.

"Oh, Harry," Kurt Gresham said. "Tony has arranged with the Immigration people for your passport. But you have to go down there."

"Sure," said Harry.

"Tony will go with you. When there's red tape there should always be a lawyer."

"Sure," said Harry.

Tony Mitchell grinned. "I've set up a date for ten A.M. Wednesday, Doctor. That all right with you?"

"Sure," said Harry.

Fifteen

Monday was the first day of August, and on Monday the first day of August, at ten minutes past two, the phone rang in the office of Dr. Harrison Brown and the operator said, "I have a person-to-person call from San Francisco for Dr. Harrison Brown." His girl transferred the call, and Dr. Harrison Brown said, "This is Dr. Harrison Brown."

"One moment, please. Go ahead, please."

A voice said, "Dr. Harrison Brown?" It was a thick voice, deeply male, with a rasp in it.

"This is Dr. Brown." He could feel the sweat spring out.

"Hi, Doc. This is Jackie Jill's uncle, her Uncle Joe. Remember me? You treated me last year when I was in New York. Hiya, Doc."

A snake of fear crept along the spine of Dr. Harrison Brown. He sat up straight. "Yes?" he said. "Yes?"

"I need a favor, Doc."

"A favor?" He groped for a tissue, swabbed his forehead.

"My brother Ben died last week. In New York. He was cremated, see—"

"Yes?"

"It says in my brother's will that he wants his ashes thrown into the ocean, the Atlantic Ocean."

"I see."

"I know this is a lot to ask, but I'm gonna be stuck here in Frisco for a long time and I couldn't think of nobody in New York but you. Suppose you could pick up the package of ashes, the urn, or whatever it is, Doc, and as a special favor carry out my brother's last wishes? I'd be awful grateful."

Harry moistened his lips. "Where is it? Where do I pick it up?"

"Well, the funeral parlor is up in Yonkers. You know, where they got the race track, the trotters? It ain't far from the track. Allerton Avenue. Smith and Smith Funeral Chapel. Ask for the head undertaker, Franklin Gregory Archibald Smith. Would you do this for me, Doc?"

"When? What time?"

"Tomorrow, one o'clock. I called Mr. Smith and I told him you'd probably be coming. After all, I did do you that favor, that time I was in New York, lending you the thousand bucks. Say, come to think of it, I could kill two birds with one stone, like they say. I heard you were doing pretty good now, Doc—could you possibly pay up that thousand you owe me? I mean now?"

"Yes."

"Great. I ain't paid Smith and Smith yet for the funeral, and they won't release my brother's ashes till they get their money. By a coincidence, it comes to just a thousand bucks. You could pay them for me and pick up the ashes and we'd be all square. Okay, Doc?"

"Yes, certainly."

"I guess you better make it cash. Can you make it cash?"

"Yes. What name? The deceased, I mean?"

"Oh, my brother. I told you—Benny. Benjamin A. Smith. Common name, huh, Doc? Undertakers named Smith, stiff named Smith. Poor old Ben—he lingered a long time with that cancer. Well! We all set, Doc? You got the name and address?"

"I marked them down."

"One o'clock tomorrow. Don't forget to bring the money. And I thank you very much."

And the wire went dead as Uncle Joe, in San Francisco, hung up.

That afternoon Dr. Harrison Brown called an associate, Dr. Manley Lamper, and arranged for Dr. Lamper to take over his practice during the months of September and October. He also drew up a letter notifying his patients that he would be away for the months of September and October and that his practice would be handled during that period by Dr. Manley Lamper, address and telephone number. He instructed his girl to go through the files and send a copy of the letter to all his patients, and to make a note to refer all calls beginning September first to Dr. Lamper.

The next morning, on his way to the office, he stopped into his bank and came out with a plain envelope containing ten $100 bills.

Sixteen

It was a two-story red brick on a nice street in Yonkers, chiefly residential. There were shade trees over the sidewalks, and neat houses with green lawns, and some stores: a supermarket, a laundry, a beauty parlor, a drugstore, a florist's, and the funeral parlor. He drove past slowly and backed into a space at the curb a hundred feet away. Before he got out of the car he touched the envelope in the inner pocket of his jacket.

He walked back without haste along the sunny street to the brick building. It had a gray marble front and wide glass doors. He pushed through the doors and found himself in a cool room with a soft gray carpet, a long gray table, gray chairs and benches, and some potted palms. At the far end of the room a blond young man sat at a small gray desk. The blond young man rose at once and came forward. He said softly, "Sir?"

"I'd like to see Mr. Franklin Gregory Archibald Smith."

"What name, sir?"

"My name?"

"Please, sir."

Harry said, "Smith."

The young man smiled, exhibiting lively white teeth.

"You have an appointment?"

"Yes."

"Please sit down, won't you?"

The young man walked sedately to the end of the room . . . through two glass doors similar to those at the entrance, but narrower. Harry remained standing.

The young man returned in thirty seconds.

"This way, sir."

Harry followed him through the narrow glass doors and along a windowless corridor to an office also furnished in gray: gray carpet, gray leather armchairs, gray steel desk, gray Venetian blinds tightly closed.

"Come in, sir." A thin man with a long wrinkled face and sparse black hair rose from behind the steel desk. His hair was obviously a toupee. His rather high voice was, to Harry's surprise, that of a cultivated man. He wore an expensive black suit and a black tie with a gray pearl stickpin. "All right, Adam."

The blond young man went out, shutting the door.

"I'm Franklin Gregory Archibald Smith," the mortician said. "Please sit down—Mr. Smith, did you say?"

"Harry Smith," said Harry Brown.

The thin man smiled and gestured to the armchair beside the desk.

Harry sat. The tall man sat.

"Common name," the tall man remarked.

"Yes," said Harry.

"Well," said Mr. Smith. "What can I do for you, Mr. Smith?"

"I'm here on an errand."

"Errand?"

"For Uncle Joe."

"Joe?"

"Uncle Joe from San Francisco."

"Oh, yes?" said the thin mortician. He waited.

"I'm here to pick up the ashes of Uncle Joe's brother Benny. Benjamin A. Smith?"

"Oh, yes?" said the mortician again. He still did not move.

"Oh," said Harry. He took the envelope out of his pocket. "Here's the money Uncle Joe owes you."

This time the man moved. He extended a bony hand for the envelope, opened it, took out the bills, and counted them. He returned the money to the envelope, unlocked a drawer of the steel desk, dropped the envelope into the drawer, locked the drawer and pocketed the key. Then he rose.

He said in his high voice, "Wait here, please," and left the room. He had a long gliding stride that made him look as if he were walking on tiptoe.

Harry sat. The room was cool. He stirred uneasily.

Was it a swindle? Why not? Smith could give him an urn containing ashes, and what could he do about it? Go to the police? The thought made him laugh, and he felt better.

The man returned with an oblong package. It was wrapped in ordinary wrappingpaper, seams secured by wide strips of gummed tape, and bound with heavy cord.

"Here it is," said the mortician. He handed the package to Harry. "I'm to remind you that it's to be thrown into the Atlantic Ocean."

"Yes," said Harry.

"A good deep place is best for its last resting place. You'll remember that, won't you?"

"Yes," said Harry. The hell I will, he thought.

"Well, good luck, Mr. Smith."

"Thank you," said Harry.

The tall man shut the door on him immediately.

The blond young man was back at his desk.

"Goodbye, sir."

"Goodbye," said Harry.

He pushed through the glass doors into the heat of the street. The package, not heavy, was heavy. He did not hold it by the cord. He held it in the crook of his arm tightly. At the car, he put it carefully into the trunk. He did not dare open it. His clothes were pasted to his body. He removed his jacket, loosened his tie and unbuttoned his collar. He got into the car and drove off.

He did not speed. He did not attempt to beat any lights. He kept strictly to the right, gave hand signals on every turn. It took him a long time to get back to his office. He had told his receptionist he would be back by two. It was almost two-thirty before he got there.

The package weighed heavily in the crook of his arm as he let himself in through his street door.

He almost dropped it. There was someone waiting for him in the waiting room.

Not a patient.

Lieutenant Galivan.

Seventeen

"Hi," said Lieutenant Galivan.

"Hello, there," said Dr. Brown.

"I was in the neighborhood, figured I'd drop in. Your girl here said you'd be back about two, so I waited. Nice and cool."

"That's air conditioning for you."

"A boon to civilization."

"Anything for me?" said Dr. Brown to his receptionist. He was trying to squeeze the package into invisibility.

"Yes, Doctor. You have three house calls to make." She handed him three slips of paper. "And Mr. Murphy will be here at four-fifteen, and Frieda Copeland at four-thirty."

"Busy all of a sudden," smiled Dr. Brown. He glanced at the slips. "Any of these emergency?"

"No, Doctor."

"Will you excuse me a moment, Lieutenant?"

"Sure thing," said Lieutenant Galivan.

"I'll be with you shortly."

"Take your time, Doc."

Harry closed his consultation room door behind him very softly. He placed the brown package in a cabinet and locked the cabinet. He hung away his jacket; took off his tie, shirt, undershirt. He went into the bathroom and stooped low over the sink and ran cold water on his head. Then he washed his torso and soaped and washed under his arms, dried himself and combed his hair and got into fresh linen and a fresh white jacket. He felt a great need for the jacket. The office jacket made him a doctor. It covered his sins.

He opened the door to the waiting room. "I feel better now, Lieutenant. Come on in."

The tall, elderly detective ambled into the consultation room.

"Sit down."

"Thank you, Doctor." The lieutenant sat down and crossed his legs.

Harry sat down behind his desk. A desk makes all the difference, he thought.

"How've you been, Doc?"

"Fine," said Harry. "Lieutenant, I don't want to hurry you—certainly not if it's important—"

"Oh, this won't take long."

"It's just that I have some house calls to make, and my office hours in the afternoon are four to seven—"

"Anything crop up on the Lynne Maxwell thing, Doctor?"

"Nothing, or I'd have called you."

The lieutenant nodded. "You know, we just came across a funny bit."

"Oh?"

"We keep poking around when the file isn't closed. You know that Mrs. Gresham you were with that night in the restaurant, with that lawyer-friend of yours?"

"Yes?" He could feel the sweat spring out of his skin again.

"Well, it turns out Mrs. Gresham knew Lynne Maxwell."

"She did? I didn't know that, Lieutenant."

Galivan brought out his pipe. He did not fill it. He held it cupped in his hands. "Doctor, there's no suspicion of murder in the Maxwell case. Just that bit about her winding up in your apartment dead, with no apparent explanation."

"We've been all through that."

"I understand your impatience. Sorry, but this is police talk now."

"Oh?" He could hear his voice rising.

"Mrs. Gresham is your patient."

"I told you that. She and her husband."

"Very attractive woman."

"I suppose so."

"Married to an old man."

He forced coldness back into his voice. "What's the point, Lieutenant?"

"Doctor, you're not going to like this question, but I've got to ask it. Is Mrs. Gresham anything more to you than a patient?"

He was not prepared for it. It was the last thing he had expected. Did Galivan know? Or was this a shot in the dark? A wrong answer now might come back to haunt him . . . afterward. He thought desperately.

Was it possible Galivan was having him followed? Possible, but unlikely. He was in the clear for the Maxwell girl's death; he had had nothing to do with it; he was sure Galivan was convinced of that. He decided it was a safe gamble.

"You mean am I sleeping with her?"

Galivan laughed. "Are you?"

"No. However, we do have more than a doctor-patient relationship, as I think I told you. We've become friends as well. Why do you ask, Lieutenant?"

"We figured that if you and Mrs. Gresham were cosying up, you might have given her a key to your apartment. And since she knew Lynne Maxwell, that key might explain how the girl got in."

"Well, it doesn't. Because Mrs. Gresham doesn't have a key to my apartment." He felt confident now; it was true.

"How about her husband? Ever give him a key?"

"Lord, no. Why would I do that? I told you, Lieutenant —there's no other key to my apartment."

Galivan produced a pouch and filled his pipe. He took his time lighting it and puffed slowly. Between puffs he asked, "How long have you known Mrs. Gresham?"

"She's been a patient of mine for . . . oh, a few months."

"Kurt Gresham, too?"

"They came to me at the same time."

"You didn't know Mrs. Gresham before that?"

"No."

"Mr. Gresham, either?"

"That's right, Lieutenant."

"How did they happen to come to you, Doctor?"

"I was recommended to them by Tony Mitchell."

"You've known Mitchell a long time?"

"Since I was a kid. He knew my father. My father was a lawyer, too."

"I know. So the four of you are buddy-buddies."

"Look, Lieutenant," said Dr. Brown. "The Greshams have become my most important patients. Kurt Gresham is a cardiac. When his old doctor retired, Mr. Gresham retained me on an annual basis at a very healthy fee. I don't mind telling you he's been a godsend to me. I wish I had a dozen patients like him . . . By the way, on the first of September he's taking me to Europe with him for a couple months, as his personal physician. Don't ask me if it's going to pay me; it will. I'm getting twenty-five thousand dollars for those two months, and all expenses paid, to boot. I'm a young guy just starting out in practice, Lieutenant, and I've been pinching myself ever since I met Mr. Gresham. For some obscure reason he's taken a shine to me, and I'm going to keep the old boy alive if I have to open him up and pump his heart with my bare hands every hour on the hour. Do you blame me? And have I been frank enough for you, Lieutenant? And will there be anything else before I make those house calls?"

Galivan rose. "Thanks, Doctor, I appreciate your frankness. You'll buzz me if anything—anything at all—crops up on the Lynne Maxwell thing?"

"I most certainly will."

"Sorry if I've held you up."

"It's all right, Lieutenant."

When Galivan was gone, Dr. Harrison Brown sank back into his swivel-chair and put his hands flat on his desk to stop their trembling.

But he felt a sense of triumph. He had Galivan under control, anyway.

There was no time to open the package from Smith and Smith.

Those damn house calls.

He slipped out of his white coat and into his suit jacket and grabbed his bag and ran.

When he got back to his office he found four patients waiting for him. By the time he finished with the four, there were five more in the waiting room. He felt like smashing something at the irony of it.

It was eight o'clock before the office was empty and his evening receptionist had left and he could unlock the cabinet and take out Uncle Joe's brother's ashes. He cut the cord and tore off the wrapping paper. It revealed a heavy cardboard box, its cover secured with sealing tape. He ripped it off, holding his breath.

The box was full of wadded plain tissue paper. Nested among the wads were several oilskin-wrapped objects. He opened them.

He had not been swindled.

He was now in possession of a revolver, a silencer and a box of twenty-five cartridges.

The revolver was a new-looking .38 caliber Colt Police Positive Special with a blue finish and a checkered plastic stock. The serial number had been ground off and the ground-off place deeply treated with chemicals. The number was gone beyond resurrection. The silencer looked new, too; it had been similarly treated.

The revolver had been freshly oiled. He checked the cylinder chambers to make sure they were all empty and then tested for alignment. He pulled the hammer back to full cock and tried to turn the cylinder in each direction. Then he snapped the trigger and held it far back without releasing it, again twisting the cylinder in both directions. In neither test was there any play. The revolver was in perfect alignment. He adjusted the silencer to the muzzle; it was a good fit.

He opened the box of cartridges and took out six bullets and loaded the chambers. Then he put out the lights, felt his way to the window, pulled up the Venetian blind, opened the window noiselessly and leaned cautiously out into the darkness for a look. The wall of the building across the tradesmen's alley was blank; he could see no one. He sighted up at a bright star and squeezed the trigger. There was a slight hiss as the gun went off; the kickback to the palm of his shooting hand felt good.

Harry shut the window, lowered the blind, made sure the vanes were shut; then he made his way back to the light switch and turned the lights back on.

He removed the silencer, put a fresh cartridge in the empty chamber, slicked on the safety lock; one full load was all he would need. He wrapped the revolver and the silencer in their oilskins, wrapped the oilskins in small hand towels, put them into the cabinet, locked the cabinet. He took a surgical scissors and cut the cord into short lengths, cut up the wrapping paper, cut up the rest of the tissue, cut up the cardboard box, cut up the oilskin in which the box of cartridges had been wrapped, then took all the bits and pieces to the apartment incinerator and fed them into the chute. He went back, counted the cartridges remaining in the ammunition box—there were eighteen—replaced the cover on the box and taped it tightly with surgical tape from his wall dispenser.

Then he changed into his street clothes, put the box of cartridges in his pocket, switched off the lights, locked his office and got into his car.

He drove aimlessly for a while, keeping an eye on his rear-view mirror. When he was satisfied that he was not being tailed, he headed downtown.

He drove all the way to the tip of Manhattan Island.

He drove onto the ferry.

When the ferry was halfway across the bay, he got out of his car and sauntered around the deck. There were only a few passengers at the rail, none at the stern.

He planted his elbows on the rail at the stern. The taped box of cartridges was now in his hand.

He looked around. No one.

With a swift underhand flip he tossed the heavy little box well out into the ferry's wake. He could not even see the splash in the foam.

"Sorry, Benny," said Harry. "This is as close to the Atlantic as I can come."

Eighteen

On Wednesday morning he went with Tony Mitchell to Immigration; on Friday he went again; on the following Tuesday he had his passport. On Thursday and Friday he shopped for clothes and luggage. One of his purchases was a pair of snug lightweight gloves. He did not have the gloves sent home; he took them back with him to his office and locked them in the cabinet with the gun and the silencer.

On Saturday he played golf with Gresham, Karen and Dr. Stone; on Saturday night Dr. and Mrs. Stone were hosts of a dinner party consisting of the Greshams, Tony Mitchell, and Harry Brown. It was an expensive dinner at a French restaurant of note. Dr. Stone explained: "In return for the many times Bernice and I have been entertained by the Greshams."

At one point, between courses, the director of the Taugus Institute called across the table to Harry, "How goes it with the decision, Doctor?"

"I'm still sitting on it," said the doctor, turning to Bernice Stone in the hope that it would discourage her husband from pursuing the subject.

But it was too late. Kurt Gresham asked with a disarming smile, "Decision, Alfred? What kind of decision would that be? This is my personal physician, you know."

"Ah," said Dr. Stone mysteriously. "That's a secret."

Harry expected Gresham to question him later; rather to his surprise, Gresham seemed to have forgotten it.

On Sunday night Dr. Brown and Mrs. Gresham dined *à deux* at Giobbe's in the Village. It was the first time they had been alone since the Saturday night in his apartment. Harry thought Karen looked thinner, her classic cheeks more hollowed out; but it only emphasized the immensity of her green eyes; she seemed to him utterly beautiful. She was poised, attentive, even gay at times; but he sensed an edginess.

Only once did they talk of the matter most important to them, and it was Harry who brought it up.

"Uncle Joe came through."

She lit a cigaret. Her fingers trembled. "When?"

"On Monday. He gave me certain directions and I followed them. Everything worked out fine."

"So you have it." He could hardly hear her.

"Yes."

"Now what?"

"The Starhurst."

"When?"

"I don't know yet. But it has to be before the first."

On Tuesday he made a dry run. He left his office promptly at eleven o'clock in the morning. He walked at a normal pace. The loaded revolver was snugged in the waistband of his trousers. The silencer was in the inner pocket of his roomy sports jacket. His feather-light new gloves were in an outside pocket. He walked west to Columbus and up Columbus to the hotel.

Ten minutes flat, the whole thing.

The Starhurst was a tall, thin, rusty-looking building with a revolving-door entrance. He pushed through and into the empty forepart of a long corridorlike lobby covered with worn red carpeting. Far up the lobby he could see a corner of the desk and a bank of elevators and armchairs and sofas and tables with dimly lit lamps. From the entrance he could not see the clerk behind the desk, which meant that the desk clerk could not see him.

The whole place was silent, damp and had a faintly dusty smell.

Directly to the right of the entrance was a short corridor, red-carpeted like the lobby, that ended at a brass-knobbed door. Harry walked down, turned the knob and pushed, and found himself in a cramped vestibule at the foot of a steep flight of stairs. He climbed the stairs; the first door facing the stairway was 101.

Dr. Harrison Brown retraced his steps down the steep flight of stairs and opened the brass-knobbed door, stepped through and walked down the short corridor and turned left into the forepart of the Starhurst lobby and pushed through the revolving door to the street and walked at a normal pace back to his office on Central Park West.

Time from door to door: Exactly ten minutes.

Nineteen

On Thursday Kurt Gresham finally appeared at the office for a checkup. Both his systolic and diastolic blood pressures were up; his respiration was shallow and his pulse rapid and irregular; his EKG was erratic.

"How do you want it, with sugar or straight?" Harry said in the consultation room afterward.

"I'm not in such good shape, eh?" Kurt Gresham lit a cigar.

"You're in lousy shape. Have you been taking the digitalis in the morning? Quinidine after breakfast and dinner? Dicumerol in the afternoon? In the dosage prescribed?"

"When I remember."

"Which, I take it, is practically never. We'd better do another prothrombin. Roll up your sleeve."

He drew a blood sample and marked the vial for the lab. "You don't have to tell me you're not following my orders, Kurt. I've seen you eating your head off—all the wrong foods—"

"And drinking too much, too, I suppose."

"I don't mind the drinking, it's the diet. What are you trying to do, induce another heart attack?"

"It's nerves, Harry. I've been under a lot of pressure."

"You're a coronary, Kurt. Keep this up and you'll be just another statistic."

"That would make a lot of people happy."

"Would it make you happy?"

"How bad is it?"

"It's not bad. But it's not good, either."

Gresham looked impatient. "What's the prognosis?"

Harry lit a cigaret, shrugging. "You can go on like this for years; the damage from your last attack is repaired. You've got a strong constitution and you seem to thrive

113

on abuse. On the other hand, carrying on as you do, you're asking for it. It's likelier than not that, if you keep abusing yourself, one of these days you'll fall down dead."

"Is it in the realm of probability?"

"Why tempt fate? I'm involved, too. If you die on me, I lose my best customer." Harry chuckled, badly.

Kurt Gresham expelled a cloud of cigar smoke. "All right, what do I do?"

"If you take off sixty pounds, and then stick to the diet I gave you—if you stay with the medication—if you don't let your business"—grimly—"run you ragged, there's no reason why you shouldn't live out your natural lifetime."

"Well," said the millionaire glumly, "I suppose I'd better start."

"How about right now?"

Gresham chuckled. "You're a good doctor, Harry. Too damn good. I'll start on the vacation. You can watch me like an FBI agent. By the way, we're going by ship—the *'United States.'* "

"Is it going to be a strenuous trip for you?"

"Strenuous on the nervous system. Now don't say it— I've already decided that, starting next year, I'm going to slow down. Sort of sit back and take the cream off the top. That means delegation of authority, and you're included in my plans, Harry. Maybe you'll be retiring from general practice, eh? Be my personal physician, business executive on the side—how does that sound?"

"Not good."

"What's wrong?"

"Nothing, except that I like practicing medicine."

"I may offer a proposition you won't be able to resist."

"We'll see," said Dr. Brown.

Gresham studied his cigar. "All right, we'll see. Starting September first I'll be the model patient. I'll last until then, won't I?"

Dr. Brown squeezed out his cigaret, smiling back. "This is one business, Kurt, where we can't guarantee the merchandise."

"I'll risk it—what choice do I have?" Gresham laughed. "Oh, Harry. I'm planning a little theater party for Dr. and Mrs. Stone tomorrow night. He really couldn't afford that check the other night, and anyway, nobody extends himself for Kurt Gresham without being matched. I wish you'd do me a favor. Can you stand in for me as host?"

"Why can't you do it?" He knew perfectly well where Kurt Gresham would be tomorrow night.

"Business."

"Always business."

"From now until we leave I'm going to be on a merry-go-round. As a matter of fact, I'm sorry to have to miss it. I managed to pick up five tickets for *Success Story*."

Success Story was the runaway comedy hit of the season. It had opened late in May, and it was sold out for two years in advance.

"How on earth did you get them?" Harry was impressed. Scalpers were charging $50 a ticket for choice seats.

"Money buys anything," said Kurt Gresham. "Five together, sixth row center, orchestra."

Not anything, thought Harry. He said, "The Stones and I make three. Who are the other two, Karen and Tony?"

"Yes. I've also ordered dinner before the show at Monique's—a private room. And I'm sending the limousine and my chauffeur up to Taugus for the Stones, by the way, to drive them in and back. Make it seven o'clock at Monique's for cocktails and a leisurely dinner. Stone has to be back in Taugus early, so you and Karen and Tony can come straight to the apartment after the theater—I should be home by then—and we'll sit around and have a few drinks and talk. All right, Harry?"

"Sounds fine to me."

"Then that's settled." Gresham rose. "Karen has the tickets. You'll talk to her about the arrangements."

Harry talked to her thirty seconds after Kurt Gresham was gone.

"He was just here," Harry said.

"I know," said Karen's voice. It sounded strained. "He told me he was seeing you for a checkup. How is he?"

"I never discuss my patients over the phone," said Dr. Brown. "Can you come down here, Mrs. Gresham?"

"Yes. When?"

"Right away."

"Right away," she said.

Twenty

She sat with hands tightly clasped and knees tightly together, an eyelid twitching, her hair a copper pile, little ears exposed, unadorned. She was wearing a green silk suit over a white blouse, plunging deep. She wore no make-up except lipstick. She looked very young.

"Are you sure?" Harry asked quietly.

"I'm sure," Karen whispered. "Business as usual tomorrow evening at the Starhurst."

"Then that's it. I'll have a full five minutes? You're absolutely certain of that?"

"Yes."

"Six fifty-five to seven?"

"Yes."

"Two minutes ought to do it."

He got up from his desk and unlocked the cabinet and slid his hands into the thin gloves and brought out the revolver and the silencer. She followed his movements, fascinated. He unwrapped them and laid them on his desk. "Good old Uncle Joe," he said dryly. "He sells a mean ash. To the tune of a thousand bucks."

"Please, Harry, put them away. You . . . they scare me."

He rewrapped the gun and the silencer and put them back in the cabinet along wtih the gloves. He locked the cabinet, pocketed the key, and sat down again at his desk and looked at her.

"Karen."

"Yes, Harry."

"You're not directly involved. Will you remember that?"

"Yes."

"I know you're frightened. It's natural. But you've got to get hold of yourself. You'll have to put on an act. If you don't think you can go through with it, now is the time to tell me."

"I can. I will. It's just—"

"I understand," he said. "Now listen carefully."

"Yes, darling."

"The alibi. Not essential, just insurance. We're all supposed to meet for dinner in that private room at Monique's at seven o'clock. Correct?"

"Yes, darling."

"With Kurt sending the limousine to Taugus to pick up the Stones, they'll certainly be there early. Correct?"

"Yes. Kurt has trained the chauffeur himself. Just to be sure, I'll tell him to get the Stones there by six forty-five."

"And you'll be sure to be there early, too?"

"Tony's picking me up. I'll see to it that we get there before the Stones."

"Now as for me. I can't possibly be on time. I have office hours until seven o'clock. Right?"

"Right."

"I'm seeing to it that I have no office appointments for tomorrow past six o'clock, and I'll send my evening receptionist home at that time. I'll dress between six and six-thirty, at the office—my usual procedure when I'm going out. I'll leave shortly after that, but nobody's going to know that. Follow so far?"

"Yes."

"At exactly two minutes to seven, you'll excuse yourself and go to the phone booth at Monique's and *pretend* to call me. Then you'll rejoin the others and tell the Stones and Tony that I said I was shaving and changing my clothes, that I'd be leaving the office shortly. You've got that?"

"Yes, Harry."

"By twenty past seven—it should be ample time—I'll have got back to the office from the Starhurst. At twenty past seven you'll be impatient about me and you'll ask Dr. Stone to phone me. Tony may offer to do the phoning —if he does, let him; I'd rather it were Stone, but if you slough Tony off it may look queer. Anyway, whichever one does the calling, I'll be there to take it. I'll apologize and say I just got finished dressing and was about to leave. I will leave, and I'll drive right down to Monique's and join the party. For the rest of the evening, of course, I'll be covered by events. Questions?"

"Yes." Karen seemed less nervous now, as if talking about it had calmed her. "Between the time you slip out of the office and the time you get back, there'll be no one here. Until seven o'clock, anyway, somebody—some passer-by—might try to get into the office to see you professionally. They'll remember you weren't here—"

"Before I go to the Starhurst, I'll turn off the lights in the waiting room, and the street-door light. I'll leave the light on in my back room. If the point should ever come up—and remember, Karen, this is all precautionary; there's no reason why I should even be questioned—I'll merely say I locked up early because of having to shave, shower and change for the evening. That, not wanting to be held up, I just didn't answer the bell, or didn't hear it. It's probably an academic point, anyway. I rarely get transients."

"Suppose a patient tries to phone you between the time you slip out and the time you get back?"

"I'll have Dr. Lamper cover for me tomorrow evening; we have a reciprocal arrangement when either of us has an important social thing on. And I'll instruct my answering service to transfer all professional calls to Lamper's number beginning at five o'clock. Incidentally, when you pretend to call me at two minutes to seven, remember that it's my private number you're supposed to be calling; and when you ask Stone to phone me here at seven-twenty, be sure to give him the private number. That way we don't get into complications with the answering service. Anything else?"

"The . . ." she moistened her lips ". . . gun."

"I'm going to ditch it and the silencer where the police will find it. That's the whole point, Karen. All identifying marks have been removed, and it will copper-rivet the professional look of the job. The gloves I'll shove down the incinerator here when I get back—they may show traces of gun oil or gunpowder, and I can't risk that. So . . . that's it." He stared at her. "What do you think?"

"I love you," Karen said.

He rose. "You'd better go home now."

"I love you, Harry."

"What time do you phone me?"

"Two minutes to seven. Private number."

"Stone?"

"Twenty after. Same."

"I love you," Harry said.

Twenty-one

The day of the murder dawned to a unity with nature that was almost Greek. Friday was made for violence—scowling skies; dripping heat; windless; almost airless. It took effort to breathe. The weather aroused savagery.

By another irony, it turned out to be a busy day professionally for Dr. Harrison Brown. He was on the run all day, either out on house calls or seeing patients in his office. During his afternoon office hours he began to run behind schedule; only the fact that at the last moment two patients cancelled their appointments made it possible for him to send his evening receptionist home at six o'clock and darken his waiting room. He had called Dr. Lamper and notified his answering service at midday.

He locked the office street door carefully and switched off the outside light over his shingle.

First he downed a shot-glass of Scotch neat. Then he drank some water and put the bottle away. He had promised himself one drink before the event in his office, and two cocktails afterward, at Monique's, no more.

He went to the dressing room at the rear and set to work. He was conscious of no particular tension or sense of excitement. His whole life hung on the nature and quality of his actions during the next ninety minutes, and he was pleased to find himself without nervousness or fear.

He undressed without haste or wasted motion and showered under warm water which he gradually turned to cold until he gasped. He toweled himself brutally and, naked, shaved without nicking himself. He purposely left the used towels on the floor of the bathroom and his discarded clothes strewn about. He put on fresh linen and a loose charcoal-gray mohair suit and a white shirt and a dark gray tie. It was six-thirty exactly when he slid the revolver into the waistband of his trousers, tucked the oilskin-wrapped silencer into the breast pocket of his jacket, locked the cabinet and made a last tour of the premises and took a last mental inventory.

For the first time he felt a quiver of fear. He had almost forgotten the gloves. He got them and put them in an outside pocket. Immediately the feeling went away.

He had one last inspiration before he left: he took the receiver of his private phone off the cradle and left it that way. If anyone should try to dial him on the private line before he returned, there would be a busy signal, as if the phone were in use.

He slipped out into the street at twenty-one minutes to seven, leaving himself a cushion.

It was ten minutes to seven when he stepped into the dark tenement hallway directly across the street from the entrance to the Starhurst Hotel.

The taxi let the familiar fat figure out half a block from the Starhurst; probably, Harry Brown thought, an automatic precaution against some cabdriver's remembering his Friday night destination. Through the dirty glass of the tenement hallway door Harry watched Kurt Gresham, carrying a brief case, go through the revolving door of the Starhurst. He glanced at his watch. It was six minutes to seven.

The millionaire disappeared.

Harry gave him fifty seconds. Then he stepped out into the street and crossed over, going not fast and not slowly. He pushed through the revolving door of the hotel without hesitation and turned right—up the long slot of the lobby there was no one to be seen, or to see—and walked along the short corridor to the brass-knobbed door and turned the knob with his gloved hand. He opened the door and stepped into the little vestibule. He glanced up the stairs; no one. He glanced into the short corridor; no one.

He took the gun from his waistband and the silencer from his pocket, fitted the silencer to the muzzle and went softly and quickly up the steep stairs. Outside the door of 101 he released the safety of the Colt.

He turned slightly to the right so that the hand with the gun would be away from the door. Then he raised his left hand and rapped, not loudly, not softly, on the worn much-painted panel.

There was the slightest pause, as if the occupant of the room was puzzled.

120

Then the door opened.

And there stood Kurt Gresham, wide open to eternity.

Dr. Harrison Brown raised his right hand.

The little red mouth in the big round pink face made a little red hole as the colorless eyes went from Harry's face to the gun with the silencer in Harry's gloved right hand.

Then Kurt Gresham slowly fell back, and Harry followed, pushing the door gently to behind him with his left hand; the door clicked, and they stood there, eye to eye, in a dreadful silence.

Harry raised the revolver, elbow loose, grip firm.

He saw the jowls shake suddenly. He saw the little bit of pink tongue flick out and back from the dry lips. He saw the colorless eyes take on a jellylike look.

And he told his trigger finger to squeeze.

And it would not squeeze.

It would not.

It would not.

Kurt Gresham took the gun from him and, grabbing his lapels with one surprisingly strong hand, swung him about and pushed him. He fell back into an overstuffed chair.

Gresham was saying, "Idiot. Fall guy. Sucker. Weak sister," over and over in a soft vicious voice. And all of a sudden somebody's fist crashed on the door panel outside and the knob began to turn. As it began to turn, the millionaire darted to the bed and shoved the gun under the pillow and was halfway back to the door when it burst open.

A giant of a man with a broken nose was in the doorway pointing a big black automatic pistol.

Twenty-two

Through Dr. Harry Brown's vacant head ran the clear, cold, futile thought, He's surprised. Whoever the man is, he expected anything but the hotel guest on his feet with an inquiring look and a visitor in an armchair.

"Mr. Curtis," the giant said. He had a bass voice, rusty-sounding as if from disuse. "Everything all right?"

"All right?" repeated Kurt Gresham. "Why, certainly, Mr. O'Brien. Come in."

The giant stepped further into the room and the millionaire reached around him and shut the door.

"Why the pistol, Mr. O'Brien?" Gresham said. "Would you mind putting it away? I have a weak heart."

The giant looked foolish. Harry thought, He's a wrestler, or an old-time fighter. The broken nose, the impossible spread of shoulder, the stupid little pig eyes under the lumpy ridges of bone, the gorilla's jaw . . .

"Oh, Doctor," said Kurt Gresham. "This is Mr. O'Brien, the Starhurst's house detective. My doctor, Dr. Brown."

"Your doctor?" O'Brien said. He breathed noisily through the broken nose. "Well, how do, Doc."

Harry nodded.

"What happened, Mr. O'Brien?" the millionaire asked, frowning.

"I dunno," the house detective growled. "Somebody's idea of a joke, I guess, Mr. Curtis. I got a call in my office. Some dame talking fast and hysterical-like, said she heard shooting in Suite 101. She hung up before I could ask her who she was or what room she was calling from. I had no time to check."

"What time did she call?" murmured Gresham.

"Five minutes to seven on the nose—you know, Mr. Curtis, I got that wall clock right facing my desk in my office?—and I guess I made it up here in ninety seconds flat—took me only a few seconds to arrange to stop the elevators and seal off the exits."

"That was quick work," the millionaire said. "It makes me feel a lot safer, knowing there's a man like you on duty around here. I'll see you won't regret it, even though it was a hoax of some sort. Let's say a Christmas present?"

"Thanks, Mr. Curtis," said the giant bashfully. "It's a fact that if this'd been a real shooting, the guy would be sewed up tighter than a drum. I'd have got him hands down . . . Well, excuse the interruption, gents. I got to go get the elevators started again and the boys off the doors."

There was a rap on the door just as the house detective put his enormous hand on the knob. O'Brien glanced at Gresham, and the millionaire nodded.

"I'm expecting somebody, Mr. O'Brien. It's all right."

O'Brien opened the door. A tall, conservatively dressed man stood outside. He was carrying a brief case. The man's eyes flickered at sight of O'Brien.

Harry automatically glanced at his wristwatch. He stared and stared at it. It wasn't possible. The hands stood precisely at seven o'clock. Only five minutes had passed since he had come through the revolving door downstairs.

"If it's inconvenient for you, Mr. Curtis . . ." the man with the brief case said. He had a neutral sort of voice, a voice to forget.

"No, no, come in. Mr. O'Brien is just leaving." Kurt Gresham waved warmly to the house detective as the giant stepped out of the room, simultaneously giving the tall man a curt nod.

The man stepped in, shutting the door. He held onto the brief case. He glanced without expression at Harry. He said nothing more.

Gresham took the brief case from him and laid it on the bed. He went into the bathroom, came out with a brief case that was the identical twin of the one on the bed, handed it to the tall man.

"That's all for today, Monte," the millionaire said in his ordinary precise voice. "We'll defer the accounting to another time. By the way, this place is finished as of tonight. I'll let you know the new place and schedule over the weekend." Gresham opened the door, and smiled. "Pleasant trip."

The tall man went out without a word.

Twenty-three

Kurt Gresham locked and latched the door and when he turned around he was still smiling. "Alone at last," he said.

Harry Brown said nothing.

Gresham heaved off the bed, refilled their glasses looking down at him and Harry did not even look up. Dimly he heard the prissy voice say, "Would you care to wash, Doctor, as we well-bred people like to put it? I don't have to tell my personal physician what an experience like this does to a man's bladder. No? Well, mine isn't as young and vigorous as yours. Excuse me."

The fat old man went into the bathroom and shut the door.

Harry Brown heard the toilet flush after a while. Then he heard the sound of tap water running. Then the sounds of sloshing and of hearty gargling. This went on for some time.

He heard the sounds and they filled his head to the brim, leaving no space for anything else. Thoughts simply were not there. Vaguely, through the sounds, he knew that a great deal, of great significance, had happened in the past few minutes, but just what it was, what it signified, what position it left him in, he was unable to grasp and retain. It was as if he had been stricken with paralysis—mental and physical. He could not have pulled himself up from the overstuffed chair and gone over to the bed to reclaim the revolver under the pillow and unlock the door and walk out of the room if his life had depended on this simple series of actions. And for all he knew, his life did depend on it.

And he did not care.

The bathroom door opened and Gresham came out pink, dry, combed. He had removed his jacket and tie, his shirt was open at the neck, showing the mattress of gray hair on his chest, and he was carrying a clean towel.

The towel landed on Harry's lap.

"Use it," he heard Gresham say. "You're sweating like a boy on his first date." He repeated, sharply, "Wipe yourself."

Harry picked up the towel and wiped his face, his neck, his hands. He folded the towel and laid it neatly on his lap. Gresham, observing him closely, took the towel from his lap and threw it into the bathroom. Then he went to the bed and lifted the pillow and brought out Benny's lethal ashes and examined it. He shook his head over the silencer, glanced over at Harry, shrugged, opened the brief case on the bed, put Harry's gun into the brief case, locked the brief case.

Then he came over to Harry and said, "Harry."

Harry stared up at him.

"Would you care for a drink?"

Harry heard a hoarse voice say, "Yes." To his surprise, he realized it was his own.

Gresham went into the bathroom again. He came out with a bottle of cognac and two water glasses.

"Twenty years old," he said. "Private stock." He half-filled each glass, put one glass into Harry's hand, went over to the bed, put one pillow on top of the other and lay down. He raised the glass and took a long drink and then he lowered the glass and immediately raised it again. But this time he sipped.

"Harry," he said. "Drink that brandy."

Harry came to with a start. He raised the glass and he did not set it down until he had emptied it. Gresham watched him from the bed. A warmth came into Harry's body, beginning at the toes. It rose through his legs into his torso and then it was in his head; and his head came alive again.

"Ah," said the old fat man. "I see you're back in the land of the living, Doctor. I'd like your opinion, Doctor. What do you think of yourself?"

Harry was beginning to think, but not of himself. He was beginning to think of Karen.

"You were the sucker," piped Kurt Gresham, smiling again. "You were the patsy in the middle. The expendable man. And they couldn't wait."

"What?" Harry asked, blinking. "What did you say, Kurt?"

125

"They couldn't wait."

"Who couldn't wait, Kurt?"

"Don't you know? You mean you still don't see it?"

"See *what*?"

"Harry."

"See what, Kurt?"

"That you've been framed by my wife and her lover?"

Harry stammered, "Lover? But—"

"I mean our friend Anthony Mitchell."

Why was everything so wrong? "Tony?" Harry muttered.

"Ah, she didn't tell you about Tony. Or she lied and put on an act about Tony. It's a damned shame. I mean, so much wasted talent. She's never realized that she didn't have to earn her living taking her clothes off. She could have made a fine career for herself as an actress. Oh, yes, Karen and Tony. Would you like me to sketch in the groundwork for you, Doctor? I mean about Tony?"

"About Tony," Harry repeated.

"Tony's been with me, intimately with me, for the past ten years. He's one of my top executives—member of my board of directors. Who do you think suggested you as a replacement for Dr. Welliver here in New York when Welliver had to retire? Your friend Tony Mitchell. It was Tony who placed your name in nomination, and that was when we started our check of your background."

"Tony," Harry said again. He groped for his glass, saw it was empty, stared stupidly at it.

"It was Tony who suggested that Karen and I become your patients. It was Tony who thought up the bank loan-cosigner approach, to be followed shortly by my paying off the loan in a lump with the flourish that was to hook you, and did. And it was Tony who must be given the credit for the *coup de grâce*—getting you into bed with Karen."

Harry Brown blinked. A soreness suddenly seized the pit of his stomach.

"You're shocked," said Karen's husband, smiling. "You slob, you're actually shocked!"

He blinked and blinked and blinked. The soreness was spreading, had spread, through his body. One great soreness.

"But if you're a slob," Kurt Gresham went on, "I'm an absolute idiot. After all, Harry, you have an excuse— you've never lived, you're a complete innocent, you're rather stupid. But I'm supposed to be a smart man, a smart experienced man. I thought Tony's idea to get you involved in an affair with Karen was good sound strategy. I didn't know that their long-range objective wasn't you, but me."

"Your own wife," Harry shouted. "You *told* your wife to become my mistress?"

"Yes, and it wasn't so easy to get her to do it, either. Here, we both need another brandy."

Gresham heaved off the bed, refilled their glasses and lay down again. "Harry, you have that damned adolescent, Sunday-school view of life. Do you think I deluded myself when I married Karen? I'm an ugly old man; she's a young, beautiful and, as you know, passionate woman. I couldn't have bought her except as part of a deal; I knew that and accepted it. Money and marriage for her; and for me, the use of her at my pleasure. But I also knew I wasn't man enough for her—I'm too old and used-up, as she likes to put it. So I gave her the right to sleep around—I knew she'd do it, anyway—on the sole condition that she be discreet about it. I've known of her affair with Tony Mitchell from the day it started, which was before I married her. What I didn't know was that theirs was no ordinary liaison. I didn't know they were planning my murder and were waiting for the right weapon to come along. And that was you."

Harry remembered the brandy. He began to drink it, steadily.

"You were their weapon, Harry. You'd kill me for them, and you'd be caught doing it, and they'd be rid of us both and live happily ever after on my money. How do you like my diagnosis, Doctor?"

"I don't believe a word of it," Harry said.

"You're a bigger imbecile than I figured you. Or you do believe it but won't admit it to yourself. Or maybe you're admitting it to yourself but for some amusing reason don't want to look lower in my eyes than you know you already do."

Old Kurt Gresham, vast sagging lump-on-the-bed, smiled at young Dr. Harrison Brown. It was not an unkind smile; it was almost a smile of sympathy. The jowls shook pinkishly.

"So let me spell it out for you, Doctor . . . It was Karen's idea that you kill me."

"No."

"No, no, reflect, my boy. Was it your idea?"

"Yes."

"No. She planted it in your head. Believe me. I know her. I know how she works . . . I'll grant you that the inspiration might not have been hers originally. It smacks of Tony. Well, it doesn't matter; whichever of them thought of it first, they were in this together. That's as dead certain as that I'm still breathing. Now then. Karen told you that between five minutes to seven and seven o'clock on Friday night I'm in this room at the Starhurst, alone. Correct?"

"Yes, but—"

"And she even got the gun and silencer for you?"

He was silent.

"Oh, gallant. And so typical. And this was all worked out to the last iota, Harry, wasn't it? undoubtedly on a split-second time schedule? My death to occur during the five minutes before my club manager was due to show up? Couldn't go wrong, could it, Harry? Only it did. And why? Because just after you stepped into this room—just after you raised the gun and theoretically shot me (and how my dear wife miscalculated in her choice of weapon, Harry, or my dear attorney, or both!)—just as I was theoretically falling dead at your feet . . . what happened? O'Brien of the hotel security staff barges in and—still theoretically—catches you with your antiseptic pants down, Doctor. So, if you'd had the guts to carry the plan out, you'd have been caught, wouldn't you? My dear innocent, that must be clear even to you."

Harry Brown closed his eyes to shut out the sight of the monster, the bloated embodiment of his conscience and ineptitude; but he could not shut his ears to its voice.

"Now O'Brien got a phone call in his office just in time to make arrangements to convert the hotel into a trap and race up here to catch you in the act. Who do you think made that phone call, Doctor? At five minutes to seven?"

At five minutes to seven he had just pushed through the revolving door downstairs, less than a minute after Gresham . . .

"A woman made that call, O'Brien said," the prissy voice went on. "A 'hysterical' woman who had heard a gun go off in Suite 101 that hadn't gone off at all. So she knew a gun was scheduled to go off. She knew you were going to be standing in that room pumping lead into me. What woman knew that, Harry? Give me a name—any other name but my wife's. Can you?"

But he could not, he could not.

"And why should Karen phone the house detective of the Starhurst—putting on another act, of course, hysteria—why should she get him to roar into this room at just the time you were supposedly shooting me? Wouldn't you say that her timing—deliberately premature to give O'Brien the opportunity to get up here at the moment of the murder—wouldn't you say it was contrived to catch you committing it, Harry?"

Yes, yes, yes, yes, yes.

"Maybe they figured you'd panic and run, Harry, and O'Brien would put a bullet in you—that would wrap it up neatly . . . both of us dead, the victim *and* his killer. Or, that when you saw O'Brien, you'd stick the gun in your mouth and save O'Brien the trouble, with the same satisfying result. And if you weren't shot running, or if you didn't shoot yourself . . . tell me, Harry, would you have dragged Karen into it? *Could* you have dragged Karen into it? If I know my wife, you'll find she's managed to leave herself completely uninvolved—"

Yes . . . All she had to do was *not* go through the motions of placing that two-minutes-to-seven phone call, was *not* to ask Dr. Stone to phone at twenty minutes past seven . . . then she was in the clear, in the clear.

"—and she'd have got away with it. How do you feel, Doctor?"

Harry licked his lips. Was it possible . . . was it possible that somehow, in some way, by some miracle, Karen was not responsible for this? That it had been Tony Mitchell all along . . . ? But this straw bent and broke even as he grasped it. The only way Tony Mitchell could have known what was scheduled for tonight would have been through Karen's telling him.

"I see you feel properly rotten, as rotten as only a fine clean-living young man could feel when he sees himself as others see him . . . a fool, an object of contempt, about as important to his beloved as a soiled handkerchief. And you'd like to find a hole somewhere, wouldn't you, and crawl into it and lick your wounded little ego? You'd like to be out of the whole thing—Karen, Tony, the organization, me? Even me? Especially me? Harry?"

'Yes." It came out stiff and dry.

"Maybe that can be arranged," Kurt Gresham said. "You know, Harry, I liked you from the start. Just made a mistake about your guts. Well, this isn't the time or place to discuss you. Right now we have work to do."

He was trying hard, very hard, to follow the sense of the old man's words. Gresham got off the bed and went to the closet and came back with one of his impossibly long, green Havana cigars. Harry watched him strike a match, puff critically, nod approval.

"We're in an interesting situation now, Harry my boy," the millionaire murmured. "Let's put ourselves in the shoes of my wife and my clever lawyer. By now I'm dead and you're killed, or alive but in custody. Of course you're not able to show up at Monique's for dinner, or to go to the theater with them and the Stones afterward. How do they explain your nonappearance? Very simply: doctors are notoriously unreliable socially. An emergency, no doubt— Dr. Stone and his wife will certainly understand *that*. You didn't even have time to phone. These conscientious young doctors, tch, tch, and so on." He took the cigar out of his mouth and frowned at it. "All right, then. Karen and Tony and the Stones finish their dinner and go to the theater. My chauffeur then drives the Stones home to Taugus, as Dr. Stone had requested. Leaving Karen and Tony alone for the first time this evening. Where do they go, Harry?"

"To your apartment."

"Home sweet home—correct, Harry. He takes her home at once. Because I'm dead and you've murdered me, and the police must have been trying to reach the widow, are likely waiting for her there. Yes, they go right to the apartment, bracing themselves for the act they've undoubtedly rehearsed and—but what's this?" The fat old man cried delightedly, "No police! No sign of police! No message! No *anything*. What's their reaction, Harry?"

Harry said, "They're puzzled. Then they get nervous. Maybe scared."

"You're certainly coming back to life, Harry," said Kurt Gresham with pleasure. "Yes, they're puzzled, then nervous, then very nervous, then scared to death. And what will they do, Harry, when they get puzzled and nervous and scared to death?" His teeth clamped down viciously on the cigar. "They'll talk, that's what they'll do! They'll talk it over."

He still doesn't think I'm convinced, Harry thought. Or

maybe he's not as sure of his theory as he's made out to be.

"They'll talk it over, Harry," said Kurt Gresham, "and we'll be there, you and I—we'll be there to listen."

Twenty-four

Gresham called the desk and ordered a pile of sandwiches and a pot of coffee. The fat man ate with a sort of abstracted relish. Harry could not eat. He drank, however. Not coffee. A great deal more brandy.

At half-past ten Gresham took his brief case and they left the Starhurst. In the taxi he said, "We'll go in through the tradesmen's entrance at the rear and walk up. I don't want the doorman or the elevator men to see us."

Harry nodded dreamily. He was floating on brandy.

"We'll set up our listening post in the blue guest room."

"Blue guest room," Harry said. In all this madness it sounded perfectly logical.

The millionaire unlocked his apartment door and they went into the black foyer at eleven minutes to eleven, by Harry's watch. It was an old watch, a gift from his father, with a black face and pale green luminous hands. He was still focusing on the watch in the dark when Kurt Gresham snapped on the foyer light.

"Hurry it up." The old man trundled ahead of Harry to the blue guest room and led him to a chair near the door. "You sit here."

Harry sat. He fumbled for a cigaret. Gresham seemed able to see in the dark. "Don't smoke," he said sharply. "And don't make a sound when they come in. Breathe with your mouth open."

He trotted out of the room. A moment later the foyer light went off. A moment after that Harry heard him come back into the bedroom.

"You all right, Harry?" the prissy voice said. Harry restrained an impulse to giggle. It was like a séance he had once attended, with voices coming out of the air.

"I'm all right."

He heard the slight scrape of another chair and a wheezy

grunt as Gresham took up his position just inside the doorway, within reach of the guest-room light switch; heard the creak of the chair spring, the thump of Gresham's brief case being set down on the floor.

Then they sat there, in the darkness, silent. Harry dozed, chin-to-chest, mouth open.

Twice he came to with a start and glanced at his watch.

They heard the key in the lock. Harry sat up quickly, peering. It was twenty minutes to midnight.

The apartment door opened and closed and then they saw the glow in the hallway from the lights in the living room. They could hear faintly, but clearly.

"Something's wrong," Tony Mitchell's voice said.

There were sounds from the bar, ice cubes tinkling in glasses, gurgling from a bottle.

"I can use this right now," Karen Gresham's voice said.

There was a pause. Then: "Radically wrong," Tony Mitchell said. "There should be cops, respectfully stuck away in the rear of the lobby. But nothing. I say to the doorman, 'How are you tonight, John?' and he says, 'Fine, thank you, sir.' No excitement, no message, no knowing looks—nothing. And the elevator operator grins and scrapes as if it were the day before Christmas."

"What do you think, Tony?" It was interesting to hear her voice. It was really a different voice—unknown to him. He was sure that if he could see her she would look different, too—equally a stranger. And wasn't she? Wasn't she?

"Either our medical pigeon contracted a severe case of chilled tootsies and ran out on the whole deal—"

"Not Little Lord Fauntleroy," said Karen. "His is not to reason why. He's one of nature's noblemen, didn't you know that?"

"—or, what's far likelier, he loused it up and the old wolf beat him to the punch. That would explain why, if Harry didn't go through with it, Big Daddy's not home to greet us. He's probably talking to his meat department right now, arranging to have our boy cut up, packaged and disposed of. That takes time, baby. And we'd better face it—if that's the way it went, you and I are in one hell of a spot."

Karen began to curse. She cursed her beloved Harry in a low, steady, unemotional way that made him writhe with shame. He could not hear Kurt Gresham's breathing at all.

"Shut up, will you?" snapped Tony Mitchell. "I have to think this out. And fast, because that old man is sudden death."

"Tell me something I don't know," Karen said viciously.

"The point is that even while the surgical saws are separating Harry into his component parts, old Kurt must be asking himself: How did Harry know about the Starhurst?"

"And also who called that house detective up?" Karen actually sounded frightened. "Tony, do you suppose he'll realize—?"

"One thing at a time, will you?"

Harry could hear Tony Mitchell's agitated steps. Beside him Kurt Gresham stirred; there was the slightest creak of the chair springs. It stopped instantly.

"We've got to anticipate Kurt's thinking," Tony said. The steps had stopped. "All right: How could Harry have known? We don't have time to give it the finesse it needs —we're going to have to play it by ear—but I have an idea."

"Pour me another drink."

There was the sound of more gurgling; then Tony Mitchell said, "Like this. You blew it, but inadvertently. The kid had confided in you that he'd been recruited by the old man. You had asked him where Kurt made the deal with him, at Kurt's office in the Empire State Building or at his suite at the Starhurst. Slip of the tongue. Natural? So like the kid knew about the Starhurst, and like he worked his own points from there. Dig?"

Karen said slowly, "It might work, at that."

"You knew nothing about it, our Dr. Brown had never dropped one word to you; but now, after the event, putting little things together, you realize that Harry must have had second thoughts or an attack of cold feet; that he wanted out and knew Kurt wouldn't let him out; that he must even have realized he could escape by only one route— Kurt's murder. You can say he must even have thought you'd marry him afterward. Anyway, Harry tried, and the gutless wonder fouled it up . . . From there we play it by ear."

Karen was quiet. After a while she said, "Pretty good. You *are* a smart operator, lover."

"Not so smart," Tony Mitchell muttered. "You'll have to put on a good act."

"You're the only man I know smarter than that lump of pork fat I'm married to. And you're a lot prettier. Come here to me . . ."

There was a long, long pause. The only sounds were the sounds of love-making, fierce and abandoned. And here we are, Harry thought, listening in—the cuckold and the cuckold, the legal one and the illegal one. He was quite sober now.

"No." said Tony suddenly. "No, Karen, not now."

"Damn you," Karen laughed. "What you do to me . . ." There was a slight, laughing scuffle. "Darling. What's the matter?"

"What about the little lump?" Tony Mitchell growled.

"What little lump?"

"Harry."

"Harry?" The total contempt in her voice made Harry Brown shiver. "Lump is right. He was a panting, ridiculous lump. Strong as a bull, which made it even worse—strong, sincere, panting like an animal. The only way I was able to take him was to shut my eyes and pretend he was you. Give me a refill, darling. I need a lot of fortification if I'm going to fool Big Daddy when he comes waddling through that door . . ."

Harry found himself on his feet, aware with detached surprise that growling sounds were grumbling in his throat. But a hand closed on his wrist, and a hiss like a snake's tickled his ear: "You stay right where you are!"

And then the hand was snatched from his wrist, and the shapeless silhouette of Kurt Gresham blocked out the faint glow in the doorway, and then it moved away, and Harry heard nothing, nothing at all, until the next eternity. And then what he heard was the muffled cough of a gun. And another.

And two thumps.

And silence.

He ran down the hall to the living room and he skidded to a stop in the archway.

"Hold it, Harry," said the old fat man. The revolver with the silencer was pointed in Harry's direction. Then the old fat man said, but not to Harry, "Scum. *Scum.*"

Two glasses, unbroken, lay on the thick-piled rug in the middle of spreading stains. Near one of them sprawled Karen Gresham, her body a glittery twist in its silversequinned décolleté gown. Blood was gushing from her neck. Near the other sprawled Tony Mitchell, dinner jacket rumpled. Blood was gushing from his mouth.

"Don't move, Harry," said the old fat man. He walked over to his wife and carefully put another bullet into her head. Then he walked over to his lawyer and carefully put another bullet into his head. Mitchell's eyes remained open. Karen's eyes were no longer there.

Gresham's pendulous cheeks were the color of well-hung beef fat, and they quivered as he spoke.

"Don't worry, Harry," he said, "my security people will take care of this. There won't be a trace on the rug. And I'm not even here, remember?"

Something was wrong with Gresham's statement, but for the moment Harry could not pinpoint the mistake.

"As for disposal, tomorrow my lawyer is going to take my wife out on his boat; a good way out to sea they'll get into the dinghy and do some fishing; they're going to capsize and drown, and none of the three bodies will ever be recovered. You know those sharks off Montauk Point."

Harry started to say something, his tongue stuck, and then he got the word out. "Three?" he said.

"Didn't I tell you, Harry? You went fishing with them."

"That's why you asked me to come here with you." And now Harry realized that he had known it all along.

"Of course, Harry. Shooting you in the hotel would have necessitated a complicated disposal operation. It's simpler from here. I've saved two bullets for you." The old man moved closer; the revolver was coming up, slowly.

"But why, Kurt? Because I tried to kill you?" He was surprised at the clarity in his head, the lack of fear in his body.

"Because you failed to kill me," said the old man. "You chickened out, Harry. I can't have a weak sister working for me. And you know too much to be allowed to live. Especially now that you've witnessed me commit two murders with my own hands."

Harry measured the distance between them. He had played football in college and he knew how far he could spring for a tackle. He tensed his leg and thigh muscles.

And now, although Kurt Gresham was smiling with his little womanish mouth, his colorless eyes flashed the glare of impersonal ferocity that Harry had never seen except in the eyes of wild animals.

"That's the way it has to be, Harry. It's going to be a

bitter blow to the old man. Out fishing, the dinghy overturned, the bodies never found, and poor old Kurt Gresham is bereft, in one foul blow of fate, of the three most important people in his life—his wife, his lawyer, his doctor. Goodbye Har—"

He leaped high and out and hard and even as he struck he knew he had no target; he struck nothing; there was no resistance; the bulk was beneath him but it had not collapsed as a result of his strike. As he recovered his balance and looked down on Kurt Gresham, he knew that the third death, which had been Kurt Gresham's dream, would be as unrealized as the dreams of the other two in that silent room.

Gresham's globe of a face was not pink but yellow-green. His left arm was rigid, clamped in cramp. There were bubbles at the corners of his mouth. The lips were cyanosed and tight back against the teeth, the mouth a fixed gape. The animal eyes were rolled far up to the lids. Dr. Harrison Brown made the clinical diagnosis automatically: coronary occlusion.

Without conscious thought, in conditioned reflex, Dr. Brown pried open the mouth, depressed the tongue, placed his own mouth on the mouth of Kurt Gresham and breathed into it. He pulled back so that the lungs could express the air he had forced into them, put his mouth back on Gresham's mouth, blew the air from his lungs into Gresham's lungs—kept up the prescribed ritual, in, out, breathe, away . . .

The lips beneath his twitched, grew salty, pulled together, had wetness.

Dr. Brown drew back.

For a moment there was intelligence in the staring pucker of the eyes. The blue upper lip writhed back. Teeth showed in a mockery of a smile.

He slapped the cheek sharply.

"Kurt," he said. "Kurt!"

A whisper drowned in phlegm produced a word.

"Human . . ."

He rubbed the wrists. Rubbed and rubbed.

"Human . . . funny . . ." Very faint.

"What? *What?*"

Now, quite clearly, through the blue lips past the leathery tongue: "Forgive . . . love . . . no . . . fun . . ."

The eyes rolled up, became slits of white.

The body jerked.

The body was still.

Dr. Brown locked his lips on the lips again, blowing with all his power, but the mouth was stiff, the tongue a nuisance, the lungs empty bags.

Dr. Brown pushed up from his knees, staggered and straightened, went past the two bloody things on the floor to the telephone and dialed police headquarters.

Twenty-five

Dr. Brown in the blue guest room, well-lighted now, door closed, vis-à-vis elderly Lieutenant Galivan, who looked like his father. Dr. Brown sipping Kurt Gresham's private-stock cognac, smoking a parade of cigarets in defiance of the coronary statistics. Telling his story from the beginning.

And Lieutenant Galivan, who looked as if nothing in this world or the next could surprise him, looking surprised.

Somebody knocked on the door and Galivan said patiently, "Come in." A beef-shouldered man came in. "We're through, Lieutenant,' he said. "M.E.'s signed the order, the meat wagon's here. All right to take them down?"

"No," said Galivan.

"No?" echoed the big detective.

"There are federal angles to this thing, Sergeant."

"Federal? And here we were, figuring it the usual: old husband, young wife, young lover."

"Let's leave it like that for now," Galivan said in his slow, tired voice. "Remember. For the papers, nothing."

"Yes, sir."

"Get rid of the technical people. Everybody. Just you and Jimmy Ryan stay. And keep the meat wagon on tap. But on a side street, off the Avenue."

"Anything else?"

"Yes. Send Sidney over to get the District Attorney. The D.A.'s an early-to-bedder, but he'll want to be in on this. Have you ever met Max Crantz, our D.A., Doctor?"

"No," said the doctor.

"Hell of a nice guy. A straight-shooter. Okay, that's it, Sergeant."

The detective went out, closing the door. Galivan sucked

on his pipe, looking at Harry through the smoke. "Well, we've come a long way from the Lynne Maxwell business, haven't we? There's nothing else, is there?"

"I've told you everything."

"You sure got yourself messed up."

"That, Lieutenant," said Dr. Brown, "I did indeed."

Galivan puffed. "Damn this pipe. Oh, that funeral-parlor setup, I'll put the Yonkers police on that. And San Francisco on Uncle Joe. I think you'll find others who'll appreciate the by-products of this thing, too. Like the Federal Bureau. I take it you intend to cooperate?"

"All the way."

"If there's anything I can do for you, Doctor, I'll do it."

"Thanks, but I'm not looking for any favors, Lieutenant. I got myself into this mess, and I'll get myself out of it, or pay the price."

"No favors," said Galivan. "But to be instrumental in cracking an operation like this narcotics setup—don't sell yourself short, Doctor. You're going to have a lot of law-enforcement people grateful to you. Including Max Crantz."

Galivan's pipe was making dying sounds. He made a face and got up and went to the extension phone. He dialed the operator and said, "I'd like to talk to Mr. Christopher Hammond, please. At the New York offices of the FBI."

Twenty-six

Dr. Harrison Brown at his office on Monday crept around like a zombie. He had hoped to lose himself in work, but it was a slow day: four patients in the early afternoon, two house calls, then nothing. He had read all the morning papers; there had been no word of the three deaths in the Gresham apartment. The FBI and the Narcotics men had sat on the story, hard.

At four o'clock he sent his girl out for the afternoon papers. Now there were headlines. Millionaire industrialist slays wife and lover and dies of heart attack. But there was no mention of narcotics, and there was no mention of Dr. Harrison Brown. There were pictures—of Kurt Gresham, of Karen Gresham, of Tony Mitchell.

At four-thirty his receptionist announced Lieutenant Galivan.

Dr. Harrison Brown leaped on him. "Lieutenant. Here, sit down. Tell me what's been happening. Nobody's come near me since that all-night session Friday night with the District Attorney and the Federal people. Not a word in the papers or on radio or TV about me—"

"And there won't be, either," said Galivan. He eased his long body into the chair beside Harry's desk. He looked tired.

"There . . . won't be?" Harry sat down suddenly.

"It's all over, Doctor. Those FBI boys . . . Lieutenant Galivan shook his head in admiration. "It's a beautiful thing to watch the way they work in an operation that requires absolute secrecy until the split second they're ready to spring. On Saturday they and foreign authorities were quietly opening bank vaults on court orders in a dozen and a half cities here and abroad. CIA code specialists were put to work on the records, and by Sunday afternoon the whole Gresham machine was stripped down to its vital parts and each part analyzed—without a single member of the ring knowing what was hanging over their heads. Then—wham!—the strike. Last night, ten o'clock our time. New York, Washington, Philadelphia, Chicago, Miami, London, Paris, Zurich, Rome, Berlin, Lisbon, Madrid, Belgrade, Athens, Ankara, Cairo, Hong Kong, Tokyo. The Gresham empire. Took thirty-five years to build up, one night to destroy. Thanks to you."

"They arrested them *all*?" Harry asked incredulously.

"Every last one. It turns out that besides Gresham's board of directors he had twenty-nine regional big shots, and, of course, the usual gang of middlemen, minor executives and just plain cogs in the machinery. The big boys are already here in the Federal Building or in custody in the countries where they were picked up, and they're all singing like nightingales and trying to make deals. The small fry are doing the same thing. The evidence is overwhelming—Gresham's empire is smashed, all right. From here on in it's just mop-up. And you're out of it."

"I don't understand . . ."

The lieutenant crossed bony knees. He took out his pipe, packed and lit it, and puffed; and then he smiled around the stem.

"There was a conference at noon today, downtown—Chris Hammond of the FBI, District Attorney Crantz, a Treasury agent, a member of the Attorney General's staff from Washington, and some other interested officials—and I sat in. Do you know what the subject of the conference was?"

"What?"

"You, Doctor. And a decision was reached by the group that I think surprised every individual there. The subject was what to do with you, and the decision was: Nothing."

Harry said hoarsely, "You mean I'm not going to be arrested, prosecuted . . . ?"

"That's exactly what I mean," puffed Galivan. "You won't even have to appear as a witness at any of the hearings or trials afterward—they've got an embarrassment of evidence as it is."

"But why, Lieutenant?" cried Harry Brown. "After all the things I've done—"

"Well, what have you done, Doctor?"

The question startled him. "Why, I joined a criminal organization—"

"Under deception and duress."

"I treated a woman with a bullet wound and didn't report it to the police—"

"There's no evidence of that, Doctor, except your confession. You know a confession requires corroborating evidence."

"But . . . I accepted a huge retainer to do similar jobs for Gresham in his New York territory—"

"Again there's only your confession," smiled the lieutenant. "And you didn't get to do any other jobs, did you? And you *were* treating Gresham as his personal physician for a chronic illness."

"But . . ." He was bewildered. "I bought a gun and a silencer illegally. I tried to kill a man with it—"

"And didn't, Doctor, when all you had to do was squeeze the trigger." Galivan held up his pipe hand. "Don't say it. It's all been thoroughly gone into, Doctor. A strict adherence to the law would call for your arrest or detention for appearance before the grand jury, but the men in that office today weren't in a legalistic mood. The fact remains that, in view of what you've contributed to the upholding of the law, in view of your total cooperation and frankness where your own acts have been concerned, those men feel you're entitled to a *quid pro quo*."

"And I have a feeling," Harry mumbled, "that one man at that conference had a lot to do with the decision."

Galivan colored slightly. "Not a lot, Doctor. Nobody influences men like Christopher Hammond and Max Crantz against their better judgments. Hammond has a brother around your age; incidentally, he's a doctor, too, at the beginning of what looks like a fine career. The D.A. has two sons in their late twenties. These men understand a lot more than the techniques of law enforcement. They know you stepped out of line, but they also know you pulled back in time. A man who can and will do that deserves a break. They're not going to crucify you, and I go along with them a hundred percent."

Harry sat numbly.

"You're not going to be needed, as I said, and your name will never be mentioned. You'll be a name in the no-touch files, no more. Unless, of course, you should get into more trouble. In that case, the roof would fall in on you. That's not a threat, Dr. Brown," Lieutenant Galivan said quietly, "It's a fact. But I don't think that's going to happen. I hope not, anyway. It would make a lot of us look awfully bad. And now Doctor," he said, leaning over to knock out his pipe in the ash tray, "I've got to get back to my job." He rose and looked down at the man behind the desk keenly. "I'm not going to say good luck. A man makes his own luck, good or bad. But I think you've learned that by now."

And he was gone.

Harry Brown sat in his consultation room with his head deeply sunk in the well of his shoulders and his surgeon's hands folded at his waistline. He could not have said what he was feeling. All he knew was that under the foggy turbulence within him lay a quietness, a peace, he could not remember ever having experienced.

He looked around his office—at the expensive furniture; at the impressive rows of medical books that constituted the practitioner's showcase, meant for display, not reference; at all the sham symbols of success. He felt the luxurious material of his trousers, stared down at the high polish on his shoes, at the $75 Tiffany ash tray on his desk.

And at the empty chair where a patient should have been sitting.

A man makes his own luck—luck? Life!—good or bad.

After a while he groped for his wallet, located a card, pulled the telephone to him and dialed the number on the card.

"Dr. Stone, please. Dr. Harrison Brown calling."

"One minute, Doctor."

Alfred Stone's voice leaped into his ear. "Doctor! I wondered when I was going to hear from you. That awful thing about the Greshams—you've heard about it, I suppose . . ."

"Yes," said Harry Brown. "Dr. Stone, is the job at the Institute still open?"

"Of course."

"I want it."

"I'm delighted."

"You may not be when you hear my story."

"Story?" repeated Dr. Stone, mystified. "What kind of story?"

"Well," said Dr. Harrison Brown, "some people might call it a kind of failure story. I think it's a success story, but I'd rather you judged for yourselves. Dr. Stone, can you arrange a meeting with Peter Gross and Dr. Blanchette?"

SIGNET Presents Ed McBain's 87th Precinct Mysteries

- [ ] **THE CON MAN.** Con men—handsome, charming, and the deadliest denizens of the city. And the boys of the 87th have their hands full figuring out the gimmicks and outconning the cons.
(#E9351—$1.75)

- [ ] **LET'S HEAR IT FOR THE DEAF MAN.** What did J. Edgar Hoover, George Washington, and a football team have in common? The Deaf Man was feeding them clues, and it was up to the boys of the 87th Precinct to puzzle it out before they became the unwilling accomplices in the heist of the century. (#E9075—$1.75)*

- [ ] **THE PUSHER.** Two corpses, a mysterious set of fingerprints, an unknown pusher called Gonzo, blackmail calls to the police, and a man who keeps pigeons—and the boys of the 87th Precinct find themselves involved in the wildest case ever. (#E9256—$1.75)*

- [ ] **COP HATER.** He was swift, silent and deadly—and knocking off the 87th Precinct's finest, one by one. If Steve Carella didn't find the cop killer soon he might find himself taking a cool trip to the morgue!
(#E9170—$1.75)*

- [ ] **KILLER'S WEDGE.** Her game was death—and her name was Virginia Dodge. She was out to put a bullet through Steve Carella's brain and she didn't care if she had to kill all the boys in the 87th Precinct to do it! (#E9614—$1.75)*

*Prices slightly higher in Canada

Buy them at your local bookstore or use coupon on next page for ordering.

SIGNET Thrillers by Mickey Spillane

☐	THE BIG KILL	(#E9383—$1.75)
☐	BLOODY SUNRISE	(#W8977—$1.50)
☐	THE BODY LOVERS	(#E9698—$1.95)
☐	THE BY-PASS CONTROL	(#E9226—$1.75)
☐	THE DAY OF THE GUNS	(#E9653—$1.95)
☐	THE DEATH DEALERS	(#J9650—$1.95)
☐	THE DEEP	(#E8688—$1.75)
☐	THE DELTA FACTOR	(#Y7592—$1.25)
☐	THE ERECTION SET	(#E9944—$2.50)
☐	THE GIRL HUNTERS	(#J9558—$1.95)
☐	I, THE JURY	(#J9652—$1.95)
☐	KILLER MINE	(#W8788—$1.50)
☐	KISS ME DEADLY	(#Q6492—95¢)
☐	THE LAST COP OUT	(#J9592—$1.95)
☐	THE LONG WAIT	(#J9651—$1.95)
☐	ME, HOOD	(#Q5964—95¢)
☐	MY GUN IS QUICK	(#J9791—$1.95)
☐	ONE LONELY NIGHT	(#J9697—$1.95)
☐	THE SNAKE	(#W9005—$1.50)
☐	SURVIVAL ... ZERO	(#E9281—$1.75)
☐	THE TOUGH GUYS	(#E9225—$1.75)
☐	THE TWISTED THING	(#Y7309—$1.25)
☐	VENGEANCE IS MINE	(#J9649—$1.95)

Buy them at your local bookstore or use this convenient coupon for ordering.

THE NEW AMERICAN LIBRARY, INC.,
P.O. Box 999, Bergenfield, New Jersey 07621

Please send me the SIGNET BOOKS I have checked above. I am enclosing $_____ (please add $1.00 to this order to cover postage and handling). Send check or money order—no cash or C.O.D.'s. Prices and numbers are subject to change without notice.

Name _____

Address _____

City _____ State _____ Zip Code _____

Allow 4-6 weeks for delivery.
This offer is subject to withdrawal without notice.